KNIGHTS OF FURY

CHANTAL FERNANDO

MILLS & BOON

Coming soon from Chantal Fernando

Knights of Fury MC

Renegade
Temper

Also available from Chantal Fernando

Wind Dragons MC

Dragon's Lair
Arrow's Hell
Tracker's End
Dirty Ride
Rake's Redemption
Wild Ride
Wolf's Mate
Last Ride
Crossroads

Cursed Ravens MC

Ace of Hearts
Knuckle Down
Going Rogue

Conflict of Interest

Breaching the Contract
Seducing the Defendant
Approaching the Bench
Leading the Witness

Published by
Mills & Boon
An imprint of Harlequin Enterprises (Australia) Pty Limited
(ABN 47 001 180 918), a subsidiary of HarperCollins
Publishers Australia Pty Limited (ABN 36 009 913 517)
Level 19, 201 Elizabeth Street
SYDNEY NSW 2000
AUSTRALIA

Printed and bound in Australia by McPherson's Printing Group

CONTENTS

For Marry
I miss you.

Saint

For Natty.

I miss you.

Every day.

Chapter One

"What's wrong, Sky?" my dad asks as I step into the clubhouse with a sad face, my pink backpack dragging behind me. My body language screams defeat, and even I know it. "Bad day at school?"

I nod at my father. Technically, he's my stepfather, but considering I never knew my biological father, Hammer's the only father I've ever known. He started dating my mom when I was just a baby. My mother has never told me about who my real dad is, and I've always wanted to know. Especially since she's so secretive about it. I don't care too much, though. I have Hammer.

"I guess you could say that."

I've been finding it hard to make friends. No one wants to play with me because they know my stepdad is in a motorcycle gang. I'm not sure why they all hate bikers. I know and love every person in this clubhouse, and they are always nice to me. I don't live in the clubhouse, but we come here pretty much every day after school. Hammer plays basketball with me and my siblings, and is always there for me no matter what. Does it matter that he chooses to ride a motorcycle instead of driving a car, or a van, like most of the other parents? Not to me, but apparently it does to them.

"Tell me what happened," he murmurs in a calm tone, but I know Dad gets mad at anyone who upsets me. I'm the youngest of six, and everyone loves to baby me. I'm also the only girl. Yeah, I feel sorry for myself too.

I sit next to him on the weathered brown leather couch. Before I can say anything, my mother speaks for me. "She got into a fight and is now suspended from school." She looks at me in frustration. "I told you that you need to stay out of trouble, Sky."

I grit my teeth in anger. Anger that she doesn't understand what it is like for me. Anger that she's talking for me. Mom lectured me on the whole drive back here, and now she's going to get Dad on her side before I can even get a word in. "But—"

"Fighting isn't the answer," she continues, shaking her head in disappointment. "I know you've been raised with boys, but you're a lady, and ladies don't fight."

"Didn't you slap that woman at the cookout last month, Georgia?" Dad asks with a smirk, brown eyes alive with mischief. He runs his fingers down his dark beard and nods. "Pretty sure you did. In front of the whole club."

"I saw that," I add, lifting my chin.

My mother scowls, sending a death stare in my direction. "What have I told you? Do as I say, not as I do."

"Becky deserved it, Mom," I say, trying to explain, and wanting my dad to understand. "She said her daddy is dead and it's our fault. He was a policeman. How would that be our fault? So I called her a liar and hit her. She shouldn't be talking bad about my family."

Dad and Mom share a look, one I can't figure out.

My mom has always told me "Do as I say, not as I do," but I can't help it if I'm the way that I am. I want to protect myself and my family.

Dad gives me a big hug. I close my eyes and sink into him, knowing that I'm safe in his arms. "You're not in trouble, Sky," he assures me gently. "But you shouldn't get into any more fights, okay? You're at school to get an education, not to get into trouble."

"I know," I grumble. "I'll try not get into any more fights."

"Promise?" he asks, pulling away and offering me his pinky finger. "We know you are going to do great things with your life. Things far away from here. But to do that, you need to be good in school, and to keep your grades up."

I wrap my pinky around his and squeeze. "I promise. I'll be good."

Funny that I'd make that promise to him, but not to my mother.

Chapter Two

Age 15

"What are you doing here?" Saint asks as I step inside the club-house, frowning as he takes in my denim shorts and white top. "And dressed like that?"

I roll my eyes at him. I've known Saint for about three years now, and normally I'd think of him as a friend, just another one of the guys. Okay, that's a lie. I've always thought he was good looking—in fact, he's probably the hottest guy I know in real life—but it was always just in a "yeah, he's cute" type of way. But recently something has changed. My heart beats faster when he's around, and I want to look nice for him. I even put on a little makeup before I got here.

It's time I admit that I have a crush on Saint, a crush that is completely one-sided.

Before we could hang out and everything would be normal, but now I get nervous every time he's around, and I think it's because I'm now seeing him in a different light. I wish things would just go back to the way they were before, because we'd just chat, give each other shit or watch movies or something, but now I'm awkward around him and don't know how to act.

Let's add that he's five years older than me and a prospect for the Knights of Fury MC.

The MC my father is president of.

So basically, he's never going to see me as anything more than Hammer's daughter. I need to nip this little crush in the bud as soon as possible, because it's a huge inconvenience to my life.

"What do you mean, what am I doing here?" I ask him, brow furrowing. I walk into the kitchen, and he follows behind me, eating a green apple. "Isn't the party tonight?"

"The party got canceled. Georgia didn't tell you?" he asks as he takes another bite, white teeth flashing, then hops up on the countertop with me standing in front of him.

"No, she didn't," I reply, shrugging. "Oh well, where's Dad then?"

"He's got some business going on here today, which is why I'm surprised that you're here," he continues, pausing and studying me. "Your eyes look really green today."

I narrow said eyes. "Are you okay?"

He jumps down and leans over to put his apple core in the garbage, his body close to mine, but not touching. He's so much taller than my five foot five, and I have to look up to see his face. Blue eyes watch me. He's always watching. There's something about him, about the way he looks at me, like he can see into my soul. It's intense, and almost a little too intense. I wonder if he looks at everyone this way, if maybe it's just who he is. I look away, like I always do, and take a step back.

"I'm fine. How about you? How did your exams go?" he asks, now leaning back against the counter with his arms crossed against his broad chest. With his shoulder-length dark hair, olive skin and those piercing baby blues, it's no wonder he has so many girls after him. I've seen it with my own eyes, once when he took me to the mall, and any time we have a family-friendly party at the clubhouse that I'm allowed to attend. Like a moth to a flame, if Saint is around, he has women around him. I hate it.

If jealously is that burn in your chest and that feeling of dread in your stomach, then yeah, I've got that. I don't say anything, though. I mean, I can't. Nothing has happened between us, and I'm a child compared to him. He probably doesn't even look at me like that; I'm sure my dad would kill him even if he did. I really hope he doesn't see me as a younger sister, though, because I already have more than enough older brothers than I can handle.

"I aced them," I reply with a wide, smug smile.

"Well done," he compliments, a grin playing on his full lips. "I'm sure it has nothing to do with the new phone Hammer promised you if you passed them all."

"Nothing at all," I reply with a straight face. "You know, it won't be long until I'm finished with school," I remind him, shifting on my feet. Before I know it, I'll be eighteen too. I wonder if that will make any difference to him. I sure as hell hope so. Maybe he will start seeing me in a different light. A girl can dream.

"I know," he replies, looking up at the ceiling. "What are you going to do then?"

While he's looking away, I take him in from head to toe. Dressed in all black, as usual, a V-neck T-shirt, jeans and boots. He has a leather cuff around his wrist, one I know doubles as a manly scrunchie.

"What was the question again?" I ask, licking my suddenly dry lips.

"Don't look at me like that, Skylar," he says with an expression on his face that I can't seem to decipher.

"Like what?" I ask, glancing down and taking a deep breath.

Before he can answer, my dad walks into the kitchen, empty beer in hand. "What you doing here, Sky?"

I purse my lips and turn to him. "What a warm welcome everyone is giving me today."

Dad grins and wraps a big arm around me. He's such a huge man, when I was little he used to remind me of the Hulk. "You know I love having you here. It's just that today we have the other chapter coming in."

"Is that why the party was canceled?" I ask, glancing between Saint and him.

Ever since I became a teen, my dad doesn't like me being here whenever anyone else outside of this chapter is around, so I usually just stay home. I live with my mom and one of my brothers, Brooks, who is closest in age to me, but still four years older. The two of us are like water and oil—we don't mix, and we never have. I have four other older brothers: Logan, Seth, Axel, and Smith. All of them, including Brooks, have the same father, some guy none of them talk to anymore. I have a different biological father; but no one knows who he is. Every time I've asked Mom about him, she has deflected and not given me a proper answer.

"Yeah, I told Georgia to tell you," he continues, making a *tsk tsk* noise with his tongue. "How did you get here?"

"Brooks dropped me off on his way to basketball."

Dad turns to Saint. "Can you give her a ride home?"

He nods. "No problem."

Dad kisses the top of my head. "I'll see you tomorrow, Sky."

"All right, Dad," I say, bummed about the fact there will be nothing going on tonight for me, no amazing food or company, I'll probably end up being home alone watching TV and binge eating pizza. I suppose I could call up one of my friends to come over and hang out with me, but it won't be as interesting.

Saint and I walk outside, heading toward his bike. I try not to get too excited, but he glances back at me, taking in my attire. "Yeah, let's take the car."

Damn it. I was looking forward to getting on his motorcycle, and it would have been for the first time. I've only ever ridden with my Dad or Temper, one of the other members of the MC, and no one else.

"Fine," I say with resignation, knowing I would have frozen my butt off if we had taken the bike.

He opens the car door for me, which surprises me, and waits until I slide in before he moves to the driver's side. I look up and into the mirror, fixing my long red hair and pushing it back behind my ear as he gets in.

"You look fine" he murmurs, not looking at me.

I close the mirror and eye his profile. "Thank you."

Tension fills the car, and I shift on my seat, swallowing hard. Saint starts the engine and turns on the radio. "Still listen to sheep music?" he asks me, amusement in his tone.

I roll my eyes. "Just because I like listening to the top fifty doesn't make me a sheep. It means I have good taste, because I happen to like popular music. What does that make you then? Liking non-mainstream music doesn't make you any better."

"It makes me a wolf," he replies, flashing his perfect white teeth.

At that very moment, "She Wolf" by Shakira fills the car, and I start to laugh, unable to stop myself.

He shakes his head at me and pulls out of the clubhouse parking lot.

He's more than just a wolf.

He's a Knight.

And that means so much more to me.

Chapter Three

Age 16

"Who is that with Saint?" I ask Brooks, scowling as I see the woman rest her palm on his chest.

"Why? She's hot, isn't she?" he says, smacking his lips together. "Saint always picks up the hottest chicks."

That is literally the last thing I want to hear. And I'm sure my brother knows it. He's such an asshole sometimes.

"She's just a hanger-on," I mutter under my breath, glancing over the yard, and then looking up at the sunset to distract myself. I don't need Saint to catch me sending daggers in his direction. It's my eldest brother's birthday party, and I need to focus on that and only that. "Where's Logan?"

"He's on his way," Brooks says, shrugging. "You know Logan. He only comes to these things because Mom makes him."

Not all of us embraced the MC lifestyle. Logan left the second he turned eighteen, and now we pretty much only see him on birthdays and holidays. I know he loves us—he just never fit in here at the clubhouse, and prefers a quieter, private life-style. And as he calls it, a less criminal one.

Our family is big, and complicated, but we try our best to make things work and include everyone, even if the birthday boy himself hasn't even shown up yet, and my crush is standing a little too close to some pretty brunette for my liking. I hate that it has to be that way, and there's nothing I can do about it. I'm younger than him, and he sees me as some kid. Yet when we hang out, there's just something there that makes me want to be around him. He shows a different side of himself to me, a side that the rest of the world doesn't see. Maybe it's one-sided, but I have to hope when I'm older, things will be different for us. If not for the brunette.

I decide to head back inside—ignorance is bliss and all of that—and help my mom with the food. "Who made these?" I ask, picking up one of the little mini quiches. "They look delicious."

"I did." She beams, standing up from the oven and turning to me. "I made everything except the cake. Can you call Logan and see where he is? I was thinking we could sing happy birthday to him the second he walks through the door."

It's kind of weird being at a birthday party without the birthday boy, so I agree to call him and see where he is, not that the men here need a reason to party. It will be nice to see Logan, even though he doesn't love being at the clubhouse. He always looked after me growing up, and I do love and miss him. I think because he was the firstborn child, my mom does seem to make more of an effort with him and hates that he has this new life without us. She tries everything to get him to come around more.

"How old is he today again?" I ask, wrinkling my nose and pulling out my new phone from my jean pocket.

"Twenty-nine," she replies, eyes widening. "Wow, I almost have a thirty-year-old."

I hit Logan's name and listen to it ring and go to voicemail. "He's not answering."

"Must be driving," she replies absently.

"Anything else you need me to do?" I ask her, looking around the kitchen.

I have a weird relationship with my mom. We get along, but at the same time we're not very close. We don't seem to understand each other or have any type of the connection I've seen some of my friends have with their mothers. I've always gotten the impression that she wished she had all boys, maybe because she seems to favor all of them. Either way, I'm definitely not her favorite child. In fact, I'm most likely her least.

Hammer makes up for it, though. He is always there for me when I need him, making sure I'm okay and spending time with me. He teaches me new things, laughs at my jokes and is slow to anger. I appreciate him more than he knows.

"No, I've got it under control, Sky. You can keep trying to get in touch with Logan, though," she says, her focus already shifting to whatever dish she's fussing over now.

"Okay," I reply, heading for the living room, and dropping down onto the couch, trying my brother again. When he still doesn't pick up, I expel a deep sigh and rest my head back on the velvet pillow.

"Come here to hide out too?" asks Temper, my dad's friend and the Vice President of the Knights.

"Oh my god," I groan, hand on my heart. "You scared the shit out of me, Temper. Jesus Christ."

He simply grins, arching his brow at me in an amused manner from where he's perched on the opposite couch. "You allowed to cuss now?"

I stick my tongue out at him. "I'm almost grown now, man. I can do what I want, when I want."

We both share a laugh, because we know just how untrue that happens to be.

"You're funny," he says, brown eyes smiling. "You know

that? I don't know where you got your personality, because it definitely wasn't from your mother."

I laugh out loud. "Yeah, she's not the funniest woman I've ever met."

In fact, I don't think she's ever told a joke or made me laugh uncontrollably. That's more my dad's job, or even Saint's. Saint can be pretty funny when he wants to be, and has a quiet yet dry type of humor, which I can appreciate.

"I'm funny *and* cute," I add, batting my lashes slowly. "How lucky I am."

Temper throws a pillow at me. "Try that shit in a few years, and I'm sure you'll have all the men on their knees." He pauses, and then adds, "Actually, none of the Knights, but you know, other men."

His comment strikes a chord with me. I've never wanted just anyone. The only man I have my eyes on happens to be in this clubhouse right now. They always say stuff like this to me, about how I'm going to get them all into shit, because I'm pretty and have a mouth on me, and how I'm trouble waiting to happen. I don't think that's the truth, though.

I lift my chin in indignation. "Are you guys really going to let me date a man who isn't a Knight?"

Because I can't see that happening. The boys at school are nothing but my friends, and it's gotten to a point where no one even bothers to ask me out because they all know I'm going to gently refuse them. I don't think I'm better than them in any way, I'm just not interested. I can't help my pull toward Saint. It's torture, and it probably won't end well, but I can't help how I feel about him. Temper doesn't speak for the whole MC, and even if he would prefer I not date any of the Knights, that doesn't mean it can't happen.

"Why the hell would you want to do that?" the man I was just thinking about asks as he walks in and sits next to me, the scent of his cologne hitting my nostrils and sending me into overdrive. "All the good men are right here."

"I don't know about good." Temper winces, tilting his head to the side, brown eyes studying me. "Badass, maybe. Good? Probably not."

None of the men inside these walls consider themselves good men. However, I've seen good in all of them, and continue to do so. They are kind to me, patient, and treat me as if I'm a family member. If that's not the definition of good, then I don't know what is, but I love them all just the way they are.

"Everyone is good to me," I reply on a shrug.

"Only because Hammer would kill us if we weren't." Temper smirks, throwing another pillow at me.

"Can you not?" I ask him, scowling. "I know they call you Temper, but you're about to see mine."

I've noticed something about Temper. The men are wary of him, and always make sure never to push him too far. I've never seen him lose his shit, but I've heard the stories, and with his large build I can see why they wouldn't want to mess with him. To me, I see him as more of the strong and silent type. He acts silly with me, and is protective, but I think that's because he sees me as a niece or something. He keeps an eye on me, but likes giving me shit too. I like him. We have good chats and he's someone I trust.

Saint chuckles from next to me, and the sound brings my attention straight back to him. "Hammer raised a little hellion."

Saint says it like it's a good thing, and when he looks over at me, I get lost in his blue eyes. They are my weakness, not that I'd ever admit that out loud.

"Would you expect any different?" Temper replies in a dry tone, then glances at Saint, a contemplative look on his face. "Thought you were with Diana. What's happening there?"

Why does Temper have to do that? I know that everyone is a little weird about Saint and me hanging out, or even us being alone together, but nothing ever happens. We just chat and joke around. He doesn't even flirt with me, not that I don't try. I guess he saves that other side of himself for women like Diana.

Saint's blue eyes are suddenly looking everywhere except at me. "We were just chatting, that's all."

"Hmmmm," Temper replies, narrowing his gaze. He is always suspicious. Maybe he thinks something is going on with us, and I wish that were true. Unfortunately, Saint hasn't so much as held my hand even when we've been alone and had the opportunity.

"Why are you being all cryptic?" I ask, looking between the two men who are having a silent conversation. I am completely lost now. "Does Diana have an STD or something?"

Low blow, I know, but I have to get my kicks somehow.

Temper barks out a laugh, his wide shoulders shaking. "Fucking hell, Sky. You're so young, you know that?" He pauses and then adds, "But maybe he *should* be worried about that."

"Seriously?" Saint mutters, jaw suddenly tense. "Thanks, Temper."

"Compared to you I'm young, I guess," I reply to Temper, ignoring Saint.

Temper laughs harder.

"Ignore him," Saint says to me, his voice instantly drawing me in, Temper and his shenanigans forgotten.

I asked him once why they call him Saint when I know for a fact his name is Thorn Benson. He said it's because compared to all the other men here, he *is* a Saint.

I call bullshit.

I might be young, and maybe even naïve, but I'm not stupid.

"I always do," I reply, snuggling back into the couch. "Logan isn't even here, and he's not picking up the phone. We might just be having this party in his honor, without his presence. I don't know why Mom bothered—she knows he doesn't even like coming here."

Another day, another dysfunctional family issue.

I think Mom was hoping, even pressuring, Logan to join the Knights of Fury MC, but in the end it backfired, and now he wants nothing to do with them. She needs to let go, as he's already chosen his own path. My mother, though, is known for her tenacity.

"Ahh well, I'm just here for the food anyway," Temper replies, standing up, his height making him look like a giant. "Speaking of."

We watch him walk away, leaving the two of us momentarily alone.

Probably not the best idea, at least not for me, because suddenly I'm finding it hard to think of something to say. I hate how it's become so hard for us to talk. It never used to be like this before.

Lucky for me, Saint speaks first. "It's not on you if your brother doesn't show up. You know he's not a fan of being here. I don't know why your mom bothers with the big parties, pretending we're all one big family."

"I know," I reply, glancing down. "We should have just done something else with him. It's like she makes it about her instead of him and what he wants."

"I think we all know the party is more for your mom than Logan, like you said. But Temper is right, at least there's good food. There's always a silver lining, and if that lining is lining my stomach I'm not going to complain."

Saint says this as he wraps his arm around me and kisses my temple. He can be affectionate, sometimes, but never in the way I crave. More like a big brother. Unfortunately. But I still enjoy times like these, knowing it's more than he gives anyone else. "You're the rose that came from concrete, do you know that?"

I'm about to ask him exactly what he means by that when my dad walks in, barking out Saint's name. I assume he's about to yell at him for being so close to me, something we do avoid when he is around, but I know I'm wrong when he says something that sends a shiver up my spine.

"Get all the men together. We have a fuckin' problem, and we need to handle it right now."

And then Saint's up, doing what he's told, and I'm left alone wondering what the hell is going on. I know they will never tell me, though. They let me in on the good times but shield me from the bad, even though I know there is plenty of bad. Sometimes I'm curious about what's going on, and other times I just block it out and leave them to it. This is their lives, and what do I know about how an MC works? As interested as I am, I don't really want to know. At least not now.

I'm just here for the family and food.

I try Logan again and he finally picks up, and before I can say hello, he yells into the line, "I'm not fuckin' coming, Sky. Tell Mom again, since she didn't listen the first ten times. Thank you, and I love you."

He hangs up, and I stare at my phone for a few moments. Well, at least he said he loved me. I don't know why Mom does this every time—she can't push Logan to be a part of something he doesn't want to. She chose the MC life, not him, and he's old enough to do whatever the hell he wants now.

The drama.

Sometimes I can see why our biological fathers left us all.

I sleep at the clubhouse that night, which isn't unusual, especially for weekends, but loud voices wake me up and I can tell that something is very wrong.

When I overhear my name, I go out to the kitchen to see what all the commotion is about. My mom is at the kitchen table with Hammer opposite her, but won't even look at me, too lost in thought.

"What's wrong?" I ask.

All conversation stops between Hammer and Mom the second they realize that I'm there, which lets me know it's something they don't want me to overhear. Damn, I should have stayed hidden and just listened in.

"Go to bed, Sky," my mom demands, tone laced with impatience and irritation. She looks away, like she expects me to just follow her orders instantly, and like I'm simply going to do as I'm told. Something in my gut tells me that something isn't right, though, and I need to know what's going on, especially if it involves me. Has something bad happened? Is someone hurt? My brothers? Saint?

"I heard my name," I explain, glancing between the two. "Is everything okay?"

My dad won't look at me, his eyes darting down to his hands in front of him. I don't know why he's remaining silent right now, when it's so unlike him. Hammer does and says whatever he likes; it's one of the things I love about him.

Why won't he look at me?

"It's fine," she replies curtly, glancing over before turning her back on me once more. "This is adult business, and you need to go back to bed."

Adult business that apparently involves me.

Hammer, who usually stands up for me any time my mom gets into one of her evil moods, continues to say nothing, but his tight jaw lets me know he's unhappy about something.

Feeling hurt, I leave the kitchen and walk back down the hallway, except this time I stop in front of Saint's door. I lift my hand to knock, but can't find myself quite able to. It's not like this is something I've ever done before, and I don't know if he would appreciate it or not. If he also tells me I should just go to bed, I think I might scream. I move to turn and just head back to my room, but then the door opens.

"Sky? What are you doing still awake?" he asks me, standing there shirtless, in nothing but some shorts. His body is amazing, muscles so defined, so deadly, he has turned himself into a weapon.

A beautiful one.

"Can't sleep," I tell him, glancing behind him with curiosity. "I'm not interrupting anything, am I?"

His eyes narrow slightly. "No, I'm just watching TV. Do you want to come in?"

I look around the hallway to make sure no one is around, then nod and enter his domain. I've never been in his room before. He has a massive wall-mounted TV and his bed looks comfortable as hell, all black bedding and plush pillows.

"Not what I was expecting," I admit as I sit on the very edge of the bed and look at the TV. "What are you watching?"

"*Supernatural*," he says, leaving the door open a bit and passing me the remote. He then opens a drawer and pulls out a black T-shirt, sliding it over his head and covering the amazing view. "But we can watch whatever you want."

He doesn't ask me what the hell I'm doing here, which is nice, because I don't know if I have an answer for that. It's almost as if I'm crossing a line here, or changing the rules on our friendship.

"Really?" I ask, arching my brow. "Just like that, huh?"

"Guest picks," he replies with a smirk. "I'm giving you the remote, not my credit card; calm down, Sky."

I have a laugh at that. "For now," I add cheekily.

He shakes his head and picks me up, moving me farther onto the bed. "You don't have to sit with one butt cheek off the bed—get yourself comfortable."

I do as he suggests, but don't lie down. Instead I sit perched on a few of his pillows and look for something for us to watch. When I settle on a romantic comedy, I expect a complaint from him, but he stays quiet and lies down next to me.

"What happened tonight?" I ask him quietly as the movie starts to play.

"Club business, Sky," is all he gives me. "Don't worry, we will take care of it, like we always do."

"Mom and Dad were fighting, and I heard my name," I admit to him, hoping that he can offer me some insight, or some answers. Anything.

"I'm not sure what that was about, but you know them two, they're always arguing about something or another," he says, lifting the blanket up over me. "Don't stress about it."

I try not to, and soon get lost in the movie.

It's not long before I fall asleep, cuddled up next to him, not a worry in the world.

I wake up to an empty bed and screaming.

I jump out of Saint's bed, the last place I want to be found—not like anything happened, but it's still not good. I rush toward the noise. My dad, Saint and my mom are yelling at each other.

"You can't do this!" Saint yells, starting to pace. "Hammer, you can't let her do this!"

"She's my daughter," my mom growls in a smug tone. When she sees me, she barks out, "Get your shit, Sky, we're leaving."

I lock eyes with Saint, who looks panicked, and almost scared.

"Don't do this," Dad pleads with her. "Leave Sky here. I'll look after her. And you know I'll take good care of her."

Confusion fills me. Leave me here? Where is Mom going? I don't know what's happening, but my first instinct is to scream yes, let me stay with Dad. I want that. I want to stay with Hammer. My father. The only father I've ever known.

"I'm not leaving my daughter behind," Mom sneers, lifting her chin. "She's just your stepdaughter, Hammer, she's not your blood, so don't even think of trying to take her, or the police will be here before you know it. And you know what I'll tell them, so don't push me. You're a dead man walking, anyway. What's the point? I tried to help you, and you didn't want it. Now you can deal with the consequences."

"That was your idea of helping me?" he growls, anger filling his gaze. "You disgust me, Georgia. And Skylar deserves so much fucking better. If you love her at all, you will leave her here! For one second stop thinking about yourself and do what is best for her."

"Go get your bag, Sky!" she yells once more. I rush to my room and grab my backpack, panic filling me. I hate when they fight, but it's different this time: for the first time ever she's not listening to anything Dad has to say, and Mom is known for giving in to whatever he wants.

She's never stormed off like this before, and something in me is telling me not to go with her. I don't have much of a choice, though.

Saint meets me at my door, and I can't hide how worried I am.

"She's making me leave?" I ask him, tears threatening to spill. I don't know what is going to happen, and I'm scared. "Are they breaking up? Oh my God, Saint. I don't want to leave. What if she doesn't let me come back?"

He pulls me into his arms, holding me tight. And when I glance up at him, before I know what's happening, he kisses me. Just a soft, chaste kiss on the lips.

His emotions hit me full force. He doesn't want me to go either. His soft lips leave gentle memories, a first kiss I will never forget, nor regret.

When he pulls back, he rests his forehead on mine. "I'm sure she will just take you to your house until they sort their shit out. You'll be back."

I want to believe him, but there was something in the way Hammer was looking at me that makes me think this is more permanent.

"Sky!" I hear her yell. "Get your ass out here right now. We're leaving!"

"They will make up. This is just a fight that they've taken to the next level," he whispers, cupping my cheek. The look in his eyes contradicts his words. He's worried too.

Shit.

"You're probably right," I tell him, nodding, wishing I could believe him. "Goodbye, Saint."

A muscle tics in his jaw. "I'll see you soon, Sky."

I swallow and follow my mom's screams. Dad hugs me and whispers, "I love you," into my ear before she grabs my arm to drag me into her car.

I stare at the clubhouse as she drives away.

My family.

What has she done?

"He's going to regret dumping me," she says, an evil tone to her threatening words. "Just wait and see. We're going to go home, pack our shit, and then we're leaving. We aren't coming back here, Sky. Ever."

Finally, I let the tears fall.

Chapter Four

Present Day

"I'll have a cappuccino, please," a man orders. I nod and write it down so I don't forget. One would think I'd be able to remember one drink without problems, but apparently with me and my usual daydreaming, that's not the case. My head is habitually in the clouds, and sometimes I'm not paying attention even when I think I am.

"No problem," I tell him, smiling. "Anything else?"

He shakes his head.

"Won't be long, sir," I say as I move away and head back behind the counter.

I never thought I'd be working at a café full time at twenty-one, but here I am. I took a gap year after high school, which turned into three, and I don't know, I thought at this age I'd be living a little more. Maybe traveling and seeing the world, with a degree behind me. Experiencing life. Instead I'm serving coffee, living with a friend and barely making ends meet. My brother Brooks moved back to the city at the first opportunity, so I'm the only sibling who is still out here in the country, isolated from the rest. But at least my mom is still here. She lives with her new husband, and we catch up once a week or so.

"Sky, can you cover my shift tomorrow?" asks Max, my roommate and coworker, blue eyes pleading. "I know it's your only day off, but I have an audition, and I need to be there."

Max is trying to make it big with his band, and I try to help him out when I can so he doesn't lose his job. He is extremely talented, and I have no doubt that they are going to make it—they just need to get their big break.

I was really looking forward to having my day off, but I can't let him miss this. It's not like I had any great plans, other than sitting on my couch. "Yeah, no problem," I tell him, sighing. "Just remember me when you make it big."

"You know I will," he says, leaning forward and kissing my hair. He steps back and looks above me, spreading his palms out, as if imaging his future. "I'll write a song about you. Sky O'Connor, the only one who had my back *before* I was a millionaire."

"I'll be waiting for it," I reply with a smile, finishing up the cappuccino and taking it over to the customer. I spend the next five hours doing much the same, until it's time for me to head home. I get on my bicycle and ride the fifteen minutes it takes to get to my house, with my red ponytail billowing behind me. Max passes me in his car, his honk scaring the shit out of me. They must have let him finish work early, because I know he wasn't meant to go home for another few hours.

"Race you home!" he calls out, and I roll my eyes at him, but start to pedal faster. There's a shortcut I take that actually makes this a fair race, because even in his car, Max has to go around the longer way. I whizz around a lady walking her dogs, then take the sharp turn to the right, rushing toward our house.

When I get there seconds before him, I jump off my bike and do a little happy dance, shaking my booty and flashing him a smug look. "Ha! You lose! Nice try, though, Max."

He gets out of his car and shakes his head at me, laughing. "Whatever, I let you win!"

I cross my arms and narrow my eyes. "You're such a bad loser."

"You're such a bad winner," he grumbles, grabbing the mail before brushing past me to the door. "I hope no one is dropping in tonight so I can run around naked and drink milk from the carton." His friends have a habit of dropping by unexpectedly, and I've somehow gotten used to it.

I wince at that vision. "Umm, hello? Even if no one else is there, I am. And I'd rather not see you naked. Again."

We've been in our apartment for about a year, and in that time we've both caught each other in some pretty compromising positions. I went from growing up surround by boys to living with one. Platonically. When I was advertising for a roommate to split the rent, I was hoping a nice woman might come along, but nope. Just an up-and-coming rock star waiting for his big break.

I'm just destined to be surrounded by men I have only platonic feelings for.

"Why not? I look good naked," he brags, unlocking the door and gesturing for me to enter. "Ladies first. But wait, you aren't a lady, so…"

He runs in first and I throw my handbag at him. "You're such a jerk! This is why you're single!"

"I'm single because I'm a player!" the idiot calls back to me, and I can't help but laugh at him. Never a dull moment when Max is around, that's for damn sure. He's like the sixth brother I sure as hell never wanted but got stuck with anyway.

I close the door and head straight for the kitchen, grabbing my bag on the way and placing it down. Picking up the bunch of letters Max threw on the counter, I go through them and pull out the ones for me, walking with them into my bedroom.

"More bills," I grumble, ripping them open. When I come to the last letter, though, it doesn't look like a bill. It's addressed to me in neat handwriting I don't recognize. I open it with caution.

As I read the first line, my heart stops.

Dear Skylar,

Five years. That's a long time to go without talking to somebody, especially someone who was such a huge part of your life. I hope you are well. I don't even know why I'm writing to you, when you're the last person I'd want to know where I am. But you're also the first person who came to mind when they said I could write snail mail. I can't even remember when I wrote something this long. I think maybe it was on your sixteenth birthday when I wrote out the lyrics to your favorite song in your card. Seems like a lifetime ago.

The clubhouse was never the same after you left.

Neither was I.

Saint

Saint.

Saint wrote me a letter. I double-check the envelope, looking at the return address for the first time, and my eyes grow wide.

Saint, my first ever crush, wrote me a letter.

From prison.

"What have you done?" I whisper to myself, reading the letter once more from the top.

"What's that?" Max asks, as he steps into the doorway of my bedroom.

"Nothing," I say quickly, folding up the letter. I left my heart back in the Knights of Fury clubhouse, with Hammer and Saint, and there hasn't been a day that's gone by that I don't think of them. I was never told what exactly happened that night, other than that Mom and Hammer were done with each other and we needed to get away so we were safe. After we left the clubhouse that night, we drove to our house and she had me and my brother Brooks pack everything. We left a day later and never returned.

Neither Hammer nor Saint have ever reached out to me, until right now.

It's not like it's a surprise for one of the bikers to land themselves in prison, but the thought of Saint being there physically hurts me. It means the world to me to hear from him, but at the same time I do feel a little resentful that it took him being locked up to reach out to me. And another thing... I wonder how he knew where I live. Has he known where I've been this entire time?

I need answers.

"Just more bills," I lie, flashing Max a forced smile, wanting to keep Saint to myself. He rolls his eyes and walks away. I get up to shut my door and walk over to my desk to pull out some paper and a pen from my top drawer. I sit down and start to write.

Saint,

I'm sorry to hear from you under these circumstances. Are you okay? If there is anything I can do for you, please let me know. You're right, five years is a long time. I didn't know if I'd ever speak to you again, but I have thought about you often.

How is Dad?

I pause, then scrub out the word *Dad*, replacing with *Hammer*.

How is Hammer?

He always said I would do great things, far away from the MC, and I guess he was half right. I'm farther away, but I don't know about the doing great things part. I've put college on hold and am just...living.

I guess in prison you'd be doing exactly the same, just living, pushing through to get to the next day.

But things will get better, right?

How much time do you have? I hate the thought of you behind bars, and I hope that you won't be in there for too long. I'm here if you need me, and even though it's probably not much, it's all I can offer right now.

And how did you get my address?

Hang in there, Saint.

Love, Sky
P.S. I still have that sixteenth birthday card.

Chapter Five

Skylar,

You replied. I didn't know if you would or not.

Hammer gave me your address. Just because you left doesn't mean we stopped checking up on you and making sure that you were okay.

I will be in here for about a year, and yes, that time will be spent just living. What's your excuse, though? You should be out there loving life and taking everything it has to offer.

Do that for me, at least, while I'm stuck here eating the worst food I've personally ever tasted. It's worse than that time you were hungry at the clubhouse and I tried to make you spaghetti. Do you remember that? It was awful, but you still ate it without complaining.

I stop reading to remember that moment. I was starving and had just come to the clubhouse after school, but Mom wasn't there and neither was Hammer, so Saint said he'd whip me up something. I remember sitting on the counter, watching him as he boiled pasta and tried to make a sauce from scratch, making do with the lack of ingredients and somehow managing to create a dish. He'd winced and flashed me an apologetic look as he tasted it, but to me it tasted fine. No, it had tasted great, actually, because he had made it.

My cooking skills have improved since then, and maybe
one day I'll be able to prove that to you.
Hammer is fine.
How are you?
Saint

Sitting back on my couch, beer in hand, I consider his words. Reading that they checked up on me is surprising. Knowing my address and checking up on me are two different things, and not once did they show up at my door and ask me if I was okay. It kind of pisses me off. Why didn't they just reach out to me? Let me know they were still there for me? Anything.

I get up and head to my room, filing the letter away and getting ready to head out to watch Max's band play at one of the local bars. Instead of putting myself out there and loving life, I've just been fumbling along, trying to adult the best I can, but I need to do better.

In an attempt to figure out what I want to do with my life and at the same time stay productive, I've started volunteering at the children's hospital in my spare time. I usually read to them, which doesn't seem like much, but they really enjoy an extra person giving them some attention. Even Max has come in and sung songs for the kids to cheer them up, which has been really rewarding to watch.

I think I've always known that I want to help people in some way or another. I just need to decide what direction I want to go with that.

Now that I am in communication with Saint, he's where my

mind tends to be focused, worrying about him and thinking about all the memories I have of the Knights of Fury. The what-ifs also cloud my head. What if my mom and Hammer had never broken up? What if I'd gone back to the city as soon as I turned eighteen? What if I'd kept in touch with Hammer and Saint?

Sliding my feet into my heels, I grab my handbag and head outside, the cool breeze hitting my face. It feels good to get dolled up and I'm excited to see Max play tonight.

After parking my car, I head to the front of the bar and show the bouncer my ID before stepping inside the dimly lit space. The loud music is familiar, chords I've heard Max play over and over from my bedroom. He asked me once if I'd fill in for their lead singer, but I declined. I save my vocals for the shower.

Lucky enough to find a seat by the bar, I glance around at the crowd, smiling as I take in all the people who have come to watch my friends play tonight. I see big things for them in the future.

Max waves to me whilst singing, which has a few women turning around and giving me the evil eye, leaving me feeling amused.

"You here alone?" a gentleman to my right asks me, eyes on me. He's tall and really muscular. He'd be pretty good looking if he got rid of the mustache, but maybe he's just rocking it for Movember. "It's rare to find a woman who won't leave the house without a squad these days."

"A squad?" I repeat, smirking. He mustn't have seen Max's wave, and is probably wondering why I'm sitting here alone. "Well, it's probably smart. Safety in numbers, right? But no, I'm not alone."

And as if any woman in their right mind would admit it even if they were.

He chuckles, sounding truly amused. "That was a terrible opening line, wasn't it?"

"Might need some work," I say, then turn to the bartender to order a drink. I've no interest in this man, or in any other man really. I'm not here to pick up or to be chatted up. I'm just here to watch Max and the rest of the band play and then to go and grab some food with him afterward, as was promised, before heading home and to bed, to sleep next to my pile of clean laundry.

Max tells the crowd they are taking a break for thirty minutes but will be back, and the DJ starts to play some hip-hop music.

"I'll keep that in mind," the guy replies, laughing to himself. He stays silent after that, but I feel his eyes on me.

"Don't even bother with that one," a familiar voice says over my shoulder. "We're pretty sure she's destined for the convent." I turn to Max, who simply grins back at me. "Can't leave you alone for two minutes."

"Well, if it isn't the star himself" I say, turning my stool to face him. "You're amazing up there."

"Thank you," he replies, smiling widely. "It's such a rush. I love being up on the stage."

This is his moment, the first of many, and he deserves to enjoy every second of it.

"And can you believe how many people are here tonight?" he asks me, shaking his head in wonder. "Holy fuck, Sky. This is the best night ever. Come on, drinks are on me."

We have a few celebratory drinks, and I notice the man who spoke to me before watching me every now and again, but I ignore him, and soon forget about it.

Max finishes up his set, and I stay for the whole thing, loving every moment. Seeing him up there, living his dream, makes me want to chase my own. I want that adrenaline rush, and I want to love what I do every second of every day just like him.

Afterward, he doesn't forget his promise, and we stop for food on the way home.

It's the small things in life.

As I sit down to write Saint, my anger at his and Hammer's silence pour out onto the page.

Saint,

   Of course I'd reply to you. You were all once my family, and that means something to me. I might not be a Knight anymore, or maybe I never was, but I'm loyal like one.

   What do you mean you all checked up on me?

   Where were you when I broke my leg at seventeen because I'd gotten drunk for the first time because I was missing my home and looking for an escape? I tried climbing back up to my room to sneak in and fell down the side of the house while trying to scale the wall.

   You didn't check up on me then.

   Where were you when, at eighteen, I lost one of the only people I connected to when I moved here? My best friend Shauna died when a drunk driver hit her on the road. It felt like my heart had broken into a million pieces, like I'd lost the sister I never had.

   You didn't check up on me then.

   I could go on, but you get the point.

   When I left, it felt like I left all of you behind.

   Kind of like you all died too.

   Sky

I drop the letter off in a mailbox on the way to work, stopping for a few moments on my bicycle. I realize how angry the letter might sound to Saint, and I didn't even know I was angry until now. I guess I feel left behind. Sad. Vulnerable. I know I shouldn't live in the past, but it's hard when I still have so many questions that have been left unanswered after all this time. I didn't realize how much I've bottled up those emotions.

I'm still early when I get to the café, so I take my time in the staff room before clocking in.

"We have the worst crew on today," Max whispers to me when I'm within earshot. "We're basically going to have to be doing the work for everyone."

"You haven't quit yet?" I ask, softly laughing. "After the weekend I thought you'd come in today with your resignation."

"Oh, I'm going on to bigger and better things," he assures me, picking up a tea towel and folding it neatly. "I'm just not going to quit until my bank account reflects my ambition."

"Smart," I agree, nodding. I glance at the roster, and cringe when I read all the names of the young, new staff. "And you're right. We're going to be doing all the work today."

"Told you."

"Lucky you're filled with ambition," I tease.

"Not for this job, I'm not," he grumbles, scrubbing a hand down his face. "Did you send the letter to your jailbird?"

I stifle a groan. Over food after his concert, I ended up telling Max about Saint, and the letters, and he's pretty much all Max has wanted to discuss ever since.

"Yes, I did," I say, dusting something invisible off my shirt and avoiding eye contact. "And don't make me regret telling you about him."

"No, it was nice to know something personal about you. You're so closed off, Sky. And between us, I kind of thought that maybe you were asexual."

"Just because my door isn't revolving like yours?" I fire back, scowling. "I'm very…uhh…sexual, I'll have you know."

He blinks slowly, then bursts out laughing. "'Uhh sexual'? I said asexual."

"You're an idiot. Besides, even if I were asexual, there is nothing wrong with that," I declare, quieting down when a customer walks in.

Just because I'm not actively having sex doesn't mean that I'm not sexual, or that I couldn't be. I think about sex a lot; I just haven't met that person that I want to experience all those things with. No one has caught my eye or held my attention. I've been on a few dates in my time, but nothing ever came of it. I don't think I've been saving myself for Saint or anything like that, but no one better than him has ever shown up in my life. I've never felt that draw, that pull, that connection like the one I had with him, even if I was only young then.

I'm still young now.

I don't know, maybe I've yet to meet the one, or maybe I've already met him.

I guess only time will tell.

Chapter Six

Skylar,

I hope you are well. I wish we could have this conversation in person. Your mother made it clear we were to have no contact with you, and that if we did, the consequences would fall on you and the MC. We didn't know what to do. She knew a lot about the MC, and we didn't know what she was capable of. At the end of the day, you were her daughter, and she held all the power. I might not have been there to get you through your loss, or be by your side while your leg healed, but you were in my thoughts.

We never forgot you.

Tell me everything else I've missed out on.

I have nothing but time.

Saint

Placing the letter down on my thigh, teeth clenched, my mind roams back to a conversation I had with my mother after she broke up with Hammer. We were on our way to the country, the city becoming farther and farther away in the rearview mirror.

"Did Hammer call you to say bye?" she asks me, tone smug.

"No," I reply, glancing down at my phone, which has zero notifications. "Did he call you, Mom?"

"He tried," she says, shrugging. "But I'm done with him. And if he cared about you like he said he did, he would have contacted you by now. Guess it was all a lie."

My chest tightens, just like it did back then, at the thought of the man I considered my father, the only father I've ever known, not loving me or fighting to have me in his life. My mother always played the card that Hammer didn't want me without her, and that because they were over, I was no longer of any use to him. Like his love of me was just an extension of her and didn't have its own depth. I'm not going to lie—it cut me, deep.

But what Saint is saying—if it's the truth, which I'm pretty sure it is—means my mother purposely and maliciously lied to me. She made it out like Hammer didn't care about me when that wasn't true. Maybe it was the other way around—maybe he didn't care about her and she couldn't take that. I don't know what to believe anymore.

There's only one person I want to talk to, so I drive straight to her house.

"What are you doing here, Sky?" Mom asks as I get out of my car. She's sitting on the grass, weeding, a large, wide-brimmed hat shielding her from the sun. At fifty-five you'd think life would be slowing down for her, but she still looks and acts like she's not a day over forty. I hope I take after her in this way when I'm older. "Is everything all right?"

It's easy to tell that I rarely drop by unannounced. Now that I'm here, the words don't seem to come. I kind of don't want to tell her about Saint's letter, because I can only imagine what her reaction will be. She will be angry and want to know every detail, and I haven't seen that side of her in a long time.

"Yeah, everything is fine. Was just passing by so thought I'd drop in and say hello," I lie.

"That's nice of you," she replies, studying me. I don't know how my mother went from leather pants and streaked hair to overalls and gardening, but she did, turning her life around and landing herself a well-off farmer. It's like she changes herself to match whoever she's with, and I don't really think that is a very attractive trait. I hope I never do that. However, I must admit that her new husband is a good influence on her, because she has changed for the better since marrying him.

"What have you and Neville been up to?" I ask her, trying to make conversation.

"Nothing much since we last spoke," she murmurs, removing her hat and wiping the sweat from her brow, her red hair pasted against her forehead. "He's in there making a roast for dinner. Do you want to stay? You look a little thin, Sky. I think you need to eat more."

"Oh, no, it's okay, Mom. I've got food at home waiting for me," I lie.

"If you insist. We spent the day feeding and watering the animals. We have a new foal, if you want to go see her. Neville said you can name her, if you want to."

"I'd love to," I reply earnestly. I think the thing I love the most about visiting here is seeing all their animals. "So, I was thinking about Dad...uh, Hammer today."

I clench my jaw as I wait for her reply.

"He's not your father," she says to me in a gentle tone, placing her handful of weeds in the bucket then turning to me. "We've had this conversation so many times over the years, Sky. That's not our life anymore, and they are dead to us. We are so much happier out here, and much safer. The best decision I made was moving us away from that life."

"I guess I just don't understand how he could just stop caring about me," I say in a voice much too small. "Did he ever try to contact me, or speak to me? Or even ask how I was?"

"No," she says instantly, jaw tightening. Her green eyes flash and show me a glimpse of the angry old lady she used to be.

"He didn't. How many years has it been? Why are you still asking about them? That was another life, and one I don't want to revisit. Hammer wasn't a good man, none of the Knights were, and they don't give two shits about you. You deserve so much better than what they gave you, Sky, and I'm sorry I made you grow up in that environment at all. It was stupid of me. I should have found a nice man like Neville much earlier than I did, instead of getting involved with a...criminal."

Swallowing hard, I nod. This is all I'm ever going to get out of her. She doesn't want to speak about them, and I can't force her. "Yeah, I guess you're right."

Neville comes out, smiling when he sees me. He's a kind man, and I genuinely do like him. I have to give my mother credit—she has great taste. She always finds men who are better than she is.

"Skylar, hello! Will you be joining us for dinner?" he asks.

"No, sorry, Nev. I was just in the area and thought I'd say hello," I say, standing up and brushing the grass off my butt. "And I should probably get going."

The foal will have to wait, because right now all I want to do is get away from my mother. I don't know why I've stayed out in the country with her when I could easily move back to the city and be close to the rest of my siblings and the life I knew before I was dragged out here. I guess I got comfortable and stayed because it was easy. In a messed up way, I also think I see my mom as the only one who has ever stuck by me, so I did the same for her. The MC didn't come for me. My brothers left me. Mom was the only one who didn't leave.

"I'll see you soon," I say, waving quickly before disappearing into my car.

I might not know who Saint is anymore, but I do know who my mother is, and it wouldn't surprise me if she's been lying to me this entire time.

Only one person can clear this up for me, and that's Hammer himself.

Chapter Seven

I don't write back to Saint, because I don't know what to say to him. That it's nice that they all wanted to reach out to me, but no one did? I still have the same number, and there's no excuse that no one called me or sent me a message. It hurts when I think of it like that.

I don't know what to think, and I don't know why they let my mom win so easily. They are a MC, but they let one woman dictate their actions? It makes no sense, and maybe everything Saint is saying is just a bunch of excuses to relieve their guilt. Even with all these thoughts running in my head, I decide to move back to the only place that felt like home. I'm doing it for me, not for them.

I reach out to someone I haven't spoken to in a while: my oldest brother, Logan. When I ask him if I can stay with him until I find my own place in the city, he agrees, and even sounds happy to have me.

After putting in my two weeks' notice at work, I know that I have to tell Max that I'm leaving. To soften the blow, I bake a cheesecake, buy some beer and order pizza. He knows something is up the second he walks in, going by the way he eyes me suspiciously.

"Did someone die?" he asks, frowning. "Ooh, you baked cheesecake. The last time you baked cheesecake was when Otis got run over. Did our cat die?"

"We don't have another cat," I remind him. "No one has died." I take a deep breath and look him in the eye. "I've decided that I'm going to move back to the city. I'm sorry, and I'm going to miss you so much, but we can all visit each other, and—"

"You're leaving me?" Max asks, brow furrowing. "Why would you want to move when your family is here? I'm here!"

"I just need a change, and I want to go back to college and reconnect with my other family, and… I don't know. I just need a change, okay? You are the only good part about living here. Otherwise, my job is shit—all I do is work and still struggle to make ends meet. My mother only sees me on her terms and we aren't even close no matter how much I try and pretend we are, and…"

And Saint.

And the Knights.

I don't know why, but they are calling me, and I need to find out the truth about everything.

Max sighs and wraps his arm around me. "I'll be doing gigs in the city soon, so it's not the end of the world, but do you know how shitty it's going to be not coming home to you? *You* make this place a home, Sky. You."

Feeling the tears prickling my eyes, I blink rapidly and glance away from them. "I'll still be your home. Just…a movable home."

Max chuckles and pulls me against him. "This better be the best damn cheesecake ever."

Smiling sadly, I grab the plastic plates and hand him one. "We still have each other." I look him in the eye. "Okay?" He nods.

After he devours the cheesecake, I head into my room to start packing my things. About two hours later, I hear Max call for me in the living room.

"What the hell are you doing?" I ask as I find Max waiting for me with a mischievous grin on his face. That's when I glance down and notice the water gun in his hands. He quickly aims for me and I duck, the stream of water hitting the wall. "Oh my god, we are so not getting our deposit back. Get outside with that!"

I run after him, trying to chase him outside, only to get hit in the face with a stream of water. "I'm going to kill you!"

Max laughs while I run to grab his extra water gun and start filling it up in the sink. "You're not going to live long enough to be famous!"

I hear him laughing harder from outside and decide to follow him out there with my now loaded gun. He has his speaker playing outside, and when I hear what he's listening to, I laugh out loud.

"Oh my god, are you playing your own music for everyone? You're such a lo—"

A bucket of water is tipped over my head.

And then he throws me in the air, over his shoulder, and my damn weapon falls to the ground. I must resemble a raging bull, because I'm fighting to be let go, kicking and screaming until he puts me back down.

"You are going to pay for that!"

"What are you going to do?" he presses, arching his brow. "All talk, Sky. You are all talk. You love it. And you're going to miss the shit out of me while you're back in the fancy city."

His words have never been more true. The truth is that Max is the only thing making me second-guess my decision. He has become my family, and even though he drives me crazy, I'm going to miss him so much. But if I stay here I know I'm not going to be moving forward. I'll be stuck in this rut I seem to have gotten myself in, and I need change.

My heart is telling me to go home.

To where it all started for me.

I throw my hands up in the air, making a promise. "I'm never living with a boy again!"

"I love you, Sky!" Max calls out.

Shit, I love him too.

Goodbye is going to be harder than I thought.

"I don't know why you are going back, Skylar. There is nothing there for you," Mom says with her chin in the air. Strategically, I'd decided to tell her about the move in front of Neville, knowing that she won't react too harshly with him there, wanting to keep her true self hidden.

"All my brothers are there, Mom," I point out, keeping my tone even. "I'm the only one who isn't."

She waves her hand in the air. "You were never even that close with your brothers. Who is going to look after you over there? And you know Neville likes our weekly dinners."

I don't miss how she says *Neville* enjoys the dinners, not her. She's changing, losing the sweet mother façade and returning to a woman I remember well.

Gritting my teeth, I manage to get out, "Well, hopefully that will change now, and I will become closer with them," without losing my temper.

I'm looking forward to reconnecting with them all again, and there's nothing she can do to stop that. I hardly keep in contact with them anymore. We call each other on our birthdays, and sometimes I see them on Christmas, but that's about it. Like Mom said, we aren't close, and I hate it. And if I'm being honest, part of it is my fault. I always had this irrational sense to stick by my mom. And look what it's given me. Nothing.

She's so against me leaving, but I don't understand why. It's obvious she doesn't want me in contact with any of the Knights, but is that the only reason? It's not like we see each other that often. I don't so much as get a "Happy Birthday" from her unless Neville is there and she wants to put on a show. I visit her because she's my mother, and at the end of the day, I get only one of those. And I respect her because she gave birth to and raised me. She's far from perfect, but yeah, she's all I really have. And she has been much nicer up until I brought up Hammer.

"I'm sure at her age she would much rather be in the city, Georgia," Neville says, rubbing his palm along her shoulder. "Must get boring out here. We don't have many shops, or clubs—"

"Or bikers," Mom mutters under her breath.

"What was that, dear?" Neville asks, none the wiser.

"Oh, nothing, honey. I'm just worried about her being in the city," Mom lies, giving me a filthy look when he's not paying attention.

"Her brothers will look after her," he continues, smiling over at me. "And I'm sure we can come for a visit once she's settled in. I like seeing you every week, but you need to do what is best for you."

"I've already applied for a few jobs, so hopefully I will have work as soon as I get there. It's a fresh start, and I'm pretty excited about it."

Because my bank balance isn't going to allow for anything else, but also because I'm going to need money to put me through college.

"Do you need any money?" offers Neville, God bless him. "Just for you to get set up. Does Logan have a bed for you? We could pay for you to get one if you like, or anything else you need for your bedroom there."

"That's very kind of you, but I couldn't accept. I will be fine, don't worry about me. Logan said he does have a bed, and I have gas money to get there, so I'm good," I assure him, thanking him again for his kind gesture. It means a lot to me that someone cares, even if it isn't my own mother.

Although the money would be wonderful, I don't feel right taking it from him, or from anyone, for that matter. I made the mistake of asking my mother for financial help right when I graduated high school. I foolishly believed she had a nest egg for me, a college fund. She told me, and I quote, "I raised you for eighteen years and I no longer owe you anything. You're on your own, kid."

I never asked again. That's part of the reason I never enrolled in college too. I had no way to pay for it.

But I'm an adult and I know how to make things work on my own. I need to figure out what I'm going to do with my life. I want more than to serve coffee every day, no offense to people who serve coffee. I just want…more. I can't be relying on anyone else, especially not my mother's new husband, because I have no doubt that she will bring it up and use it against me at some point. Mom has never worked a day in her life and has always lived off men, and I want to make sure I'm never like that. I want to be independent, earn my own money and have a future. It's time I figure out what that future is.

"Are you sure? You know I don't mind—"

"I'm sure she will be fine," Mom cuts him off, shooting me a *you're on your own now* look. "She's an independent woman, aren't you, Skylar?" she asks, as if she can read my mind.

"I like to think so," I reply, squaring my shoulders.

The second Neville disappears into the kitchen to get us some coffee, Mom is on me. "You came here the other day bringing up Hammer, and now you're telling me you're moving back there? If this has anything to do with him, you're more of a foolish girl than I thought. If you think you can just walk into that clubhouse…he will kill you, Skylar."

Hammer would never hurt me, and I know that for a fact. She let that man raise me, but the second they broke up he's bad news? It makes no sense, and I don't really believe anything she says anymore.

"I never said anything about walking into that clubhouse or even seeing them," I say. "I know I'm not one of them anymore, Mom. I want to make something of myself, and here I'm just wasting away."

"The only thing you want to make of yourself is some biker's slut. If you think Saint still even remembers who you are, you have another thing coming," she whisper-yells.

My jaw drops.

One, because I never knew that she knew I had a thing for Saint, and two, because how dare she say that to me? She couldn't possibly be more hypocritical if she tried.

"A biker's slut? You mean what you were?" I fire back, unable to contain my anger any longer. She was an old lady, so I know it's not exactly true, but she was still with a biker and lived that lifestyle, so she can't talk. "Bit hypocritical of you, isn't it? I wouldn't have even known that life if it wasn't for you, so don't act like any of this is my fault. Perhaps if you told me who my real father was I wouldn't have to go around looking for father figures. Or is it that you don't even know, mother dearest?"

With that, I stand and head to the kitchen to tell Neville I have to leave early. I give him a hug and tell him thank you for always being so kind to me, and then get in my car and drive back home.

Home. Or at least my home for the next few days.

Can I still call it that?

Chapter Eight

Happiness is wind in my hair and a road trip leading to a fresh start. Music pumping, I try to push away the sadness at saying goodbye to Max, and leaving him standing outside watching my car disappear down the road. I know I'll see him again, but it's the end of an era, and I can't pretend that it's not.

I'm not sure how I'm going to navigate life without him, but I'm going to find out.

I finally answered Saint's letter, telling him about the move and not to reply to my old address anymore. I didn't give away too much information, but I wanted him to know that I could no longer be reached there. I guess I did want him to know I'll be closer to him too, even if I don't know what that is going to mean just yet.

I see a familiar face when I stop for gas, the man with the mustache who tried to talk to me at the bar. He pretends like he doesn't notice me, and I'm more than okay with that, so I too ignore him, pay for my gas and leave.

I arrive at Logan's a few hours later. I'm ashamed to admit I've been to his house only once before, and that was when we all had Christmas together about two years ago. His wife, Sabrina, seemed nice enough the one time I met her, and I hope that she doesn't mind that I'm going to be staying here for a while. Knocking on the door, suitcase dragging behind me, I take a deep breath and wait as I hear the door opening.

"Sky, you made it," Logan says, green eyes smiling. He pulls me in for an awkward hug, then steps back and gestures for me to enter. "Come in."

"Thanks, Logan," I reply, stepping through with my suitcase.

"Here, let me take that for you."

"Thanks. Where's Sabrina?" I ask, following behind him into the kitchen.

"She's at work. Do you want something to eat or drink? Or should I show you your room first?" he asks, running his hand through his brown hair, looking a little unsure.

"I ate on the way, so I'm okay."

"Room it is," he murmurs, gesturing upstairs. "You have the whole upstairs area to yourself."

"Thanks for letting me stay here, Logan," I say as he carries my suitcase up the stairs. "I know we haven't spoken much recently, and—"

"We're still family, Sky," he says, cutting me off. "And if you need me, I'm here for you. All right?"

"All right, thanks," I say softly, not expecting such kind words from him.

He shows me my bedroom, which is larger than I had anticipated, with a queen-sized bed and walk-in closet for my clothes. It even has a bathroom attached.

"I can't remember the last time I didn't have to share a bathroom," I admit, smiling over at him. "This is amazing, Logan."

"Good thing I bought a four-bedroom house, right?" He grins, glancing around. "We planned it so we wouldn't have to move when we had kids, but..." He trails off, shrugging. Mom had mentioned to me that Logan and Sabrina were trying to conceive, but were having no luck. He hasn't said anything to me about it personally, though, so I decide not to comment. If he wants to talk to me about it, that's up to him.

"Hopefully I will find a job this week and be out of your hair before you know it."

"There's no rush," he quickly says, placing his hands in his pockets. "It's been a while since I've gotten to spend some time with you, especially with Mom not around. It will be nice. I told Brooks and Seth to come over for dinner this weekend, so it will be a mini-sibling reunion. Shame the rest of them aren't around."

Smith and Axel are currently overseas, traveling and working together around the world. Last I heard they were in Northern Ireland. They both used to have corporate jobs, but one day they packed up and left, starting their own travel blog, which is increasing in popularity every day.

"Yeah, but that still sounds really nice, actually," I say, sitting down on the bed. "It's been a while since we've been together. And whenever Smith and Axel get home, I'll be around to catch up with them properly." I haven't seen them all since the last Christmas we spent together, which was two years ago.

He nods. "It has. Too long. Well, Sabrina changed the sheets for you and put a fresh towel in the bathroom. Anything else you need, let me know. Make yourself feel at home."

Before he heads back downstairs, I stand up, step toward him and give him a big hug.

A proper hug.

One with my arms around his waist, my cheek pressed against him, and my eyes closed.

He didn't have to look after me like this, but I'm grateful that he is.

He squeezes me back, then steps away, flashing me a sheepish smile.

"Thank you," I say once more.

"Don't mention it, baby sis," he replies, then disappears.

Lying back on my new bed, I stare up at the ceiling and smile.

* * *

"Why aren't you in the kitchen cooking?" Brooks asks me that weekend, smirking. "Is Sabrina in there doing all the work?"

"No, actually, Logan is cooking. Sabrina and I did the dessert, though. Also, stop being a pig—it's 2019," I tell him, frowning. "Let me guess, you're still single?"

Brooks and I still rub each other the wrong way, but in a sibling way. We are only a year apart, so you'd think we'd get on better, but nope. Fire and ice.

I'm fiery, and he's cold. But I still love him.

"Yeah, he is," Seth laughs, taking his own cap off then resettling it back on his head. "I've never even seen him with a girlfriend."

"The type of women I like aren't the ones you bring home," Brooks adds, raising his brows suggestively. He then looks around the room. "And I don't see your woman here anyway, Seth. Where is she?"

"At work," Seth replies, returning his gaze to the TV and then toward me. "You never told us why you suddenly decided to move here, not that we aren't happy you're close to us now. Mom driving you crazy?"

Now all eyes are suddenly on me.

"Okay, well, there was nothing there for me in the country. I want to make a career for myself, and I want a change. I only had Mom there and it's not like I was spending more than an hour a week with her, so…" I trail off, shifting in my seat.

"Are you going to go to college?" Seth asks, pushing his glasses back up on his nose. He's the only one of my brothers who has a degree, so of course it's him asking me that. "You're a smart girl, Sky. You could do anything you want. Didn't you want to be a vet growing up?"

I nod. "I did, yeah."

"So why don't you make it happen?" he asks, studying me. "I told you that working in that café was a waste of your time."

"Having money to eat and pay rent was kind of necessary,

Seth," I tell him, rolling my eyes. "And I didn't come here for an interrogation, okay? I am going to go to college. I want to do something where I can help people and actually make a difference."

"Leave her alone," Logan chastises, and it feels so good to finally have someone on my side for once. "She's here, and that's all that matters right now. She's trying to do something new. She's never even been away from Mom before, so let's cut her some slack, all right?"

"Excuse me, you guys are acting like I've been living with Mom all of this time when I haven't. I've just been in the same town as her. She hasn't been supporting me, financially or otherwise, for a long time. Just because you guys all bailed long before I was of legal age doesn't make my situation any different," I tell him, frowning. "So don't give me any shit just because I'm a girl and the youngest."

They all stay silent for a few seconds, and then Brooks says, "Is it too early to crack open that bottle of vodka I bought?"

"You only brought one?" I ask, lip twitching, glancing at each of my brothers' faces.

He throws his head back and laughs, then stands up and heads to the front door to go to his car, I'm assuming. "This is an O'Connor gathering. Of course I didn't just bring one bottle. I'll go and get my stash."

"He has a bottle shop in his car?" Seth asks, looking a mixture of impressed and horrified.

"Georgia O'Connor raised him. Of course he does," Logan mutters.

I don't miss all the digs made at Mom, but no one says anything directly to me, and I'm not sure how they feel about her.

However, I feel like there's something I'm missing, and I'm going to find out what it is.

Chapter Nine

"Well, that's what Hammer said," Seth says to Brooks, making my ears prick up.

"You've spoken to Hammer?" I ask him, sitting down next to him on the couch and looking him in the eye. We've all been vegging out in the living room, catching up on life, eating and watching movies. I forgot how much I love hanging out with all of them. "How is he?"

"Yeah, he checks in on us every now and again," Seth says, biting the inside of his lip. "Makes sure we aren't in any trouble. Not that we tell Mom that. She'd kill us if she knew."

So Saint was right. Mom didn't want Hammer to have anything to do with us, not the other way around.

"She told me that he doesn't care about any of us, and that he never once tried to make contact," I say, glancing between them.

"That's bullshit. He's always asking how you are," Seth admits, eyes softening on me.

"How come no one told me about this?"

"I don't know. You were over there with Mom, and we didn't

know what you were thinking, or if she had gotten into your head about Hammer."

"Mom never wanted to give up her control of you, Sky," Brooks adds, shrugging. "Trust me, it was just easier to stay away from all of that."

"You're an asshole," I tell him, digging my fingers into my palm. "You all had some kind of brotherhood going on and I was left in the dark, being told that Hammer and the MC washed their hands of me the same time they did Mom."

"You were only sixteen when you left, Sky," Logan adds, sitting down and joining the conversation. "We didn't want you dragged into some drama, and thought maybe it was best that you were away from it all out there in the country. Neville is a sweet guy, and Mom has been playing nice because of him, so we figured we'd leave it be."

"Why did you want nothing to do with the MC?" I ask him, something I have always wondered.

Logan winces and rubs the back of his neck. "You know that I never felt at home there. I remember walking into the clubhouse one time with Mom. I was like seventeen, but we were a little early and I saw something I wasn't meant to." He shakes his head, as if trying to forget the memory. "And Mom acted like it was fucking normal, when it wasn't. I just remember thinking, what the fuck am I doing here? It wasn't the life I wanted, and I never really clicked with any of the men. I remember you as a kid, coming home after you got into a fight, because the other kids judged you because of your parents. I didn't like that. I don't know. It was just never my home, Sky. Ever. I know it was yours, and that's okay, but it wasn't for me. Hammer was a different man to you than he was to the rest of us. He saw you as his daughter, but we weren't his sons. We never called him Dad, and he never did for us the things he did for you."

"I never thought of it that way," I whisper, not knowing what to say. He's right, they never did call Hammer "Dad," and I guess it's because they're older and remember their own father.

Hammer obviously cared about them all, I don't doubt that for a second, but maybe he didn't have the same bond with them that he did with me. I suddenly feel a little sad about that. We should have all been treated equally no matter what. We should have always stuck together, but we didn't.

"And we knew when you were old enough you'd get sick of Mom's shit," Brooks says, smirking. "Took a bit longer than we thought, but that's okay."

"How about a fucking invitation or something? I had no idea if I was even welcome here. Our family isn't exactly the Brady Bunch, and nothing was the same after I moved away. You barely kept in touch with me, and now I feel like the baby, the lone black sheep or something," I grumble, crossing my arms.

"Ah, come on, don't pout," Seth grumbles in return, reaching out and touching my shoulder. "We should have put in more effort to keep in contact with you. It was just hard, because then we had to deal with Mom, and that's not always easy. Especially when it comes to you."

"What does that even mean? Especially when it comes to me?" I ask him.

He glances away, looking to Logan for some help.

"Mom's just really weird when it comes to you," Logan admits, a look of sadness passing in his gaze. "It's like if we ask about you, or show interest in you, she doesn't like it and wants to bring the attention back to her. I don't know...it's almost like she sees you as competition. And I know this isn't a really nice thing to say or whatever, but that's just how I see it. I feel like she's jealous of you, and always has been. She was the queen, surrounded by all these boys doting on her, and then you came along. The last sibling, beautiful, smart. We all fell in love with you. Including Hammer and his men. And she didn't like that."

Eyes wide, I sit back in my chair and take a deep breath. I've never thought about this from that perspective before. I knew I wasn't Mom's favorite, but it never crossed my mind that she was jealous of me.

Why would she be? It's true that the men in the MC tended to spoil me growing up, and my brothers always cared for me. Could it be possible that my own mother didn't like that? The thought is foreign to me. What kind of mother feels that way about her only daughter?

"I don't even know what to say right now…" I glance around at my brothers, taking them each in individually. Brooks looks more like me, with his red hair and green eyes, but Seth and Logan have brown hair and brown eyes like their dad.

"Which is why we never said anything," Logan continues, running his hand through his dark brown hair. "How do you tell your little sister something like that? It's complicated, makes no sense and is kind of twisted."

"It's not like Mom was mean to you or anything," Brooks adds in, shrugging. "She just…is more of a boys' mom."

I roll my eyes at him. "Seriously? All of you seem to think she's crazy, so she can't have been that great of a mother to all of you, either."

"She *is* crazy," Logan agrees, making the others chuckle. "She has her good moments. She's not evil. She just has a very… unpredictable side to her. She's manipulative and can be quite conniving when she needs to be."

"Understatement," Seth adds, standing behind me and resting his hands on my shoulders. "You're out of her grasp now, that's all that matters. And if you want to go and see Hammer, you can. She doesn't control your life anymore."

"Have any of you seen or spoken to Saint?" I dare ask. I have no idea if they knew about my crush on him or not.

"Nope," Logan replies, shaking his head. "We've only spoken to Hammer. Why? Still have that stupid-ass crush on him?"

I'll take that as confirmation that they knew.

"I have no idea what crush you're talking about, but yes, Saint was a big part of my life once upon a time," I admit, accepting the ice-cold glass of vodka and lemonade that Seth passes my way. "Thank you, Seth. So what else have I missed out on while I've been segregated?"

"Nothing much on my end," Brooks answers first, downing his glass then giving me his attention. "Still working at the sandalwood factory."

We chat for a bit, and then we have dinner, a lasagna and salad that Logan made for us. Sabrina comes back from work just in time to have some of the dessert we both made earlier today, chocolate cheesecake and strawberries, before the boys start heading home. It's been so long since I felt like I could open up and be close to my brothers, like when we were little, but after tonight I realize how much I've missed them all. Even Brooks, who is generally a total asshole.

I already feel like I've made the right choice by moving here. There's no going back now.

Saint,

    Sorry it's been so long since I've written to you. I've been settling in at Logan's house and found a new job at a bar, so I've been pretty busy. I've been looking at different colleges too, trying to figure out what my passion is and what I'm meant to do.

    How are you doing? I've been thinking about going to visit Hammer, but I'm not sure if I should call him or just show up. Am I even welcome there anymore? Maybe calling would be safer. I don't really know what to expect, but I do want to see him, and I do want some answers. How would you feel about me coming to visit you?

Sky

I write this letter, but then decide not to send it. Some things are just better said face-to-face.

I'm going to go see Hammer.

And then I'm going to go and see Saint.

* * *

Feeling extremely nervous, I step onto the Knights of Fury MC turf. The last time I was here I was being dragged away and put into Mom's car, which was five years ago. So much has changed since then, but the clubhouse building remains exactly the same, the brown brick, the rickety metal fence and the worn wooden door. There's a few bikes out front, making me pause for a moment as I scope them out, trying to see if I remember any of them but coming up short.

Slowly, my white canvas shoes take me to the entrance. I knock once, and then twice, louder, when no one answers the first time.

"Is that someone knocking?" I hear a masculine voice ask. "Jesus Christ. Those knocks were too polite to be the cops. Who the fuck could it be?"

I don't know if anyone has even knocked on this door, other than police, because normally everyone just walks in like they own the place. However, I don't really feel comfortable doing that, especially when I don't even know if Hammer is in there.

"I hope it's someone selling chocolate or candy," another voice adds, just before the door opens, and I see Renny, aka Renegade, and Temper standing in front of me. While I wasn't that close with Renny growing up, Temper was one of my favorite bikers. The man has a heart of gold for the select few he lets in. For everyone else, though…if Temper doesn't like you, you should get the fuck out of Dodge.

"Sky?" Temper asks, brow furrowing. "Is that you? Holy fuck, it is! What the fuck happened to you? You grew up on me."

He opens his arms, and I run into them. "And you grew old on me, Temper."

"Only you can get away with saying shit like that, trouble," he mutters, voice husky. "What in hell are you doing here? You're the last person I thought to see on the other side of this door."

I let go of him and turn to Renny, offering him a shy smile. "Renny."

"Sky," he replies, stroking my hair. "Hammer is going to be fuckin' happy to see you."

Relief fills me, and my shoulders release all of their tension. "Is he here?"

Temper nods and pulls me gently by the wrist. "Come on."

He leads me through the house and outside to the yard, and that's where I see him on a chair, smoke in hand, staring out at the sky.

"Hey, Prez, look who the cat dragged in," Renny calls out ahead of us.

Hammer doesn't even turn around. "If it has tits I'm not in the mood," he calls out, tone irritated.

"I mean, she does have them, but I'm not gonna look at them if I wanna live to tell the story," Renny says, chuckling deeply.

This seems to get Hammer's attention. His slow head turn has my nerves racing. He looks the same. A little grayer, a few more wrinkles around his eyes, but he's exactly how I remembered him.

Sky? he mouths, shaking his head slightly, as if to clear it. He looks surprised, shocked…but also happy. Standing, he opens his arms and smiles widely, approaching me. When he reaches me, he hugs me so tightly that all of the pieces fit back together.

Home.

I'm home. I'm safe.

"Dad?" I whisper, feeling emotional, tears prickling at the back of my eyes. I bury my face into his worn brown leather jacket and just hold on to him for dear life.

He kisses the top of my head. "I knew you'd come back."

Lifting my face up, looking him in the eyes, I say, "Did you? Because I didn't."

Sadness fills his brown gaze. "I hoped that you would. Does your mother know that you are here?"

I shake my head. "No, and I'm not going to tell her. My brothers told me what happened. I know she didn't want any of us to have any contact."

Which is quite the understatement. Mom is the one who took me away from Hammer. She didn't want me to have a relationship with him because she no longer did.

I pull back from him and wipe my eyes with my palms. "Is someone cutting onions?"

They must be. I'm sure of it. I'm not much of a crier, and I'm the type who tends to bury her emotions as much as she can. Suffer in silence, that's my motto.

"I've missed you," I admit.

The man standing before me is the only parent who has ever shown me love, the only one who made me feel like I'm not a failure. Up until we left, Hammer had done nothing but love, support and be there for me, and even though it's been years, all of those feelings and emotions come back. They say you never remember what a person says, you remember only how they made you feel, and right now I feel loved and cherished, and it's all coming back like it was yesterday.

This man took me to the hospital when I broke my arm.

He made me soup when I was sick.

He threatened the parents of the boy who was mean to me in fifth grade.

Through all the years he was the one who got me through everything, and now I have him back.

"I've missed you too, Sky," he replies, cupping my face and smiling down at me. "Welcome home."

Chapter Ten

The next voice I hear is one I didn't expect.

"Skylar?"

I look around Hammer to see Saint himself, standing at the door. He's dressed in a pair of low-slung jeans and he's not wearing a shirt. My eyes linger on his body, one that was once bare but now is covered in tattoos and muscles, and I don't know where to look right now. He's beautiful. He seems older, more mature, and there's a weariness in his eyes that wasn't there before.

"What are you doing here?" I ask him, lost for words.

I thought I'd have a little time to prepare myself before seeing him, and when I did it was going to be at the prison, so this whole meeting has caught me off guard. I'm still drawn to him like no other, and I can't seem to look away from him. It's been so long since I laid eyes on that face and heard that voice, and now that he's finally in front of me I don't really know what to say or do. The last time we saw each other we were friends and I was a child. Yes, I was sixteen, but it was a schoolgirl crush. But now...seeing him as an adult woman has me feeling all sorts of things I don't know if I'm supposed to feel. I'm still very much attracted to him. Is this normal?

As I study him, I can see he's looking at me in that same inscrutable way he always did. But this time, there is something else. It's like he's seeing me for the first time. He's never looked at me this way before.

"I could say the same about you," he murmurs, stepping toward me.

Hammer backs away and lets us have our moment, and when Saint's arms come around me, his warm skin pressing against me, I don't have words to express how I'm feeling. I've thought about this moment for so long, but it's so much more than I ever thought it was going to be.

"They let you out early?" I surmise, looking up at him. "I didn't expect to see you here, that's for sure."

He nods. "Yeah, early release. Long story."

"I have all the time in the world to hear about it," I reply with an arched brow.

Lip twitching, he smiles down at me. "I can't believe you're standing here right now. When you never wrote back to me, I just thought that you'd given up."

Staring at the tattoo on his chest, a knight with a grim reaper ax, I say, "Nope. I was actually going to visit you at the prison next, after I got the details from Hammer, but looks like you beat me to it. I'm glad you're back home; I didn't like the thought of you locked up."

"I didn't like the thought of it either," he replies, lip twitching. "And I've never been happier to be home than I am in this moment. You're a sight for sore eyes, Skylar. I feel like I'm fucking dreaming or something."

I think that's a good thing.

"I feel like this is a cause for celebration," I hear Renny mutter to Temper. "Is she old enough to finally attend one of our parties?"

"We don't want to scare her off just yet," Hammer mutters in a dry tone. "She just got here."

"Think the last thing she needs is to be around half-naked women and lots of bikers, Renny," Temper replies, smirking. He slaps him on the back. "But if you need that, we can make it happen."

"Excellent," Renny says, rubbing his hands together in anticipation. "It's been a while."

Saint touches my cheek, bringing my attention back to him. "Come on, let's go sit inside. I'll make you a coffee, or see if we have anything to eat in the fridge."

"Good luck," Hammer calls out, laughing softly. The other men don't follow us, which I appreciate, giving me that little alone time with Saint.

"There used to always be food here," I point out, remembering the days I'd open the cupboards and fridge and think I'd won the lottery.

"There used to be women around here," Saint replies, opening the door for me. "It's just us now, and well. The place has a more bachelor vibe to it. None of us have old ladies, and the older members don't live here anymore—they're with their families—so it's just about ten of us now."

"Bachelors don't need to eat?" I tease, heading for the kitchen with him at my heel. "And I highly doubt it that there aren't any women here."

As much as I don't want to think of it in regards to Saint, I know that the Knights are notorious ladies' men. I've seen it with my own eyes, even if I wasn't allowed to officially attend any of their club parties, and I heard the rumors about Saint and how he got his name. He just has this allure to him; I don't think he needs to even try with women—they just fall at his feet.

It sucks to think that I also might be in that same category, but I like to think that I'm different, because we also have a genuine friendship, or at least we had one. I don't know where we stand now, but we're both here right now and that means something. He reached out to me, and now I've found my way back. If Saint didn't want anything to do with me romantically, I'd happily still be in his life as a friend, and I truly do mean that. I want to see him happy no matter what, and if that's not with me then I'd accept that.

"None that stay around and feed us," Saint replies, opening the fridge and scanning its contents. "If I knew you were coming, I would have run to the store. How about I order us all pizza or something?"

He turns the kettle on, then sits down at the table, so I do the same. "I'm fine, Saint," I tell him, grinning.

I'm too excited to eat, nerves and happiness mixing together into a giddiness.

"I can't stop looking at you," he blurts out, and then ducks his head. "You're so different since the last time I saw you."

"Good different?" I ask, wishing that I knew what he was thinking.

"Yeah." He smiles and just stares at me, our eyes locking. After a while, he shakes himself out of a daze. "Tell me how you ended up here, because I bet it's a fuckin' story."

I tell him about my conversation with Mom, my decision to move and the sadness at leaving my roommate. We talk about my brothers and how I decided I was just going to show up and hope for the best.

Blue eyes watch me as he listens intently and then says, "Well, there you go. Even I had no idea Hammer was checking in with your brothers."

"Glad someone else was in the dark with me."

A man steps into the kitchen, and I recognize him instantly. "What the fuck?"

He waves, a sheepish grin on his face. "I'm Dee."

"Dee?" I ask, confused. "You're a member? Why the fuck were you following me?"

Did Hammer ask him to watch me?

"I'm a prospect," he admits, looking to Saint to explain the situation, I guess.

"He was checking up on you to make sure you were all right," he explains, wincing and running a hand through his dark hair. It's a little shorter than I remember it. "I know it sounds bad, but like you said in your letter, we aren't there with you, so we wanted to make sure you were okay, and to do that we needed eyes on you."

"You or Hammer could have come yourselves!" I point out, scowling. "Or Temper. Renny. Any of you. And you could have come and actually said hello to me."

"We couldn't send someone your mother was going to recognize—that would bring a hell of a lot of drama we don't need. So we sent someone she wouldn't know," he explains, shrugging like it makes perfect sense to him. If he wasn't sitting here all sexy, shirtless, and if it hadn't been so long since I'd seen him, I might have slapped him.

"So you sent some guy to come and talk to me in a bar?" I mutter to myself, shaking my head. "Next time a phone call will suffice, Saint."

He throws Dee a look that says *bye* then turns back to me. "I'm seeing you for the first time in five years and you want to fight?"

"How did I know you were going to play that card?" I groan, quieting when he reaches out and touches my arm.

"Let me get used to seeing you all grown up before you rip into me, all right?" he asks, flashing me a charming smile. He then stands to make our coffee. "Do you have any plans tonight?"

"No. I have to work tomorrow, but that's about it."

"Where are you working?" he asks, sounding confused. "More like *why* are you working?"

"You know, to do things like eat," I say slowly, arching my brow. "And buy things. I only just started at this new bar, but it's a pretty cool place."

Saint, mug in hand, comes over and places it on the table. "What did you do with the money Hammer gave you? Are you saving it? I thought you'd go to college and just live off that so you didn't have to worry about anything else except your studies."

Confusions hits me. I dare to ask, "What money?"

Saint's brows draw together, and concern fills those blue eyes. "The college fund Hammer set up for you. He's been putting money into it ever since you came into his life."

College fund? I've never heard the words *college fund* in relation to me. My mother never gave me a cent, and always made me work for anything that I wanted. "I didn't get any money, Saint. Mom never told me that there was any money."

"Nothing?" he asks, jaw going tense.

I shake my head. "No, nothing."

"That fucking bitch," he mutters, slamming his hands down on the table, making his coffee drip down the mug. "Hammer!" he calls out. Studying me, he murmurs, "Stay here a second," then disappears outside.

I can hear the two of them yelling before they come reappear in the kitchen. "Georgia didn't give you any of that money?" Hammer asks me, searching my eyes.

I shake my head. "No, nothing. I had no idea I had any kind of savings anywhere. I've always just lived paycheck to paycheck." Not a luxurious life, but I've always gotten by.

"There was a hundred thousand dollars in that account for you," he growls, fist clenching. "I made it so you could access it when you turned eighteen."

Wow, that's a lot of money. A hundred thousand?

Wrapping my arms around myself, I don't know what else to say. This woman I thought I could trust, even if we weren't as close as some kids are with their mothers, has lied to me over and over. And now she's had money that was supposed to be mine while she knew I struggled to pay my bills? And never told me about it? I'm speechless.

"Guess she thought Sky would never speak to us again, so she'd never find out about the money," Saint says, shaking his head. "The nerve of her, honestly. That money was for Sky-lar's future!"

"I asked her for some money once," I say in a whisper, re-membering the day so clearly. "She told me that she was done taking care of me and I was on my own. That she had five other children, and how could I expect there to be anything left for myself? That I was ungrateful. It's why I didn't go to college right away…"

My brain cannot process this. I cannot understand how she can lie to me and make me feel that it was my fault. This can't be true.

"Maybe there is more to the story. Maybe she still has it and was waiting to give it to me," I say, but the words sound stupid even to my own ears. It's just embarrassing that my own mother would manipulate me and use me so easily, and I was none the wiser, visiting with her every week, playing my role as the good daughter, the only child she had close by to her.

The men don't even bother with a response, and I don't need one, because I know the words I just spoke are lies. I take a deep breath. "It's fine. Thank you for thinking of me, Hammer. I think it's the nicest thing anyone has done for me."

Swallowing hard, I look down at my hands.

Don't cry.

Don't cry.

Don't cry.

Strong arms come around me. "I'll fix this for you."

Glancing up, I smile at my dad.

Saint steps closer, touching my shoulder, silently giving him his strength. "No one is going to hurt you anymore, Sky. We've got you now."

The tears fall.

Chapter Eleven

"Safe to say today has been an emotional day," I state, sighing heavily. I must look like crap, after crying and rubbing my face, I imagine my mascara must be everywhere, and I'm feeling completely overwhelmed. Seeing Hammer and finding out my own mother doesn't have my best interests at heart has taken its toll on me. I mean, I shouldn't be surprised, but that doesn't mean that the reality of it doesn't hurt.

And then there's Saint.

I want to hold him, to be held by him, but with Hammer here it's kind of awkward, and just because we've finally reconnected doesn't mean we are anything. Yeah, he wants to do dinner tonight, but that could just be to catch up. It's not like he's ever said he had any feelings for me other than friendship. Oh god. What if he still thinks of me as a little sister?

My life is a fucking mess, and I almost feel like I need to go home and crawl into bed right now to process everything.

"Been a bit of a surprise for us all," Hammer mutters, then smiles at me with gentle eyes. "Don't worry about anything, Sky."

He says that, but I still have so many questions. Is now the time to bring them up or should I wait?

"Why didn't you fight for me?" I blurt out, unable to keep myself quiet. "With your reaction today, it's like you missed me and wanted me to come back here. So why didn't you fight for me? Call me? Visit me? Send me a fucking message? Something. Anything?"

"It's complicated," he says, sharing a look with Saint, who appears to want to make a quick exit from this conversation. "Your mom held all the power with you, Sky. You were *her* daughter, no matter how much she didn't deserve you—"

"I was your daughter too," I cut him off. "I *am* your daughter. Or don't you feel that way anymore?"

"Of course I do," he says quickly.

"Then don't play that card. You not being my biological father doesn't mean anything to me," I say, looking him in the eye. "I know there's something you aren't telling me. I'm not stupid. There's no way in hell the whole MC is so scared of Georgia O'Connor that they never want to go up against her. Sending me a message or calling me wouldn't have upset anyone except her. So what does she have on you?"

That has to be the only reason: Mom must have blackmailed them with something. It's that or they simply didn't care enough about me and gave up. There's no other explanation.

Hammer rubs the back of his neck. "Fucking hell, Skylar. There's some things that are better left unsaid, and this is one of them. Don't push this, because you won't like the truth, and I won't be able to fucking sleep at night knowing that you know. So please, let it be. I'm so fucking happy to have you back— don't make me break your heart on the same day."

He cups my cheek, smiles sadly, then leaves the room.

"He's really going to say all that and then bail?" I ask Saint, shaking my head. "What could possibly break my heart any more than it's already been broken?"

Saint wraps his arms around me. "Your mom and Hammer

had a complicated relationship, as I'm sure you remember. They hated each other half the time and were obsessed with each other the other half. It was unhealthy. Who knows what went on between them that we don't know about?"

I breathe easier knowing Saint has been left in the dark with me. "I do remember."

Unhealthy is the right word. The two of them had a passionate, yet volatile relationship, one with a lot of drama. I've blocked out most of it and pretended it was normal, but it wasn't. Hammer was always the stable parent in my life, and considering he's the president of an MC, that's saying something. We did have plenty of good times as a family, though, and they are what I try to remember.

Saint holds me tighter.

After having not seen him for so long, I can feel that we are still connected.

But in what way is to be determined.

Saint and I head out to dinner, but I requested something low-key and casual, so we decide on a little Indian place that we used to all eat from back in the day.

"Nice to see that some things around here don't change," I say as we walk inside, smiling at the familiar décor. Saint pulls out my chair, waiting for me to be seated before doing the same. Looking over the small table at him, I start feeling a little shy. It's just us now, no distractions, and it feels more intimate than I imagined it would be.

"Your hair is so long now," he muses, staring at it. "It's beautiful."

"Thank you," I say, feeling myself blush a little. "Yours is just how I remember it, just a little shorter, though."

He runs his hand through his thick, dark hair. "Yeah, I cut it but it grew back. It grows fast. Do you like it like this, or think I should get rid of it?"

"I like it," I say, wanting to run my own fingers through it.

"I don't think many men can pull it off, but it suits you. It always has."

Between all the dark hair, piercing blue eyes and his body, I must say he has a lot going for him, and I know that there's no way in hell that I'm the only one who notices that.

"Okay, I'll keep it then," he says with a wolfish grin, picking up the menu in front of him.

"So when did you get out exactly?" I ask.

"Two days ago," he replies. "So good timing on your behalf."

The waitress comes over, and we order our drinks and meals.

"How's it been moving in with Logan?" he asks me, changing the subject away from him. "You know you can always move into the clubhouse with us."

"Thanks for the offer," I say, grinning. "But it's pretty sweet at Logan's, and it's nice to have my own space. He and Sabrina have given me their entire upstairs—it's a really cool setup. Because of our age difference, I never really got a chance to get to know him. I feel like this is my second chance to get to know my brothers in a different way. I saw Seth and Brooks as well. It's great to be surrounded by family."

"I'm glad you have them, then," he replies, studying me. I notice a freckle on his olive skin, on his left cheek, one that wasn't there before.

"Yeah. I do miss my best friend and old roommate, though..."

Saint shakes his head. "You couldn't go live with a bunch of girls, could you?" he grumbles, lip twitching. "It had to be with a dude, and one who is a rock star."

"How'd you know that?" I ask, wondering how he knew about Max. But then I remember my stalker. "Did Dee tell you?" I roll my eyes. "Max is family to me. There is nothing between us but friendship."

He nods, and I take a moment to bask in the fact that I'm sitting here. With Saint.

"You're the same, but different," I announce, looking away from his intense blue gaze. "Like, I know you, but at the same time I don't anymore. I've missed out on so much, Saint. You need to catch me up."

We're both different, older people now, and hopefully more mature. I want to know everything I've missed out on, and what has happened in his life in the last few years.

"I feel the same way about you," he admits. "You were just a girl back then."

"And now?"

"And now you're a woman," he replies, lip twitching. "Those few years were good to you."

"Are you saying I was ugly back then?" I joke, laughing.

"No," he replies, laughing with me. "But you were young, Sky. I only saw you as a girl, because that's what you were. We were friends."

"I know," I admit. "Although I did have a bit of a crush on you."

"I know," he replies, grinning. "But you know how difficult a position it put me in. I had to balance not hurting your feelings with not leading you on. It's why I never flirted back. It's like I programmed myself to see you as Hammer's kid daughter and that's what you were. Besides, Hammer would have killed me."

I nod. "I can understand that. But I always thought…" I stop myself.

"No. Tell me," he encourages.

Well, Sky, it's now or never. "I always thought that there was this connection between us. I mean, I knew you never looked at me in a romantic way, but there was something more than friendship. I don't know what I'm saying…" I trail off, afraid to look into his face.

He's silent for a while, and then he grabs my hand. "Sky, look at me."

I do as he asks and see nothing but sincerity and gentleness in his eyes.

"There *was* a connection. You weren't wrong. But you were

a kid, and no matter what you felt or I felt, it never would have happened back then, even if you had never left."

And just like that my heart shatters. He's telling me that we're destined to be just friends. I try not to cry.

"I understand," I whisper, trying to hold in the pain that I feel after hearing that.

He looks at me and shakes his head. "No, I don't think you do. What I'm trying to say is it never would've happened then. But you being gone all those years, and coming back as an adult woman...it changes things."

I process what he's saying to me. "So you're saying that it's good that my mother took me away from my only family and stole money meant for me, and that I lived a pitiful existence for five years," I joke.

He laughs. "Well, I'm not saying what happened to you was good. But I'm saying that it changed the course of things. Now we get a fresh start. Now you are an adult. Now I don't have to hold back."

Holy shit, did my childhood crush just tell me that I have a chance?

We're silent as our drinks come.

"So what else have I missed out on? The MC has consumed my life," he admits, a distant look in his eyes. "I've been working my ass off to prove myself, and to slowly work up the rank. How about you? How was country life?"

"Pretty good, but it was the same thing every day, you know? After I moved out of Mom's, she met Neville and they got married and moved in together, and then I kind of fended for myself. Worked at the café to make ends meet, spent a lot of time with my friends." I pause, thinking of Shauna. "I told you about Shauna. She was my best friend, and for a little while there it was always her, me and Max—the Three Musketeers. If I wasn't at work or with them, I was volunteering at the children's hospital. I think I was kind of just buying time while deciding what I should study at college."

"And what did you decide on?"

"Still contemplating," I say, grinning. "Terrible, I know. I'm twenty-one and still have no idea what I want to do with my life."

Saint laughs softly, and reaches over the table to touch the bracelet on my wrist. "Is there anything you're leaning toward? Anything you are passionate about?"

I think about what he is asking me. No one has ever asked me that and I don't think I ever asked myself this either.

"You know I never stopped to ask myself that. I'm not very creative, so being an artist or poet is out. I have issues with authority—let's blame me being raised in an MC for that one—so that's a no to law enforcement," I joke. "But in all seriousness. I think I want to help people. I like helping people. When I was volunteering at the children's hospital, I got a huge sense of satisfaction after my shifts there. Like I was doing something to make another person's day better. Like I was making a difference."

"That doesn't surprise me at all, Sky. You've always been so empathetic. Always wanting to put a smile on someone's face."

"Yeah, but now the question is, how do I turn that into a career?"

"You're still young, and you have time. You'll figure it out."

"You sound so confident," I whisper, eyes on his fingers.

"You're destined for great things," he replies, bringing my gaze back to his. "I've always known it, and I believe in you. That mind is a weapon."

Ducking my head just as the waitress brings us our meal, I thank her then wait for her to leave before saying, "I guess only time will tell."

"And you have all the time in the world," he says, taking a sip of his soda.

"You say the MC has consumed your life. How so? No one ever told me about how the MC was run back then, what you guys did to make ends meet. What exactly do you do for the Knights?"

He studies me for a few seconds before answering. "We have a few different businesses. Security, for one. We do security for high-profile people. We also own and run a bar. We do a few little things on the side, but those are the things I'm not going to mention right now."

My eyes widen. "At least tell me it's not drugs."

He shakes his head, but says nothing else. If they aren't selling drugs, maybe it's weapons, guns or something.

"You're not a pimp, are you? Because that would kind of be a deal breaker."

He shakes his head again, this time with amusement dancing in his eyes.

"Okay, good. What does twenty-six feel like?" I ask, changing the subject to something a little lighter.

"Pretty good," he admits, flashing his teeth in a grin, and placing his glass back down onto the table. "My back's not hurting yet. I think I'll give that another five years or so."

"Nope, it does look like your body is in fine form," I say, leaning forward and lowering my voice. I'm trying my hand at this flirting thing. "Looks like you've spent a lot of time in the gym while I've been gone."

He flexes his arm. "Nice to know my hard work hasn't gone unappreciated."

"Nice to know your ego is still intact," I fire back, amused.

"I don't know what you're talking about," he replies, laughing out loud. "I'm as modest as they come."

"Well, Mr. Modest, are you going to tell me what happened that got you locked up?"

"Got into a fight," is all he says, shrugging. "I lost my cool, hit a guy, and then was arrested. I took a plea deal that gave me only a few months in jail. And here I am."

He makes it sound like it's not a big deal at all, when it clearly is.

I let it slide, though, and figure he will open up about it in due time.

It's always been so easy to talk to Saint, and it's good to know that that hasn't changed. We eat, and laugh and joke through the entire meal. It's like I'm getting to know him all over again.

The butter chicken was amazing, but the company was even better.

Chapter Twelve

"Where have you been?" Logan asks as I step inside the house, key still in my hand. "It's ten o'clock—you left hours ago."

"I hung out at the clubhouse then went to eat dinner," I explain, locking the door behind me. "Why, what's wrong?"

"Nothing, I was just worried when you didn't answer your phone."

"Shit, sorry," I murmur, pulling it out of my bag. "It was on silent."

"Hey," Sabrina says as she pokes her head out of their bedroom. "How was your rendezvous with the bikers?"

"Good," I say, smiling. The smile drops as I remember the whole money fiasco. "And also bad. I found out that Hammer left me some money for college, and Mom never gave it to me."

And to think of all the nights I was eating two-minute noodles because I couldn't afford anything else. That hundred thousand would have come in handy. Hell, one thousand dollars would have come in handy.

"Wait, what?" Logan asks, frowning. He follows me into the kitchen, where I put down my bag and grab some water from the sink. "He left you money and she took it? How much are we talking here?" He pauses, and then adds, "And how come the rest of us didn't get any money?"

"It was for me to go to college," I tell him with a shrug. "And because I'm the favorite."

"You totally are, you little shit. With Hammer, anyway. I'm Mom's favorite," he responds, sitting down.

"Is that something to brag about?" I ask, smirking. "And even if you did get any money, Mom probably would have taken that too. Maybe he did leave money for you all. I remember he used to pay for everything for all of us. Anyway, I don't know if I should call her out on it or just let it be. Maybe it's still sitting there in her bank, growing interest. Neville pays for everything for her, so it's not like she has to reach into her own pocket. I knew she was shady, but this is next level. No wonder she never cared when I couldn't decide what to study in college."

"She probably tried to justify it," Logan agrees, shaking his head in shock. "If you ask her about it, that's what she's going to say, that you never enrolled in college so you didn't need the money. Plus if you call her she's going to know that you spoke to Hammer."

"So basically I have to let go of the largest amount of money I'd probably ever see in my life?" I sulk, pouting my lip out. "Damn, I was almost rich there for a second."

"Now you'll actually have to go to college and get a job that pays well," he adds, amusement dancing in his eyes. "Ain't that a bitch?"

I expel a deep sigh. "The search for a desirable career path continues."

Sabrina joins us in the kitchen, her long silk robe trailing behind her. "Man, I'm thirty and I still don't know what I want to do."

"You guys aren't giving me much hope here," I deadpan. "Don't you like your job at the retirement center, Sabrina?"

She shrugs and moves to stand next to Logan. "Pays the bills.

I don't love it, though. I always wanted to get a job in fashion, design my own clothes or something."

"Why don't you?" I ask. "If I knew what I wanted, I'd be going after it."

"I don't know, I guess I didn't think it was something that was realistic," she admits, sounding saddened by that fact. "Only a few people would be making money off those type of jobs. Working as a nurse's aide is steady pay, and there's lots of work. Fashion is a gamble. But maybe I should look into it. I'm in a more stable place now, or I could even take it on as a hobby."

"You should," I encourage.

A gamble.

Why do I feel like anything worth pursuing is usually a gamble?

"What are you doing here?" I ask Saint, smiling up at him. He looks like a damn snack, dressed in black from head to toe, his bound hair off his face.

"Wanted to check out your new workplace," he replies, glancing around the bar before bringing his eyes back to me. "And I wanted to ask you out on a date."

My eyes widen. "A date?"

I can't stop the smile spreading on my face. I had hoped after getting dinner the other night that he was into me, but I didn't really know for sure. When we got back to the clubhouse to get my car he just gave me a hug and said he'd see me around.

He nods, eyes pinning me in my place. "Things are different now, Sky. Do you understand what I'm saying?"

Talk about putting me on the spot. "So the Indian food wasn't a date?"

"More like a pre-date catch-up," he replies, shrugging. "So are we on the same page?"

"Yes," I say, swallowing hard. "I mean, I think so."

"You think or you know?" he asks, lip twitching.

"You want me," I state, boldly so.

And he's letting me know it, clear as day.

He nods and flashes me that smile of his, the one that makes me feel weak in the knees. "How about tomorrow night? I thought maybe I could take you for a ride on my bike."

I know the men are weird about who they let on their bikes, and once they're taken they want only their old ladies on the back of theirs.

"That sounds nice," I reply, happiness filling me. "Do you want something to drink while you're here?"

"Sure, I'll have a whiskey. Neat, please," he says, taking some money out of his wallet while I make the drink. He gives me a hundred dollar bill, then shakes his head when I try to give him the change, so I put it all in the tip jar.

"You're ridiculous, you know that?" I tell him as I slide him his drink.

He simply grins. "Thank you."

"You're welcome. Are you going to stick around?"

"Yeah, for a bit anyway," he says. "I've never been here before."

And I bet he wants to suss the place out, probably see what type of crowd we get. It's pretty much a standard bar, though, with a dance floor thrown in. "It's a pretty easygoing place, Saint. I'm fine. It starts to get busier in about an hour."

"Let me do my thing, and I'll let you do yours," he murmurs, lip twitching, making my eyes narrow.

"You going to start trying to boss me around before we've even gone on our first date?" I ask, arching my brow with my hands on my hips. "I didn't take any of your shit before I was even legal—don't think I'm going to take it now."

He throws back his head and laughs.

And it's glorious.

"I don't know what's so funny," I grumble, grabbing a cloth and wiping down the counter so my boss doesn't see me doing nothing. "I might not have had many boyfriends, but I know what I'm not going to put up with."

"Boyfriend, hey?" he teases, leaning forward over the counter. "I think you're moving a little too fast for me, Sky."

I throw the cloth at him and storm to the other side of the bar, shaking my head in amusement and embarrassment. He's such a shithead.

Saint follows me, glass of whiskey still in his hand, and glances out over the dance floor, where there's only a couple of people enjoying the music.

"You still like singing?" He turns back to me to ask, finishing the rest of his drink and placing the glass down.

"You remember that?" I ask, eyes widening in surprise. "Yeah, I still like singing. Just not in front of anyone. I'm more of a bathroom singer."

"Yeah, you used to sing while doing your homework at the table in the clubhouse," he reminisces, leaning over the table and touching my cheek. "You were in school while I was prospecting."

"It was a big age gap at the time," I admit, shrugging. "But it doesn't feel that way now. Does it to you?"

"It doesn't feel that way now, no," he agrees, pushing an errant hair back behind my ear.

Some customers appear, and I take a step away from him, pull myself together and go do my job, while Saint faces the crowd. I don't actually mind him being here, but I realize it's going to be a problem when the place starts to fill up and the women start to approach him.

The first one—who is very beautiful, might I add—strolls up to him confidently and speaks to him with her hand on his arm. He removes it, which I appreciate, and shakes his head at her, refusing whatever she had on offer.

Scowling, I make two espresso martinis, trying not to glance back over at him. I know he's here because he's being protective, but apart from the eye candy, he's not helping, and I'm perfectly safe. I also seem to be paying more attention to what he is doing than the customers lining up for drinks. The man is a distraction.

The next time I look there's two new women trying to speak to him.

"Do you want to have a break, Skylar?" Camilla, the bar manager, asks me.

"Yes, please," I tell her, not moving my eyes from Saint.

"Is that your man?" she asks me, whistling under her breath. "He's fine."

"Not yet, but he will be," I reply, walking around the bar and straight to him. His eyes widen as he sees me, but it doesn't stop me from my mission. I step through the women, right in front of him, get up on my tiptoes and kiss him.

I wanted this kiss long before I was ever going to get it, so different from the innocent kiss Saint gave me all those years ago before I was ripped out of his arms.

And fuck.

His soft lips respond immediately as he takes control, gently gripping the back of my neck and pulling me closer to him. I have goose bumps on my skin, and my heart is racing out of my chest as he kisses me like I've never been kissed before, sensually yet hungrily. The kiss gets a little too hot for public, his tongue teasing me and our bodies pressed up and close as they can get with our clothes on.

It's me who pulls away. "Wow," I whisper, licking my lips and staring up at him.

He swipes his thumb along my lower lip. "You're moving too fast for me, Sky," he teases again, wrapping an arm around me and kissing the top of my head. "What was that for?"

I decide to stay silent, because anything I say right now isn't going to make me look good. Instead, I glance at the two women, who are still standing on either side of him, watching us. Apparently they just can't take a hint.

Saint leans down and whispers into my ear. "And by the way, these are my cousins."

His cousins?

Shit.

"This is Skylar," he says to the two of them. "Skylar, this is Jamila and Daisy. They're my mom's brother's daughters."

Fucking hell. Clearing my throat, I manage to get out a "Nice to meet you both." I can feel my face heating, embarrassment creeping in.

"This is all your fault," I whisper-yell at Saint.

"What is my fault?" he asks, amusement written all over him.

"You were standing here distracting me all night," I say, not wanting to mention how worked up seeing all the women trying to hit on him got me, even though he must know that's the reason I stormed over here in the first place.

As I start to calm down, I realize how stupid I must look right now, and what a mistake I've made.

He's not even mine—he just asked me on a date, and I'm already marking my damn territory. I might as well have peed on him right here in front of everyone, including the new people I work with.

Fucking hell, Skylar.

Chapter Thirteen

I can sense his amusement while I make small talk with his cousins, who are gracious enough not to hold my behavior against me. They don't seem too surprised by what I did, seeing as they have apparently heard about me from Saint before and are happy finally to have met me.

"I better get back to work," I tell them both. "It was nice meeting you."

And sorry about being a dickhead.

"I'm going to head off too," Saint says, lowering to kiss my forehead. Butterflies fill my stomach. I don't know how it's so natural for us to be affectionate after everything we've been through. I had a crush on him and he was too old for me, but now we are on an even playing field, which is hard to wrap my mind around. "Call me if you need anything, and let me know if you need a ride home. Anything, all right?"

"I'll be fine. And don't even think about sending Dee or someone else to come here and keep an eye on me," I tell him, shaking my head at the thought.

"Damn, when Dee shows up here tell him to go home," he jokes, saying goodbye to his cousins and walking me back around the bar. "Do you want me to pick you up after work?"

"No," I tell him, rolling my eyes. "My car is here. I'll be fine."

"Okay," he grumbles, leaning me back against the counter and kissing me properly. Melting into him, I suddenly wish I wasn't at work, although who knows if I'm even going to have my job after my display tonight.

I'm breathless when he lifts his head, blue eyes filled with heat. "I better go."

"I think you should," I whisper, clearing my throat.

He flashes me a wide smile, then leaves.

Dusting off my work shirt, I turn back to see Camilla watching us with wide eyes. *That was hot*, she mouths, fanning herself.

Cheeks heating, I step back behind the bar, in professional mode once more.

Saint is a bad, bad influence on me.

The next morning, staring at the word *Mom* on my phone, I let it go to voicemail. She's the last person I want to talk to right now.

It rings again, this time from Neville's phone, but I ignore that too. I'm not that stupid.

There's a knock on my bedroom door. "Come in!"

Logan peeps his head in before stepping inside. "What you doing?"

"Nothing much," I admit, glancing down at my phone next to me on the bed. "Wondering what Mom wants."

"Yeah, she tried to call me too," he says, sitting down in the cane chair opposite my bed. "So what's been going on?"

"You mean besides the whole Saint thing?"

"You always liked him," he grumbles. "What's going to happen with the two of you?"

My mind flashes back to last night, when we had our first kiss—and better yet, it was me who kissed him and not the other way around. "I don't know," I reply, sitting up and studying him. "It's too early to tell. Why? You don't approve of him?"

"I didn't say that. I'm just wondering," he muses, keeping his expression blank. "Is that what you want to do with your life? Be a Knights old lady? I know that you grew up with the club, but a lot of what goes down there was shielded from you."

"I know you think I was shielded from most things, but I'm not stupid," I tell him, frowning. "I do have feelings for Saint, though, and if it doesn't work out with him, I wouldn't try to find another Knights member. I mean, my end goal is not to be somebody's old lady, but I can't help who I feel a connection with. Saint has always been one of my favorite people. It's not about the club, it's about him."

"I didn't mean that you just wanted to be an old lady to anyone, Sky. I just wanted to ask if this is how you want your life to be. Being with Saint comes with a lot of shit, and I just don't want you to be blinded by a teenage crush and distracted by all that hair and muscle. You do know what kind of shit they must be involved in, right? That much money doesn't come from a nine-to-five."

I laugh out loud at his description of him. "Thank you for the concern, Logan. I do know what you mean and are worried about. But with Saint, it's not really a choice, you know? I mean, I don't know if things will work out or if we will end up together, but I do know that if I don't try then I'm always going to wonder what if. So if this whole thing ends up being one huge mistake, I'm going to have to live with that and take that chance."

And because I haven't met any other man who so much as holds my attention.

It's always been Saint.

Maybe Logan is right and I *am* blinded by some crush that started years ago, but it still doesn't change how I feel and what I want.

"When's the last time you saw Saint?" I ask Logan. "With all his hair and muscle."

He rolls his eyes. "It's been a while. I stopped coming by the clubhouse, what, six months before you left for the country? So it would have been then."

"Years, then."

"Yep. Almost same as you. Okay," he says, nodding. "As long as you know what you're getting yourself into. I just don't want to see you get hurt. I feel like Mom got even crazier after Hammer ended things with her. You have to be strong to deal with those men."

"And you don't think I am?" I ask him.

"No, it's not that. I just don't see why you have to be," he admits, tapping his fingers on the arm of the chair. "Why do you need to become tougher, and more resilient, when with an average man you wouldn't have to? You wouldn't need to get used to him being around women and all the hangers-on, you wouldn't need to worry about where he is every night and if he's safe, or if he's gotten himself locked up again. You wouldn't need to worry about any of that. The road you're choosing is yours to decide, but you're choosing the harder path."

He smiles to soften the blow, and leaves my bedroom.

But his words linger long after his exit.

Later that night, I'm climbing on the back of Saint's motorcycle in tight ripped jeans, a Freddie Mercury T-shirt, black block heels and Saint's leather jacket. He hasn't told me exactly where we are going, other than to go for a ride and get something to eat, so I thought I'd wear something that would work no matter where the night takes us.

It's been so long since I've been on the back of a bike, and that was only on Hammer's or Temper's, so this is a whole different ball game. After Logan's words this morning, I must admit I'm a bit more on guard. But I need to make my own choices and decisions. And I need to try.

"You ready?" Saint asks, placing his hands on mine when I wrap my fingers around him.

"Yep!" I call back to him. The helmet feels a little more claustrophobic than I remember, but as soon as he takes off and the wind is hitting me, it's not so bad.

I take in everything—the smells, the sights, the sounds, the wind on my face and in my hair, and the sense of freedom that comes from the ride—just enjoying this little moment, after having missed this elated feeling for so long. As we breeze through traffic, I notice a lot of people looking at us, even without Saint wearing his Knights cut, and wonder what they are thinking.

When Saint slows down and pulls over onto the side of the road, I have no idea what he's doing until I see what's happening on the other side. Two cars have collided, and it's the biggest crash I've seen with my own eyes. One of the cars doesn't look too bad, but the other one is completely smashed, the windshield and windows all broken and the whole front bumper crushed.

"Shit," I whisper, removing my helmet and jumping off the bike after Saint stops on the side of the road. "That doesn't look good."

"Call the ambulance," Saint tells me, heading over to the car wreck just as more people stop to help, examining the car for any other survivors.

I pull my phone out of Saint's jacket pocket and dial 9-1-1, watching as Saint opens one of the car doors and speaks to the person inside. After telling the lady on the line about what happened and where we are, I hang up and follow Saint, who has a man in front of him lying on the ground.

"How bad is my head?" I hear the man asking Saint, touching the blood on his forehead. "My chest hurts too. Is everyone else okay? Oh my God, I hope they're okay."

"Keep this on there," Saint tells the man, ripping cloth off his flannelette jacket and using it to stop the bleeding. The man holds the blue material against his wound, which is soon drenched with blood.

"Fuck," I hear Saint mutter, then quickly moves to help the next person, who is screaming out with a leg injury.

Just as Saint moves away, the man loses consciousness. When I check on him, I notice that he's not breathing.

Fuck.

Following the first aid training I recently did at my old job at the café, something I thought was a waste at the time, I clear his airways and proceed to give him CPR. Pumping down on his chest, I count each push in my head then lower my mouth to his to breathe into it.

When I pull back and he starts to breathe again, I close my eyes and look up at the night sky in relief.

The ambulance pulls up shortly, and Saint and I watch as they take away the four people involved in the accident, all with varying injuries.

"You were amazing," he says to me, pulling me closer. "You saved that man's life, and you didn't panic. I'm so proud of you, Sky."

"You helped all of them," I say in return. "And you were the first to stop and help. Lots of people didn't even bother."

"Some did, though," he mutters, absently touching my waist.

As I pull back from him, I notice something. "You have blood on you. Do you want to go and clean up before we do anything else?" I'm not really in the mood to go and sit at a fancy restaurant after everything that has just happened anyway. I feel like having a steaming hot shower and curling up in bed with soup or something.

"Yeah, maybe we should move date night to another night,"

he says, exactly what I was thinking. "Come on, let's go back to the clubhouse."

We get on the bike and ride back the way that we came.

A lot slower, this time.

Chapter Fourteen

After my long, hot shower, I leave the bathroom in a towel, another one wrapped around my hair. I pretend I don't notice him watching me. "Shower is free."

"Thanks," he says, standing up from the bed, bloody T-shirt gone and nothing but smooth skin and muscles left in its place. "I ordered us some food in."

"Sounds perfect," I reply, eyes lingering on the indentation under his pecs, and down farther to the vee right underneath the top of his jeans.

"Don't look at me like that, Sky," he rumbles, walking past me and into the bathroom. I turn to catch an eye of his muscular back before the door shuts. I never even knew backs could be sexy, but boy, they can.

My body starts to overheat, and I feel a little clammy. After sliding the towel off my body and onto the bed, I change into the T-shirt he left for me to wear as I hear the shower turn back on.

We haven't really had a talk about my lack of experience in the bedroom, and I know it's something that is very different about us. He's older and has slept with plenty of women, while all I've done is kiss and had a few hands go wandering. While I'm not embarrassed about the fact that I'm still a virgin, I know it's just a reminder of how young I am. Still, if he wants me he's going to have to deal with whatever I come with, and me the same with him.

I'm sitting on the bed going through my phone when Saint walks out in his towel, and I can't help but stare at him. I may be drooling and I really don't care. He shakes his head at me, but the little smile on his mouth lets me know he likes the way I look at him.

"What?" I ask, not ashamed in the least. "You are sexy." Feeling bold, I add, "Can I touch you?"

I know it may sound like I'm inviting him to bed, but I genuinely just want to touch him. I've imagined touching him for years and here he is, with us in this weird limbo place. I figure it's worth the ask.

He stays still, so I move toward him and reach out to touch his shoulders and the soft skin there, then his hard biceps, then down his chest and ripped abs. He is all muscle, and I could touch him all day, the concept so foreign to me.

"Any farther and you're gonna be in trouble, Sky," he says in a husky tone, eyes locked on mine.

Now would probably be the right time to tell him.

"I'm a virgin," I blurt out, anticipating his reaction. "So you're going to have to take it slow with me."

Blue eyes widen, and his fingers reach out to touch my face. "You're the most beautiful woman I've ever laid my eyes on, and you've managed to get to your twenties a virgin? You're a fucking unicorn, is what you are." He rests his forehead against mine. "You control the pace, Sky. I want you, but I'm not going to rush you. We can go as slow as you want to."

He kisses me then, a sweet, gentle kiss. The kiss of a man who is going to enjoy the journey instead of rushing to the end. The thing is, I'm more ready than I let on. I haven't stayed a virgin because I wasn't ready for sex; I stayed one because no one was Saint, and now that he's here and he's said exactly what I want to hear, I don't think I'm going to last long without wanting him to be the first man inside me.

"You'll wait for me," I ask, smiling against his lips.

"You're worth it," he replies. "You know you were the only one who ever understood me, even back when we were just nothing but friends and I was a prospect. You always said just what I needed to hear."

"You can be pretty closed off," I say gently, placing my palm on his chest. "You know you can trust me, right? You don't need to have your walls up around me."

"I know," he whispers.

"What did Hammer say about us?"

"That if I hurt you he will skin me alive," he admits, cringing. "But he knows that we've always gravitated toward each other. I don't think anyone is surprised, to be honest. If anything I think I'm more surprised than anyone else."

His hand roams down the back of the T-shirt I'm wearing until it rests on my ass. "Are you wearing any panties?"

I shake my head.

He makes a deep sound in the back of his throat. "You're not going to make this easy on me, are you?"

"I feel like you've had enough easy," I tease, stepping back and winking at him. "Time for a bit of a challenge for once."

"You're making a lot of assumptions here, Sky," he murmurs, gaze on my thighs.

"And are they true or false?" I ask.

He laughs out loud. "True, but still, you don't need to call me out on it."

Picking me up, he throws me back on the bed, his T-shirt going up in the air and flashing him before I can pin it down, making me squeal.

Saint simply laughs, our eyes cutting to the door as someone knocks.

"Stop giggling away in there!" Hammer shouts out. "The food is here!"

We laugh harder.

Saint makes me wear a bra and jeans under his T-shirt before he lets me leave the room. When I enter the kitchen and see everyone, I can understand why. Temper arches his brow when he sees me, glancing between Saint, me and Hammer before shaking his head in an "I don't even want to know" manner.

"Hello, Temper," I say cheerfully, sitting down and glancing around the table. "Dee," I say in a less excited tone. "How are we all?"

Dee just laughs and Temper throws a chip at me.

"Not quite the date night I had in mind," I say to Saint, who grins and kisses my cheek. "I'll make it up to you later this week. I didn't plan on getting covered in blood before we could even have dinner."

"What happened?" Temper asks, and Saint recaps our night for him.

"Sky was amazing—she gave one of the men CPR and literally saved his life. She was solid."

"I was terrified, but I knew panicking wasn't going to help anyone," I admit. "And the feeling of saving someone was exhilarating. Like I would have done anything to save that man. I don't know how to explain it."

I glance around the table to see all the men staring at me. "What?" I ask.

"Your eyes just lit up," Hammer says, sitting back in his chair. "Maybe you're meant to be a doctor or nurse, or a paramedic. I know you were up in the air about what you want to do, but I think this might be your calling."

"Yeah, and we could always use a doctor around here," Temper adds, smirking. "Someone is always getting hurt, or shot, and no one wants to go and see a doctor and have to explain that shit."

The men all make sounds of agreement.

"Don't try and make this about you," I tease, sitting back and contemplating Hammer's words. He might be right.

Saint agrees. "You have it in you, if that's what you want to do, Sky. Honestly, you surprised me tonight. Most people freak out and panic in situations like that."

Interesting. Could I see myself in the medical field? The excitement that fills me at the thought says yes. It's about time I did something with my life—working in hospitality isn't my calling and I've always known that.

"I'll have to look into it," I say, smiling wide.

"And don't worry about money," Saint says to me quietly. "I'll cover anything you need."

I open my mouth to object, but Hammer interrupts me. "Money isn't an issue, Skylar. Find out what you want to do and enroll in it. And you can even quit the job at the seedy bar too."

"Yeah, or I'll be in there more to check on you, and you know how that went the other night," Saint adds, chuckling to himself.

"What did we miss?" Renny asks, looking between us.

I sit there red-faced as Saint tells them the story about his cousins and me being jealous, thinking that they were random women trying to hit on him.

"Very funny, guys. Just wait until the tables are turned—I bet it won't be funny then," I tell them all, huffing.

"It will still be funny, actually," Temper adds, shoving a chip dipped in salsa in his mouth. "Watching Saint beat the shit out of someone and get arrested is pretty amusing."

"What?" I ask, confused.

"How do you think he got arrested the first time?" Dee adds, shrugging. "He lost his temper."

That's right. Saint told me this at dinner, although apparently it was seriously downplayed. "Temper, maybe you and Saint need to swap road names," I mutter.

This is what Logan meant. This is everyday life for them,

and I knew Saint went to prison, obviously, but hearing them play it off like that and turn it into a joke is hard to listen to.

And the question is, will it happen a second time?

Chapter Fifteen

"Who did you attack that got you locked up, Saint?" I ask the next morning. We had spent the rest of the night watching a movie and then fell asleep cuddling. And now that the sun is up, I realize we have to have this discussion. I can't not ask.

He sighs deeply and rolls over to face me. "I got drunk and was out at a club, and I got into a fight. They arrested me. I told you this. I accepted the plea deal, did my time and now I'm out."

That doesn't answer my question.

"Does stuff like that happen often?" I press.

"No," he replies quickly. "Sometimes other shit happens, though. I'm not a saint, Sky." His lip twitches when he realizes what he just said. "I mean, I'm a biker, and you know sometimes we get into trouble, and it's not always my trouble. I protect and defend all of my brothers, just as they do with me. You know all of this."

"I do, and I guess I just want to know exactly what I'm getting myself into," I admit. "I haven't been here, and when I was, you guys never let me see the bad. I don't know if you getting into a fight is a common occurrence or not, so I'm just asking so I know what to expect."

"Are you thinking you might not be able to handle this before anything has even happened?" he asks me quietly, tucking my hair back behind my ear. "I've only been arrested one time. It's not an everyday thing, and I'm not going out there looking for fights. I am able to control myself, but yes, that time I was drunk and lost my shit, and I have paid for that. I have no desire to go back to prison for anything. I didn't have anything to lose before, and now I do, okay?"

"Okay," I breathe, considering his words. "And no, it's not that I'm not going to be able to handle whatever happens, I just want you to be honest with me, that's all. I don't like hearing information from the other people; I should hear it from you. I might not be a professional at relationships, but I know that communication is key."

He looks away from me, then sits up and stares ahead. "Yeah, you're right. Communication. Loyalty. Honestly." He turns back to me. "I want all of this with you, all right? I'm not fucking around here. You mean something to me. You always have. You're not just another woman."

"Good, we're on the same page then," I reply, pulling him back down and onto me. "Tell me something."

"Like what?"

"Anything," I whisper.

"Okay." He thinks, laying his head on my chest without putting all of his weight on me. "I had a dream last night, and it was weird. We had a son together."

"That's an interesting dream to have," I whisper, smiling to myself.

Saint goes quiet, and I run my fingers through his hair.

As much as Logan's words had truth to them, I know in my heart he is wrong.

And I'm going to prove it.

* * *

I find a two-year degree program in paramedic training. I looked into nursing and even becoming a doctor, but that would be something I need to dedicate my whole life to, and I'd have to be willing to move to wherever I'm needed. I think working in paramedics I'd enjoy being on the go and the adrenaline of being the first at different scenes instead of being stuck in a hospital. Something new every day.

I'm glad Hammer said money isn't an issue, because the paramedic program is almost ten thousand dollars in fees. Although compared to going to med school, that's basically nothing.

"So you're serious about this?" Logan asks as we sit and have a coffee in front of the TV. "I think it's pretty cool."

"Yeah, I think so. I'm really excited about it, actually," I tell him, blowing on the hot liquid. "I feel like maybe it is my calling. Nothing else has got me motivated like this. Normally I'd just check out the courses, do the research but then do nothing about it."

"Are you going to enroll?"

"Yeah, I'm going to go in this week. There's a month before the next program starts, so I have time to sort everything out. Hammer and Saint want me to quit the bar, but I don't think I'm going to. I need my own money; I don't want to rely on them for everything."

"Probably smart," Logan agrees. "I spoke to Mom. The entire time she was asking about you and whether you tried to see Hammer."

"What did you say?" I ask, rolling my eyes at how nosy she is.

"I told her I had no idea, that you got a job and work a lot," he says, shrugging. "If I tell her about Hammer and Saint, she will probably drive straight here just to stir shit up."

"What, and bring Neville? Hammer will chew him up and spit him out. And he's a nice guy—he doesn't deserve to be dragged into Mom's shit," I admit, feeling bad for him.

"She could come here without him. She'd just say she wants to see you," he replies, pausing and then adding, "But yeah, he'd definitely try to tag along. He's a bit of a stage-five clinger."

"Or he's just smarter than we give him credit for and doesn't trust leaving Mom alone," I mutter, taking a sip from the Harry Potter mug, then putting it down on the coffee table in front of me. "I should have just answered the phone because now she's going to know something is up. I shouldn't have to play these games with her, though. It's bullshit."

"She's never just going to accept that you are back in the MC life and she's not," Logan concludes, running a hand through his hair. "She hated that she got dumped and lost everything, all her power. No more connections, money, nothing. She was suddenly just a normal woman with a heap of kids and no man again."

"She needs to let it go," I grumble, picking up my phone and smiling when I see there is a text message from Saint.

I miss you. What are you doing tonight?

Working, I type back, then add, And no, that wasn't an invitation for you to join me.

What a shame, I wouldn't mind one of those kisses again, he instantly replies, making me laugh out loud.

"You have it bad," Logan says, shaking his head at me. Sabrina comes into the room and cuddles up next to him.

"So when am I going to meet this man of yours?" she asks me, kind brown eyes curious.

"I don't know," I tell her. "Next time he picks me up I can bring him in and introduce you."

"Sounds good," she replies, perking up. "I've heard about the Knights, but I've never met any of them. I know Logan speaks to their Hammer on the phone, but that's all the fun we get around here."

"Probably for the best," I mutter, and Logan makes a sound of agreement. "Logan, remember that birthday party Mom threw for you in the clubhouse?"

"The one I never turned up to?" he asks in a dry tone, nodding. "Yeah, I remember. I told her I didn't want a party, especially not there, I just wanted a dinner with the family, but she went and did the party anyway. Not really my scene, so I said fuck it and decided not to show. I spent the night with Sabrina instead." He turns to her and says, "Remember? You took me out for the quiet dinner I originally wanted."

"Yeah, and your phone kept going off with everyone asking you where the hell you were," she says, amusement in her eyes. "That was such a long time ago. I think we'd pretty much just met and weren't even exclusive then."

"Wow, I thought the whole nonexclusive thing was just with modern dating," I muse, laughing when Logan sends a glare in my direction.

"I'm not that old, thank you," he replies, softening as he looks back to Sabrina. "But yeah, we were just casual when we met. I wasn't really looking for a relationship. I had so much family drama going on and wasn't in the best place, but I couldn't let her pass me by. She's a once-in-a-lifetime type of woman, so I had to man up."

"That's a bit cute," I whisper, chin resting on my palm and watching the two of them. "And you guys have lasted for so long. If I need relationship advice, I'm coming to the both of you." I pause, and then amend, "Well, maybe just you, Sabrina. I don't think Logan wants to know too much information."

Sabrina laughs, shoulders shaking. "I'm always here if you need advice or someone to vent to. It's actually nice having another girl around. I'm an only child, and before you moved in it was just your brothers randomly dropping in with alcohol and eating all of our food."

"I'm still eating all of your food," I point out, grinning. "Speaking of, I want to take you both out for dinner to say thank you for letting me stay here, and for being the family I always wanted, pretty much."

"You don't have to—"

"I want to." And now that I've made a little money from working, and with tips, I can afford to.

"Don't worry about us, Sky. You should be saving your money," says Logan, always the wise one.

"Just let me say thank you," I say. "I know it's not much, but let me do this, at least. I'm very grateful to you both for making my move here such an easy, amazing one."

"Okay," he says, grinning. "When do you want to do this? Tomorrow night? We can go to McDonalds."

Rolling my eyes, I say, "I was going for something a little fancier. You two can choose."

I stand up and kiss Logan on the cheek, then head up to my room.

I have a program to enroll in.

Chapter Sixteen

The next night after dinner with Logan and Sabrina at a Sri Lankan restaurant, Saint texts and asks me if I can come to the clubhouse to spend the night.

I bring some takeaway food with me for him and Hammer, and step into the clubhouse. There's loud music playing, so the men must be drinking or maybe having people over, who knows. I didn't see Hammer's bike out the front, so he may not be here tonight.

More food for me.

I put the food in the kitchen, and then find Saint sitting out back with a beer in his hand, laughing with Renny about something or another, but he stands with a wide smile when he sees me.

"Hello, beautiful," he murmurs, strolling over to me and lifting me up in his arms. He gives me a quick kiss, and then pulls me down onto his lap. I notice that there are other members here tonight, new faces, and a few women around the place. All eyes are on me.

"How was dinner?" he asks.

"Good. I brought you some food," I reply, turning on his lap to face him.

"You spoil me," he says with a grin. "Do you want something to drink? Beer? Juice? Soda? I stocked the fridge and cupboard for you. I think I might have gone overboard."

"I'm fine, but thank you," I say, kissing him again quickly.

"Hey, Sky," Renny calls out.

I move my face around Saint, who was blocking him with his body. "Renegade. How are you?"

"I'm good. Even better now that we're eating like kings since you came back," he teases, lifting a beer up in cheers. "Although I'm going to have to do extra hours in the gym," he grumbles, raising his white T-shirt, showing off a very toned six-pack of abs. I don't think he has to worry about that just yet.

"Happy to be of service," I tell him, grinning, then glance back up at Saint. "What kind of stuff did you buy?"

"I didn't know what cereal you liked, so I got a variety. Bacon, eggs, stuff to make pancakes, juice. Snacks. Everything," he says with a shrug. "I remember you used to like strawberry-frosted cupcakes, so I got some of those too. And mangoes."

"You are so fucking cute," I say, warmth filling me. "Mangoes are still my favorite, and I still love those cupcakes."

The fact that he remembers all these things means so much to me. We're both getting to know each other again, but a lot of me is still the same. He knows who I was, and now he's getting to know who I am, and vice versa.

"Good," he murmurs, scanning my face. "Thanks for coming to spend the night with me. I missed you today."

"I missed you too," I say. I'm about to open my mouth and tell him about how I enrolled in the paramedic course when the door opens and Hammer walks outside.

With none other than my mother.

"What is she doing here?" Saint asks, standing up and putting me next to him, protecting me.

"I asked myself the same thing," Hammer growls, jaw tight and face redder than I've seen it. He must have just arrived at the clubhouse. "I found her standing out the front and demanding to see Skylar, because otherwise she's going to call the cops and tell them that we're keeping her against her will."

"I'm fine, Mom," I tell her, frowning. "And Logan told you I was fine. You didn't have to come all this way."

We all know this isn't about me—this is about her. She never wanted me to reconnect to the MC, because it meant leaving her behind in a different world. I think she sees this as her territory, her old family, and without her I'm not allowed to be in it.

"My own daughter, a traitor," she muses, shaking her head. "I should have known. I never trusted you, you know. From the day you were born, I wished you'd been another boy."

Anger fills me. "How am I a traitor? You are the one who brought Hammer into my life, to be my father figure and to raise me. Just because he broke up with you doesn't mean he broke up with me, even though that's what you wanted!"

"Don't let them fill your head with their lies, Skylar. I am your mother!" she shouts back, pointing at me.

"Why are you here?" I ask, scowling. "No one wants you here, Mom."

She glances around the outdoor area, taking in all the faces and people, before bringing her gaze back to me. "Leave with me right now or you are dead to me, Skylar. If you don't walk out of these doors, as far as I'm concerned, I have no daughter." She lifts her chin and narrows her eyes. "And you will have no mother."

"Has she ever had a mother?" Hammer asks her, tone as violent as I've ever heard it. "I tell you what, the truth about what happened needs to fucking come out. I wanted to protect Sky from it, but maybe it's better that she knows the truth. So she can understand what happened back then when you took her away from us."

I step closer, needing to hear this. "I want to know the truth."

"Don't listen to a word he says," Mom spits out, but I don't miss the flash of fear in her eyes.

What has she done?

Hammer tells everyone to clear out, except me, Saint, him and Mom. I'm starting to feel really fucking nervous right now, and scared. As Hammer prepares to tell me the truth, hesitating and rubbing the back of his neck, I realize words can't be taken back, and I feel like shit is going to change.

He moves closer to me while my mother just stands there, knowing that she invited this. "Five years ago, we were having a lot of trouble with a rival MC, the Destined Killers," he starts, looking me in the eye. "We'd always coexisted peacefully, but something happened that had them coming after us. Targeting us. Fights broke out, property destroyed, all of that bullshit, until eventually shit went too far. After being hit on the head, one of their members died at our hands. It was an accident. No one meant for anyone to die."

Swallowing hard, I don't know what to say, so I say nothing. One of the Knights killed someone? Hammer doesn't say who it is, and I don't ask. I'm curious to know who, though. Saint's hands squeeze into fists, as if the memory frustrates him.

"Their president, Killer, was out for blood over it, and said he wasn't going to stop until I was dead," Hammer recaps. "This man is known for liking younger girls, younger than is legal, if you know what I mean. And your mother here suggested, to save my ass..." He trails off, struggling to say the next words. "That we offer you up to him instead."

My jaw drops open. "Offer me up as in..."

As in give me to a fucking adult man?

I eye the woman who gave birth to me, so much pain and anger and betrayal filling me. "You'd give me up to be raped to save your boyfriend? Is that how much I mean to you?"

"No, it's how much he—" she looks to Hammer "—meant to me. He was going to be killed. I was desperate and—"

"You're a monster. I was sixteen years old!" I scream, cutting her off. Saint's arms come around me and I melt into him. I thought I was safe with my own mother, but I was wrong. I was never safe, and she never loved or cared about me. "So that's why you broke up?"

Hammer nods. "That's when I realized just how fucking evil she is, even by my standards. I had fucked up, though, because she knew a lot of shit about the club, and after I dumped her, I told her I wanted to keep you here with me, that she didn't deserve to have you as a daughter. She said if we tried to contact you in any way, she was going to the cops with the information she had on the club. And she knew about every deal we were a part of, our contacts, everything." He looks at me, sadness in his eyes. "I couldn't risk the club."

"So you knew that she didn't give a fuck about me, would have given me to your enemy, but you sent me off with her anyway just so the club didn't get into any shit?" I recap, my chest tightening.

I know the MC is everything to him, but I was just a girl. A girl he claimed to love like his own flesh and blood, and I can't help but feel betrayed over this. They knew, even more than me, what she was like and what she was capable of, but they allowed themselves to be blackmailed by her. They, in all their power, didn't come up with a way to save me from her.

"It's complicated, Skylar," he says, voice soft and broken. "The whole MC could have ended up in prison, and because I'm not your biological father, I wouldn't have been able to keep you without her agreement anyway. She's a spiteful bitch, so she would have fought just so I couldn't have you. She'd have taken me to court, and I wouldn't have a leg to stand on. They'd take one look at who I am and laugh in my face. There was nothing I could do."

Something. He could have done something. Or tried something.

Anything.

No one thought of me.

No one tried to save me.

Yes, Hammer wanted me to stay here, but in the end, he chose the club over me, and I guess this is the point Logan was trying to get across.

The club will always be first.

"Saint rode down to the country to try to see you without us knowing, did you know that?" Hammer asks me.

"You men are all the same!" Mom yells, starting to pace. "Skylar is my daughter—you aren't her father, Hammer, no matter how much you want to be. She is *mine*."

I push down my anguish at Hammer's admission to face my mother. "What about the money, Mom?" I ask, moving closer to face her. "What did you do with my money?"

"I was owed that money," she sneers, pausing to look at Hammer. "For all the bullshit I did for you, and for this club. I walked away with nothing. I know how much you had in your bank, Hammer. You didn't leave me a cent!"

"I left that money for Skylar's future," he says to her, remaining calm somehow. "Not for you. I knew she wasn't going to see all of it, because you're a selfish bitch, but I thought you'd give her something. Something! I wish I never gave you that account, and I only did it because it was before that bullshit, before I saw you for who you truly are."

She lunges at Hammer, but I move quickly, stepping in front of him. "Don't you dare touch him!" I yell, hands shaking.

She stops, but I know she wants to hit me. She looks me right in the eye, and I don't miss the hate there. Maybe it's always been there, but I'm noticing it only now.

"Touch her and see what happens," Saint says from behind me, his tone as lethal as I've ever heard it. The threat is clear. If she puts her hands on me, she's going to regret it.

"That money was mine," she maintains. "I clothed you and fed you, and you have never had anything to complain about, so don't act all woe is me, Sky. It doesn't suit you."

"So you took my college fund as child support? Or so you

keep saying," I fire back, jaw tight. "Have some dignity. You are pathetic—I'll never be like you."

I look back at Saint, who looks as sad as I feel right now. "You came and saw me?"

He nods. "I just had to see you with my own eyes and make sure you were okay. You were at school and with a girl, and the two of you were laughing."

"Shauna," I whisper. I would have been laughing with Shauna, my best friend who passed away.

"I left after that. I wanted to speak to you, but I know I would have jeopardized everyone, and Hammer would have fucking killed me," he admits. "We just needed a little time to bury some shit; we weren't going to let Georgia hold something over us."

"So she doesn't have anything on you now?" I ask.

Hammer shakes his head, glancing over at her with a smug look. "Nope. Nothing. It took us a while, but we handled what we needed to and got us some legitimate businesses. Everything she once had on us has no validity anymore. We made sure of it."

But even after they sorted shit out, they didn't come for me. They waited for me to come to them, and that really does hurt.

I absently rub my chest, which suddenly feels tight. "I don't even know what to say right now," I admit, looking Mom in the eyes. "But I know I never want to see you again, you disgust me, and you're right. I don't have a mother."

I storm into the clubhouse, straight to Saint's room, where I dive into his bed and cry.

Fuck everyone.

Chapter Seventeen

About ten minutes pass before Saint quietly slips inside and closes the door behind him. He slides into bed next to me and pulls me against him, kissing the top of my head.

"I'm so sorry, Sky. I didn't know the truth of what happened back then either, but then Hammer finally admitted it to me the other night. I told him he had to tell you. He's right, it's fucked up, and I can see why he never wanted you to know, but now at least the truth is out there. I think you're right to be angry. I'm so fucking sorry this happened. Now you know why we never fought for you and why they broke up in the first place, and it might just sound like a bunch of excuses, but fuck. I'm just sorry, okay? If I could do it over, I'd do it differently."

I don't know what he means by that exactly, but I don't ask. If he means that he'd go against the club's wishes and come for me, it's best that he not say it out loud. It doesn't change anything anyway. It's all done, and now I just need to decide what I'm going to do with all this new information.

"Maybe Hammer was right—ignorance is bliss. I don't think this wound is ever going to stop hurting," I admit, wiping my eyes. "I just don't understand how someone could even suggest doing that to their own flesh and blood. I don't get it. She never loved me, Saint, and that proved it. She said she never trusted me, but I never did anything to her."

"She's crazy and jealous," Saint tells me, rubbing my back in soothing circles. "You can't expect rational thought from her, and you did nothing wrong, Skylar. She is the number one person meant to protect you, but she only cares about herself. Good fucking riddance, I say. Georgia is something else."

Great, I win the worst mother award. "Fuck my life," I whisper, taking a weak moment to just feel sorry for myself. "I don't want to see her ever again, Saint."

"She won't be stepping in here again that's for sure," he says, kissing my temple.

"What happened to the rival MC president? Hammer is obviously not dead, so did he just give up?" I ask, wondering what happened to the war between them.

"Killer got put in prison," Saint explains. "So no retribution happened. Not that he would have been able to kill Hammer, but he would have tried. And we would all have to watch our backs every second of every day."

"So it all worked out in the end."

For everyone except me.

She loved Hammer more than she loved me. I don't know why that hurts, because if I'm being honest I loved him more than I loved her too, but I'd never hurt her or throw her under the bus. I wouldn't do that to anyone, never mind my own flesh and blood. Saint is right—she's clearly not right in the head, or maybe she is just pure evil.

Drying my tears, I look at Saint and gather all of my strength. I'm here right now, and I'm fine. I'm strong. I don't need that woman, I guess I never did.

I can't change what has already happened. I'm going to do something with my life. I'm going to thrive, and I don't need anyone in my life who isn't going to cheer for me, celebrate with me, and just simply love me.

Everyone else, blood or not, is being left behind.

"I have to admit, I didn't see that one coming," I admit, closing my eyes and taking a deep breath. "At least it's all out in the open now. I hated not knowing what had happened, and why you or Hammer didn't even try and contact me."

"Hammer and I actually got into a fight over it," Saint admits, pushing my hair back off my face. "I didn't understand why we were letting Georgia dictate our actions. I was pissed. But Hammer said it was the only option for now, and before we knew it you would be eighteen and could do what you want. He said you'd come back to us."

"And what if I hadn't? Would you have come to me?" I ask him. "Because I'm a little older than eighteen, and you only reached out to me when you were locked up."

"Because it made me think about what was important in my life," he says, wiping away a tear from my cheek. "I didn't know who you were anymore, if you wanted to talk to any of us after what had happened. I didn't know much. Yes, we kept an eye on you from afar as best as we could, but we didn't really know all the details of your life." He sighs deeply.

I ask the question that I'm not ready to hear the answer to yet. "Would you have done what Hammer did? Would you have put the club before me? Would you do that now?"

"Things aren't always as easy as you make them sound, Sky."

"They are to me," I whisper, feeling uneasy by how noncommittal that answer was.

He holds me closer, and eventually, I fall asleep.

When I wake up in the morning I jump in the shower and replay last night in my head. I can't let this affect me or my life—I need to feel the pain and then let it go.

Mom would want me to feel weak, helpless, and maybe even run back to her, but I'm not going to do that. I might not have been a perfect daughter, but no one deserves a mother like that one, and when I have children I'm going to make sure I'm nothing like her.

Saint opens the glass door, seeing me naked for the first time. I don't cover myself up; I let him have his fill, the look in his eyes making me feel sexier than ever.

I ask, "Do you want to join me?"

He nods and undresses, and I realize he was waiting for an invitation. I have to set the pace, not him, and I know if I told him to leave, he would have. I get distracted as my eyes land on his body, such masculine perfection.

He steps under the scalding hot water, but doesn't complain as he puts some bodywash on his hands and starts to massage my shoulders. I close my eyes and let him, enjoying the touch and the pampering. "How are you feeling?" he asks, tone husky.

"Better," I whisper, then clear my throat. "I'm not going to let her win. Yes, it's shitty and she's shitty, but now I just have to keep moving forward and try not to let her impact my life at all."

I can only control *my* actions. I can't give myself the mother I always wanted, but I can let go and move forward and not use her as an excuse for anything.

"She's a twisted woman," he mutters, now rubbing my back. "But you're nothing like her. At all. And I think that's why she has a problem with you, because she knows you're better than her. You're kind, and smart, and witty, and we all fucking adore you."

Smiling sadly, I turn around and look up at him. "I just want to pretend last night never happened. Just for a little bit."

Cupping my cheek, he drops his head and starts to kiss me, pushing me back against the tiles. "I think I know a way I can distract you."

"Go on then," I manage to get out, watching as he drops to his knees in front of me, water dripping down his skin.

"Now I know you said you're a virgin," he says, lifting my thigh up and around his shoulder, so I'm balancing on one leg up against the wall. "But just how innocent are we talking? Has anyone ever tasted you here?" he asks, running his finger along my sex.

Swallowing hard, I shake my head no.

"So I'm going to be the first to taste this sweet pussy?" he asks, flicking his tongue out and licking me once before delving in a little deeper, sliding his tongue inside me.

"Yes, you're the first," I tell him, watching his head bob up and down as he starts to lick and suck on my clit. "Holy fuck."

I've never felt anything like this, and watching him pleasure me is so sexy. I couldn't look away if I tried. My thighs start to tremble, my breaths turning into pants.

I brace my hands against the tiles to hold me up as pleasure hits me. "Okay, wow, you're really good at that," I mutter, unable to help the moans that escape my lips.

Saint starts to laugh a little at my narration, and I don't know if I should feel offended or not. Is it normal to laugh during this? I forget my train of thought as the pleasure starts to get more intense, building with each second, until he makes me come, and my thighs are trembling, shaking with the power of my orgasm's intensity. He doesn't even stop then, not until I push him off me, gasping for breath.

Saint stands, his giant erection looking right at me, begging for attention. I want to give him what he gave me, even though I've never done it before. However, I have watched a few instructional videos on it.

Still, I feel a little shy, especially thinking about all the experienced women he must have been with. But then watching him, knowing how much he wants me, is a confidence boost, and I feel comfortable enough with him to explore and test the waters a little.

Reaching out, I begin to stroke him, watching him get even harder in my hand. His penis is really big and thick, and I honestly have no idea how that is going to fit inside my mouth, or anywhere else.

"Saint?"

"Hmmm?"

"Why do you have to be so big?" I ask him, making him chuckle under his breath, eyes darker than ever on me. "I'm serious. I'm pretty sure this isn't normal. It's like the size of my forearm."

Hesitating, I move to my knees, which embarrassingly happens to make that cracking sound, and explore him a little more before tasting the tip and twirling my tongue around him. "Well, that's better than I thought it was going to be."

More laughter, this time choked.

Taking the head into my mouth, I swirl my tongue around him again, getting the taste of him. Then, feeling a little bold, I try to take as much as I can down to the back of my throat, but my gag reflex kicks in and I push him straight out. "I think I need a little practice."

"Sky, you are doing fine," he murmurs. "Just you touching me and looking at me like that is about to have me explode, trust me. There's nothing you can do that is wrong or will turn me off."

"Okay," I say, then continue to suck, tease and lick, getting into a rhythm and figuring out what he likes by his moan and body language. When his fingers tighten in my hair, I know he's loving what I'm doing. I continue to suck and tease until he's about to explode, and when he does he stays true to his word and pulls away, coming all over my breasts while I watch in fascination.

"Fuck," he whispers, face a mask of pleasure. It's a good look for him, and one I plan on seeing many more times in the near future.

He washes me off once he's finished, and we scrub ourselves again, this time to actually get clean before we get out.

"I liked that," I say as he wraps a towel around me. "I wonder what your come tastes like."

He makes a choking sound. "Fuck's sake, Sky. If you don't stop you're about to find out."

"You can go again so fast?" I ask him, staring down at his cock, which is hardening. "Oh…my."

But I pretend I can't see it, because I'm kind of hungry and need to sate my other desires now.

"Do you think someone ate our food?" I ask, making him laugh out loud.

Chapter Eighteen

Hammer's at the breakfast table, and I start to feel extremely awkward when I think about what I was just doing under his roof.

"Good morning," I say to him, turning the kettle on and then sitting down.

"Morning. How are you?" he asks, brow furrowing in concern. "Your mom left straight after and I told her not to ever come back or she's going to regret it."

"Thanks," I say, smiling sadly. "I'm okay. Much better than last night, anyway. I'm glad I know the truth, but I can see why you didn't want me to know. It's pretty damn fucked up."

"Understatement," he says, reaching out and touching my arm. "We've got you, all right? You're my daughter, I don't care what your birth certificate says, and I don't want to lose you again. I love you, Sky."

"I love you too... Dad," I say, realizing that I've started calling him Hammer instead of the usual Dad. I don't know why, I guess I'm still figuring out where the hell I stand here. "And

I'm not going anywhere. But I have to admit, I'm a little hurt about the whole thing."

"I understand," he replies, glancing down at his hands.

"You chose protecting the club over me," I whisper, swallowing hard. "You say you love me and that I'm your daughter, but you were willing to let me go with her, knowing what she was capable of."

I hold up my hand when he tries to speak, because I need to say what I have to and get it off my chest. "It's true that she never hurt me or anything like that, but you didn't know that. And I wasn't in a loving environment with her. She just tolerated me, and I took it because she is my mother and the only person I had left. I knew she didn't really love me the way a mother should. But I always thought you loved me like a father should. But I can't help but feel like you didn't. You picked a club over me—that's something I expected from her. But not you."

"I'm sorry, Skylar," he says, sounding sincere. "The men rely on me to protect them, and if Georgia fucked us over that would have been on me. I brought her here, and I trusted her at one point. Which was a huge mistake. I couldn't let her hurt the club, all that I have built, and possibly get us arrested and put away. However, I should have found a way to keep her off our backs and still have kept you. I'm so sorry, Skylar. When things settled down, I should have come for you. I didn't know if you'd want to see me, or what lies Georgia had been feeding you. I was a fucking coward. But don't you think that because I let you go with your mom that I don't mean it when I say I love you, because I do. I thought about you a lot, and I fucking missed you, and—"

I lean over and hug him, cutting off his apology. He hugs me back, squeezing me tight. "I'm sorry," he says again into my hair. "It's hard being the president, but it's even harder being a dad. And I fucked it up."

What happened will always hurt, but I know I'm going to

forgive him. It's either that or walk away, and that's not going to happen. I love the man, and he's the only parent I have left.

"I forgive you, Dad," I tell him, pulling back and smiling.

He looks me in the eye. "I will never put anything before you again. Please believe me when I say that. I got your back and I don't want to lose you again."

"I know."

He smiles in relief, and stands up. "Good. I don't know what I'd do if you didn't. I'm not going to let you down again, Sky."

He makes me a coffee just as Saint comes in. "Did they eat the food from last night?"

"I didn't check." I smirk, watching him while he does.

"Seriously, you can't leave food anywhere in this house," he grumbles, scanning the contents in the fridge.

"I'll have a mango," I tell him, and thank Hammer for the coffee.

I start to think about what I'm going to say to Logan about this whole thing with Mom. I know I need to tell him and the rest of my brothers, but it could end badly. What if he says that she would never do something like that and doesn't believe me? Or maybe he will take my side. I don't expect him to, though. This is my battle, my war, and I'm not going to make my brothers choose.

Saint slides a cut-up mango in front of me. "Thanks. Do you want to go for a ride or something? I just have to be home in the afternoon so I can get ready for work."

"You haven't quit yet?" Hammer asks, frowning. "I thought you were going to."

"Not yet," I tell him, eating a piece of the fruit. "My paramedics program starts in a few weeks, so I'm going to keep working and make some money. And no, I don't want any of your money. You're doing more than enough for me as it is."

"You enrolled?" he asks, sounding surprised. I remember then that Mom showed up just as I was about to tell them all, and I only ended up telling Saint later that night. "I'm so proud of you, Sky. Congrats. You know you don't need to work, though, right?"

"Yes, I do," I fire back. "I've always worked; I don't even remember a time when I haven't worked. It's all I know. And I like working, I'm not a lazy person."

"You think I don't know that? I just want to make your life a little easier, especially when money isn't an issue for any of us," Hammer says, looking to Saint. "Your man here is loaded too. If you don't want to take my money, take his."

Saint smirks at me and raises his brows. "She's going to be stubborn about it. There's no point trying to convince her— she's just going to say no for the sake of it now."

My eyes narrow on him. "That is not why I'm saying no. I'm saying no because it's my life and I get to choose how I want to live it." I pause, before adding, "Not that I don't appreciate the offer. I just want to make my own money, not take it from someone else like some... I don't know..."

"A kept woman?" Saint suggests, while Hammer says, "Spoiled little daddy's girl?"

"All of the above," I say with a laugh. I don't know how the hell I'm even able to laugh after everything.

Maybe I've lost my damn mind at this point.

But could anyone blame me?

After lunch and a long ride with Saint, I head back home and run into Logan just as he's coming in from work. "You look tired," I say as he unlocks the door.

"Working in the sun is a killer," he admits. "I was helping fix a fence." He lets me enter first. "Did you stay at the club-house last night?"

"Yeah, and guess who dropped by," I say, placing my bag down on the kitchen counter.

"Who?" he asks.

I wait a few seconds to make it extra dramatic. "Mom. She

came to tell me that if I didn't leave with her, she's going to disown me."

Logan's jaw drops open. "Mom came to the clubhouse? With Neville?"

"No, she came alone. Unless he was waiting for her in the car. She probably told him she had to run in and drop something off for charity or something," I add in a dry tone.

He snorts, knowing that it is probably something our mother would do.

"And that's not all. Everything came out, about why Hammer and her split up, about how she didn't want them contacting any of us, especially me."

"So what happened?" he asks, which sobers me as I realize I'm going to have to tell him everything.

I start at the beginning of the night, and don't miss out details. By the end of it, my brother is fuming. I don't think I've ever seen him this mad in my life.

"Are you fucking kidding me? Tell me this is some sick joke, please!" he yells, pacing. "I knew she was crazy, but that is something else. How the fuck did this woman birth us?"

I jump up on the counter and sit there, watching my legs dangle. "I don't know. Apparently she's only really terrible to me because she wanted another boy." Telling the story again stirred all those feelings from last night. There are tears in my eyes. I hope one day it will hurt less.

"I'm so sorry, Skylar," he says, coming to stand in front of me. "I'm not going to have anything to do with her anymore. That is…" He trails off, shaking his head. "Despicable. What kind of person does something like that?"

We talk a bit longer about the whole thing, and he wants to call our brothers. I give him permission to fill them in, but I can't bear to hear or retell the story again, so I head up to my room. I know they say blood is thicker than water, but in this case that's not the truth. Betrayal from your own blood is painful.

* * *

When Saint's cousins come back at my work that night, I figure this must be their local. "Hello," I say to them both. "How are you?"

"Good," Daisy replies, showing off the huge diamond on her finger. "Brad proposed! After only six months! Can you believe it? And look at the size of the rock."

"It's a huge rock," I admit. After chatting with them for a little longer, I realize why Saint isn't that close to them. I almost feel like the two of them should have their own TV show where they get to talk about themselves and how much money their men have spent on them recently.

I'm about to excuse myself and get back to work when Jamila says something that gets my attention. "I hope Thorn brings Tory to the engagement. It's been ages since we've seen her."

Tory?

I want to ask them who the hell Tory is, but they're acting like I should already know, so maybe it's one of Saint's ex-girlfriends. He hasn't mentioned any of the previous women he has dated, so I have no idea what his history is like. He's acting like I'm his first real relationship, like he is mine, but I doubt that is the case. I make a mental note to ask him about this, and about Tory specifically, the next time I see him.

"Maybe he will come to the next one?" I lie, smiling at them both. "I better get back to work, but you both have a good night, and congrats on the engagement, Daisy."

"Thank you." She beams, lifting her ring up at me again, just in case it didn't blind me enough the first time.

The two of them head to the dance floor, and I look over at my manager, who is smirking at me. "How do you know those two?"

"They're Saint's cousins," I admit, shrugging. "He's not that close to his family, so I only met them for the first time the other night. They come here much?"

She nods. "Yeah, I see them here a lot. They spend a shit load of money on drinks, that's for sure."

"Yeah, but whose money?" I mutter.

She laughs out loud. "Not theirs. But stupid men's money is still money."

"Ain't that the truth? Hopefully it picks up tonight," I say, glancing around the mostly empty bar. "Or is this what we should come to expect on a weeknight?"

"It will pick up," she assures me, carrying some clean glasses over to the counter. "Everyone comes here after the casino, usually."

"Just a casual night of gambling and drinking."

"Yep," she laughs.

"My best friend, Max, is the guitarist and lead singer of a band—I could get them to come and play here, if you're interested?" I ask, doing a quick search on my phone and showing her a video of them. It would be good to get Max more exposure, and also another reason for him to come visit me.

"Hey, I've heard of these guys," she says, nodding. "We'd love to have them here. We're pretty booked up for the next month but after that, hell yeah!"

"Awesome, let me know what date, and I'll see if they're free."

The place soon starts to fill up, keeping me busy for the rest of the night.

However, my mind is on Saint, and whoever this Tory is.

Chapter Nineteen

"Have you seen that hot chick who lives near the clubhouse?" I overhear Renny ask Temper as soon as I step outside, looking for Saint. "Her house is the closest one to us. She's fucking sexy."

"Nope, but you should probably stay away from her. Don't shit where you eat. Or even down the road from where you eat," Temper replies, glancing up as he notices me. "Hey, Sky, what are you up to? Did we miss any more family feuds?"

"Nope, just that final battle," I say, dropping into the chair next to them. "Where's Saint?"

"He went to grab some shit from the store," Renny explains, offering me one of the beers from the six-pack he's holding. "Whenever he knows you're coming here he goes and buys aisle four for you."

"Thanks," I say, accepting it and opening the lid on my T-shirt. "What can I say, a girl's gotta eat."

"Don't know where it goes, though," Temper adds, downing half his beer in one mouthful.

"When are you going to settle down?" I ask Temper in return, watching, amused as he starts to choke on his beer. "What?

Is the concept that foreign to you? Don't you want a wife and kids?"

"Never met anyone worthy of making her my old lady," he admits with a shrug. "I'm not the easiest man to deal with, Skylar."

"You're nice to me."

"You're a kid," he fires back. "And you're family. You see a different side of me that not many get to see."

I consider his words. "Okay, so if you did meet someone you liked, you could show her that side too? You aren't getting any younger. And yes, that was payback for the kid comment."

He chuckles at that. "I haven't been on a date in five years, I think it is now. I don't think the whole dating thing is for me. I'm old school. And not just a few decades ago old school— more like caveman."

"Even cavemen brought women home to their caves," I point out.

He nods sharply. "Yeah, by hitting them over their heads."

I laugh, but he doesn't. "Okay, well, maybe don't do that."

Renny laughs out loud from beside him. "He's a little psychotic. But I wouldn't have anyone else at my back."

"Don't think that's on top of a woman's checklist these days," Temper says to us both. "None of the pretty ones are asking for a man to cover their back while they are doing shady shit."

"Are the non-pretty ones asking for that?" I ask, confused. "I'm sure there are some pretty criminals out there that would love that about you, Temper. But maybe you should go for a nice woman. Someone with quiet strength. Maybe she could balance you out a little."

"Why aren't you giving Renegade any shit about this?" he grumbles, finishing his beer and placing the empty glass bottle down on the table.

"Because he was talking about some hot chick when I walked in, so he's still in the game," I point out. "You I've never heard talking about any woman."

"I'll talk about one when I have something nice to say about one," he declares.

Saint walks in, and Temper eyes him in irritation. "Thank fuck you're back. Your girl here is giving me relationship advice, and I'm not drunk enough yet to deal with that."

Saint leans down with a cheeky grin, and kisses me longer than he should in front of company. "I'm sure she has some good advice for you, Temper. Come on, Skylar, I'm going to cook for you, just like I told you I would."

I remember what he wrote in the letter, smiling as he pulls me to stand up and leads me to the kitchen.

"You shouldn't poke Temper, you know," he says, lifting me up on the counter. "I know he's nice with you, and calm, but I've seen him flip the fuck out. Don't get me wrong, I'd take him on if he ever directed that at you, but I'm just saying be careful."

"I've heard that about him," I admit, remembering Hammer giving me a similar warning. "I don't know, I feel safe with Temper. I don't think he'd ever hurt me."

"You feel safe with all the monsters," he grumbles, getting a frying pan out of the cupboard and placing it on the stove. "How was work last night?"

"It was good," I tell him as he starts to get busy in the kitchen. "Your cousins were there again. What are you making, exactly?"

"Spaghetti," he says, turning to look at me in excitement. "A do-over for the shitty one I made you years ago. And yeah, they go out a lot, those two. They consider themselves socialites."

"Daisy has a huge rock on her finger," I tell him, and then linger a little before trying to casually drop the question I've been meaning to ask him. "And they mentioned that you haven't been to a family function since the last one you went to with Tory."

He fumbles in his onion cutting, then pauses for a second before continuing.

"Who is Tory? Is that your ex or something? You haven't

said much about anyone you've dated and..." I trail off, waiting for him to chime in with answers.

"No," he replies, dragging out the word. "I've never brought a girlfriend home to meet my family. I haven't really had any serious girlfriends aside from one, and that never worked out." He turns around and glances at me. "You have nothing to worry about, Skylar."

"You didn't answer the question. Who is Tory then?" I ask, narrowing my eyes. A bad feeling settles in my gut, something not sitting right with me.

With a sigh, he pulls out his phone from his pocket and presses a few buttons. I'm about to yell at him when he walks over and shows me a picture.

"This is Tory," he says, a little hesitantly.

I glance down at the little girl with bright blue eyes and a cute, dimpled smile. She is beautiful, the poster child for the perfect baby girl, and looks to be about two years old.

"This is Tory?" I ask, confused.

Until it hits me.

I do a double take of those blue eyes.

"She's yours?" I ask, breath hitching. "You have a daughter? And you didn't think it was a good idea to mention that?"

My voice gets higher with each word, until I'm yelling loudly. I'm sure the whole clubhouse can hear me.

"It's complicated," he says, glancing at the picture himself, then sliding his phone away. "And I didn't want you to walk away because you knew I had a child with someone else."

"So what, you were just going to bring her to our wedding one day and yell surprise?" I ask, standing up and stepping closer to him, being confrontational. I'm hurt, and I'm sick of feeling this way. It's like when it comes to me no one can be honest. They all care more about how they feel and what's best for them. But no one stops to think about me. In the end I'm left feeling betrayed, *every damn time*. So much has happened recently and I've shared all of that with him, and he didn't feel the need to be open and tell me about this? I just don't understand.

"And what's complicated exactly, Saint? Because the only thing that's complicated for me is the fact that you purposely didn't tell me this huge bit of information. I've been talking about honesty, communication. We even discussed having children in the far-off future, and you didn't think any of those times were good enough to bring up the fact that you already chose to have a child with someone else?"

Saint grabs my shoulders and gets me to look at him. "I didn't choose anything. She got pregnant—it was an accident. She was on the pill, but forgot to take it."

These things happen, I know. But he could have been more responsible.

Thorn Benson, the love of my life, has a child with another woman. And he lied about it.

I don't understand why he lied to me. He could have told me about Tory in his letters, or when we first saw each other again. He could have told me, but he specifically chose not to. This isn't a small deception. And then there is the other thing...

He has a child. While he's been my firsts for everything, my first kiss, my first lover, and one day I thought the father of my children, I was none of those to him.

I wasn't his first kiss, his first lover, and I didn't give him his first child.

"You saved nothing for me," I whisper, feeling empty all of a sudden.

"I saved *everything* for you," he growls, eyes scanning mine. "I never gave anyone all of me, no one, and even if I wanted to, I couldn't. Because deep down inside, I knew that I was meant to be with you, and no one else. I would never make anyone else my wife, Skylar. I've saved that for you."

Nothing.

"Skylar, are you listening to what I'm saying?" he asks me, cupping my face, begging me to look at him.

I keep my eyes on his chest, because I don't want to look at him anymore.

I can't.

He's a liar.

First my mother, and now him.

Is there anyone I can trust?

Chapter Twenty

Hammer steps into the kitchen, looking at us both like he'd rather be anywhere else but felt like he should check up on me.

"Are you okay?" he asks me, brow furrowing.

I turn the heat on to him. "You obviously knew Saint had a fucking child, and you didn't think *I* should know about it? How come no one can just tell me the truth, straight up, as it happens? Why does no one think about my feelings first? You're *my* father."

"Sky—"

"I'm the last person to know everything, and then I get some bullshit story about not wanting me to get hurt. Well, guess what, guys? Lying to me, it hurts! Being kept in the dark, yeah, that hurts too. And having to hear from two women in a bar that the man I thought was my fucking soul mate has a child, yeah, you guessed it, that also fucking hurts. So save me any speeches the two of you have, because I'm leaving."

Hammer blocks the door with his large build. "I told Saint he needed to tell you. That was up to him, not me, Skylar. The two of you are in a relationship, and it's between both of you.

And it's a complicated situation with Tory. I'm sure if you let him explain—"

"I'm not listening to shit," I state, hands on my hips. "I get that it's between me and him, but you know what I've been through recently! How much more shit am I going to have to take by the men who claim to love me?"

I turn to face Saint. "It doesn't matter what explanation you have—you had your chance, many chances I might add, and you still didn't tell me about it. You have a real fucking problem with communicating, and you are still so closed off with me. You say I'm the only one you want, that we have a connection that has lasted years of separation and change, then why won't you let me in?"

Hammer steps aside, and Saint follows after me as I make my swift exit to my car. When I open the door and get in, he sits in the passenger side.

"Please leave. I do not want to speak to you at the moment, so please get out of my car," I growl.

He stays silent for a few seconds.

"I don't know if she *is* my kid," he says quietly. "My ex, if you can call her that, we slept with each other only a handful of times. She told me that Tory wasn't mine a year after she was born. For that whole year I spent so much time with her, loved her, and spoiled her, and then Carol decided to drop that on me."

That...was not what I expected. I don't even know what to say to that. While I'm still angry over finding out about the child in the first place, I can't help but feel awful at what he's telling me now.

Confusion also fills me. Why is everything so complicated with this man?

"I didn't not tell you about Tory because I wanted to keep it from you. I didn't tell you because I don't talk about it, or her. I haven't seen her in months, and I'm just fucking pretending everything is fine when it's not, because I don't know what the hell is going on. And yeah, I miss my little girl. My little girl who apparently isn't even mine. And I'm sorry I didn't tell you."

He pauses, letting his words sink in. "Yes, there was an element of it that I didn't tell you because I thought you would get angry or walk away from me because it was too much to handle. No one wants to deal with baby mama bullshit, and no one wants to find out that the person they want to be with has a child already with another woman. Skylar, you put me up on this pedestal, but I'm not perfect. This isn't some forbidden romance story. I'm just a man, a biker, and yes, I've been with a lot of women over the years, and maybe even knocked one of them up. But I never loved them. I love you, and I always will."

He reaches out and touches my face. "I love you, Skylar. Don't give up on me, not just yet, okay?"

Swallowing hard, my heart breaks for everyone in this situation.

For him, for not knowing if the daughter he loves is his.

For Tory, who hasn't seen her dad and must be missing him.

And for me and my teenage dream that Saint would be mine and mine only, and when I finally had to share him, it would be with our own children. It might sound petty and unrealistic, but I do feel saddened about this.

"Maybe I *have* put you on a pedestal, or maybe my expectations are set too high, I don't know, but I never, ever, for one second thought that you would have gotten another woman pregnant," I admit, being a hundred percent honest.

"Sky," he whispers, ducking his head, like my words hurt him.

Well, his actions have hurt me, so I guess we are even.

"I know that sounds stupid and immature. But you just sprang this on me and it's a lot to process. And unlike some people—" I give him a glare "—I want to be honest in how I'm feeling, no matter how foolish my thoughts are. I can be mature about this and admit that part of my anger is unjustified, but—"

"You have nothing to feel stupid about," he tries to assure me, cutting me off. "This was before you, Sky. You can't be mad at me about something that happened before we were together. There's nothing wrong with having high expectations—fuck, you deserve the world—but can you judge me for my actions now, not what I've done in the past?"

Closing my eyes, I rest my head back on my car seat, sighing deeply. "I *am* judging you for your actions now. You never told me the truth, Saint."

"I knew it would upset you."

"That doesn't give you a free pass not to tell me," I quickly reply.

"I'm fucking this up," he whispers. "I love you, Sky. I'm beginning to think I always did, even when I forbid myself to even go there. I'm sorry, all right? And I know it seems like I'm always fucking apologizing, but I'm trying. I'm going to do better, and I'll be more open and honest."

Saint is trying to love me.

But he needs to try harder if this is going to work.

"I love you, too, Saint. I always have," I say, opening my eyes and turning to him. "I'm sorry about the situation with Tory and her mother, but yeah, you should have told me."

"I know."

Half of me wants to help him sort out the situation and be there for him through it, and the other half of me just wants to be selfish and make it about me. Right now, I just want to go home and cry, and feel sorry for myself because although I'd never admit it out loud, my perfectly constructed future has been shattered.

It's so ridiculous that I feel this way, so I think I need to cry it out. I need to vent to Max, even though I know he's going to tell me that I'm overreacting and I need to get over it.

Saint just hasn't let me in emotionally, and how can we move forward if he isn't going to?

"I'm all in in this, Saint. I moved here and found you. I'm here right now, for you," I say, feeling emotional, my voice breaking a little. "And now I'm here, and you're saying all the right things, but you have this irrational need to protect me from everything that will hurt me, even though I need to know it. It's not fair."

I hold up my hand when he's about to speak, stopping him. "I do not need someone to protect me. I need a partner who will be my equal and who will respect me."

He's silent for a few second before he speaks. "You're right. And you know what? If the roles were reversed, I'd hate it. I'd be furious. I'm not as open as you are, but I'm trying to be. It doesn't come naturally to me, but I'm willing to work on it for you. I'll do whatever I have to to make this work. I'm so fucking sorry I didn't tell you the truth."

If Tory is Saint's—and going by her eyes, I think she is— she is a part of him. This isn't about me, and wouldn't be my perfect plan for us, it would be about loving Saint's kid like I would my own, because I do love him.

"Sky, can you please say something?" he rumbles, and glances at the door. He wants to leave too.

How is this going to work if we can't communicate properly? It's way too soon for us to be having these concerns; we should be in the honeymoon stage, not fighting about issues way too big for me to handle.

I open my mouth to say I want to go home, and we can talk about this later, but I know that if I do that Saint is just going to close off even more from me. I need to show him he can trust me and that I'm not going anywhere unless he lies to me about something or betrays my trust again, because there's no coming back from that. Yes, I want to make this work, but I'm not going to be treated any less than I deserve. I can forgive him this time, but only a fool would a second time.

"I won't be lied to again, Saint," I say, looking him in the eye, expression blank. "I deserve honesty from you. And I will give you that in return, that and more. I know you only trust your MC, but you also used to trust me, and I need you to get back to that place where you aren't scared to tell me something because you think I will run away, or that I can't handle it. I *can* handle it." Not that I expected something like this to come up.

"I should have told you," he agrees, taking my hand in his. "I just... I knew you'd be disappointed."

That's an understatement. I think it was more of a shock than anything. I honestly didn't see it coming, and I just wish I had gotten to hear it from him. I don't think I'm a hard person to speak to, and I don't understand what he was thinking when he decided not to tell me. It was always going to come out; it's like he was just buying time.

"It doesn't matter what my reaction is—you still need to be honest," I whisper, staring down at our now joined hands. I've romanticized my relationship with Saint so much, but the truth of it is exactly what Logan was trying to tell me. I'm going to have be stronger to be in a relationship with him than with just a normal guy. Not that they don't do things like this either, but with Saint so much more can be tested.

Everything is going to be put on the line.

The question isn't how much I can handle, it's how much *will* I handle.

Chapter Twenty-One

"How are you, Sky? I miss you," Max says, putting on a sad voice.

"I miss you too," I say into the speakerphone, rolling over onto my stomach on my bed and resting my face on my palm, legs in the air. "There's been so much going on here, I really wish you were here right now."

"Is everything okay?" he asks, sounding concerned. "Your room is still empty here if you decide you want to come home."

"Saint has a kid. Or, well, he maybe has a kid," I blurt out, rolling over onto my back and staring up at the ceiling.

Max is silent for a few seconds. "And how do you feel about it?"

"Honestly?"

"Always."

I bite the inside of my cheek. "Disappointed. He never even told me about her. I had to find out for myself."

"Okay, how would you feel if he just told you straight up about his kid?" he asks.

I think about it. "I guess I'd still feel a little...surprised and kind of let down, but I wouldn't question our relationship over it. Him hiding it just makes me wonder what else he is hiding or chooses not to tell me."

"Yeah, the lying thing is pretty sketchy. I think you have every right to be upset over that aspect."

"Good, I needed to hear that," I admit, taking a deep breath. "Things just weren't meant to be this way."

"So what are you going to do? You do love kids, though. You're great with them. You know every time there was a crying baby or toddler having a tantrum in the café, you were always the one we sent in to help," he says, chuckling softly. "I know that it's not ideal, but you'd be great around any kid, never mind the child of someone you love. I don't think you have anything to worry about." He pauses, then asks, "Or is it the fact that you aren't the one he waited to have kids with that's the real issue here?"

"It's not that he didn't wait for me," I explain. "I didn't expect him to wait; that's unrealistic. We didn't even know if we'd see each other again, and we weren't even dating or anything romantic before. I guess it's just not how I thought we'd ever be. Saint thinks I've made up unrealistic expectations and put him on a pedestal, and now he feels like he has to live up to my idea of him."

"Maybe you have? You just said you didn't expect him to wait for you, and I'm sorry, but in case you didn't know, having sex can sometimes equal babies," he says, whispering down the line like it's some big secret. "It happens to the best of us."

"Hasn't happened to either of us," I point out.

"You're a virgin and I'm not stupid," he says, chuckling to himself again.

"See! You just called Saint stupid."

"I did not," he says, laughing harder now. "Look, sometimes shit happens. You can think you are being a hundred percent safe, and a baby still happens. The only way to guarantee not getting someone pregnant is to not have sex. And we all know your man—and I, for that matter—are not going to not have sex."

Now I'm laughing. "You're right. I know you're right. And yes, when you put it that way it seems ridiculous to be upset over something like that."

I know I can't hold on to this. I need to forgive and move forward, or if I can't accept things, I need to walk away. It's not fair for me to pretend to forgive him but then bring it up at any opportunity. At the end of the day I need to think rationally, and although it hurts—and boy does it—he didn't betray me. It has nothing to do with me, really, and maybe that is what hurts the most. I wasn't here, and what he did or got up to, and the decisions he made, had nothing to do with me.

But keeping the truth from me, though—that part hurts and I can't pretend it doesn't.

"Like you said, you love him. So don't be petty and hold grudges, Sky. I know you. For someone so sweet, you can hold a grudge worse than anyone I know. No one is perfect," he says.

"You're right," I say, still not ready to let this go.

Max sighs heavily. "Let's do a little role reversal here. Let's say you got pregnant out here in the country. But then you reconnected with Saint years later. How would you feel if he was upset and mad at you for getting pregnant with someone else's kid when he was never in your life during that time?"

Shit. When he puts it that way, I feel like a complete idiot. If roles were reversed, I'd feel horrified if he were mad at me for something I couldn't control or change. Leave it to Max to put things in perspective.

"You shit. Okay, okay. You're right. I'll let it go," and when I say it, I mean it. I need to move on and not throw this in his face again. I am not my mother; I refuse to be manipulative and petty.

"Good. Can we talk about me now?"

I laugh hard. "Okay, tell me about you. When is your next gig? Who are you dating? And most importantly, when are you coming to see me?"

Talking to Max makes me realize how much I miss him. We speak for another hour and when we hang up, I feel lighter, and see things much clearer.

That's the power of a best friend.

Saint picks me up from Logan's in his car the next afternoon, and tells me he has a surprise for me. I know with all the tension between us recently, we do need some alone time together to figure it all out. Now that I've calmed down and thought about everything, I want to try to see where his head is.

"So where are we going?" I ask as we pass the street that leads to the clubhouse.

"Surprise, Sky," he replies, flashing me a cheeky grin. "But you're going to find out in about thirty minutes."

"I'm intrigued," I murmur, glancing out the window. We haven't really spoken properly since he got out of my car the day before, just because I wanted a little time to reflect on everything. It's nice that he's putting in effort; he obviously wants to sort everything out just as much as I do. It's not a nice feeling when things are all up in the air and you don't know where you both stand. "We're heading half an hour out of town?"

"You're asking too many questions," he teases, nodding to the glove box. "I put some snacks in there for you for the ride."

"Are they to keep me quiet?" I tease, opening the compartment and pulling out a few of my favorites: chocolate, pretzels and marshmallows. "Because it's probably going to work. Man, I'm going to get so big the longer I hang around you."

"You'd be beautiful no matter what size you are," he replies as I rip open the wrapper on a chocolate bar.

"Do you want a bite? It's the least I can do after that little comment," I say, grinning and offering him the first one. He takes a chunk out of it, almost half the bar, leaving me staring down at it. "You have a big mouth."

"The better to eat you with, my dear," he mutters, making me laugh out loud. I remember the shower and how he made me orgasm, and other thoughts enter my mind. I can't wait until I get to be with him like that again.

"Yes, you are pretty good at that," I say, chewing and swallowing. "I guess you being experienced comes with its perks."

"I'm glad you see it that way," he replies, trying to keep a straight face. "You always could see the silver lining in everything, glad to know that hasn't changed."

"Well, there's no point being bitter about everything. That's hardly a way to live your life," I say with a shrug.

I'm on to the marshmallows when we pull up to a place in the middle of nowhere. "What are we doing here, Saint? Because this looks like a place someone would stop at to dispose of a body. I'm ride or die and all, but I don't know if our relationship is ready for burying a body together."

He laughs and gets out of the car, so I do the same, following him to the trunk. He takes out a tent first.

"We're going camping?" I ask, glancing around the deserted grounds. It looks like it could be a camping site, but there's nobody here except us. "Are we allowed to camp here?"

"Better keep our clothes on so if we aren't we can run back to the car," he jokes, pulling everything we could possibly need from the back of his car—blankets, pillows, food, the whole nine yards—then starts to set up while I watch. He leaves the car lights on so he can see.

"Do you want any help?" I ask, hoping he doesn't take me up on the offer, because I've never put up a tent in my life and have no idea how to do so.

"I'm good," he calls out, chuckling under his breath.

I pop another pink marshmallow into my mouth, then realize I should save them for s'mores tonight. "Okay, if you're sure."

He doesn't take long, and soon we have our own little glamping setup, with a blowup mattress and warm, thick blankets inside the tent. He even put a little welcome mat at the front. When he pulls out a portable gas stove, my jaw drops open.

"Done this before, have you?" I ask, impressed by his preparation and the effort that goes into sleeping in the wild.

"I love camping. I asked you about it once, and you said you've never been but wanted to go one day," he tells me, and I smile because he did remember. "Did you end up going?"

"I did actually, once," I admit, lying down on the mattress and watching as he does the same. "Max wanted to go for his birthday one year, but we stayed on a camping grounds so they had showers and toilets. Speaking of, where are we going to shower and go to the bathroom?"

"There's a lake down that way," he says, pointing to the right. "But we will head back tomorrow, so I'm sure you'll survive if you skip a shower for one night."

Luckily I had one this morning, but I usually have one every night as well. "And the toilet?"

"In the woods," he says casually, grinning at my reaction. "If you need to poop, I will dig you a hole."

I blink slowly a few times. "There's no way in hell I'm pooping in the bush, in the middle of nowhere, with you nearby."

"You'll change your mind if you really need to go," he says with confidence. "This is going to be a bonding moment for us."

I roll closer to him, so our noses are almost touching. "No amount of bonding will let you see me poop."

He laughs at me and pulls me closer. "I love you," he says, kissing my lips. "I felt so shitty after you drove off, and I know a lot of what you said is true. I can be closed off, and from now on, for you, I'm going to be an open book. Nothing is off limits, and everything you ask will be answered, brutal fucking honesty and all. And I'm going to assume that anything I tell you won't make you run away."

"Good," I say, reaching out to touch the stubble on his cheek. "And I thought about a lot too, and I want you to know that whatever happens with Tory, I'm going to be here for you and support you."

"Thank you," he says, the relief in his voice evident.

"Why don't you get a DNA test done once and for all so you can find out for your peace of mind?"

"You'd really be okay with that?" he asks, studying me, as if making sure I'm being honest. "I haven't requested the DNA test because if she's not mine I don't know what the fuck I'm going to do. But you're right, something has to give and I can't just live in limbo like this forever."

I nod. "Yeah, I mean, I don't know the situation with her mother, but whatever you choose I'm going to be right here next to you. I agree, I think you should find out the truth."

"Carol is…difficult to deal with. She does love Tory, and I mean, she's not the worst mother, but she won't hesitate to use her as a weapon to get what she wants either. I don't mean to be a walking fucking stereotype right now, and I know that most men say this about their exes, but she is crazy."

"How so?" I ask, brow furrowing. "Like 'wants money, gold digger' crazy, tries to fight any woman she sees you with, or stalker type?"

"All of the above," he admits, cringing and rolling onto his back, staring up at the roof of the tent. "Well, maybe not the stalker part, but everything else. We were never actually together, we were just casually fucking, and…" He trails off, scrubbing a hand down his face. "I want to say yeah, I fucked up, but then Tory wouldn't be here. So it's a hard situation. Basically Carol said she was protected, and we were using condoms anyway, but then one time…" He glances over at me. "Do you know how fucking hard it is to speak about this to you? You, of all people."

"It's hard to hear too," I admit, taking a deep breath. "But it's our reality, so keep going."

"She told me she was pregnant and it was mine. We didn't get together after that, but I made sure she was looked after, gave her money and went to all the appointments and everything with her. I might not have loved her, but that was my child inside her and that meant something to me."

"As it should," I whisper.

"Tory was born and she was just a bright light, you know? I loved her the moment I saw her, and I told myself I'd do whatever I could to be a good father. Then a few months ago Carol told me I'm not even the father, said it was the man she's with now." He sits up with his knees to his chest. "And then I went out and got drunk, and lo and behold, the fucker was also there. He's the one I hit and got arrested for. He pressed assault and battery charges. I was facing at least three to five years minimum."

"Then how'd you get out in less than six months?"

"My plea deal was for a year. But, I don't know, overcrowding or some shit," he explains, shrugging. "My lawyer is one of the best, and he knows his shit. Carol hasn't been in contact, and I haven't seen Tory in months. I know you're right, I need to figure out what I'm going to do, because I just can't pretend this whole thing doesn't exist anymore. I miss her. And it breaks my heart that she's probably thinking this other douche is her dad, because he's living with them now and taking on that role."

"She has your eyes, Saint," I tell him quietly. "When I saw her, I knew she was yours straight away, and if she is, you need to fight for her."

He turns to me, and lies back down, facing me again. "Fuck, I love you so much, Skylar. I know this isn't what you would have wanted—"

I cut him off, shaking my head. "It doesn't matter. I was being selfish. This is a little human we're talking about, and it was wrong of me to think of her as ruining some epic love story between us that I've created in my head these last few years. But you not telling me about her, on the other hand..."

"We can still have the epic love story," he says, rolling me onto my back with him on top of me. "We just might have a little princess with us now and again. And it will only be honesty from here on out."

"I'm okay with that," I say, looking into his eyes. "Like you said, she's a part of you, and I love all of you."

He slams his lips down on mine, kissing me deeply, but slowly. Hungry kisses that let me know I've made the right choice and that things are going to be okay.

We are going to be okay.

Chapter Twenty-Two

Glancing up at the clear night sky and the stars, which are so visible tonight, with a warm campfire in front of us, I whisper, "Now that is a view." I love being here, and can't wait to spend the entire night with him like this. We're all alone, with not a soul in sight, and with the fire going it's a beautiful atmosphere. "Thank you for bringing me here tonight, Saint. I'm really enjoying myself."

And I've decided that tonight is the night.

I want Saint to make me his. I want him to be my first.

"Me too," he says, eating his marshmallow off a stick. "I think I really needed to get away, and even more than that I needed some alone time with you. You know I'm never going to give up on you. No matter what, I'm going to be here, fighting for you, fighting for us. So in the moments you don't believe in us, I'm going to believe in us for the both of us."

My eyes widen at the stark sincerity in his tone.

"Thank you, Saint," I say, moving closer. "I adore you, you know that, right?"

"And I fucking adore you," he replies, lifting his blanket

up and pulling me under it. We cuddle up together, just lying there for a little while, enjoying each other's company before Saint cooks dinner on the portable stove, frying sausages and onions to eat in a bun.

"Hot dogs under moonlight, who knew this could be romantic?" I tease after we finish eating and pack up everything. Except now I need to pee, which I've been holding in for a little too long. "Can I have the flashlight?"

He hands it to me. "Do you want me to come with you?"

"No," I say, staring out into the darkness. "I won't go too far."

"Call me if you need me," he murmurs, amused, while I traipse into the woods armed with nothing but a flashlight and some toilet paper. I go behind a tree and pull my pants down, do my business and stand back up.

I'm about to pull up my pants when I feel something the size of my palm crawling on my leg, so I start to scream, "Oh my God!" picturing some huge ass spider on me and shaking my legs, before running toward the camp.

Pants falling back down to my ankles, I end up tripping over and land on my face.

"Ouch."

Just great.

Lifting my head, I dust my face off with my hands, grimacing at the sand.

Of course Saint finds me lying there, and helps me up. "What happened? Are you okay? Are you hurt?"

"Something crawled up my leg," I admit, as he pulls my pants up for me and fastens them. "It was probably a killer spider. This is how it ends for me, Saint."

"Did you actually get bitten? I told you I'd come with you," he sighs, dusting some more sand off my face. Lifting me up in his arms, he carries me back to the camp where I wash my face and hands. He checks me for bites, but there's nothing there. "Do you want to go for a swim in the lake?"

"To drown the spider that's potentially still on me? What's in there?" I ask warily.

"No idea," he replies a little too cheerfully. "And there's no spider. It was probably a leaf or something. The water will probably be freezing, but we can clean ourselves up."

Considering when we were sitting around the fire I decided I want to have sex with Saint tonight, freshening up probably isn't the worst idea. "Yeah, I guess so."

We walk down to the water hand in hand, and Saint undresses me, chuckling before doing the same for himself.

"What's so funny?" I press.

"You, lying there on your face." He laughs out loud. "I knew I should have come with you. I thought maybe with all that time in the country, you'd become a little more accustomed to nature."

I open my mouth, then close it. "I don't like bugs. No amount of country living is going to change that."

He pushes my hair off my face, chuckles dying down. "You're so fucking beautiful," he murmurs, running his hands down my arms and the sides of my body. "How did I get so lucky?"

Something hard pokes me in the stomach. "Wow, you're really happy to see me."

"Ignore it," he replies, amusement lacing his deep voice. "I know I am."

I dip my toe into the icy water and shiver. "Fuck me dead."

Saint mutters something under his breath, but I don't catch it. "What did you say?"

"Nothing," he replies, laughing softly. He splashes some water on him, washing his body and brushing his teeth, and I do the same, then wrap myself in a thick towel.

"Surprisingly refreshing," I mutter, glancing up at the moon. "It's a full moon tonight. Doesn't that make people crazy?" Seth told me that his girlfriend told him that nights with a full moon are crazy at the hospital, and the weirdest shit happens with the most random and over-the-top medical encounters.

Saint lifts me in his arms like a bride and kisses me. "I don't know. I guess if you believe in all of that shit."

I cuddle against his chest. "Tonight has been so fun. Even if I had to pee on the ground then fell over on my face with my pants around my ankles. Not my finest moment."

"At least you didn't knock yourself out or something, because the closest hospital is back in the city," he rumbles, kissing the top of my head. "You're a menace, you know that?"

"I'm not usually such a damsel in distress, I promise," I add, grinning to myself. "But I guess I do have my *Knight* in shining armor now."

Saint pauses in his steps. "Did you just make a Knight pun?"

"I did, and how great was it?" I ask, wrapping my arms around his neck.

I can't remember the last time I felt this carefree. Saint and I are good, I've made a decision in regards to my future career path, and I don't have to worry about my finances and whether I'm going to make rent this week or not. I have a family who loves and supports me. Hammer is back in my life, along with all the men in the MC, and... I'm happy.

When Saint puts me on my feet, I drop the towel on top of my clothes and turn to him, pressing my palm against his soft, smooth chest and tracing the tattoos there. When I glance up at him, he must see the hunger in my green eyes, because he makes a deep sound in his throat and cups my face kissing me deeply. His towel drops, and we press our bodies together, skin on skin. He leads me backward and onto the blowup mattress, our lips never leaving each other's.

It's not long before he starts to trail his lips down my body, and gently spreads my thighs. I start to get excited knowing what's coming, something I've been craving since we had that shower together, but I want more from him this time.

I want everything.

"Yes," I whisper, as Saint kisses up my thighs, teasing me and turning me on even more. He has me arching my back, silently begging him for more as he kisses my inner thigh, nibbling the sensitive skin there. Goose bumps appear on my flesh, my nipples pebbled to the point of pain.

By the time he puts his mouth on my pussy, I'm all but begging for it, so turned on that I can't even think straight. Using his talented tongue, he brings me to ecstasy by licking, sucking and eating me. My thighs start to quiver, my breathing so heavy anyone would think I'd been running in a marathon. He makes a growling sound in the back of his throat, letting me know that he's enjoying it too, which is so sexy to me. I didn't even know men enjoyed going down on a woman, but Saint has shown me otherwise.

He pays special attention to my clit, running the tip of his tongue over it repeatedly, but just before I'm about to come he stops and raises himself over me, rubbing his cock against my entrance. I'm so on edge, and so needing to come right now.

"Are you sure, Sky?" he asks me, sounding gruffer than I've ever heard him.

"Yes, I'm sure," I reply, breathless. "I want you, Saint."

He gets up and pulls out a condom from his bag. I'd give him shit for being so hopeful, but I'm just glad that he's prepared because I'm not on the pill just yet.

After ripping the condom packet open with his teeth, he rolls it down his length and returns to the position he was in before, stroking my clit and then gliding the tip of his finger inside me, touching my wetness, before slowly sliding his hard cock inside me, inch by inch.

He sucks my nipple, sending pleasure through me. At the same time there's a little bit of pain. He stills, waiting for me to get used to him before he starts to move. It feels so good, the pleasure so much more than the slight dash of pain.

"Are you okay?" he asks, tone husky. I look into his eyes and see so much there. Heat, pleasure, and concern. He doesn't want to hurt me, but little does he know he's making this an experience for me that I'm never going to forget.

I nod. "I'm fine. More than fine."

Then I kiss him, deeply, my fingernails scoring down his back.

I finally see what all the fuss is about.

Suddenly, he pulls out of me and puts his mouth back on my pussy, licking me over and over until I come, his name on my lips.

Only then does he slide back inside me, thrusting gently, kissing me, letting me taste myself.

When he comes I love watching him, looking into his eyes and seeing the desire there, listening to the sexy growling sounds he makes, which only turns me on further. After he's finished, he rests his forehead against mine and kisses my lips.

He then lies back next to me, breathing heavily, and silently reaches out his pinky finger to touch mine. "That was…"

"Worth the wait," I finish, rolling closer to him and resting my head on his chest. I feel a little sore, but in a good way, and I know he made it the best for me as possible, his experience paying off once again.

"I fucking love you," I think I hear Saint whisper.

I fall asleep with a smile on my face.

Chapter Twenty-Three

For the first time since getting this job, I start to feel a little uneasy about two men at the bar. It's not like they have been unruly or overly rude or anything, but I just don't like the way they are looking at me. It's almost like they're studying me, or memorizing me, and it's making me feel really uncomfortable. They both grin at me, and then at each other, and something about them makes me nickname them Dumb and Dumber in my head.

"Hey, sweetheart, can we get another one?" one of the men asks, even though my manager is closer to them.

"Sure," I reply, forcing a smile and making another two gin and tonics. After I deliver them, I take my break in the staff room, not wanting to be around the bar until they leave. Checking my phone, I find a few messages. Three are from my mother. All the same.

Sky, I'm your mother. You have to talk to me eventually.

Why are you being a little brat about this?

Can you call me? Can we talk about this?

I ignore them all and read the message from Max.

Got a gig in the city next weekend, so I'll see you then! I'll
send you the details.

"Yes," I cheer to myself, typing back a quick reply. Something to look forward to.

Can't wait to see you! I'll make sure I have next weekend off.
You still need to play at my work too!

Lucky for me, the men are gone by the time my break is over
and the atmosphere is back to normal. An hour or two later I
see a familiar face, bringing an instant scowl to my expression.

"Seriously? Tell me Saint or Hammer didn't send you here,"
I ask Dee, crossing my arms. Every time I see Dee now, my
guard is up. He reminds me of being babysat and spied on at a
time when I had no idea the MC had any kind of involvement
in my life. I know it's not his fault, he was just following orders, but the sight of him sets me on edge.

He puts his hands up in submission. "Calm down, feisty
one. I'm actually here on a date. She suggested the place. Don't
worry, my time following you is over. I've moved onto bigger
and better things now."

"From spying on women in bars to going on dates instead?"
I ask him, arching my brow. "Do you want a drink? Or maybe
I should be offering your date a drink instead." She's the one
who has to put up with him for the night.

"I'll have a beer. You know, Sky, I think you and I got off
on the wrong foot. I was following you because Hammer made
me, yet you're still angry at me but not him. How is that fair?"

The man has a point. "Okay, I guess you're right. Every

time I see you now I just assume you're here being a spy, and I'm sorry."

"I appreciate that," he replies in a dry tone. He places some money down on the table and eyes the busy dance floor. "I should probably message her and tell her that I'm here."

"Where did you meet her?" I ask, wondering what his type is going to be.

"Online," he replies, flashing me his teeth. "Is there any other way these days? We can't all meet our true love in a clubhouse."

"Yeah, I don't think love is really what they're distributing out there," I agree, laughing out loud. I notice that Dee has taken the time to dress up and is in a navy blue shirt with his hair slicked back. "So what is Dee short for? Derek? Damion?"

He starts laughing, loudly. "No, my real name is Wade."

"Why do they call you Dee then?" I ask, grabbing the beer I almost forgot to get him, and taking the money from the counter. "Because you can be a dick?"

"Closer," he replies, glancing at his phone. "Okay, she says she's here and wearing a white dress."

Nosy, I glance around, trying to spot anyone with that description. "Over there," I say, pointing to this girl sitting in one of the corner booths. "Good luck."

"I don't need luck," he says with a cocky wink. As he turns around to go to her, he bumps right into another woman, and she spills her drink down his shirt.

Oops. I grab a cloth and hand it to him over the bar. "Are you sure you don't need any luck?"

If looks could kill.

Miss White Dress spots Dee and makes her way over to him. "Wade?" she asks, voice soft and feminine. She's beautiful, with blonde curly hair and a full figure.

"Yes," he murmurs, turning to face her. "Nice to meet you, Maryanne."

Feeling like I'm a part of the first date awkwardness, I want to move away, but I can't seem to make myself, instead glancing between the two of them and eavesdropping without shame. Dee has forgotten about his alcohol-soaked shirt, now lost in Maryanne's eyes, the two of them seemingly taken with each other.

"Can I get you a drink?" he asks her, placing the cloth back down on the bar.

"I'd love one. A tequila sunrise, please," she says, smiling up at him like he's her prince charming.

"Tequila sunrise, please," he echoes to me, before turning his attention back to his new woman.

I make her drink and place it on the table. "That's fifteen dollars, thanks."

He gives me his credit card this time, and it's true his name is Wade. Wade Simpson, actually. No D in his surname either.

Swiping the card, I look up at him and sigh. "Oh no, your card declined."

"What?" he asks, glancing down at the eftpos machine and then at Maryanne, surprise written all over his expression. For a moment, I consider playing this out, but it is kind of mean, so I relent.

"Just kidding," I smirk, handing his card back to him.

"I'm going to kill you," he mutters under his breath.

"Now, now, Dee, don't be showing your true self on the first date—she will run," I reply quietly, laughing and moving to serve another customer.

The rest of the night goes quickly, and Dee says bye before he leaves with his date.

Wrap your willy, I mouth to him. He simply shakes his head at me and pulls Maryanne outside as fast as he can.

Saint picks me up from work on his Harley, and he truly looks so sexy on it. The bike is black, and he's dressed in all black too—jeans, leather jacket and biker boots. He removes his helmet and jumps off, coming toward me as I stand out front of the bar, under the moonlight.

"The night I've had," he growls, scooping me in his arms and dipping me backward with a kiss. "I've missed you."

"I missed you too," I reply, holding on to his neck. "What happened?"

"Just some shit with the club," he says, giving away nothing. "It's been a long day and all I want is to be in bed with you next to me." He pauses. "Or on top of me."

"Well, we better get you home then," I reply, grabbing my helmet off the back of his bike and putting it on. After I get on behind him I squeeze him tightly and feel his stomach.

Yeah, I can't wait to be in bed with him either.

"So I messaged Carol and told her that I want to do a DNA test," Saint tells me as we're naked in bed after a very long session of showing each other how good it felt to see one another. He's running his finger up and down my arm, sending goose bumps all over my body.

"Not my idea of pillow talk, but go on," I tease, kissing his shoulder. "Did she agree?"

"No," he replies. "She didn't, which makes me think she has something to hide, or doesn't want a certain outcome. But I spoke to a lawyer, a good family lawyer at the Bentley and Channing law firm. I can get a court-ordered DNA test, so I'm going to do that."

"Good," I whisper against his skin. "I'm glad you're going to fight for her."

I don't know why this woman has decided to punish Saint, but I can only guess. He most likely ended things with her or she saw him with another woman, something like that to make her turn spiteful and put her needs above her child's. Or maybe it's the truth and she's not sure who the father is. I guess everything will come out with time.

"As long as I have you by my side, I can fight for anything," he replies, tracing my lips with his thumb. "Thank you for being the angel on my shoulder, Sky. I think you've always been that for me."

"Thank you for loving me like you do," I reply, kissing him

on the lips. "I'm sure it will all work out for you. Maybe Carol will come around and let you see Tory in the meantime."

"She might. There's only one thing she loves other than her daughter, and that's money. I could try offering her some money if she lets me see Tory once a week or something."

"You shouldn't have to pay to see your own child. I mean, you already do pay child support, right?" I ask him.

"Yeah, I pay child support for her. Which I should tell Carol she can kiss goodbye if Tory isn't mine," he adds, frowning. "Pretty shitty how that works out, isn't it? Some men don't even get to see their kids but have to still pay, by law. The system is fucked. If Carol is determined to keep Tory from me, I know I'm not going to win in court. I can use the court for the DNA test, but if it came down to a custody battle, they'd take one look at me and I'd lose. I'm a biker, I'm covered in tattoos, I'm big and I've recently been to prison for assault."

"We'll worry about that when we get to it," I tell him. "Let's just get the DNA test sorted, and maybe you starting to see her again. I'd love to meet her."

"I'll try make it happen," he agrees, nuzzling my head. "I never choose the easy route, do I? It's always something, and I know I've fucked up with my choice of baby mama, and I'm sorry I'm dragging you into this with me."

"It is what it is," I say, yawning. "You don't have to keep saying sorry. We will handle it all together." He squeezes me tighter. "Oh, and Max is visiting next weekend, so me and him are going to catch up. He's doing a gig here—do you want to come with me? You can meet him."

I feel Saint stiffen a little, so I open my eyes and look at him. "He's family to me, and one of my closest friends. Don't act all weird just because he has a penis, because trust me, friendship is all we have, and is all we will ever have."

"You really think heterosexual men and women can be friends, and just friends?" he asks me. "Usually one person wants to fuck the other, who is friend zoning them. I don't think I've ever met a guy and girl who are just genuinely best friends, with a purely platonic relationship. Usually someone secretly has a crush. Unless you grew up together or are childhood friends or something, maybe."

"You're so cynical. Just because you don't have any female friends you don't want to fuck, doesn't mean that other people don't," I fire back, feeling a little annoyed at his comments. "I've been friends with Max for years, and I think I'd be able to tell if there was a little something more there for either of us, but there isn't. We're basically like brother and sister—we give each other shit, and I could comfortably be around him in any situation."

"Don't get angry at me, I'm just telling you what I think," he grumbles, lifting my hand to his mouth and kissing the back of my palm. "All right, if it means that much to you, I'll meet this guy, and I'll be on my best behavior."

"He's the one who was there for me, Saint," I tell him, my stern tone letting him know how important this is to me. "He held me together, and that means something to me. So please don't be weird about it. He's important to me and I want the two of you to get along."

"Okay," he agrees. "I'm hearing you, Sky. Relax."

Melting back into him, I hope he keeps to his word, because the last thing I need right now is more drama.

I think I have my fair share as it is.

Next weekend comes up fast, and soon I'm pushing through a crowd of women screaming and loving Max and the band. Saint is at the bar, ordering us a drink. I was hoping to catch Max before his set began, but we ended up running late because Saint and I ended up in bed together, almost like he was reminding me that I'm his or something—as if I need the reminder.

"Max!" I call out, wanting him to see that I'm here.

"Max is mine," some girl next to me says, elbowing me out the way.

"You psycho," I say, elbowing her back and glancing up at the stage to find him waving at me.

"You know him?" she asks, suddenly my best friend. "He's so dreamy! Can you introduce me to him?"

"Fuck no," I reply, heading back to the bar and away from the crazy-ass fans he's accumulating the more popular his band gets.

"It's a warzone out there," I say to Saint as I reclaim my seat next to him. "I almost feel sorry for Max." If I didn't know how much he loves the attention.

"Their music is pretty good," Saint admits, sliding my cocktail my way. I can't stop looking at him in his white shirt tonight. He looks sexy as hell, and since he usually wears black it's something different.

"Yeah, they are amazing," I agree, bringing the margarita to my lips and taking a sip.

"This song is one I wrote for my friend, Skylar. Skylar, this one is for you," Max calls out, making me almost spit out the liquid in my mouth.

Saint throws me a look, one that clearly says *I told you so*, but when Max starts singing it has nothing to do with anything other than him being friends with a girl who is funny, loyal and loves to give him shit all of the time.

"If I needed to be brought back down to earth, she'd be the one to do it..."

The song seems to be about him climbing the ladder to fame, and about me being the one who helped get him there, which is very sweet of him. As Saint listens to the lyrics, he loosens the hold on his glass, which was about to crack in his hand, and relaxes a little. I don't know how I'd feel if a woman wrote a song about Saint, and I can't believe that Max wrote one about me. It's very nice of him, but I wish I was given a heads-up about it. I was trying to make a point to Saint that we're just normal, close friends, and a song isn't working in my favor right now, even if it is just about a close friendship.

"See, just a friend saying thank you to another friend," I point out, taking a casual sip of my drink.

"He has some balls, I'll give him that," Saint growls, then turns to me with a fake smile. "Just a friend saying thank you."

I laugh at his expression. "I love *you*, Saint. You have no competition in this whole world. You could send me anywhere, with the hottest men on the face of this earth and it wouldn't matter. I'd still choose you, every single time."

Blue eyes soften. "I'd choose you too, Skylar. No matter what."

"Good," I murmur, lifting my glass up. He clinks his against it. "To us, forever."

"To us," he says, our eyes locked as we drink once more.

We turn our attention back to Max and enjoy the rest of his songs.

When they take a break, Max comes straight to me and gives me a giant hug. "Fuck, man, it's so good to see you, Sky."

"You too, Max," I say, smiling at him. "This is Saint. Saint, this is Max."

Max turns to Saint and smiles widely, offering him his hand. "Nice to meet you, man. I've heard a lot about you."

"All good things, I hope." Saint grins, flashing his teeth.

"Yep, all good. Except the whole baby mama drama, but hey, you can't win them all right?" Max says with a casual shrug. Saint laughs, while I cringe and down the rest of my drink.

"Come on, I'll order us a round," Max says, slapping Saint on the shoulder.

Saint flashes me a look that says "he's not so bad after all" and the two of them get talking.

Almost makes me feel like the third wheel after a while, but as long as they aren't killing each other, I'm happy.

Chapter Twenty-Four

"What the hell is going on in here?" I ask Saint as we step into the clubhouse a few nights later. All I can hear is music, cheering and laughter. After just having a night out with Max, I didn't think I'd be attending another outing so soon. "Are they having a party?"

"It's Renny's birthday today," he explains, closing the door behind us.

The scene I step into makes me laugh out loud. Renny is sitting there, blindfolded and in nothing but a pair of boxer shorts, and there are two women in front of him, feeding him cake.

"What birthday party game is this? Whatever it is, Saint, you aren't playing it," I declare, glancing around at the giant happy birthday sign and the balloons. There are two cakes on the table, so I step forward and grab a piece. "Who made the cake?"

Saint chuckles and wraps his arms around me. "I don't know, but I think he's blindfolded because he has to choose which cake tastes better without looking at it."

"So the women are here as cake models?" I ask, brow furrowing.

"This is Renny's party after all," Saint reminds me, and yeah, it does seem like something Renny would appreciate.

"Maybe we should have invited the woman next door he has a crush on," I say, taking a bite of the chocolate cake. "Do you want to party with them? I can go home and sleep," I ask him, not minding. Saint and I have been spending so much time together, I'm sure he would love some time with his brothers without me there, and I'm totally fine with it. Women around and all.

"No, they're going to be drinking all night, and I want to take you to your first day tomorrow," he replies, leading me away from the laughter and toward his room.

Tomorrow is my first day in the paramedics program, and I can't wait to start this new chapter. Over the last few weeks everything between Saint and me has been amazing—we've been communicating more and just talking about everything, and he has really opened up to me, which I'm grateful for. I think even Logan is coming around now, especially after I brought Saint in to talk to him and meet Sabrina. I haven't heard anything else from my mom, so I guess she's sticking to her word about disowning me, but it's peaceful now, and I'm not upset about it anymore. My life is better without her in it. She's a toxic person, and although it's sad, it's just how things need to be. Sorting out my schooling was the final part I needed to make my life exactly how I want it, and now that I'm here I'm never looking back.

"Are you sure?" I ask as we enter his room, and I drop down onto his bed, kicking off my shoes, removing my clothes and climbing under the sheets. "Or you can leave me here to read a book and fall asleep."

"I have a little something more interesting than reading a book—"

"You obviously don't know how good this book is," I cut him off, teasing.

He takes off his shoes and shirt, standing there in a pair of low-slung jeans and a smile. "Can't be more interesting than this."

He slowly undoes his belt and then pulls down his jeans, his cock straining against his briefs. Arms folded back behind my head, I lick my lips and watch the show as he takes it all off, standing there naked before me.

When he starts to stroke his length up and down slowly, then faster, I sit up and crawl toward the end of the bed. On my knees, I take over the job for him, using my hands and then my mouth to pleasure him. He gets harder the second my mouth is on him, and his fingers tangle in my hair, encouraging me.

When he starts to get impatient, he steps out of my reach and comes around to the bed, lifting me up and tossing me back against the pillow. Lips slam down onto mine, kissing me while he rubs his engorged penis against me, and every time he slides against my clit I can't help but moan a little, lifting my hips, begging for more. He pushes inside me, just the tip at first, then the rest of him.

"Saint," I whisper, nibbling on his ear.

He lifts his head up and looks at me. "Yes? You feel fucking amazing."

"So do you," I say with a smile, cupping his face and bringing it back down for me to kiss. Going on the pill was the best decision ever.

He pulls out of me and turns me over onto my stomach, lifting my hips up and sliding back into me in one smooth thrust. At the same time he reaches between my legs to stroke me there. He's so generous in bed—he never makes it just about him, and I know that every single time he's going to make sure I'm satisfied, the mark of a true gentleman.

My nipples rub against the bed with each thrust, adding extra sensation. He kisses the back of my neck, sending shivers up my spine, and I'm so wet I can literally feel how damp I am, wetness spilling out onto my inner thighs.

"Fuck," I moan, as he gently pulls my hair back, turning my head to the side to kiss me. He lets go of me and grips my hips, sliding in and out of me in a slow grind, while I push back against him.

I bite down on the pillow as he makes me come, and seconds later he follows me, finishing inside me.

He pulls out and lies back, grabbing me and spooning me, his chest moving up and down. "See, much better than drinking with the men."

The men choose to laugh loudly at this exact moment, and we can hear them all the way from outside.

"Are the walls really thin, or is it just me?" I ask, wondering how much they can hear.

"Is that why you suffocate yourself with a pillow when you come?"

"Yes," I reply, laughing. "I don't want anyone to hear me, especially Dad. That's traumatizing. For both of us."

"But I love hearing you and the little noises you make," he admits, biting down gently on my neck. "You are so sexy, you know that?"

"I do now," I reply, rolling over and getting as close to him as I possibly can. "And thank you for making me feel that way."

Don't get me wrong, I've always had a healthy self-esteem, but with Saint I just feel beautiful, wanted and loved all the time. It doesn't matter what I look like, whether I've just woken up or I'm all dolled up, he always looks at me like I'm the most beautiful woman he's ever laid his eyes on.

"I love you," he whispers, tucking my red strands back behind my ears. "Are you excited for tomorrow?"

I nod. "Yeah, I am. Feels good to finally have some direction and a plan, instead of just being flaky and hiding behind random jobs."

"Does this mean you're going to quit the bar?"

"No."

"Stubborn," he says with a head shake. "I'm going to make

you an additional cardholder for my credit card, so if you need anything, just use it and I'll pay it off."

"Why the hell would you do that?" I ask him, lifting my head. "That's so unnecessary. Dad is already paying for me to do this program, and I don't need you paying for anything for me either."

"Sky, it's not a big deal," he replies, brow furrowing in confusion. "Just keep it for emergencies if you're feeling weird about it."

"Saint—"

"Stop being stubborn," he says, interrupting my rant. "Choose your battles, Sky. I read that somewhere. That's what relationships are all about, choosing your battles. I feel like this one isn't one you should pick, because I'm just trying to look after my woman a little, even if she doesn't want me to or need me to."

I open my mouth, then close it. "Okay, I'll save my battle for something else, then."

He's right, he's just trying to take care of me, even if I prefer to be more independent and not expect anything from him. It's not like I *have* to use the credit card. If it makes him feel better, there is no harm in accepting it. I know that some women specifically look for men who will do this for them, but I'm not one of them. I don't need lavish gifts or lots of money to make me happy, but I can appreciate the fact he wants me to have a backup in case of emergencies.

"Good girl," he replies, grinning at me. "Look at us, not killing each other and compromising."

"I just compromised, actually," I state. "And I hope it's going to be reciprocated at some point soon."

He kisses me, stopping me from saying anything else. "You have a smart mouth."

"You love it."

"And I have compromised already. I didn't say anything when you went to go hang out with Max all alone. Even though I don't love it, I know he means something to you, so I stay quiet and don't give you hell over it."

Yeah, he didn't love it, but he just told me to call if I needed him and message him when I got home safely, which I appreciated.

"You're right," I reply, grinning. "You've been toning down the whole alpha overprotective bullshit, and I appreciate it. Anyway, I'm going to jump in the shower—would you like to join me?"

He responds by getting out of bed and picking me up, carrying me to the shower.

So much for toning it down.

Chapter Twenty-Five

I see Carol from a distance before I see Tory, the little girl standing next to the swing set at the park. She's a pretty, petite blonde, pretty much the total opposite of me. Maybe Saint doesn't have a type, or hell, maybe I'm not even his type at all. It's been a week since he requested the DNA test, and suddenly Carol is playing nice, being flexible and letting Saint see Tory whenever he wants, but of course it comes with a price.

He squeezes my hand, bringing me back to reality. Today is about meeting Tory, and nothing else. It's not time for me to start feeling insecure, or questioning things because I'm finally getting a look into his life before I came back.

"There she is," he murmurs, and my eyes drop to the most beautiful little girl ever. Her dark hair is in pigtails, and she's wearing a pink dress with gold strappy shoes.

"Tory!" he calls out, and the little girl spins and looks in our direction. When she sees Saint, her blue eyes light up and she runs over to him.

"Daddy!" she calls out in her baby voice, holding her little chubby arms out. Saint picks her up and gives her the biggest hug.

"How are you, Tory?" he asks her, kissing her cheeks.

"Good," she replies, beaming up at him. "I good, Daddy."

Saint turns to me and steps closer. "Tory, this is Sky. Can you say Sky?"

"Sky!" she calls out, giggling.

"Nice to meet you, Tory," I say, smiling.

Carol walks over, and up close I can see that life hasn't always been kind to her. She looks tired, her face weathered and worn. I don't know if she's just much older than Saint, or if maybe time hasn't worked in her favor.

"So, you're the new flavor of the month," Carol remarks, eying me.

"So you're the woman using her child as a weapon," I fire back, my temper getting the better of me. I regret it as soon as the words leave my mouth, both because Tory is present but also because I should be the bigger person and just not say anything, because she's just not worth any of my time or energy.

"That's enough, Carol," Saint says to her, holding on to Tory. "I'll bring her back in two hours, like we agreed."

"Did you put the money in my account like *you* agreed?" she asks, pursing her lips.

"Yes, the money was transferred."

We walk back to our car, and the whole time I can't help myself from judging Carol, and even judging Saint for sleeping with her. Forget looks or anything else—Carol is obviously not a nice person. She has no dignity or self-respect and is blackmailing Saint for money to see his kid. Also, if she were so certain Saint wasn't Tory's father, why would she still let her see him?

Out of all the women Saint could have been with and gotten pregnant, why did it have to be this one? I know he says Carol loves Tory, and that might be true, but it can't be healthy for Tory being raised by this woman. Although I could be still grappling with my own mother issues and projecting onto Carol and Tory.

I don't verbalize any of my thoughts—it's not going to help the situation in any way—but that doesn't mean I'm not thinking it. Saint puts Tory in her car seat and the two of us get into the car, a weird tension between us.

"Did we decide on where we are going to take her?" I ask, turning on the radio.

"How about the aquarium?" he suggests, reaching out and touching my thigh. He lowers his voice so only I can hear. "Don't listen to anything Carol says. You know what you are to me."

"I know. And I'm sorry for engaging with her. I'll be better around Tory."

The situation is far from ideal, but it's not my situation to fix, it's theirs. All I can do is try to be there for Saint, and to put in effort with Tory and try to be a good role model whenever I'm in her presence, which means no more snarky remarks from me, no matter how much Carol tries to bait me.

We go to the aquarium, and Tory's face lights up when she sees the starfish and the turtles. I don't know much about two-year-olds, but she seems very clever.

"Pretty," she says, and I turn around thinking she's talking about one of the starfish again, but she's looking right at me. She reaches out from Saint's arms and touches my hair. "Pretty hair."

"Thank you," I say to her. "You have pretty hair too."

She giggles and puts her arms out, trying to come to me, so I let her all but jump into my arms. As she buries her face into my neck, Saint and I look at each other. This isn't what I ever would have asked for, but with this little girl in my arms I feel like I don't even care if Saint is her biological father. She's his.

And she's perfect.

After class I head straight to the clubhouse. "This has been the best week ever," I tell Saint, Hammer and Temper, who are sitting outside chatting. "I'm so happy I decided to do this." I love going to class every day, learning all these new skills on saving people, and it's just such an empowering feeling. I stop my rant when I realize something isn't quite right, going by how tense the men are.

"Is everything okay?" I ask. I must have interrupted some club business, or some other conversation that stopped the second I made an appearance.

"It's fine, Sky," Hammer says, reaching out to touch my hand. "I'm glad you found your calling. It makes me happy seeing you happy. And soon you won't have to serve drinks for a living." He turns to Saint and smirks. "And now because you have a man, I don't even have to pay for it."

"What do you mean?" I ask, confused.

"Saint paid for it. Didn't he tell you?" Hammer asks, glancing between us.

"No, I didn't tell her, because I knew she was going to give me shit about it," Saint mutters, throwing Hammer a dirty look.

Hammer simply shrugs. "He's your man and he wanted to pay for it. Don't need my bank anymore when you have his."

Fuck's sake.

This program was a hell of a lot of money, but I didn't feel that bad about Hammer paying for it—he's my dad and has paid for and bought many things for me growing up.

But Saint paying for it? That's different.

"I'm going to pay you back," I announce to him.

"See?" Saint growls.

"At least she's not a gold digger like the last one," Temper adds, chuckling to himself.

Pursing my lips at that comment, I turn to Saint but before I can open my mouth he starts talking. "Sky, you don't need to pay anything back; don't be ridiculous. You just study and then save some lives."

"Some biker lives," Temper adds. "You're basically an investment."

I throw my hands up in the air. "I can't deal with the lot of

you, seriously. But Saint..." I turn to my man. "I can't thank
you enough. You really didn't have to do that."

"I wanted to," he replies, brushing it off. He lowers his voice
and says, "I don't know what you think we're doing here, Sky,
but I'm in this forever. That means we're going to look after
each other and support each other, and that's what I'm doing."

I feel a little bad that he didn't even want to tell me because
he knew I'd have something to say about it, but it's not that I'm
ungrateful. I don't ever want him to think that. It's just that I
don't like feeling like I owe someone.

"Thank you," I say, kissing his stubbled cheek. "I appreciate it."

"I know you do," he says, leaning in and pressing his soft
lips against mine.

"Okay, get a room, you two," Temper adds, looking uncomfortable. "I don't know where the fuck to look right now. How'd
you deal with it, Hammer?"

Dad just shrugs. "At least she's with a Knight. Imagine her
bringing some banker or businessman home. This way she's
here almost every fucking day and I get to see her."

"I'd come and see you anyway," I point out. "Are you sure
everything is okay?"

I can tell when it's not, because the change in atmosphere
is so obvious.

"Yeah, just club business," Dad replies, glancing up and
flashing me a smile, as if to reassure me.

"Okay," I reply, lips pursing. I know they aren't going to tell
me anything else, so I change the subject. "What are we having for dinner?"

"I'm going to make the spaghetti I never got to make last
time because we had that huge fight and you went home," Saint
replies, glancing around the table. "If anything goes wrong this
time, one of you please stop her from leaving."

"What could go wrong this time? Unless you have more

baby mamas and secret children, I think we're good," I say, arching my brow.

"None that I know of," he replies, the men chuckling at his smart-ass answer.

"I'm going to kill you," I threaten, eyes narrowed to green slits. "This better be the best fucking pasta that has ever entered my mouth."

"It's pretty good," he says, standing up and winking at me. "You going to come help me in the kitchen?"

"I'll supervise," I agree, standing up and following him. "Do we have any wine?"

"Is he driving you to drink already?" Hammer calls out.

"Yes," I call back, and then all I can hear is laughter. Whether it's at me, or with me, I have no idea.

"Yeah, I'll get you a glass," Saint says. I sit back and watch him work the kitchen, first getting me wine, then starting to cook. "How was your day?"

"Good," I tell him, perking up at the thought. "We're doing anatomy right now and there's so much to remember, but it's interesting, so I don't mind it. I'm going to have to do some studying tonight."

"Oh, need someone to help you study?" he asks, turning around from the stove with a wooden spoon in his hand.

"Yeah, actually. I was thinking of asking Reece, this really cute guy from class," I reply, getting him back for his baby mama comment outside.

Now he's the one with narrowed eyes. "You're giving this Reece guy a death sentence if you decide to continue."

I sip my wine, pinky finger sticking out. "Now, now, Saint. Let's not get violent. Also, he's a martial arts expert."

I put my glass down just in time for Saint to grab me and lift me up. I wrap my legs around him and hold on to his neck.

"You just don't want to eat my spaghetti," he says to me, lip twitching. "That's what all this is about, isn't it? Or has the spaghetti left you traumatized after last time?"

"No, it hasn't left me with PTSD, don't worry." I smirk, kissing his nose. "I'm just feeling a little…"

"Sexually frustrated?" he offers, laughing out loud. "Is that why you're pushing me? Babe, if you want me, all you have to do is ask. Hell, all you have to do is look at me. I'm always wanting you and I will always be ready for you."

I put my hand over his mouth when I hear footsteps near us. If my dad heard that, I'm going to die a little inside.

It's Renny who sticks his face in the kitchen. "What the hell is going on in here? You're supposed to be cooking, Saint, not having your way with the prez's daughter in the middle of the day." He barks out a laugh before disappearing. "You have some balls, brother. Balls of fucking steel. I'd be pretending I was a virgin while Hammer is around."

Saint puts me down and I pick up my glass once more, resuming my position. When I down the rest of it, Saint murmurs something about needing some of the wine for the pasta.

Maybe he's right and I am sexually frustrated, but it's not like I'm going without. Saint and I have sex pretty much every night we spend together. He's created a monster. Or maybe I'm just hangry, which is also a possibility. When I glance over at him he's picking up a tea towel that fell on the floor, and I can't stop looking at his ass, his strong thighs…

Fuck, he's right.

I'm addicted to his D. This is going to be a problem.

Speaking of D… "Why do you guys call Wade *Dee*?"

Saint turns to me with brows furrowed. "How the hell do you know his name is Wade? I didn't even know that."

"I saw his credit card when he came into work once. Remember, I told you—his first date with Maryanne," I explain.

He nods. "Oh yeah, that's right. They call him Dee because he's the biggest dick."

"Biggest dick or he has the biggest dick?" I ask, dead serious. Why else would they call him that when his name is fucking Wade?

And guess who decides to walk in just as I say that?

All I can hear is the bastard's laughter, like a fucking hyena, absolutely losing his shit.

"What the fuck is so funny?" Temper asks as he comes to see what all the commotion is about.

Dee can't breathe at this point, so when he tries to tell Temper what I said, it just ends up in more fits of laughter.

"Sky is asking how Dee got his nickname," Saint says, scrubbing a hand down his face. He looks like he's torn between laughing and killing me. "And she's come to the scientific conclusion that he's either a huge dick or has a huge dick."

Pointing my finger in the air, I sophistically state, "I believe it's a valid conclusion. I mean, Saint got his name because he's a man whore, right? You guys were trying to be funny."

Saint always tried to maintain that he got his road name because he was a Saint compared to the others, but I learned long ago that it's because he always had a way with the ladies.

"I'm reformed," Saint adds in, finally admitting the truth.

"Temper got his because…well. He's apparently a psycho."

"And how did I get my name?" Dad asks as he joins us, amusement plainly written on his face.

Hammer?

Ew.

The only thing I can come up with is something I'd rather not think about.

Ever.

"I need more wine," I declare, looking for the bottle.

And this motherfucking conversation is over.

Chapter Twenty-Six

I can tell that something is wrong the second I step inside the clubhouse—the atmosphere so thick and tense, it's a struggle to breathe. There is a tension in the air that's just festering. Searching for Saint, I find him sitting outside at the table with the men.

All of the men, and all of them looking very serious.

After all the time during my childhood spent at the clubhouse, I know this isn't a time to intrude. I walk back inside and wait in his bedroom. I hope no one is in trouble with the police, and that no one is in danger. Did one of their deals go wrong? I know that they run several businesses, like Saint said, and not all of them are legal.

Things have been so lighthearted around here recently that it's easy to forget what they do to earn their money; they don't exactly have a nine to five. I don't really think about what each of these men I call my family are capable of. I just go by how they treat me, and that's all that I focus on. Maybe it's naïve, but it's how it needs to be.

I fall asleep with my book in my hands, and wake when Saint

opens the door and comes in. "Sleeping beauty," he says, lying down next to me. "Sorry to keep you waiting."

"Is everything okay?" I ask, reaching for him. "Seemed pretty heated."

"Yeah, there's an issue, but we're going to sort it out, so don't worry. Unfortunately I'm going to have to go and do the rounds tonight with Temper, so I'm not going to be able to stay in and do all the things I want to do with you. Will you stay here, though? I want to come home to you in my bed," he asks, kissing me softly, which soon turns heated.

Lifting myself up, I lower my body onto his and straddle him. "Do you have to leave right now?"

Someone bangs on our door. "Saint! We're leaving!"

"I guess that's a yes," I whisper, leaning over to kiss him and then roll off.

"Well, you just made my night that much harder," he groans, glancing down at his cock.

I bury my smile into the pillow. "Great pun. I'll see you later tonight then."

He groans again, gets out of bed and comes around to my side, kissing my cheek. "Just wait until I get back, you little tease."

"Be safe."

"I will. Renny will be here if you need anything."

Another kiss, and then he's gone.

Not knowing what is happening or what we are dealing with is hell. I know I could push and get more out of him if I wanted to, but I'd rather him just tell me what he feels comfortable with. The MC is my family, but I'm not a member, and I know there's a difference. I trust them, and that they will handle any situations that arise.

While I study, Renny locks up the clubhouse and makes sure everything is closed. They should really amp up the security here. I know they only have security cameras and the big fence, which they usually just leave open because there's so many people coming in and out. I think they live by the "no one is stupid enough to come in here" law, but they should be smarter about it.

I fall asleep without Saint, and when I wake up in the morning he's not in bed, either.

Finding him in the gym, I watch as he punches the shit out of a boxing bag, shirtless. "You didn't sleep?" I ask when he stops to take a break.

"I did, but just for a couple hours," he explains, wiping his face with a towel. "You were knocked out so I didn't want to wake you, although trust me when I say I was tempted."

"You could have," I say. "I'll go and make us some breakfast."

I'm frying bacon, and the smell brings in Dad and Renny, so I end up making breakfast for everyone. "Bacon, eggs, toast, mushrooms and hash browns," I say, placing the plates full of food on the table for them to serve themselves.

"Thank you," Dad says, and I don't miss the bags under his eyes. "Looks like none of you got any sleep last night."

I know Saint said he had to do the runs with Temper, which means he was checking on their businesses or whatever, but there's obviously something going on because they all look exhausted and their morale seems kind of low. I open my mouth, but decide to close it and make some coffee instead. Coffee might perk them up a bit.

"Is there anything you guys want me to do before I head to class? I could drop off some lunch for everyone on my break," I offer, glancing around the table.

"We're okay, Sky," Saint assures me, standing behind me and massaging my shoulders. "You just worry about your class, and we can sort ourselves out. Are you here tonight or at Logan's?"

"Logan's," I tell him. "Tonight is family night with my brothers, so basically we're all going to eat, drink and talk shit and rip on each other until we call it a night."

I clean up and then head to class, but I can't shake off this bad feeling in my gut. Something is going on.

* * *

"So we actually have some news tonight," Logan announces, clicking a spoon on his bottle of beer. He has Smith and Axel on video chat, so I know this news must be big.

"You won the lottery?" Seth screams.

"You're visiting us here in Ireland!" Axel says enthusiastically.

"You're getting a dog," I add hopefully.

"You found out you were really adopted?" Brooks asks, garnering a smack in the back of the head from Seth.

Logan rolls his eyes at Brooks. "Sabrina is pregnant! You lot will finally have a niece or nephew."

"What?" I shout, jumping up and running to Logan to hug him. I know how long they have tried for a baby, and I'm so happy for it to finally happen for them.

"What about me? I'm the pregnant one," Sabrina teases, so I give her a hug too.

"Congratulations to you both. Just telling you now that Skylar is an amazing name, and I'm not against having another one in the family."

"One Skylar is enough, thanks!" Brooks calls out, eyebrows high on his smug face.

"Hopefully it's a girl because I'm tired of being outnumbered," I say, looking back at him. "And also surrounded by assholes."

"Are you sure? Because you have the same thing at the clubhouse," Brooks fires back, chuckling to himself. The rest of my brothers join in.

I throw daggers at Logan, the most mature one, but he just shrugs. "Oh, come on. That was funny."

We all speak to Smith and Axel, who are over the moon for Logan, and it's really nice to see their faces. Axel tells me that they'll be coming back soon and will try to stay in the city long enough for me to spend actual time with them, which warms my heart.

The pizza Seth ordered us all arrives, and we sit in front of the TV and eat. It's the quietest it's been since we walked into the house.

"How's class been?" Seth asks me. He's the brother who has been the most interested in my education from the get-go, and when he found out I have decided to become a paramedic, he was so proud of me.

"Really good, I'm learning so many new things every day," I tell him, swallowing my mouthful of pepperoni. "It's both mentally stimulating and physical when we do the practical stuff, so it's really interesting."

"I'm glad you're studying again. You're such a smart girl, Skylar. You always have been," he continues, reaching over and touching my shoulder. Seth isn't very affectionate, so him actually touching me of his own free will is kind of a big thing. Usually it's me hugging him, and him awkwardly standing there and taking it.

"Thanks, Seth," I reply, beaming. "It feels good to be moving forward instead of being stuck in the same place and routine like I was in my last job. And the bar job I'm in now, I actually don't mind it, maybe because I know I won't be there forever."

It's going to be nice having some options for a change, and some sort of qualifications behind me, not to mention financial security. I don't want to have to live paycheck to paycheck for the rest of my life, and I also don't want to have to rely on Saint for anything. Logan told the rest of my brothers what happened with Mom, and I don't know if they're in contact with her or not, but I'm fine with it either way. They haven't asked me anything about Saint or Hammer, so it's not like anyone is trying to get information out of me to pass on to her. She's just like the elephant in the room, and no one wants to bring her up or discuss what happened so we're all just going to pretend she doesn't exist.

And I'm more than okay with that.

It's easier this way.

Chapter Twenty-Seven

"I have it all under control," I hear Dad say. I've shown up un-announced at the clubhouse, and with the loud talking they mustn't have heard me enter.

"They aren't going to stop—it's not safe for any of us right now. Either we take him down, or we're sitting ducks," Temper chimes in.

Instead of making myself known, I step back and listen to their conversation. They will never tell me what's going on, and although I feel bad, I really want to be included this time.

"I know," Hammer growls, a large bang, one that sounds like him slamming his fist on the table, makes me jump. "I fucking know, all right? We need to make a plan, and we need one now. It feels like five years ago all over again. When will this end, though? His brother died, and he wants revenge. But if we take him out, then what? Is there another fucking brother we have to look out for?"

"Nope, just the two of them," I hear Saint add in. "It's not safe right now, and yeah, we need a plan. I don't want Sky in any kind of danger."

"And you think I do?" Hammer fires back, tone lethal. "No one we care about is going to get hurt. We just need to find this guy, and… Fuck. Why did he have to get out of prison? I know we can handle him. The question is, can we handle him without any of us doing time?"

Silence for a few seconds.

I step back a little then walk to Saint's room instead, my head buzzing with everything I just overheard.

Revenge?

Sitting ducks?

Could they be talking about the man Mom offered to hand me over to? It makes sense, because that man did end up in prison. The past has come back to haunt us all.

This time I'm older, and there's no one to throw me under the bus like last time. But I still have no idea how I can help. I don't want anything to happen to any of the men, and I don't know what I'd do if it did.

Saint comes in about thirty minutes later and I pretend to be fast asleep.

"I didn't even hear you come in," he whispers as he jumps in bed with me.

Snuggling up to him instantly, I struggle between ignoring everything I just heard and acting normal or confronting him. I decide on the latter. "I heard what you guys were talking about."

Saint sighs and lifts my face up to look him in the eye. "We will handle it, all right? You don't need to worry, but I just want you to be a little more vigilant than usual. Don't trust anyone you don't know and just be extra street smart in all situations."

"What's happening exactly, Saint? No more bullshit. This affects me too," I say to him, frowning. "Is this the same guy that was after Hammer when I left? The one Mom wanted to use me as a bartering tool with?"

"Yeah, that's him. Killer. He's been in prison all of these years, but he's finally been let out and apparently hasn't let go of his vendetta. His brother died, so I guess it's understandable," he says, words turning to mumbles.

"His brother was hit," Saint says, wincing. "And he fell back and knocked his head and died. It was a big group brawl, so we don't even know who hit who, but it was us they were fighting, so Killer decided to take it out on our president and swore Hammer would pay for him losing his little brother."

"But then he got locked up," I whisper, finally understanding the situation. "So what are you guys going to do? We all have to protect Hammer."

"Yeah, basically we're all going to be on guard," Saint says, kissing my forehead. "He might want Hammer, but none of us are safe until the threat is stabilized. If Killer sees his opportunity, he's going to take it."

"What did he go to prison for?" I ask, trying to formulate a plan. I might not be able to fight or anything like that, but I'm smart, and I'm good at problem solving.

"Assault. But that was his second offense, so he didn't get a lenient sentence like I did."

"Okay, so he's on probation now, I'm assuming, which means he can't step out of line. What if we try to get him locked up again? I don't want any of the Knights having to go to prison because of this guy."

Or getting hurt, or worse. I don't want any of them having to end someone's life to protect my dad's. I don't want anything to happen to my dad, either. It's hard to win in this situation without someone being sacrificed.

"And what about my brothers, are they all safe?" If something happened to any of them, I wouldn't be able to live with myself.

"Your brothers will be fine, but we will give them a heads-up just to be safe. If it gets bad we will have a shutdown, where anyone we love can come here and be safe. Trust me, we don't want that either, but if it's us or them, it's going to be them," he states, a hard look in his pretty blue eyes. "I don't want you to worry about anything other than keeping yourself safe. If it gets to a critical point, we're going to go into lockdown, and you will be escorted to classes or work, or wherever. It's better to be safe than sorry, all right?"

I nod. "All right." I love my freedom, but I'm not stupid. These men aren't messing around and I'm going to be careful.

"Good girl," he whispers, sighing. "I'm sorry you have to deal with all this."

"Don't worry about me," I tell him. "I'm just worried about all of you. I can't lose you, Saint."

"You won't," he replies, sounding confident. He even manages to flash me a cheeky grin. "When I have you in my bed, there's no way I'm not going to return to it."

"Be serious."

"I am being serious," he says, rolling me over and holding my wrists down against the mattress. "I love you."

"And I love you."

The sooner this whole situation comes to an end, the better. Killer needs to go back behind bars where he belongs.

"Tory, what are you doing?" I ask the energetic toddler as she runs around the clubhouse, leaving a spiral of disaster everywhere she goes. I don't know how moms do it, because this looking after a small person thing is no joke, and I'm watching Tory only while Saint's out to get us some lunch and run some errands.

"Don't you like the new toys I bought you?" I ask, eying the discarded pile. Instead she seems to enjoy playing with the box one of the dolls came in.

"I like," she says, nodding, but continues to drag the box around. I follow her into the kitchen and watch as she tries to open up the cupboard.

"Are you hungry?"

She looks at me with those blue eyes and nods again. "Yes."

"Okay," I say opening the fridge. "How about some yogurt?"

She cheers, so I'm guessing that's a yes.

I sit her at the table with a spoon and watch her shovel the yogurt into her mouth. She really is a cute little kid. Her mom did the DNA test, so we're just waiting on the results now, but I think it's obvious that Saint is her dad. I don't know why she said otherwise—maybe she just wanted to hurt him and get more leverage over him.

"Yum," Tory mumbles, placing the cup down and looking up at me. "More?"

"More, please?" I suggest to her.

"More pweese."

Grinning, I grab her another tub and some blueberries. "Your dad better hurry up with the food or you're going to be full by the time he gets here."

I hear the rumble of his motorcycle just as those words leave my mouth. "Oh, he's here. Can you hear the sound of his bike?"

Tory nods, eyes going wide. "Bike loud."

"It is pretty loud, isn't it?" I agree.

Saint comes in with bags of food, smiling when he sees both of us sitting there. "Sorry it took so long."

"That's okay. Your little girl got hungry, though, so she had some snacks," I tell him.

He comes over to me and kisses the top of my head. "Why do you do that?"

"Why do I do what?" I ask him, lifting my head back to look up at him.

"You always say 'your little girl' or 'your daughter,' emphasizing the 'your.' I'm going to marry you one day, Skylar, which means she's yours too. Just because you didn't give birth to her doesn't mean she's not your family. You should know more than anyone that blood doesn't always mean the most."

"I didn't even realize I was doing that," I admit, and never would I have thought my wording would upset him. I don't see Tory as mine in any way—at least I don't consider myself her second mother or anything like that—but I do care about her and would do anything for her. So I think that has to count for something. Saint is right, of course. Blood isn't everything—loyalty is.

"You're a part of this family," he says, kissing me again, and then unloading the food. I know he's making sure I feel included and I appreciate it, but he doesn't need to. I've accepted the situation as it is, and I'm going to make the best of it.

"I know, Saint. And thank you for making me feel that way."

We have lunch, and then I head off to work, leaving Saint to have some alone time with his daughter. Carol seems to be slowly letting him have her more, and I wonder if it's because the results are going to arrive within the next few weeks and we're all going to know the truth about Tory's paternity. Or maybe she's just in a good mood with all the extra money she's been getting.

Either way, we get to see Tory, so that's all that matters.

Chapter Twenty-Eight

As I'm leaving class, the last person in the world that I want to see is standing next to my car. After having such a good morning—spending some much needed alone time with Saint and then a great class where I got high marks on a test—I feel like my day is about to be ruined.

"What are you doing here, Mom?" I ask, searching for my keys in my handbag. "You have no daughter, remember? So why don't you go and visit one of your sons? You have plenty of them."

I don't know how she knew I'm doing this program or what time I'd be here, but I hate that she does. She's obviously still keeping tabs on me, which annoys me to no end.

"I just want to talk," she says, pursing her lips. "Can you give me that, at least? I want to apologize. I know I'm not a perfect mother and that I've messed up, but I want a chance to apologize and explain some things to you. This is all my fault, and it's time that I told you who your real father is. Do you have time for a coffee? I'll explain everything from start to finish."

"I thought you didn't know who my father was," I remind

her, frowning. She's dangling the bait right in front of my face, but it's the one thing that I've always wanted to know. "Was that a lie too?"

I don't know how much more of this I can take. The back and forth, it's so exhausting. I wouldn't be surprised if she knew this whole time who my biological father is and just didn't tell me. Not that it would matter. Hammer is my father.

"I have my reasons, and when I explain, you'll understand everything," she promises.

"Okay, I guess we can have a coffee," I decide, willing to hear what she has to say. "There's a place down the road. We can walk there or drive."

"Let's drive. I'll walk back once we're done," she suggests.

"Okay," I say, opening the car door. She gets in, and we buckle up and leave.

"I really am sorry, Skylar. I took you out of that world for a purpose, and when I found out you had gone back there, I just lost it," she says, sniffling a little. "And I'm sorry about the money. I still have some of it and I will give it to you. I'm sorry about everything. I've been a terrible mother. I hope you can forgive me."

She got dumped—she didn't choose to leave and save me like she is now claiming—but I don't bring that up to her. You can't argue with crazy, and she's the queen of talking shit, so she's going to have an answer for everything.

After parking my car in the coffee shop lot, I turn to her about to ask her if she really knows who my dad is.

Instead, I'm greeted with a sharp knock to my head, and all goes black.

When I wake up, my head is pounding. I don't think it has ever hurt so much in my life. Rubbing the back of it gently, I force my eyes open and glance around at my surroundings. I'm in a room, which is bare except for a mattress on the floor. The windows have been barred with big pieces of wood, blocking any light from getting in.

A sick feeling in my stomach, I sit up and remember how I got here—because I trusted my mother when she said she wanted a fucking coffee and an adult chat about everything that has happened. I'm here because I wanted some closure, and in return, I get knocked out and kidnapped by the woman who gave birth to me. This takes family drama to a whole new level.

Moving to the locked door, I bang on it loudly. "Mom! Let me out!" I yell, banging harder.

What the hell is she going to do with me? I have no idea what she has planned, but I know it can't be good. The fact she has crossed this line means she has clearly lost her mind—I need to never underestimate her again.

Wherever she's decided to put me, she obviously thought about this. I try to pull the wooden planks off the window, but they don't budge. There's nothing I can use as a weapon, and no way I can break out of here except through the door.

I was going straight home after class and not to the clubhouse, so the MC isn't even expecting me, and I don't even know if Logan is home to realize that I'm missing.

Basically, I'm fucked.

I scream until my voice is broken, then fall back onto the mattress in a pile, not sure what the hell I'm meant to do or how I'm going to get out of this. Why didn't I just drive off and leave her there? I thought I was fine and had accepted my situation with her. But no, I'm still a little girl who needed her mother to love her, who wanted to know the truth behind the father who I've never known. Stupid idiot that I am.

Hand on my forehead, I curse myself for thinking there was even an ounce of good in her. Getting back up, I place my ear against the door and listen for any sounds or movement but hear nothing. Is she out there? Deciding all I can do is play the waiting game and see what she has in store for me, I sit back on the bed and pray that Logan has called Saint or Hammer.

I don't know how much time passes, an hour maybe, but the door finally opens, and it's not my mother. A man stands there, one I've never seen before. A very large man. He's dressed in black and worn leather, and looks like his personal hygiene isn't a high priority with him.

He grins evilly when he sees me, revealing teeth too big for his mouth, surrounded by a beard that needs a good wash. "Skylar O'Connor," he says, cracking his knuckles.

"Who are you?" I ask, back literally against the wall. "Where's my mother? And what do you want with me?" I can't believe that once again, my own mother has thrown me under the bus. At this stage, I don't know why I'm so surprised, but the hurt and betrayal is still there, ripe as ever. I never should have given her a second of my time, or thought that she was human and wanted to apologize.

I've fucked up, big time. My stupid bleeding heart that wanted her mother to love her. Idiot.

"You, my girl, are going to be used as bait to bring Hammer here," he tells me, booming with laughter.

"Killer?" I guess, starting to panic.

"Oh, you've heard of me then? Good. You're about to find out how I got my road name," he declares, stepping closer to me. "You're a pretty little thing, aren't you?"

Fucking creep. "Don't fucking touch me," I warn him, placing my hands in front of me. "Besides, aren't I a little old for you?"

He laughs harder. He clearly belongs in a mental ward and instead he's been let out of prison to ruin other people's lives. "I like you, Skylar." He leans forward and adds, "And that's probably not going to end well for you."

Great.

He moves back to the door, and I relax a little, my shoulders slouching. Movement from behind him brings none other than my mother into view.

"Mom, don't leave me here!" I call out, pleading with my eyes. "I am your only daughter—how can you do this to me?"

"You'll be fine," she replies with a shrug. "It's just Hammer we want, Skylar. And after we have him, we will let you go. No harm will come to you."

She acts like that makes all of this okay, that just because I will be able to walk out of here, it's no big deal. She's batshit crazy.

"How can you do this to him?" I ask her, feeling tears threaten. "He raised me! You loved him more than your own kids at one point—how can you do this to us?"

"Don't bother begging, little one," Killer says to me, his beady, dead eyes looking right into mine. "My brother died, and now someone has to pay. A tooth for a tooth. If not Hammer, then who? Would you rather someone else take his place?"

I feel bad, but my mother does come to mind.

"Killer, give it a rest." She pushes him aside and steps toward me. I instinctively take a step back. "I told you I was going to tell you who your father was," Mom says, looking at me unflinchingly in the eye. "I never wanted you to find out the truth, but I agree. It's time you knew the whole truth.

"When I met Kieran—that's your father—I was a single mother with five boys at home. I fell for him, and I fell for him hard. When you were born, you were the apple of his eye. He looked at you like you hung the moon."

I want to smile at the thought that my biological father, whoever he is, loved me. Truly loved me, but I bury those feelings for another time.

"I hated that he loved you so much. Loved you more than me and my boys. He didn't want anything to do with your brothers. I don't even think they remember him." She sneers. "I couldn't let him ignore my sons and I couldn't let him put you before me. So I took you away from him. I left and changed my name, and met Hammer a few months later. And Hammer loved *me*. Sure, he loved you too, but he loved me in a way Kieran didn't.

"When you were sixteen, Kieran found me. And he was furious that I had kept you from him for years. I knew he'd come after you and he'd make me pay for what I did."

"Mom, this is a great story, but I have no idea what that has to do with the fact that you basically kidnapped me." I glare at her.

"He was my brother," Killer says. I look at him in confusion. "Kieran was my brother."

And just like that all the pieces fit into place. The reason why the Knights of Fury started catching heat from Killer and his MC. The reason why my mother never told me, or Hammer, who my biological father was.

For just a moment, Killer looks almost human as emotions cross his face. "Kieran was the best part of me. He hated your mother for what she did, but he loved you." He stares at me. "You look like our mother, actually." He actually sort of smiles.

My own mother rolls her eyes. "The Knights killed Kieran, Skylar. They killed your father. When I offered you up to Killer, I knew he wouldn't hurt you, because you are his blood."

"You have got to be kidding me. You want me to think that you were doing me a favor? You're nothing but a selfish, sad woman…"

She slaps me across the face. "Listen to me. If Killer had you, a piece of his brother, they'd leave the Knights alone and I'd be able to stay with Hammer. I loved him and—"

"And you offered up your daughter in exchange for your own happiness."

She opens her mouth to speak but then closes it.

"So what do you want now? Why are you working with him? Why after all this time?" I point over to Killer.

"I found her," Killer simply says. "I spent years in prison planning what I would do when I got out. Every plan I had came down to finding your mother. She is the reason why my brother is dead. She is the reason my brother missed out on sixteen years with his daughter. But then she changed my mind, and offered me something better."

I look at her. Shocked that she once again offered up her own daughter to save herself. "And you told him what? That I'd go with him?"

"No, I told him I'd get him Hammer. On a silver platter. But he promised he'd let you live your life, without any interference. See, I'm not as evil as you paint me out to be, Skylar. I was thinking of you."

I look to Killer. "Is this true?"

If it is, the monster standing before me is none other than my uncle.

"It's true," he admits. "It's the only reason you aren't bleeding out on the floor right now. That and because of my brother." He looks at Mom and points to his watch. "You have a few hours or else our arrangement will have to change." He turns to leave and slams the door closed.

"Mom, what the fuck is wrong with you? What are you doing?"

"I'm doing what mothers do. I'm protecting you," and with that she turns and leaves.

I'm left alone once more with all these new revelations. I can never tell if my mom is lying or not, but I feel like she might have actually been telling the truth. It's such a twisted end to the story that is my life, my biological father dead by the hands of the men who actually raised me and cared for me. I try to feel sad for him, but it's hard to grieve a man you never met. The worst part of this whole thing is that Kieran seemed like a decent guy. It's my mother who was the problem. She is to blame for all of this. Her and Killer.

Pushing Kieran out of my mind, I concentrate on the task at hand: getting out of here and not letting any of the Knights fall into the trap that my mother has set.

I need to trust in the Knights right now, and know that they're going to come up with a plan and save me. A plan that will get us *all* out of here safely. And alive.

And if not?

I'm going to save my damn self somehow.

When Killer opens the door and leaves some water and a sandwich on the floor, I feel like I'm in prison. Both the food and the company are shit.

"I need to pee," I tell him, because even prison has a toilet in their cell.

His jaw tenses, but if I'm such an inconvenience, then he shouldn't have kidnapped me in the first place. I regret my request as soon as he comes closer, grabs me by the arm and hauls me up. "Try anything, and trust me when I say you're going to regret it."

Swallowing hard, I let him drag me outside the bedroom, revealing an old, messy, and what looks to be abandoned house. The type of house that should have been knocked down years ago, and now is being used for nefarious under-the-radar purposes.

"Nice place you have here," I say, unable to keep my mouth shut.

I get a grunt in return.

When I see the bathroom, my jaw drops open. "This is worse than prison."

"Yeah," Killer agrees, clicking his tongue. "It's dirtier, isn't it? Enjoy, princess."

He throws me in and slams the door shut. I place toilet paper on the seat before sitting down, then wash up after I finish my business. I guess I should be grateful there is toilet paper and soap.

I check the bathroom for anything I could use to defend myself. It doesn't even have a mirror, or I could have tried to smash off a piece of it, like I once saw in a movie. Instead, I'm left with a toothbrush. I know professionals would somehow turn that into a shank, but I'm not on that level, so I don't bother.

"Fuck," I whisper, hands clenching to fists.

Think, Skylar, think.

The bang on the door makes me jump. "Hurry up!" he yells in his booming voice, banging once more. "Your bladder can't be that big."

Opening the door, I step outside, given up on the toothbrush, only to be grabbed by the neck and hauled back toward the room.

Starting to panic, I realize this might be my only time to escape, but how the hell am I supposed to fight off this huge-ass man? He's easily three times my size, built like a tree house and as muscley as any man who is trying to compensate for his small penis. Still, if I don't try now, I'm going to be put back into that room and will be just sitting there waiting on other people to save me.

Fuck it.

I wait until we are just before the room, and glance down the hallway which must lead to either a front or back door—hopefully the front—and then spin around quickly and kick my leg up as hard as I possibly can, hitting him right in the nuts.

He might be a fucking beast but even that takes him down, and he falls to his knees while I run down the hallway and out the door, only to run into two men. Men I've seen before. They are the ones I saw at my workplace, Dumb and Dumber, watching me and giving me the creeps.

I try to escape them by running, but quickly fail, one man grabbing me and throwing me over his shoulder.

"And where the hell do you think you're going?" Dumber rumbles, slapping me hard on the butt. "We aren't done with you yet."

I scream, I kick, I hit. I do everything I can to make it harder for them to drag me back inside, but between the two of them, they manage to do just that, and I'm thrown back into the room, landing on my back, which fucking hurts.

"Try that again, and we won't be so nice," Dumber threatens, slamming the door shut. Thankfully, Killer doesn't come back in, but I hear his booming voice and he sounds extremely unhappy with me.

Shit.

Things are not looking good.

"Saint," I whisper, lip trembling.

Where are you?

Chapter Twenty-Nine

I get hungry, so I eat the damn food Killer left me, hating that I couldn't hold out for any longer. But with nothing to do except plan different scenarios in my head and how I would react in each one, I'm bored and nervous and waiting for the pin to drop.

What feels like an eternity later, the door opens and Killer stands there, a smug smirk on his gruesome face. "Today is your lucky day," he says, resting on the doorframe, his leather cut pressed against the powdered walls. "You get to go home."

"What happened?" I ask, standing. He looks way too happy to have lost in any way, and I'm almost too scared to find out what has happened.

He stays silent, so I yell, "Tell me!" If something has happened to Saint, or to Hammer, I don't have anything else to lose.

Killer closes the door, laughing. I call out, demanding answers, suddenly feeling bold and strong. I need to know if the men are okay.

When it comes to saving myself, I might have failed, but when it comes to saving someone that I love...

I'll never stop fighting.

When the door opens again, it's not Killer's face I see, or even my mother's.

It's Hammer's.

Relief fills me, but when I don't see Saint with him, confusion sets in. Is Saint okay?

Running to his arms, I jump against his chest and hold on tighter than I ever have before. "What the hell is going on?" I ask him. "How did you get in here? Where's Saint?"

I imagine the whole MC out in front, Killer and his henchmen no match for the Knights of Fury.

No one is.

"Saint is fine," he assures me, rubbing my back soothingly. "Everyone is fine, you don't need to worry, but I need you to listen to me, okay?"

I nod.

"I love you," he says. "You're the daughter I always wanted. I'm so proud of the woman you've become, and...yeah, I love you, Skylar. I've always loved you, and I want you to remember that."

He then whispers numbers into my ear—a code maybe? "Six, one, seven, three."

"Why are you telling me that?" I ask, confused.

"Just remember it."

So I memorize it: six, one, seven, three.

"I love you too, Hammer," I reply, holding on to him even tighter. "But we can tell each other this when we both get out and are safe back at the clubhouse."

He smiles sadly, and then slowly he slides his phone into the front pocket of my jeans, which I quickly cover with my T-shirt.

And then Killer appears behind him, and Hammer steps aside. Killer grabs my arm and starts pulling me toward the door, but I fight against him.

"No! Hammer! I want to stay with you, I'm not leaving you here!" I scream out.

Dumb and Dumber stand on each side of him. He could take them both, I know it. But all three? Probably not.

He'd put up a mean fight, though.

I realize he's not going to fight back until I'm safely outside, or maybe with the deal he's made he's not going to fight back at all. I don't want to think that he has given up, I don't want him to be a martyr, I want him to come home to me.

As I continue to fight Killer off, he grabs me by the neck and starts to squeeze, obviously tired of my shit.

"We had a deal," Hammer calls out, tone furious. "She is to be left unharmed!"

Killer loosens his hold, muttering a curse. "Can't wait to be rid of you, bitch."

The feeling is motherfucking mutual. "Fuck you. You're going to regret this, especially if anything happens to Hammer."

The last thing I see before stepping outside is Hammer mouthing my name.

It hits me then, that no, he's not going to fight back.

He's sacrificing himself for me. *We had a deal*, he said.

He put me before anything. Before the club and even himself. He put me first.

There's a car already waiting for me, with the door open, and a man dressed in all black stands next to it.

"You can't blame him for your brother's death, you piece of—"

Suddenly, something is pressed against my nose and my sight goes blurry, and then everything turns to oblivion.

When I wake up again, I have sand on my mouth, and I'm lying on the side of the road on my stomach in shrub. Sitting up and wiping my face, I stand up and eye the road, realizing that they have dropped me off not too far from the clubhouse. I have no idea how long I've been here, or how much time has passed. Remembering what happened, and Hammer, I force myself to run the full way back. I can only hope I'm not too late.

"Saint!" I yell out as soon as I reach the front. "Saint!"

The gate, which is usually unlocked, isn't budging. I try yelling out a little longer, but when there is no sign of anyone, I glance around, trying to think of what else to do next.

My mouth is dry, and I don't know how much time has passed or how long I was lying on the side of the fucking road. My phone was in my car, and the clubhouse doesn't have a land line anyway, so I don't know what the hell I'm supposed to be doing right now.

Running across the vacant blocks of land next to the clubhouse, I keep running until I come to our closest neighbor. I need a phone. Banging on the door, I realize I must look awful, and I hope they don't slam the door in my face and call the cops.

The door opens, and a woman stands there, taking me in through the screen door. She opens it too, eyes roaming over me. "Are you okay?"

"I'm Skylar, I'm from next door and I was wondering if I could use your phone. It's kind of an emergency," I rush out, bouncing on my feet in impatience.

"Next door as in the clubhouse?" she asks, frowning. "Yes, of course you can use my phone. Come on in."

I follow her inside as she grabs her phone from a wooden coffee table and hands it to me. "Thank you," I say to her, dialing Saint's number, which thank God I memorized, and putting it against my ear.

"Hello?" Saint asks, and I can hear some sort of commotion in the background.

"Saint?"

"Skylar? Where are you? We've been looking everywhere!" he says, tone panicked and laced with desperation.

"I'm next door to the clubhouse," I tell him. "At that woman's house—you know, the one Renny thinks is hot."

"Fuck, stay there. I love you," he says, hanging up the line on me.

"Thank you so much," I say to her, handing her phone back.

"No problem. I'm Isabella," she says, arching her brow. "And whoever Renny is, tell him I'm flattered."

I'd laugh in any other situation.

Isabella makes me a cup of coffee and sits with me out front on her swing until I hear the familiar rumble of motorcycles.

"He's here," I say, standing up and giving her the mug back. "Thank you so much. I owe you a beer or something. You're a lifesaver."

"No problem," she replies, standing up with me. "I hope everything is okay."

"Me, too," I say, waving to her and running toward Saint's bike. Temper and Renny are with him, and I have so many questions, but all I do is jump on his bike and ride off with him, squeezing him from behind in relief. Even if all we are doing is riding back to the clubhouse, being near him is what I need right now.

Saint is okay, and I'm back where I belong.

Now we just need to go back for Hammer.

Chapter Thirty

Saint stops at the clubhouse, and I get off his bike and hold on to him.

"Are you okay?" he asks, lifting me in the air. "I've never been so scared in my life, Skylar."

"I'm fine, and I wasn't hurt. Where is Hammer?" I ask. "He saved me and then stayed back, and I need to know if he's okay. Did he get out?"

Saint looks away, swallowing hard. "He left here without us. We don't know where he went—only he knew the address. We showed up at Killer's clubhouse, broke inside and raised hell, asking where our prez was, but he wasn't there. Killer was smart; no one there knew his location. No one."

I realize that while I know what the abandoned house looks like I don't know how to get there, either. I was out both times, going to and from the house, and now I know that was done on purpose, not just because I was carrying on and not making shit easy for them.

"Fuck!" I yell, stamping my foot. "It's an old abandoned house."

Temper and Renny come and stand around me. "What else can you tell us?" Temper asks.

"Mom was there, Killer, and two men. I've seen those two men before—they came into my work."

And then I remember something.

Lifting up my T-shirt, I pull a phone out of my pocket. "I'm such an idiot, I had this the whole time. Hammer gave it to me."

And only I know the pin. I type it in.

Temper holds out his hand. "Fuck, he knew this would be the only way we could track him. He turned his GPS tracking off." He goes through the call list. "This has to be Killer's number. We can try to track it down. Dee knows how to do all of that shit; I'll get him on the line. Rest of you get ready, we're going to go find him."

Saint turns to me, resting his arms on my shoulders. "I'm going to drop you at your brother's. It's not safe being here alone."

"No, I want to come. I can tell you if you're at the right place or not, I know what it looks like from the front," I say, watching Saint shake his head. "I'm coming. He's my dad, and he's only there because he saved me. I'm coming."

"No, you're not," Saint growls, fingers tightening on me. "I only just found you safe—you aren't going back there. It's too dangerous."

"It's dangerous for everyone, and you're all still going. Saint, if something happens to you and Hammer, I have nothing left. I want to be there. I know I can't do much, but you can't expect me to sit at home twiddling my fucking thumbs not knowing if any of you are dead or alive," I say, standing my ground.

"She's right. We need her to ID the building," Renny says to Saint, slapping him on the shoulder. "We'll all be there, brother. And she's a Knight too—you can't expect her to sit on the side-lines."

"You have no idea, Renny," Saint snarls back to him, stepping away from his touch. "When you find your old lady, you will, but right now you have no idea, and you need to stay out of this. Skylar is not coming, and that is that."

"Then I guess I'll ride on the back of Renny's bike," I say, walking toward it.

Saint grabs my by the waist and pulls my back against his chest. "I can't lose you, Skylar, and I almost did today. I won't..." He trails off, sucking in air. "Don't do this, please."

I hate seeing him like this, and I know that it's because he's scared something is going to happen to me and because he loves me, but I'm not backing down from this.

"I can't lose you either, Saint. Do you think I like you riding off and potentially never coming back? It goes both ways. Instead of fighting me, why don't you take me with you? We can protect each other," I say, turning to face him and looking him in the eye. "I'll try not to be a liability."

Temper runs out of the clubhouse, sliding a gun into his jeans. "Let's go. I've got an address. Dee and the other men are going to meet us there, and a few of them are bringing cars instead of bikes, so we can bring Hammer home."

Bring Hammer home.

I've never wanted anything more in my life.

Saint kisses me, deeply and hungrily, and then hands me a helmet. I put it on without any hesitation and get on the back of his bike. The engines start, like a chorus, and determination fuels me. I'm scared, terrified even, but I'm not going home without my dad.

We ride for about twenty minutes and then come to a stop in front of a house.

The house.

I look at Temper and nod. Dee found it.

"Shouldn't we have parked down the road and walked or something?" I ask Saint as we get off the motorcycle.

Saint passes me a handgun. "No time for being subtle. We're going in there and shooting, and asking questions later." He glances up and down at me. "Dee is here in his car. Go in there and wait with him."

"Okay." I nod, kissing Saint. "I love you."

"I love you too."

I run toward Dee's BMW and jump in the front seat. He parks across the road, keeping the engine on, ready to make a quick exit. Looking down at the gun in my hand, I turn to him. "What if they need more backup?"

"Five men went in," he says, lifting his own gun up and placing it out the window. "And I'm the sniper. So we're good. This isn't all done at random, Sky. We've planned this in case some shit went down. Every member knows what they're supposed to be doing and where they're supposed to be. You don't need to worry—this isn't our first rodeo."

"Interesting," I whisper, staring at the now open door of the house where they all entered. "And what is Saint's job?"

"Protect Temper, and to shoot first and ask questions later," Dee admits, eyes through the scope of the gun. "Temper protects Hammer. There's a hierarchy, and we always have someone watching out for us, like little brothers looking out for the big brothers."

We hear shots firing, and I find myself on the edge of my seat, praying that the men aren't hurt.

"Please let them be okay," I whisper, my fingernails digging into my palms.

Minutes later, I see them all coming out, and Temper and Saint are carrying Hammer in their arms. He's covered in blood and looks like he's taken a few too many hits to the face, but he's alive, and that's all that matters.

They put him in the back of the car and slam the door shut, telling Dee to take us to a hospital. I sit next to him, covering him with Dee's jacket, which I find in the back seat. "We have to go to the hospital!"

"I'll follow you," Saint tells me, running back to his bike.

Hammer reaches over and strokes my face. "My beautiful girl, what are you doing here?"

"Came to save you," I tell him. "From the car, though, because my SWAT skills are seriously lacking."

He laughs, then winces and coughs. "Don't make me laugh, Sky. It hurts."

Bracing myself, I lift up the jacket and see the gunshot wound. Holding the jacket on it to stop the bleeding, I look him in the eye, scared for him, but quickly turn my expression blank, not wanting him to see that in me.

"For once in my life, I've got you, Dad. It's always been the other way around," I say to him, smiling sadly.

"No it hasn't," he replies, closing his eyes. "I never should have let Georgia take you away from me. It doesn't matter that she was your mother, I always loved you more, and I shouldn't have ever let you leave your family."

"It doesn't matter now. I'm here, and that's all that matters," I tell him, kissing his cheek.

He nods, but I can see that he's slowly spacing out and might lose consciousness soon. "How far away are we?" I ask Dee, keeping the pressure on the wound.

"Five minutes," he replies.

"We're almost there," I tell Hammer, trying to keep him awake. "Don't worry, okay? We're almost there."

"What's the code I told you, Skylar?" he asks me.

"Six, one, seven, three," I whisper, scanning his eyes as he opens them and looks at me. "Why? What is it for?"

"Just remember it, okay? It's important."

I'm curious, but now is not the time to worry about small details like this one.

"I won't forget," I promise him. "But you can remind me what it is after we leave the hospital, okay? Trust me, I'll have plenty of questions about what it means."

"You were never one to shy away from questions," he mutters, but his lip twitches, like it's something he likes about me.

"Speaking of questions, what happened to Killer?" I ask Hammer.

"Let's just say he needs to change his road name," he replies, panting, his face etched in pain. He takes a deep breath before continuing to speak. "You don't have to worry about him, or any of them anymore, Skylar. I can rest easy now. You'll be safe, and the MC will always look after you. You always have a home there, for life, all right?"

My heart breaks with each word he utters, and fear starts to take over me.

"There will be no resting easy for you just yet. You're speaking like you're not going to be here when that's not the case, Dad. We're almost at the hospital, aren't we, Dee? Look, I can see it in the distance. We're all going to be fine, including you, and tomorrow you're going to yell at me about bringing a gun and pretending I'm some fucking heroine when in reality I have no idea what I'm doing, and I probably almost died a few times today, and…"

I stop my rant and look at Dad, cupping his cheek tenderly, my fingers trembling.

No.

"Dad?" I whisper, shaking him gently. "Dee, he passed out. Dad?" I repeat. "Wake up, you need to wake up."

"Fuck. We're here. Hide the weapons, Skylar, I'm going to run in and get a doctor," he says, parking the car, then handing me his rifle and bolting inside. I hide the guns under the seat and keep talking to Dad, hoping he can hear me.

"You know I was curious about my biological father, but I never cared about him, because I had you. If I wasn't curious about what Mom had to say, maybe we wouldn't be here right now. I don't know why I cared. This is my fault," I whisper, tears streaming down my face, my voice quivering. "I love you, Dad. More than anything."

Dee appears with two nurses and a stretcher. I get out of

the car and watch as they place him on the stretcher, and rush him inside.

"I'll go wait with him," I say to Dee.

"I'll make sure everyone else is okay and meet you back here," he tells me, giving me a hug and a kiss on my temple before he leaves.

After I rush into the hospital, the nurse tells me to sit down in the waiting room and they will let me know when I can go in to see him. So I sit there, staring at nothing, just wondering how the fuck my life came to this moment right here. Glancing down at the blood on my hands, I realize I must look how I feel.

This year has been a whirlwind, and so many things have happened, but all I want to do is walk through those clubhouse doors and annoy the men, and see what they're up to. I want to cook for them, and I want to laugh with them, and have a beer with them. Everything I took for granted, I want it back. I want Hammer to be okay.

"I'll never ask for anything else," I whisper. "Just please let him be okay. Please. Don't take away the only parent that I have left."

I've never prayed as much as I have today.

And maybe that's why I didn't get what I wanted.

Chapter Thirty-One

The doctor comes straight over to me and by the look on his face, I can tell that he doesn't have good news.

"Are you with Xavier Dixon?" he asks, looking at my blood-covered hands. I should've gone to the bathroom to clean up, but I couldn't move.

It takes me a moment to respond. I'm not used to people using Hammer's real name. "Yes, I'm his daughter."

Words have never been more true. I don't care what Mom said about Killer's brother—Hammer is and always will be my dad.

"I'm sorry. We tried as best we could, but his injuries were too severe," he says, and the second those words leave his mouth, my body freezes. I feel cold throughout my body. The tears have stopped and I'm just frozen.

"We tried to save him," the doctor continues. "He was shot through the stomach and in the lung, and he lost so much blood..." He glances away from me, like he can't bear to continue talking and looking at me at the same time. "He's gone. I'm sorry."

My head spins. There's a sudden loud noise in my ears as

what he's saying hits me, like I'm trying to block the words out. Like that can save me right now.

Shaking my head, I say, "Can I see him?" I won't believe that he's gone until I see it with my own eyes. He can't be gone.

The doctor nods and a nurse leads me to a room. Hammer lies there on the bed, blood still covering him. Stepping closer, I take his large hand in mine and hold it. I think I'm in shock, because I don't say anything, I just stand here, numb.

He honored his promise to me. He was the only person who loved me enough to put me first. He was the only loving parent I ever had. And now he's gone...

He's not gone, he can't be. He's right here in front of me. I refuse to accept this.

I don't know how long I stand here like this, but then I'm surrounded by those I love. Saint's arms are around me, and Temper's burning anger and utter devastation. Renny's warmth and Dee's silent strength. I truly thought we were going to get out of this unscathed. I was naïve, and hopeful. I didn't think we'd be losing Hammer, the glue that holds us all together. Without him, I don't know who we are, or who I am.

I don't know if I'm a Knight. He's the one who made me feel like I was one of the family. He was the only parent who has ever truly loved me, who wanted the best for me, and now he's gone.

I miss him already.

I also miss myself, because now there's a piece of me gone.

Letting go of Dad's hand, I turn around and cry into Saint's chest.

Hammer's reign as the President of the Knights of Fury MC is over. All the men lower their heads and show their respect.

The Knights' leader is gone.

I don't leave the clubhouse for two whole weeks. Saint brings me food and tries to force me to eat. I skip my classes, and I don't see my brothers or answer calls from Max, or anyone who

I would normally make time for. They try to come to the club-house to see me, but I won't see them. Not yet.

I'm a mess.

I've blocked everything and everyone else out, and all I do is keep replaying what happened that day in my head. Could I have done better in the car to help him? I'm training to be a paramedic and I couldn't do anything.

If I'd never fallen for my mother's bullshit, would Hammer still be alive? I cannot believe I went with her. I need help. I must be so desperate for my mother's love that I sacrificed my own father. The whole situation might have played out differently had I not gone with her, and that's what kills me. One little difference could have changed the outcome and Hammer would still be here right now.

The good die young.

Which means my mom is probably going to live forever. If I hated her before, after Hammer's death and the part she played in it, I'll never forgive her as long as I live.

"You need to eat more, Skylar," Saint says, pushing the fruit platter toward me. "I know everyone grieves in their own ways, but you need to take care of yourself. Hammer wouldn't have wanted this."

"Well, he's not here, is he?" I reply, then instantly feel guilty. It's not just me who is grieving—they all loved him and were family to him too. They were here with him all those years I wasn't, and they trusted him above all others.

Saint told me how Hammer pretended he was going to take them all into war but lied to save them, sacrificing himself to get me out of there. He knew what he was going into, but he did it anyway.

The man was fearless.

He didn't want me or any of his men to get hurt, but if he had let them help, he might still be alive. But then again, we might have lost someone else, and I know that wasn't a risk he was willing to take. Like the captain of a ship, he took it as his responsibility and no other's.

And he was the only one left on that sinking ship.

"I'm sorry, Saint. I'm just not myself right now. I'm a mess," I admit, rubbing my eyes. "I just keep thinking about how it didn't need to go this way and driving myself crazy with the what-ifs. And with everything that Mom told me, that's messing my head up too."

I'd told Saint all about everything my mother had shared with me, but I'm not going to tell anyone else. It doesn't matter, and it doesn't change anything.

"I know," he replies, bracing his elbows on his knees and glancing down at the floor. "I keep wishing that I followed him when he said he was going to sort it out. I would have seen him leaving in the car and could have followed him. So I know exactly what you mean, Skylar, but it's not helping. He's gone, and now we have to live with that. We will never forget him. He wasn't just the president of the Knights, he was the founder. He made this family himself."

I open my arms and Saint falls into them. I stroke his back, offering him the comfort he's been giving me this entire time. "You're right, Saint. It's just so hard here without him. I keep expecting him to stick his head inside my room and ask me if I'm hungry, or if I want to come sit outside with him and have a chat."

I know things will get better. When I lost Shauna, I felt exactly like this, and while the pain never goes away, you learn to live with it. You adapt. You survive. You bury that agony, pushing it all the way down until it can resurface only in moments of weakness.

I survived losing my best friend, and I will also survive losing my dad.

It's just going to take me some time before I'm ready to face the world again.

* * *

A week later I'm back in classes, playing catch-up because I missed so much that I had to beg not to be kicked out. Using it as the perfect distraction, I bury myself into school and work, keeping myself so busy that I don't have time to think about anything except the task at hand. I finally quit the bar job Hammer always hated, wanting to honor one of the many things he wished for me.

I visit with Logan, Sabrina and all my brothers, who have come to spend time with me. That includes Axel and Smith, who are finally back in town. I fill them all in on what Mom did. I've never seen grown men so upset and sickened before. Logan had to excuse himself and Brooks broke a glass. They couldn't believe everything she had done. Logan tries to remember my biological father, but according to him, my mother had a lot of male "friends" back then.

I love my family, but I don't think I'm going to live with Logan and Sabrina anymore, preferring to be at the clubhouse with Saint now. We talked about getting our own place, but for now, I want to stay. I feel closer to Hammer there, and I love being with Saint every night, and waking up to him every morning.

Life is short, and from now on I'm going to live my life how I want to, not how I'm told I should.

Renny told me that Killer and his two henchmen were on the news, reported as missing people. The abandoned house also somehow caught on fire, and because it's in the middle of nowhere, it was a long time before anyone called the fire department to contain it.

I don't know who actually shot who, and I want to leave it that way. Temper said that if the police come knocking, he already has a plan on how to handle it. I'm guessing if any of us are going to get pinned for the deaths or the fire, it's going to be Hammer. I doubt he'd mind. The fire would have gotten rid of the bodies but not the teeth, so I don't know what Temper did to cover their tracks, but he told me it's all under control and I have nothing to worry about.

The world is better off without Killer and his thugs anyway. I don't know where my mom disappeared to after I saw her, but she wasn't in the house when Saint and the men got there. Bitch is probably back on the farm feeding the horses and pretending she's the quintessential housewife to an unsuspecting Neville. She got what she wanted—Hammer is gone—but I don't think she realized what she was giving up by her selfish actions. All of my brothers have cut contact with her. They've blocked her numbers and told her, in no uncertain words, that they never want to see or speak to her ever again.

I wish I felt satisfaction at that. But I don't. There is no way for me to take legal action against her without implicating the Knights, so that is also out of the question.

I feel nothing when I think of her, other than disappointment mixed with anger.

"Temper is stepping up as our president," Saint tells me one day when we're sitting outside, staring at the sky and having a drink.

I nod. "I thought that would happen. Does that mean you move up to vice president?"

"Yeah," Saint replies, reaching out and touching my arm. "Means I'll be busier, taking care of things for the club, and have more responsibility. Temper wants to reach out and get more members as well. Hammer preferred us to be a smaller, tightknit chapter, but we want to expand. The more people we have behind us, the less likely someone will want to fuck with us. We want to be a force to be reckoned with. Are you going to be okay with all of this?"

"I'm by your side all the way," I say. "And I trust Temper. He will be a great president."

"Good," he replies, exhaling. "I was worried you'd say you wanted out. And I wouldn't blame you. If you didn't want this, I'd leave it for you. So don't think it's ever me and the club or nothing. You are the most important person in my life, and I'm never going to fuck this up. I'm not losing you."

"Thank you for saying that, but I knew what I was getting into with you when I came back, Saint. I'd never ask you to choose between me and the club. I love the club. This is my family, too, and I'm not going anywhere. After Hammer died I felt as though I didn't know if I belong here without him, but I do. As your woman, and more than that too. I love all the men here," I reply, lifting my bottle of beer to my lips, then to the sky.

"I love you, Dad," I whisper, smiling sadly.

I can almost hear his voice replying in my head. *I love you too, Sky.*

Chapter Thirty-Two

When the DNA results come in, I'm not surprised. I knew Tory was Saint's the second I saw the photo of her.

I kiss the top of Saint's head as he sits down on his bed, letter in his hand.

"How do you feel?" I ask, smiling down at him. "Carol can no longer say that Tory is not yours whenever she feels like holding that over your head."

"I'm really fucking relieved," Saint admits, placing the piece of paper next to him on the bed. "I love that little girl and it broke my heart when Carol started saying that she wasn't mine. Now I know for sure, and there's nothing she can say. Hunter, my lawyer, said we should get a child custody agreement in place so we have set times to have Tory. This way Carol can't go back on her word and decide one day that she doesn't want to let me see her."

I'm so glad Saint has gotten help from one of the best family lawyers in the city. "That sounds good," I say to him. "It's good if you can come to an agreement out of court, so she doesn't try to bring the whole MC thing into it."

Saint agrees. "Yeah, but it's not like she's mother of the year, and her criminal record is on par with mine."

"You sure know how to pick them," I grumble, sitting down next to him.

"Hey, I picked you, didn't I?" he replies, pushing me back on the bed and pinning my arms above my head. "When are you going to let that go? I didn't make the best choices while you were gone. I didn't think I deserved any better, if I'm being honest, and now I know I have to pay for those decisions, but we got Tory out of it, so I can't have any regrets. And one day I will have more kids with you, the love of my life, and I can't wait for that day."

"I have let it go, but that doesn't mean I'm not allowed to make a little petty comment every now and again," I joke, laughing out loud when he starts to tickle me.

"Yes, actually that's exactly what it means. If you forgive me for my past, it means you can't throw it in my face anymore, even if it's a joke." He clears his throat, and then adds, "It hurts, because I don't like that I let you down, or that I was that person in the first place, the kind who gravitated toward toxic people. I'm not perfect, and trust me, I know that more than anyone."

"I know, Saint," I reply, sobering. "I'm sorry."

"You know, Hammer said something similar to me when he found out Carol was pregnant," Saint admits, smiling sadly, his eyes distant. "He said it's a woman's mentality that raises those kids, nothing else. Not their looks, not how fun or exciting they may be. And that line stuck with me. Because Carol's mentality isn't what I want for Tory. End of the day, she is her mother, though, and now I need to live with that and be civil for Tory."

I nod. "Yeah, you do. Both of your lives are now entwined forever, whether she's the woman you want to raise your child or not. However, I was raised by Georgia, and I turned out okay, so maybe there's hope for everyone."

Saint lowers his face to mine. "Yeah, but you were also raised by Hammer, and everything he taught you, all that time he spent on you, obviously made an impact, because you are amazing."

"From now on, I'll keep quiet and leave your past in the past," I say, not wanting to fight with him again over this. I shouldn't have brought it up again and it was immature of me to do so, when I told myself I would leave it all where it belongs. "If we don't solve this it's just going to keep coming up again and again. It's something I'm going to have to deal with it because I want to be with you forever, and nothing is going to change that." I pause, and then add, "Except cheating."

"I'd never cheat on you," he declares, blue eyes narrowing. "There's no one else I'll ever want, Skylar. I have no doubt about that."

"Good," I say, lifting my head and pressing my lips against his. "And right back at you."

"You better get to class," he murmurs, kissing down my neck. "Which is a shame, because I really want to show you just how much I love you right now."

Grinning, I push him away and get off the bed. "You're right, I'm going to be late otherwise. I'll see you later tonight."

I give him another quick kiss and then head to my car, only for Temper to stop me before I can get in. "Hey," he says, shifting on his feet. "I just had a visit from Hammer's lawyer."

"Hammer had a lawyer?" I ask, eyebrows raising as I throw my handbag on the car seat and turn back to give Temper my full attention. "I guess you guys would need one. What did he want?"

Temper holds out a bank card to me, one that already has my name on it. "Hammer had this card made for you, as an additional cardholder on his account. If anything happened to him, he had it in his will that all of his money, property and assets go to you. The lawyer said you can start using this right away, that you just need to use the pin code. Do you know it?"

Six, one, seven, three. The numbers he made me memorize.

Hammer left everything he owned to a little girl he raised, one who was not of his blood, but of his heart.

"Yeah, I know it," I reply, looking down at the card. "What am I supposed to do with it?"

The thing is, I don't want any of his things or money, and I'd give them all up to have him walk through those clubhouse doors just one more time.

"Whatever you want," Temper says, shrugging. His big build shields me from the sunlight, and I have to look up to speak with him. "Maybe live a life of luxury."

"I don't want to live a life of anything with money I never earned myself," I tell him, feeling a little overwhelmed suddenly. "I don't know what I'm supposed to do with this information."

"There's no rush for you to decide," Temper reminds me, resting his big hand on my slight shoulder. "Just keep it for a rainy day for now, or make it another's day problem. Either way, you'll want for nothing now, Sky. Hammer has you covered for the rest of your life."

"Thanks, Temper. I better get to class. I'm already late, so you're right, I'll just worry about this later."

I wave and jump in the car, thinking about the money the whole way to the campus. Hammer was so adamant I remember that code, and I thought it would have been for something more important than money, but maybe he just wanted to make sure I was looked after forever. If he couldn't be here to make sure that I was, he's now given me enough money that he will never have to worry.

He loved me so much he planned for this, maybe even expected that one day it would come, considering his lifestyle and who he was. I'm grateful, but I didn't love him for what he could give me. I love him for how he hugged me, made me feel safe and actually listened to me when I had something to say. I mean actually listened, like he had all the time in the world for me every single time I spoke, and that's so rare nowadays.

I love him because he put his phone down when he saw me, because he didn't judge me for choosing Saint, because he knew I was nothing like my mother.

I love him because he loved me, and that was it. It was that simple.

Wiping my tears away, I get out of my car and rush to class.

I'm going to make him proud, and I'm going to think of something to do with the money that involves more than shopping and living in luxury. Maybe donate to charity, such as the hospital I used to volunteer at, and of course pay off the rest of my paramedic program. I'd like to buy something for the MC, and save the rest for a rainy day.

"Hey, Skylar," Reece welcomes me as I drop into the seat next to him. "Is everything okay?"

"Yeah," I say, forcing a smile. "At least, it will be."

Knights don't lie down for long.

Epilogue

Two Years Later

Glancing up at Max on stage, I smile before turning back to Saint, who has his hands a little too low for my liking, considering everyone is watching us for our first dance as a married couple.

"Can you keep it PG until we're alone?" I whisper, lip twitching. "Your mother is watching us."

"So?" He shrugs, dipping me backward and smiling when everyone starts clapping.

"I'm so glad we did those dance classes," I say, feeling confident as I move with him. "Or else you probably would have almost dropped me like in the lessons."

He kisses me, smiling against my lips. "I'm used to moving with your body in a different way."

"Well, we *are* good at that," I reply, letting him spin me around before pulling me close against his body again. "I think I could get used to seeing you in a suit."

"Prefer this to my leather?" he asks, arching a brow.

"No." But I've never seen him look as handsome as he does right now. The black suit and white shirt fit him like a second skin, and it shows off his build perfectly. When I walked down the aisle with Temper—I wanted Temper to walk me down the aisle so I didn't have to choose between my brothers, and because Temper was the closest to Hammer—I couldn't stop staring at Saint. I just feel so lucky that I now get to call this man my husband. "But you do clean up very nicely."

"And you're the most beautiful woman I've ever laid my eyes on," he replies, glancing down at my white lace dress. "You always were, Skylar. I'm the luckiest man alive."

"I was just thinking how lucky I am," I say, and we share a look.

This is where I've always meant to be, this is fate, and this man is my soul mate.

Saint dances with Tory next, and it's the cutest thing ever.

"She's adorable," Logan says, offering me his hand. "Can I have the next dance?"

"You may," I say with a smile, accepting it. He leads me to the dance floor where he shows me his skills, which I find quite charming.

"You look so happy, Sky," Logan says, eyes gentle. "After everything you've been through, you're still one of the best people I know, and I'm so proud to be your big brother. I love you."

"I love you, too, Logan," I say to him, my heart full. Mom wasn't invited to the wedding, obviously, and I feel no guilt about that. I don't even know if she is aware that I was getting married, since no one talks to her anymore. I hope she stays away from me and my family.

My brothers, in order of age, all have a dance with me, followed by my adorable nephew Bronson, Logan's son. After I hand him back, Temper takes a turn, his stiff moves making me giggle. "Hammer would be so proud of you right now, Sky," he says quietly. "He loved you so much, you know that, right?"

"I do," I reply. "Thank you for giving me away today. It means everything to me."

"Always stepping in for Hammer," he jokes, leaning forward to kiss my forehead. "Was happy to do it."

Saint steals me back from Temper, and the two of us dance closely, bodies touching.

I've never been happier.

Three Years Later

I've never been more exhausted.

"Why the hell did I decide this was a good idea?" I ask Saint, breathing heavily. "No, wait, this was your idea! Oh my God, it hurts so much, Saint. No amount of orgasms is worth this…"

He strokes my sweaty forehead. "It's fine, Skylar. Just keep breathing."

If he says that to me again, I'm going to attack him. When I came to the hospital, I was already six centimeters dilated, so I couldn't get an epidural, which was what I was hoping for. Instead, I'm feeling childbirth in its full, raw glory, and it's unlike any pain I've ever experienced before.

"There's no way that getting kicked in the balls hurts like this," I tell him, digging my nails into his palm. "I don't have balls, but I just know it. There's no way. Whoever made that up is a man and a dickhead."

Saint, the bastard, laughs out loud at that.

I'm going to murder him.

When I fell pregnant, I was over the moon. I was already a qualified paramedic, and I love what I do. I will always be grateful to Hammer for suggesting that I should become one. My eyes lit up when I spoke about it, he said, and he was right. I love going in every day and saving as many people as I can. And now when a member of the Knights gets hurt, I'm the first one they call. With my career sorted, and no financial stress on us because of Hammer's money, the timing was perfect to add to our family, to give Tory a sibling and for me to experience being a mother.

"You're doing so well, babe," Saint assures me, moving to glance down at my vagina, which I imagine looks really fucking interesting right now, especially when I feel the baby crown.

"Fuck," he whispers, unable to look away.

He was never at Tory's birth—he arrived after—so this is the first time he's witnessing a baby push out, and going by his expression, it just might be the last.

"Can you look at my face, please?" I cry, pushing with all of my might, using the pain of each contraction to bring my child into the world.

Suddenly I hear crying, and see a thick head of dark hair in Saint's arms. Overwhelmed with emotion but also relieved because I'm no longer in agony, I close my eyes and take a moment. When I open them again, Saint is in front of me, handing me this beautiful bundle of joy.

"We have a son," he says, eyes filled with sentiment, happiness and pride. "He is perfect, Skylar."

My son stops crying as soon as he's laid on my chest. "He really is perfect."

Tears drip down my cheeks, but this time they are happy ones.

"Xavier," I whisper. Same name as Hammer.

Blue eyes open and look directly at me.

And that's when I learn for myself that love at first sight is a very real thing.

* * * * *

Acknowledgments

A big thank-you to Carina Press for working with me on the Knights of Fury MC series!

Thank you to Kimberly Brower, my amazing agent, for having my back in all things.

To my family, my sister Tenielle, and my three sons, thank you for bringing joy to my life every damn day.

And to my readers, thank you for loving my words. I hope this book is no exception.

Renegade

Happy thirteenth birthday to my firstborn son.
You are *so* loved.

Chapter One

"You have got to be kidding me," I groan, slamming my hands down on the steering wheel in frustration. After a week of nothing but bad luck, from locking myself out of my house to smashing the screen on my phone, I shouldn't be surprised that my car has decided to die on me just as I'm about to leave for a road trip to visit my nine-months-pregnant sister, but I am.

After getting out of the car and opening the hood, pretending like I know what I'm supposed to be looking for, I realize that I don't.

Shit.

My car is old, but it's been reliable up until now, and I'm pissed this is the moment it has chosen to be disloyal. I'm going to have to call a mechanic and hope that it can be fixed right now, or I'm screwed.

I type *cheap local mechanics* into my phone when I hear the familiar sound of a motorcycle rumble, a sound I've gotten so used to that it is just background noise. I've been living near the Knights of Fury Motorcycle Club for a few years now, and even though there's a block of vacant land between us, I still call them my neighbors.

My mother and sister told me I was crazy for knowingly moving next to a bunch of bikers, but my house was such a good price, I couldn't turn it down. I suppose I have them to thank for that, because no one else wanted to live near them. Besides, what really is a motorcycle club? I suspect it sounds a lot more nefarious than it really is.

And it hasn't been all bad. Our interactions have been limited to the casual head nod as they ride by. There was one moment where a woman was in a pickle and dropped in to use my phone. There's been no crime in the area, and I surprisingly feel pretty safe.

I start dialing a mechanic and the rumble gets louder as a black Harley comes to a stop behind my car. It's kind of been our unspoken rule that the bikers and I live harmoniously, but don't really engage, so it surprises me when someone gets off the bike and removes his helmet.

Hello, Mr. Biker. He's one good-looking biker, that's for sure. Dark hair, dark eyes, stubble and a tall, built body dressed in all black. He slowly approaches, eyes on my car.

"Need some help?" he says, his deep timbre sending a shiver down my spine.

"That would be great." I'm desperate at this point, especially when the phone rings with no answer from mechanic number one. "I don't know what happened. It only made it down the road before it just stopped."

He comes to stand next to me, and fiddles with the engine before getting in the car and trying to start it to no avail. "I'm going to have to take it in to the clubhouse," he says, frowning. "We can fix it and get it back to you ASAP."

"I appreciate the offer," I say, shifting on my feet as he stares at me. "But I'm kind of supposed to be in Vegas today."

I'm going to have to call the last person I want to call to ask if I can borrow his car.

My father.

Ugh.

"Vegas? We're actually heading that way ourselves. We can give you a ride, if you want," he says, shrugging. "I'm Renny, by the way." He holds out his hand for me to shake.

Renny?

I vaguely remember hearing this name before. Maybe it was when that woman used my phone.

"Isabella," I reply, shaking the tattooed hand. It's big, yet warm and soft, despite the calluses on it.

"I know who you are," he murmurs. "You helped Skylar when she needed it." Skylar, that was her name! "Now why don't you let us return the favor? It's the least we can do."

"I didn't really do anything," I say, surprised he remembers something so small. I mean I let her inside to use my phone, and that's about it. Anyone would do that for someone that they see is visibly in distress.

"You helped. That day…" He pauses with a far-off look on his face. "It was a tough day. We lost someone important and you helping her… Well, it meant a lot. So thank you."

"You're welcome," I say, knowing that arguing would be pointless. "What are neighbors for, right?"

He grins at that, a little dimple popping up on the right side of his cheek, distracting me. "So what about my offer. Do you want to hitch a ride to Vegas?"

His offer sounds tempting, but I really don't know these men, and I'd rather drive there by myself. Even if that means I have to call my dad.

Who am I kidding? While I wouldn't feel comfortable driving to Vegas with Renny and his friends, I'd probably still choose that option over asking Dad for help.

My phone rings, bringing me back to reality, especially when my sister's name pops up on the screen.

Shit.

"Ariel, hello?" I say, raising a finger to Renny apologetically.

I turn my back a little for privacy, glancing down at my shoes, silently praying that everything is okay.

"Izzy, have you left? I'm in labor, it wasn't just Braxton Hicks. You need to be here now!" she says in a panic. "The way these contractions are coming on..." She starts to scream in pain, and I hold the phone away from my ear, wincing. "Fuck!"

Man, I am never having a baby if that is what I have to go through. My older sister is one of the strongest women I know, and she has a high pain threshold, so anything that makes her sound like that gets a nope from me.

"I'm leaving now," I promise, turning back to Renny. "I'll be there as soon as I can, Ariel. I love you."

"I love you, too," she says before hanging up.

I weigh my options and the likelihood that I will make it to Vegas in time. I may not know Renny, but I promised Ariel I would be there for the birth of her child. My niece or nephew. And I will not let her down.

"So when are you leaving?" I ask before I can give any more thought to what I am doing. I need to go, and I need to go now. It's a five-hour drive, and maybe, just maybe, I will make it before the baby's head crowns and ruins Ariel's vagina.

"Was going to be in an hour or so, but we can make it right now," he says, pulling out his phone. "I'll tell the men."

"Just how many men are we traveling with?" I ask as he types out a text message. "And what about my suitcase?"

"Three of us, and don't worry, you can trust me, and the rest of them. You'll be safe, I promise you. Skylar can vouch for us, if that makes you feel better," he says, brown eyes pinned on me.

Oddly enough, I believe him. I'm not afraid for my safety around them. I mean they've been my neighbors for over a year and they haven't bothered me once. "Suitcase?"

"We'll get there faster on the bike," he replies with a shrug.

If this means the five-hour drive could be cut shorter, that means I'll get to Ariel sooner. I don't need anything in my suitcase.

"Fuck it," I tell him. "I'll buy new clothes there."

His lip twitches, and he nods toward his black motorcycle. "Get on. I'll try my best to get you there on time."

"Thank you, Renny," I say, grabbing my handbag from my car and crossing the strap over my body. I have my purse, ID and credit cards; anything else can be bought.

"Have you ever ridden before?" he asks as he helps me climb on, his large hands on my waist sending shivers up my spine.

"Yeah, I have actually," I tell him, smiling fondly, remembering the times I'd ride with my cousin before he passed away. "On the back of one, anyway."

"Okay," he murmurs, studying me with a slightly narrowed gaze. I've always had a weakness for men with blue eyes, but suddenly brown is looking extremely appealing. "I'll skip the debrief then. We need to stop at the clubhouse first, but then we will head off. You have the address of where you need to be?"

"Yeah, I do," I reply, reciting the name and address of the hospital to him.

He nods and hands me his spare helmet. "I'll have your car towed to the clubhouse and it should be ready by the time we get back from Vegas."

"That's great. Thank you," I say, feeling grateful it's one less thing to worry about. "I just need to get there."

The thought of Ariel in labor alone makes me feel sick to my stomach. The baby decided to come two weeks early, otherwise I would have been with her this entire time. The father is my sister's ex and wants nothing to do with the baby, which makes my role even more important.

Renny gets on in front of me and fires up the engine. "Let's do it then."

Feeling awkward, I put the helmet on and hold on to the back of his leather vest, very aware of my personal space, knowing that I'm about to be pressed up against this man for the next few hours at least. I'm not exactly sure how I've found myself in this situation, or how this Renny ended up being my knight in shining armor, but I'm glad he was around.

I've heard a lot of things about the MC—like that they engage in criminal activities and are dangerous womanizers. I know they are judged in the community and that no one wants them here, but I want to form my own opinion. Even the real estate agent who sold me my house told me that he wished they would move away, because they are nothing but trouble.

But from what Renny is doing for me, they don't seem too bad.

Or at least I hope they aren't.

Because I just signed up for the next few hours at their mercy.

Ariel, I'm coming.

Chapter Two

We stop at the clubhouse, where I meet Temper, Saint and Dee, our travel companions. While Temper is older and stoic, Dee is kind of goofy and playful, which lightens the mood.

"Trust you to pick up a hot chick to take on the ride," he says to Renny, grinning. "Nice to officially meet you, sweetheart. Please note that I am also single, after my last online dating experience left me feeling lonely and rejected."

Saint, on the other hand, is the epitome of cool. "Do you really say stuff like that to women? No wonder you're single."

"Renny's single," Dee points out.

"By choice," Saint replies with a smirk, bringing his blue eyes to me. "Renny is just waiting for the right woman to come along."

The clubhouse looks completely different than what I had imagined it—it's neat and tidy, for one, decorated very masculinely, but it has a homey feel to it that I didn't expect. Saint thanks me again for helping Skylar, who I learn is his girlfriend, or "old lady" in motorcycle speak, but we don't linger to chat for long because Renny kindly tells them that we're in a rush and need to leave right now, which I appreciate.

"You all ready?" I hear Temper ask the men.

"Yeah, Prez. We're ready," Dee says.

I take in their all-black getup, mostly comprised of leather, and then my light blue skinny jeans and mustard-yellow sweater. Along with my white Converses, I'm going to stand out like a sore thumb on this ride.

"Let me know if you need a break," Renny says as he packs the leather satchel hanging off his bike with water, clothing and his wallet and phone. "We're all used to riding long distances, so we probably won't stop unless you want to."

"Just hit him across the head if you want to stop. He'll get the point," Saint teases with a smirk.

"We definitely have to stop for some food," Dee says, frowning. "What do you mean we ain't stopping?"

I hide my smile at the banter between them. I was expecting a grumpy bunch of brooding assholes, but now I can relax a little. Don't get me wrong, Temper is brooding and kind of scary, but I don't feel like I'm unwanted here, and the men seem to genuinely not mind that I'm tagging along on their road trip. Besides, they seem to speak so highly of Skylar. It's obvious they love and care about her deeply.

Lucky woman.

And I don't think I've ever been so easily accepted in my life.

Bikers, who knew?

"I'm not opposed to a quick food stop," I reply, winking at Dee, who chuckles. These men are all helping me get to where I need to be, and in record time, so a little stop won't kill us. "I'm partial to doughnuts and bagels with extra cream cheese, but I'm not going to say no to any food at any point."

With all the men packed and ready to go in record time, I climb on Renny's bike and hold on to his leather once more.

"You can hold me tighter," he says to me, bringing my arms

around his waist. "I'm not going to bite, and you better get comfortable because it's going to be a long ride."

Sliding forward and holding on to him the way he suggested, I try to pretend that I don't notice how hard his stomach is, and nod, even though he can't see me. The familiar rumbles have my own stomach in a knot, because everything just got real.

I'm going on a road trip with the Knights of Fury MC.

I last an hour before my ass starts getting numb and my lower back starts to ache a little, but I don't complain. If I ask Renny to stop more than once or twice, I know it's going to take much longer to get there.

During the ride I worry about Ariel and whether or not the baby has arrived. I'm going to be so sad if I've missed the birth, but it's completely my fault.

I know that some labors can be quick and others can take hours upon hours, so maybe I will make it. Even if I don't, I'll still get to be there with her, see the baby and take care of them both, helping in any way I can. I'm lucky that working as a freelance graphic designer allows me to be flexible with my work and be my own boss.

Not that I brought my laptop, which is packed in my luggage. So apparently I don't plan on working until I get back.

After we've been riding for what seems like ten hours, but is probably only two, Renny stops in front of a gas station and restaurant. I'm off the bike the second it comes to a halt, removing my helmet and shifting on my feet, trying to get the feeling back into the lower half of my body.

Renny takes off his own helmet and studies me. "Why didn't you tell me that you needed to stop? You're stubborn, you know that?"

I do know that, and I don't want to bring up the fact that my lower back isn't my friend right now, so I simply shrug and play it off. "I'm fine."

He purses his lips, clearly disagreeing with me, but he lets it go. "Come on, let's get something to eat."

He holds the door open for me, waiting for me to pass him before also stepping inside.

"Thank you," I say, glancing up at him. Brown eyes watch me a little too closely, but he stays quiet. "I said, thank you," I repeat, arching a brow.

"You're welcome," he replies, lip twitching.

With him standing behind me, I turn and stare up at the menu. I'm starving, but more than anything I need something to drink.

"What do you want?" he asks, coming to stand beside me.

"I can get it," I tell him, frowning. "In fact, I should be buying your lunch since you're the one doing me a favor."

His eyes narrow, and a scowl twists his full lips. "What do you want to eat, Isabella? And don't forget we're on a time crunch, so don't even bother trying to argue because we'll be here all day. I've never let a woman pay for anything for me, and I'm not going to start now."

"What about your mom?" I ask, lifting my chin.

He scrubs his hand down his face and gently pushes me to the front counter with a hand on my lower back. "Tell the lady what you want."

The rest of the men walk in and we all order together. I quickly head to the restroom while we're waiting and send Ariel a text message saying I'm on my way. When I return, they are all sitting at one of the tables with burgers and sodas in front of them.

"How was the ride for you?" Dee asks me, grinning. "I saw you holding on for dear life there."

"It felt like we were going so fast," I tell him, sitting down next to Renny. "But you were going the speed limit."

"Check that, did you?" Renny asks, arching a dark brow.

"Yeah, of course I did. I'm a law-abiding citizen."

They all laugh. Narrowing my green eyes, I look around the

table and stare at them each in turn. "What's so funny? I'm being serious."

"Nothing," Renny replies, lips still slightly lifted. "How have we not spoken until today? You're hilarious."

"I guess we run in different circles," I state with a straight face.

More laughter.

"What do you do for work?" Temper asks me, leaning back in his chair.

"I'm a freelance graphic designer," I tell him. "So I'm my own boss, which is pretty cool. What do you all do?"

"We are business owners and entrepreneurs," Dee replies, grinning. "And motorcycle enthusiasts, of course."

"Of course," I say, laughing softly. "Any businesses I would have heard of?"

"You want us to give away all of our secrets right off the bat?" Renny teases, lifting his coffee cup to his lips and taking a sip. He's a smooth operator, this Renny, and I knew that from the second he first spoke to me. He has a lot of swag to him— every move is sensual, graceful and…just cool.

"Sure. You can tell me all of your real names while you're at it," I throw in, flashing them a sweet smile.

They laugh, so I'm guessing that's a no.

Renny is a cool guy, and I find myself wanting to press my palm against his stubble to see what it feels like. I'm a very affectionate, touchy-feely type of person, but now is not the time, especially in front of all these men, and this is not the man for me to push boundaries with. He's a friend, helping me out because I helped one of their women, and nothing more. He's the last type of man I need to be showing any interest in.

"I guess I can wait until the ride home," I say nonchalantly.

We eat our food quickly before getting back on the road. This time when I hold on to Renny, I don't feel as shy or as awkward, in fact, I enjoy being pressed up against him, and even though my mind is with my sister, I allow myself to enjoy the moment.

After all, it's not every day that you have a good-looking biker escorting you to another state.

Chapter Three

By the time we pull up to the hospital, I'm utterly exhausted, and all I had to do was sit and hold on for the entire ride. I can only imagine how Renny feels. Still, excitement fills me, and I can't wait to run inside and see Ariel. Jumping off the bike, I remove my helmet and hand it to Renny.

"Thank you so much for getting me here," I say, stepping closer and giving him a warm hug. "You're a lifesaver."

"You're welcome. Why don't you give me your number and message me whenever you need a lift home? We'll be here," he says, pulling out his phone.

"Are you sure?" I ask, feeling bad that he's going to try to work around my schedule for when I want to leave.

"Yeah, I'm sure," he assures me, running his hand through his dark, messy hair. "We got you here, and we'll get you home, too."

I tell him my number and he saves it into his phone. Waving goodbye to him and the other guys, I run into the hospital and ask for my sister at the front desk.

"Room fifteen," the nurse tells me and points down the hall to the right.

"Thank you," I call out as I start to jog to the room. Looking up at the number fifteen, I knock on the door quietly. I don't hear her screaming; the room silent. When the door opens, I see Ariel looking tired but beautiful, and a gorgeous baby wrapped up in a pink blanket.

I missed it. For a small moment, I'm sad that I couldn't be there for Ariel and welcome my niece into the world. But I'm here now, and I'm going to make up for it.

"Sorry I'm late," I say to Ariel, bending down to give her a kiss on her forehead. "You look too beautiful to have just given birth."

She smiles, and glances down at her daughter. *Daughter*, that sounds so crazy. "Isn't she amazing, Izzy?"

"She's perfect," I reply, holding my arms out so I can carry her. Ariel hands her over to me and I sit down with her in my arms, tears threatening to fall from my eyes as I stare down at my niece.

"You are so loved," I whisper to her, gently trailing my finger down her soft, chubby cheek. I now know that love at first sight is a very real thing, because there's nothing I wouldn't do for this little girl in my arms.

Nothing.

"And so beautiful. What did you name her?" I ask, gently rocking as she starts to fuss. "Did you go with any of the names we had on the list?"

We've been compiling this list since we were little, the names on it always changing whenever we hear a new one we love.

"I did. Mila Isabella," she says, beaming.

"You gave her my name?" I whisper, blinking quickly as this time the tears do fall, dripping down my cheeks. "If it's possible, I love her more now."

Ariel laughs, and then tells me about her labor, which lasted about three hours. "I sent you a message to tell you that she had arrived, but you must not have checked your phone. But you got here pretty fast."

"I rode here on a motorcycle," I drop casually, handing her back Mila when she starts to cry, probably hungry.

Ariel takes her daughter to feed her. "What do you mean you rode here on a motorcycle?"

"Well, when I was about to leave my car decided to break down," I start, leaning back in the chair and studying her. "I had two options. One, to try to get it fixed quickly then drive, or two, try to book a flight, but you know how I feel about planes."

Although I did have a third option, and probably the easiest one, which was to call my father and ask him for his help.

But my pride wouldn't let me even consider that option.

It's actually pretty sad, because he should be here, present for his firstborn daughter giving birth to his first grandchild, but he's not.

"You would have gotten on a plane for me?" she asks, green eyes going wide, knowing my terrible fear of flying. "If that's not love, I don't know what is."

"If I had no other option, then yes, I would have." But I wouldn't have liked it.

"But you didn't come in your car…"

"Nope. One of the bikers next door saw me on the side of the road, offered to help fix my car and give me a ride to you. They were already heading in this direction, so made a slight detour for me," I explain, laughing at the look of shock on her face.

"You let one of the bikers from the MC near your house drive you all the way here? And he did it from the kindness of his heart?" she reaffirms, brow furrowing. "And he just happened to be riding toward Vegas?"

"Yes, yes and yes," I reply, shrugging. "You have serious trust issues, you know that? I helped one of their girlfriends out. Do you know they actually call their girlfriends 'old ladies'? Can you believe that?" Ariel is still looking at me like I grew a second head. "I needed to be here, Ariel. I hated the thought of you having to be in labor alone, and after everything, you had to do it alone anyway. I'm sorry."

She waves her hand in the air, dismissing my concerns. "I was fine, Izzy. I was in so much pain I couldn't really think of much else, and you're here now, which is all that matters to me. I know how much you wanted to be here. I mean, shit, you even took a ride with some random criminal biker to get here."

Shaking my head with a grin playing on my lips, I add, "Yeah, and I didn't bring my suitcase so I have nothing except my handbag and the clothes on my back, so I'm going to need to borrow some shit."

She laughs softly. "You can go to my place and borrow whatever you need. My car is in the hospital parking lot."

"You drove yourself here?" I ask, feeling like absolute shit.

"Yeah," she says, scanning my eyes. "Izzy, it was fine. I only live ten minutes from here and the contractions weren't too bad when I drove in."

"I feel so bad."

"You can't help that Mila decided to come early," she says, looking down at the baby with awe in her face.

"I know," I mutter, but I still hate the fact she went through this time alone. "You never should have moved out here."

Ariel moved to Vegas to be with Merve, her then boyfriend and Mila's father, but they broke up when he found out she was pregnant, and she hasn't heard from him since.

"I know. Actually I think I'm going to move back home to California in a few months, when Mila is a little older," she says to me. "I'll need some time to pack my house up and sell everything."

"I'll help you with whatever you need," I promise. "And there's a spare room at my house with your and Mila's names all over it."

"You sure?" she asks, brows drawing together. "You going to be able to live with a crying baby? You work from home. It will probably drive you crazy."

"I'm sure," I reply, scowling at her for second-guessing it. "I'd love the company, and even if she cries all night, we can take shifts so we both get some sleep. We'll work it out. I'd love having you both there, Ariel. I can't think of anything better."

She smiles, eyes lighting up.

She might be my older sister, but I've always looked after her, and I always will.

"Did you call Dad?" I ask, not sure if she was going to want him to come and visit her or not.

"I sent him a message, but he didn't reply," she admits, shrugging. "Either he's busy or he just doesn't care."

Our dad has been so in and out of our lives that it's hard to keep up. You'd think for this occasion he'd put in the effort, though, and be on a plane, but you never know with him. How much interest he shows in us usually depends on his own agenda, and it's always been that way. We've always come second to his career, but when he left our mom for his now wife, we became lower on his list of importance. Even more so now that he has kids with her.

I remember once sending him a copy of my report card when I was twelve, hoping he would be proud and want to see us more, but the next time I saw him he asked me why I didn't get an A in math. I had gotten a B, and even though the rest of my report card was straight As, that's the grade he had to point out.

That's the kind of man he is.

"It's his loss. Can I hold her again?" I ask after Mila finishes eating.

"Sure," Ariel replies with a yawn. "Maybe I'll have a nap now, knowing she is in safe hands."

I lift her up from my sister and cradle her against my chest. "She's so little," I whisper, sitting back down and smiling at her. "I can't believe you made this. I think she looks just like you, too. Maybe even better looking."

"And look at you being so complimentary with her," Ariel laughs, while I roll my eyes. It's a known fact that I struggle giving compliments to people, but that clearly doesn't apply with babies. It's a weird thing to have an issue with but with my family history, can you blame me?

I can't believe Merve is missing all of this. If I ever see that man... Let's just say I'm going to show him my old Muay Thai moves.

It doesn't matter, though, because Mila is going to be the most loved child who ever did exist, and she doesn't need Merve, because she's not going to miss out on a single thing.

"She even has the same birthmark as you, the one inside her wrist," I point out, glancing up at Ariel to find her already fast asleep.

The poor thing must be exhausted. She should be so proud of herself and everything she has accomplished all on her own, without ever complaining once. She worked throughout her pregnancy as a legal secretary, saving money for when Mila came along, and I never ever heard her even say she was tired.

She is Superwoman.

"I guess it's just me and you now, little one," I say, running my thumb along Mila's birthmark.

I've never felt more content.

Chapter Four

Unlocking the door, I step into Ariel's apartment and take a look around. The place is just as I remembered it, a two-bedroom, one-bathroom apartment that is quite luxurious and spacious. My sister has a completely different taste in interior design to me, hers more natural, with neutral colors and modern elegance.

Yawning, tired after the ride and spending a few hours with Ariel and Mila, I head toward her room, searching through her dresser. Finding some jeans and a top, I head into the bathroom and turn on the shower. I've been looking forward to this moment. Putting some music on my phone, I undress and step under the scalding water, closing my eyes and tipping my head backward.

What a day. So much has happened in such a short period of time, and it's nice to have a silent moment to just process the whole thing.

I'm an aunty. It's still so hard to wrap my head around it.

Once I'm dry and dressed, silently thankful that Ariel and I are the same size, I tidy up her kitchen, which she must have left in a rush, the dishes in the sink and toast on a plate. The rest of the apartment is spotless, and I'd expect nothing else from Ariel, her obsessive neatness well-known. When my phone vibrates with a text message from an unknown number, butterflies find their way into my stomach.

You all good?

I'm assuming it's from Renny, checking in, or at least I'm hoping so, but I message back asking just to make sure. Renny?

How many other guys from random numbers do you have texting you?

I laugh and type out, Too many to count.

I told the men you weren't as sweet as you seem.

Unable to stop the smile on my face, I jump up on the counter and type back. Apparently you're smarter than you look.

I don't know if I've crossed the line with that one, roasting a scary biker guy, but he just comes off as fun and playful and I don't feel scared of him at all.

Smartass.

Phew.

Yes, I'm all good, and a very proud aunty.

Congrats. Let me know if you ever need anything. We're staying in Vegas for a little while.

I'm good, but thank you. I think I might stay here another week to spend time with my sister and help her out.

Sounds good. Message me the day you want to leave and the address and we will be there.

He's like my very own Uber.

I reply with a thank-you, jump down off the counter and grab the few things Ariel asked me to bring back to the hospital—an extra pair of pajamas, her phone charger, some books and some snacks that I'm meant to smuggle in—and then head back to her.

Ariel and Mila are both fast asleep when I get there, so I curl up on the chair with a book and watch over them.

And I don't mind for a second that this is going to be my life over the next week.

After two nights in the hospital, Ariel is given the all clear to go home with Mila. With the nursery all set up and waiting, I decide to cook in bulk and do some food prep to freeze for her so she will have prepared meals when I leave.

"You don't have to do that, Izzy," Ariel says as she watches me with Mila in her arms. "I want you to relax. I didn't ask you to come here to be my house elf."

"I want to," I tell her, continuing to chop vegetables without missing a beat. "Let me look after you. It's the least I can do considering I won't be here to help you until you move back home." I pause, and then add, "Actually I could come back here. I just need to go home and get my laptop so I can do some work."

"Who's the older sister here?"

"Don't worry, if I ever have a baby, I'm going to expect you to return the favor. Tenfold," I tease, placing the knife down and washing my hands in the sink. "Do we have everything you need for Mila? Or do we need to go on a shopping trip? I still want to buy her a gift."

"You sent her a box of stuff," she argues, shaking her head. "You literally bought her most of the clothes she has to wear for the next six months. What else does she need?"

"Clothes to wear after six months?"

"You're terrible, you know that? You should be saving your money," she chastises, gently tapping Mila on the back to burp her. "Mila has everything that she needs."

"I finally have a niece, Ariel. Do you know how long I've been waiting for this moment? Don't try to steal it from me," I fire back, sticking my tongue out at her. "I only wish Mom was here to see her. She would have simply adored her."

Ariel goes silent, and I instantly regret saying anything.

We lost our mom to cancer four years ago, and it was the hardest thing we've ever been through in our lives. I still miss her every day, but especially in moments like these. She raised us all by herself for the most part, and we were all really close, always just us three, having each other's back through everything life would throw at us.

The cancer was the one thing that won.

"I know," Ariel finally whispers. "And Mila will know it, too."

I lean forward and kiss the top of Mila's dark, fuzzy head. "Yes, she will. Now, why don't you go and rest? Or have a nap? I read that you're meant to sleep while she does. I'm going to be in the kitchen for the next few hours getting all of this sorted."

"Are you chasing me from my own kitchen?" she jokes, yawning. "I love you, you know that?"

"I do know that," I reply, grinning.

She flashes me a sleepy smile, and then heads to her room with Mila, leaving me to cook up a storm. She's still asleep when I'm done, so I plop down on the couch and check my phone, laughing when I see a picture that Renny sent me, one of him with one of those giant alcoholic slushy drinks, the caption reading When in Vegas.

It's not a selfie, so one of the other guys must have taken it. I can't imagine Renny taking a selfie, he doesn't seem like the type. But me, on the other hand, I have no problem doing so, so I send one back of me in my pajamas with the caption Not the usual Vegas experience. I didn't expect him to maintain any contact, and especially not to send any pictures, giving me insight into what he's doing, but I kind of like that he is.

"What are you getting yourself into, Izzy?" I mutter to myself. I know it sounds like a bad idea having any involvement with a motorcycle club, not that I know anything about them other than what I see in the media, or the whispers I've heard from the locals. But once you meet and hang out with these guys it's so different, and doesn't feel like you're at all doing anything wrong. At the end of the day, they are my closest neighbors and I should be on good terms with them, friends even, but that's probably where the boundary line should stay. That would be the smart thing to do.

Friends message each other, though, right?

And send cute pics to each other.

Mila starts to cry a little later, so I rush into her nursery and pick her up, hoping Ariel stays asleep so she can get some more rest.

"Hello, beautiful," I whisper, cradling her and breathing in her baby scent. She stops crying as soon as I pick her up, so I sit back down on the couch and have a cuddle. Just as I sit there's a knock at the door, so I quickly move toward it, frowning when I glance through the peephole and see Merve standing there, the bastard.

"What do you want?" I call out, scowling. There's no way in hell I'm letting him in here, especially without the okay from Ariel. From what I've seen and heard of this man, he's unpredictable, and I'm not going to put my sister and niece at risk.

"I heard that Ariel had the baby and I want to see it," he replies, stepping back and crossing his arms over his chest. "Let me in, Izzy. They are my family."

Family? This man wouldn't know what that was if it hit him in the face, which it just might. I can't believe the nerve of him. This is the man who deserted Ariel when she found out she was pregnant. The man who hasn't shown any interest in being a father, never mind giving zero support to my sister in any emotional or financial way. If you look up *Deadbeat Dad*, a mug shot of this guy will show up.

I cover Mila's ears and tell him to kindly fuck off.

The commotion wakes up Ariel, who walks out of her room looking like she had a good sleep, her dark hair sticking up in every direction. "Who are you telling to fuck off?" she whisper-yells.

Merve, I mouth to her, glancing down at Mila. "What the fuck is he doing here?"

She looks as confused as me. "He must have heard I had the baby."

"From who? You have no friends here," I whisper back at her, frowning.

"I made a social media post." She shrugs, regret flashing in her eyes. "I didn't think he'd show up. Why would he? He's been missing in action for eight months now, but someone must have told him."

"What should we do?" I ask, pursing my lips. "I vote for calling the cops."

"I can hear you guys," Merve calls out through the door. "Can you let me in, please? I just want to see her. I am her father, after all."

Ariel and I share a look.

"I told you that you should have gotten a German shepherd, or something," I mutter, gritting my teeth. "Then we could have just let it loose on him."

"I can still hear you," he continues.

"I don't give a fuck," I call back, still covering Mila's ears, like she'd understand the obscenities leaving my lips. "What do you want to do?" I ask Ariel. As much as I want to tell him to take a hike, I know it's not my decision here.

"Should we just let him in? He can see her and then leave. I have no doubt he won't want to step up and be a father, so it might get rid of him," she suggests, coming forward and taking Mila.

"It's your call," I tell her, but really I want her to just tell him to fuck off. It's going to be like this for the rest of Mila's life, him coming in and out whenever he feels like it, I just know it. He is her father, though, so I know that that means something to Ariel, especially growing up without a father for most of our lives. She wouldn't want Mila to grow up without a father, but who needs a man who doesn't give his whole heart over to his child?

"Shit," she whispers, then steps toward the door. "If you try any bullshit, I'm going to call the cops, Merve!"

"No bullshit, I just want to see her," he says back. I'll admit, he sounds sincere enough, but the man is a master manipulator.

Ariel opens the door and he steps inside, eyes on his daughter. I take a step closer to her, my protective instincts kicking in.

"Can I hold her?" he asks, holding out his arms. Merve is a good-looking man. A little too good-looking, which should have been the first hint that he was going to turn out to be a douche, but at least Mila got some pretty genes running through her.

"Sit down," Ariel tells him, glancing down at her daughter, hesitating. She sighs, takes a deep breath and then hands her over to him, making sure that he's supporting her neck and holding her correctly.

"She's adorable," he says, smiling down at Mila. There seems to be some emotion in his gaze, so maybe he does care for her. I guess only time will tell.

"How did you know Ariel had her?" I ask, studying him closely.

"Gina told me," he explains, referring to one of their mutual friends. "She said you named her Mila. Beautiful name."

My jaw goes tight. How dare he step up in here like he has every right, and act like father of the fucking year? Ariel's expression tells me that she's highly unimpressed, too, but I know she's trying to be mature about the situation and handle everything the best way she can. She's going to have to deal with this for the rest of her life, forever tied to him through her daughter.

"Yes, her name is Mila Isabella," she says, tapping her foot on the floor. "And what do you want from us exactly, Merve? Do you want to be in her life? Or are you going to just drop by whenever you feel like acknowledging her? Because we need to do whatever is best for her, not what's best for you."

"I don't know," he admits, which is at least honest, but doesn't sound promising. "I just knew that I had to see her. She's my child, too, Ariel, but I have a lot going on in my life right now and I don't know if I'm cut out for the whole father thing. My business is just taking off, and that needs to be my focus right now. I'll come and see her when I can."

My fingers close into a fist. I know that some might have sympathy for him and his situation, but I have nothing. My sister is the hero in this story, and Merve has done nothing but think about himself, not wanting to give up his playboy lifestyle for changing diapers and supporting a baby.

"What are you doing?" she asks as he pulls out his phone.

"Taking a photo of her to show my family," he says, capturing the image of her in his arms. "They will want to see her, too."

"The same family that hasn't made contact once to ask about her?" I blurt out, unable to hold my tongue. "Or to see if Ariel is healthy, or needs anything?"

"This has nothing to do with you, Izzy," Merve growls, sliding his phone back into his shirt pocket and pinning me with a death stare.

"You sure? Because I'm more her parent than you've been," I fire back, daring him to challenge me again.

He stands and hands Mila back to Ariel. "I'll be back to see her."

He doesn't say when, so I guess it's going to be whenever he feels like it. He's such a piece of shit. We both watch him leave the house, then lock the door behind him.

"I don't regret Mila, but boy, do I regret sleeping with that man," Ariel mutters, sighing deeply and looking worried. "It was easier when I thought he was hiding from us."

"If you hit him up for child support, I'm sure he will," I tease, sitting down. "I'll bet you any money he will post the pictures on social media and have everyone commenting about how cute she is. He's probably acting like a proud, involved father."

"Some people have no shame," she groans, shaking her head and sitting down next to me. "Thanks for having my back. It would have been so much worse if you weren't here."

I reach over and touch her hand. "I'm always in your corner."

Because that is what family is for.

Chapter Five

The rest of the week passes quickly, with no more drama from Merve. In fact, we don't hear from him at all. I don't know if I should be annoyed or relieved, but I think it's the latter.

Ariel settles into motherhood like a pro, and I feel sad that I have to leave her, but I really do need to get back to work and my home.

"Are you sure you don't want to come with me?" I ask, frowning. "You can stay at my house for a while."

She shakes her head. "I'll be fine, Izzy. I need to start packing and tie all loose ends here before I move back. I have enough money saved that I don't need to work for a few months at least, so I'm good. I don't want to rush around right now. I just want to spend this time bonding with Mila and enjoying being a mom without any unnecessary stress."

"Okay, but you say the word and I'm coming to get you," I promise, pausing and then adding, "The second I get my car fixed."

She laughs. "Let me know if you need some money."

"I'll be fine," I tell her, using her words back at her. "I have a lot of work lined up." That I probably should have been doing this whole time.

"That's good, because you're super talented and if I were you I'd be raising my prices."

"You're my sister, you have to say that." I grin, wrapping my arm around her. "I'm going to miss you and Mila so much."

"Me, too, but I will be seeing you soon enough," she promises, looking toward the door when she hears the sound of rumbling motorcycles. "Looks like your ride is here. Are you sure you trust them?"

"They brought me here in one piece, didn't they?" I remind her, picking up my handbag and draping it over my shoulder.

"Yeah, I guess so. I'm just a little concerned that you might be taking 'love thy neighbor' a little too literally," she grumbles, moving toward the front door with me.

"What do you mean?"

"You're crushing on Renny," she says, frowning like it's obvious. "And don't act like you're not. You smile like an idiot every time he messages you, and you talk about him a lot. And I'm your big sister, you can't fool me."

I open my mouth and then close it. "I think he's a nice guy, yes."

"He's a biker," she reminds me.

"The two aren't mutually exclusive," I say, rolling my eyes.

"I know, I'm just a little worried. You're out there on your own, and if something happens, I'm hours away. Just how much do you know about these men because you're putting an awful amount of trust in them? Is it dangerous being tied to them? I don't know what to expect with this whole revelation."

She's right, and I know it. I *am* trusting them, but they haven't given me any reason not to as of yet, and I'm running with it.

"I feel the same about you, which is why I was suggesting that you move home sooner," I point out, touching her shoulder and sighing. "I'll be fine, the bikers won't do anything to hurt me, and you'll be fine, too. Merve might go MIA again so he doesn't have to pay any child support, and then soon enough we'll be living together and can be so far up each other's business that we wish we lived in separate states again."

"Sounds like the perfect plan," she replies, smiling widely.

I rush to the nursery and kiss a sleeping Mila goodbye, and then head out front, where Ariel has boldly already gone, staring down the men. They all stay on their bikes except for Renny, who approaches us both, helmet in hand.

"Hello," he says to Ariel, offering her his hand. "I'm Renny."

"Ariel," my sister introduces herself, and I don't miss the firm grip she offers him. "You'll get her home safely, won't you?"

"Of course," he replies, nodding. "We would never let anything bad happen to her. You have my word."

She lifts her phone up and takes a photo of him. "Good, but just in case something does happen to her, this is the photo I'm going to show the police so they can hunt your ass down."

Renny tries to contain his amusement, but I don't miss the flash of it in his eyes. "I'll remember that, but you have nothing to worry about. I'm sure she will check in with you so you don't have to worry."

"I will," I promise Ariel, giving her the biggest hug and kissing her on the cheek. "I love you, and I will call you as soon as I get home, all right?"

"Okay," she says, sounding a little emotional. "Thank you for everything."

"You don't need to thank me," I tell her, stepping back and smiling. "What's family for, right? Love you!"

"Love you, too, baby sis," she says back.

I wave at the other men, then get on the bike and put my helmet on, once again pressed up against Renny.

I keep my eyes on my sister until she's out of my sight, waving goodbye to her, and then look ahead. We'll be reunited soon enough, and I know that, but it still sucks leaving her alone with her daughter when I know she doesn't have anyone around to help. Sure, she has a few friends, but nothing compares to family.

Renny and the guys soon make a pit stop, parking their bikes near a busy street.

"What are we doing?" I ask, taking my helmet off and fixing my hair.

"Thought we'd get something to eat," he says, offering me his hand. "It's going to be a long ride home. You aren't in any rush, are you?"

I shake my head. "I guess not." Food sounds good, and because we were so busy with Mila, Ariel and I didn't exactly get to explore Vegas or do anything adult-y, so it's kind of nice to get out.

"How was your visit?" Temper asks as Renny and I reach him.

"Really good. How was yours?" I ask. I'm not sure what they did or where they went, and I doubt I'm going to get much of an explanation, but I'm not really expecting one. Temper does look to be in a good mood, though, so maybe he got laid or something.

"Uneventful, but relaxing. It's nice to get away," is his reply.

"It is," I agree.

We walk toward the Strip, me in the middle with Renny and Temper on each side of me, Dee and Saint on the outskirts, and I don't miss the looks everyone is giving us.

"Must be the all black and leather," I mutter, glancing down at what must be the signature look of Renny and the other men, and back at my new ripped jeans and denim jacket. Underneath is my sister's royal blue top, one I've been eying for a while that she finally let me steal.

Renny glances over at me and winks. "You sure they're all looking at us?"

"Yes." I nod. "Or maybe they're wondering if you're holding me hostage, or something."

The men laugh, but hey, it could be true. I'm surrounded by

dangerous-looking men, and everyone must be able to tell that there's something about them, and not just because of the leather cuts they are wearing. They are just a bunch of strong, tall, dominant alpha males, and anyone can see that from a quick glance.

"What do you feel like eating?" Renny asks, glancing at the many options.

"How about that place?" I suggest, pointing to a pub.

"You always surprise me, you know that?" he murmurs, shaking his head. "I thought you'd choose something like that." He points to some posh, expensive-looking restaurant.

"Someone needs to keep you on your toes," I reply, feeling bold and oddly comfortable. We get a table at the back, and order food and drinks.

"You better not have too many of those," Renny quips, watching me take a sip of my mango daiquiri. "Pretty sure your sister will skin me alive if you fall off my bike because you're drunk."

"I can't go to Vegas and not have one alcoholic beverage," I state. "It would just be rude, don't you think?"

When Renny and the rest of the men order water, or soda, I feel like I may be the bad influence at the table. When my steak arrives, though, I know that it's going to soak up any ounce of alcohol in my system, because it is *huge*.

"There's no way you're going to eat all that," Renny remarks.

"Your eyes are bigger than your stomach," Dee adds, chuckling. "That steak is the size of your head."

"How was I supposed to know it was going to be this big?" I defend, picking up my knife and fork and studying it.

"I bet she doesn't even get halfway through it," Renny declares, unknowingly tapping into my competitive side. "I'm calling it now."

"I'm going to prove you wrong," I tell him, cutting into it. "You obviously haven't seen a Beck woman eat before. Me, my sister, and even my mom when she was alive—all big eaters."

"Where the hell does the food go?" Dee asks, frowning.

"To all the right places," I think I hear Renny mutter, but I can't be sure.

"What did you say?"

"Nothing," he says quickly, drinking from his water. "You much of a gambler?"

"I've never gambled before," I admit to him. "I don't have much luck."

"You've never gambled before?" he repeats, looking shell-shocked. "But you have family in Vegas. How many times have you been here?"

"A couple," I admit, shrugging. "My sister isn't really the partying type, so I've never even checked out any of the clubs here."

They all stare at me, dumbfounded.

"You know what, fuck it," Renny says, glancing around the table. "We need to show her how to do Vegas, the right way. A little gambling, a few drinks, and a hell of a lot of food."

I hate to admit that I'm tempted, and I wouldn't say no to spending more time with Renny before I'm back to reality. "What do you have in mind?"

He calls over the waitress and orders the table a round of beers, then turns back to me. "You okay with us going home tomorrow morning instead?"

I don't know what comes over me. I know that I should tell them no, that this isn't the best idea, but I don't want to. I want some excitement, and I want to experience a fun night out in Vegas which, according to them, I'm really missing out on. When I lost my mom, my party days came to an end, and I guess I've just kind of become a boring adult who spends all her time working, and whose idea of a fun time is eating out and online shopping.

Fuck it.

I deserve to let loose.

"Yeah, I'm okay with that," I reply, anticipation filling me.

"Fuck, here we go," Temper grumbles, but accepts the beer

that's handed to him and takes a quick drink. "You sure you want to do this, Isabella?"

"I'm intrigued now," I tell him, taking a big bite of steak. "You only live once, right? And call me Izzy, everyone does."

I think that's the first time I've ever used the saying YOLO, but it's never been so fitting. It's been a long time since I've let loose, had a few drinks and danced the right away, and I think it's just what the doctor ordered.

Right after I demolish this steak.

Chapter Six

"What are these?" Renny asks, taking the shots I hand him.

I deadpan, "Wet pussies."

He almost chokes, making me laugh hard, alcohol dripping down my hands. "Taste them, they are amazing."

He downs the two shots and lands them on the bar. "Not bad."

After finishing my steak and impressing the table, we had a few drinks then headed to the casino, where Renny tried to teach me the ways of gambling, starting with roulette. I'm not going to lie, it's definitely not my thing, but he did prove me wrong about not having any luck. Somehow I turned fifty dollars into seven hundred. Still, he hasn't let me pay for anything all night, and told me not to waste my winnings.

"Your lips say not bad, but your sour expression says that a wet pussy isn't your cup of tea," I reply, laughing harder when I realize how that sounded.

"I don't think any women who know me would say that." He smirks, amusement dancing in his brown eyes. He leans his elbow on the bar, facing me. "Are you having a good night?"

"Are you kidding me? I won money and have eaten and drunk

my way down the Strip. Not to mention that somehow you guys have all the right connections and we don't have to even line up anywhere or pay for entry. This is like the VIP treatment."

"With the way that you look, Izzy, trust me, I doubt you'd be lining up or paying for anything here," he says, scanning the dance floor.

"The way I look? I'm dressed in casual clothes, Renny. I was expecting a ride home, not a night on the town, and now I look extremely out of place."

The women around me are dolled up to the nines, with short dresses, stiletto heels and makeup and hair that looks professionally done, and I'm here in jeans, a blue top and rosy cheeks from alcohol instead of product.

"Yet you're still the most beautiful woman in the room," he states, offering me his hand. I know I'm not an unattractive woman, but if he honestly thinks that, he must be blind. There are more beautiful women here tonight than I've ever seen in one place at the same time, but I guess that's Vegas for you.

"I love this song. Do you want to dance?"

"Depends. Are you a good dancer?" I ask, teasing him, but taking his hand at the same time. He pulls me to the busy dance floor and presses against me, not too close, which I like, just enough that it's sexy, and I can feel how his body moves.

"I've heard I'm pretty good," he whispers into my ear, sending shivers down my spine. "But why don't you tell me?"

I can tell instantly that he's right, he does know his way around a dance floor. He moves sensually, in rhythm to the music, but doesn't overdo it, so it doesn't even look like he's trying. It just comes natural to him.

Lifting my arms above my head, I spin around and press my ass against him, gyrating my hips. I haven't danced with a man like this in years, and it feels so freeing, so…naughty. Which is kind of sad, because lots of people do stuff like this every weekend. I'm buzzing from the alcohol and suddenly life has never been easier, or more fun.

I can see why people like to party.

Renny spins me back around and cups my cheek, smiling at me. "Looks like I've finally met my match."

"Impressed, are you?" I ask, placing my palms on his chest and slowing down my moves. "I used to be a dancer in high school."

"I believe it," he says, and my eyes lower to his lips. Perfect, full, kissable lips. I bet he'd be an amazing kisser, too. I bet he'd be amazing at everything.

"We should have another drink," I tell him, because that suddenly sounds like a wonderful idea. "My treat."

"Nice try," he says, following behind me back to the bar.

I order us another round, this time vodka mixed with an energy drink—because that's always a good idea—and two shots on the side. Renny, clearly more responsible than me, also adds two bottles of water onto the order.

"So is Renny your real name? I mean, I've heard of the name Remy, but not Renny, or is that just short for something?" I ask, tilting my head to the side and studying him. At this point I have no filter, and am probably making no sense, but I want to know everything about this enigma of a man while I have the chance. While there are no guards up between us. Who knows if I will ever get another chance like this?

"No, it's not my birth name, actually," he admits, lifting his drink to his mouth and taking a sip. When he licks a drop off his lips, my thighs squeeze together of their own accord.

Control yourself, Izzy.

"What is it then?" I push.

"Jasper," he answers, lips kicking up at the corners. "Jasper Steel."

My eyes widen. "Why do they call you Renny?"

"It's short for Renegade," he admits, ducking his head as he says it.

"So they gave you a nickname of a nickname?" I ask, smiling with him. "Well, Jasper, I happen to think that's a great name for you."

"No one has called me that in years," he states, running his hand over the stubble on his cheek. "Almost seems like a different person."

"So why Renegade?" I ask, downing my shot and placing it back down on the bar. "Or do these biker road names get chosen at random?"

He laughs at that. "Something like that. Do you want to go and sit back at the table?"

I nod and let him lead me back to where the other guys are all sitting, drinking a bottle of expensive whiskey. Temper has a woman trying to get his attention, but he's flat out ignoring her, concentrating on his phone instead.

"Having a good night?" I ask him over the music.

He puts his phone down and replaces it with his glass. "Trying to. This is not really my scene."

"Really? I couldn't tell," I reply sarcastically, studying him. He's a good-looking man, but it's like he either doesn't notice that or he doesn't care. Either way, there's something about him that screams power, and it's almost like the women around him can sense that straight away. "There's so many women staring at you."

His brows come together, like he's confused. "You're drunk."

"I am, but it's still the truth," I tell him, leaning back onto Renny. "They stare at all of you. It's weird."

"Maybe they're staring at you," Dee states, shrugging and flashing me a charming smile. "Wondering what you have that they don't."

"A broken-down car and luck," I reply, making him laugh. "And damn, Dee, you have a healthy ego on you, don't you?"

He laughs again at that.

"You have much more than that," Renny says, pushing my hair back behind my ear. "Don't forget, you're also our neighbor."

I nudge him with my elbow and roll my eyes at his smart-ass comment. "I just want to say thank you for taking me out and allowing me to let loose. I'm almost embarrassed to admit how long it's been since the last time I went out and had some fun, so thank you for bringing me here and showing me a good time. And thank you for taking me back tomorrow, when I'm going to be hungover and a huge pain in the ass."

"And thank you for being a fuckin' awesome neighbor and never complaining about the loud bikes and music," Renny replies, casually wrapping his arm around me. "And for giving us some eye candy every time we need to drive down the road and you're out the front of your house."

"Man, he almost crashed that time you were out washing your car," Dee adds, laughing at Renny. "I was right behind him, and the bastard swerved and almost went into a tree."

I chance a look at Renny's expression, which is extremely unimpressed with his friend. "Is that true?"

He shakes his head but grins, giving himself away. "You were in a fuckin' red bikini. How could I not almost crash my bike?"

Resting my cheek against his shoulder, I can't contain my smile. "That's a pretty cute compliment."

He brings his eyes to mine. "You're a pretty cute woman."

"And it wasn't a red bikini, it was a one-piece," I point out, smirking. "And I'd just gotten home from the beach, so the car was filthy."

"Hey, you don't need to make any excuses," Renny adds, bringing his glass to his lips.

I look down and realize that I've finished the drink I had in my hand. "More shots?"

Renny shakes his head at me, so Dee steps up and offers to take me to the bar. "Let her live a little, brother," he says, nodding toward me. "It's her first night out in fuck knows how long, and we're all here to look after her, so nothing can happen to her. Let her be wild for one night, before she's back to being responsible."

"Come on, Renny, have some fun," I say, offering my hand and pulling him up from the booth to come and join us at the bar. "Let's have one more drink and one more dance, and then we can go if you like."

Famous last words.

Chapter Seven

I wake up with the hangover of all hangovers, my head feeling like it's splitting in half. Why do I make such bad decisions? It's like one taste of freedom and I just run with it, going way overboard and having just a little bit too much fun. This is what happens when you don't go out in a long time, or at least where I'm concerned, apparently.

Lifting my head and forcing my eyes open, I glance around the empty hotel room.

A *really* nice, empty hotel room.

Man, it's lovely having rich friends.

Everything hurts as I sit up, my whole body hating me for drinking so much last night and being so irresponsible. When I see Renny asleep on the floor next to the bed, I glance down to make sure that I'm dressed, which I am, but not in last night's clothes. I'm wearing what must be one of Renny's T-shirts. It's black and loose on me. I'm wearing panties and no bra.

Drunk me got really comfortable last night.

Feeling parched, I reach over for a bottle of water next to my bed, crack it open and drink half. My loud swallowing rouses

Renny, who sits up and glances around the room, eyes narrowed as they land on me.

I hand him the other half of the water, which he drinks greedily. "Remind me never to party with you again. I feel like crap."

"How was this my fault?" I grumble, sliding back into bed and under the sheets. "This was not my idea."

"The shots were." He groans, standing up in nothing but a pair of black boxer shorts to walk to the bathroom. My eyes widen as I take in his body in all its bare glory—the tattoos, the muscles, the toned, smooth skin. When he turns around, I see the huge knight on his back, the same one I've seen on the leather cut he wears.

He's a beast, a machine, a piece of fucking artwork.

I don't realize my mouth is open until he glances over and catches me looking at him. He points a finger at me, brown eyes narrowed to slits. "Don't you look at me like that."

I close my mouth, and then open it again. "I need a shower, food and some painkillers."

And I mean, I wouldn't say no to a little foreplay with Renny, with him looking like that. I mean, I'm sure it would make me feel better to have his body pressed up against mine, my fingers exploring that Knight while his explore my…

Bang. Bang. Bang.

The loud knock has me jumping and pulling the covers up to cover everything but my head.

Renny answers the door but only opens it a little, so no one can see inside.

"Are you ready to go?" I hear Dee ask, tone a little too fucking happy for so early in the morning. It sounds a little smug, too. "Or are you two both staying to enjoy the honeymoon?"

"What?" Renny asks him, sounding just like I feel, grumpy, tired and a little bit horny.

Okay, maybe the horny bit is just me, but I can't help it when he's walking around like *that*.

"You don't remember what happened last night?" Dee asks, quiet for a few moments before he starts laughing.

Hard.

He pushes the door open and steps inside, Renny locking it behind him with a harsh curse.

"Mrs. Steel," he says to me, smile wider than I've ever seen it. "How are you this morning? You don't seem to be glowing. Did Renegade here not blow your mind with his bedroom skills?"

Renny slaps him on the back of his head, which I really appreciate, until I start processing what he is saying.

We're in Vegas.

Honeymoon?

Mrs. Steel?

I think we all know what he's getting at here, but no, just fucking no. There is no way I would do that. I rack my memory, flashing back to every place we went, every club and every bar, every laugh. I remember doing Fireball shots with Renny, and then I remember...

Nothing.

What happened after the Fireballs at Hakkasan?

We share a look, and he looks just as concerned as I feel.

I glance down at my hand and see a wedding band. One that wasn't there yesterday. Dread fills me.

I eye Renny's hand and see a plain gold band on his.

Fuck.

Renny studies me for a moment, then shakes his head. "No. I don't know what fucking *Punk'd* shit you're trying to pull on me, Dee, but we drank, we danced, and then we fucking came back to this hotel room, where I was a gentleman and slept on the floor."

"Since when are you a gentleman—"

"Dee, what the fuck," Renny growls, crossing his arms over his chest.

Dee hands him his phone. Renny stares at the screen, and I

jump out of bed and rush over to him, needing to see this, especially after hearing my obnoxious laughter blazing through the speaker.

I'm silent as I watch me, in my clothes from last night, standing opposite Renny, holding his hands and staring into his eyes.

"Fuck," I whisper as it all comes back to me.

"I'm having so much fun!" I say, smiling widely. I'm clearly very drunk, but I haven't had this much fun in a while. "I can't believe you've been so close to me this entire time and we've never hung out."

"I know," he replies, stirring the ice in his drink. "I knew you were beautiful, but I had no idea you'd be like this..."

"Like what?" I ask him, leaning closer to him, my chin resting on my palm.

"Funny," he says, scanning my eyes. "Smart. Witty. I don't know, just different."

"You like me," I reply with a smug grin. "I'm glad my car broke down, you know that? We wouldn't be here right now if it didn't."

Renny reaches his hand out and cups my face, my own hand dropping away. When he leans closer to kiss me, I don't stop him. Instead, I all but jump onto his lap and kiss him deeper, pressing my body against his, holding on for dear life and enjoying the ride. My heart races, and when he pulls away I can't help but smile against his lips.

"Yeah, you really like me," I say, smiling, my heavily lidded eyes locked with his.

Wincing, I cover my face with my hands, remembering how bold I was, and the fact that I didn't care who was watching is a testament to how much I'd been drinking, because I'm usually not one for public displays of affection. More flashbacks hit me as I remember exactly how I got myself into this predicament.

* * *

Stopping in front of a wedding chapel, I stare up at the sign. Renny stops ahead of me, turning to see why I'm no longer next to him.

"What are you doing?" he asks, walking back over to me. "We need to get back to the hotel."

"Do you know what would be a great idea?" I ask, sighing happily. "If we proved just how perfect we are for each other."

Mind buzzing, I'm clearly not thinking straight by this point.

Pulling at Renny's arm, I glance up at him. "You said you'd show me a true Vegas experience."

"I did say that, didn't I," he murmurs, staring down at me and grinning. "We need rings. We can't do this without rings. And we need my brothers here. It isn't a wedding without the Knights."

"All we need is each other," I slur, laughing to myself. "But yeah, we also need those things."

What the fuck.

Dee takes his phone back, and then takes a picture of both of our expressions. "I wish you could see your faces right now," he chuckles, and then presses a few buttons on his phone. "Everyone is going to lose their shit when they see this."

I'm speechless, my mind racing, not knowing how the fuck I have managed to get myself into this situation. Last night I messaged my sister and told her the new plan, that I would be staying here one more night to have a little fun, but there's no way in hell I'm going to tell her about this clusterfuck.

I'm just going to fix this and bury it under the rug, along with memories of the douche lord I lost my virginity to, the fact that I have my ex's name tattooed on my ass and any other generally bad decisions I've made over the years.

Not knowing what to do or how to react to this, I decide to blame the only other person I can. Pointing a finger at Renny's chest, I narrow my eyes and scowl. "This is all your fault."

He rubs the back of his neck. "You just saw the same video as I did. You weren't exactly saying no."

Opening my mouth, and then closing it, I step away from him and puff out a tired breath. "It's fine. We can get it annulled, we didn't even consummate the marriage." I pause and then add, "Did we?"

"Not that I know of," he groans, pushing Dee toward the door. The bastard is still laughing like a fucking hyena. "What time are we leaving?"

"We're waiting for you two," Dee admits. "I'll tell them you'll be ready in thirty? Or do you need longer?"

I'm going to need longer.

"Thirty is fine," Renny grumbles, closing the door on him.

I've got a change of clothes that I luckily shoved in my handbag, and I've never been more grateful to have planned for the unexpected.

"I need to have a shower," I state, moving past him and into the bathroom. When I close the door, I lean my back on it and close my eyes. I can't believe I allowed something like this to happen, and I can't remember the last time I was so reckless.

After stripping down and having a scalding hot shower, wishing it would wash away my sins, I realize I left my bag on the bed and now I have to exit the bathroom in nothing but a towel. I open the door and stick my head out, seeing Renny sitting on the bed with his face in his hands, probably having the same mental lecture I just gave myself in the shower.

"Can you pass me my bag?" I ask him in a soft tone.

He lifts his head and takes me in before standing, picking up my bag and bringing it to me. He looks tired, which is understandable, but I hope that he's going to be okay to ride.

"Do you want to rest? We don't have to leave with everyone else if you're not up for it," I say, taking my bag from his hands and lingering.

"I'm fine," he says. "We slept for seven hours, it's already lunchtime. I'll just get us something to eat before we head off. How are you feeling?"

"In general, or about the whole being a walking cliché and getting drunkenly married in Vegas thing?" I ask in a dry tone, hiking up my towel.

"Both." He grimaces, running his hand through his hair in frustration. "I don't know, tell me what you need from me right now. I'm not good at this shit, so you need to tell me."

I'm not sure what he's asking me exactly, but it sounds like he wants me to tell him what to do to fix this, and to make it all okay. I think the only thing we can do is get our asses home and get an annulment, or whatever we need to do to get unmarried. I'm too hungover to even try to attempt to fix this right now. I just want to get home, survive this bike ride and collapse onto my bed in a pile of relief and regret. What's done is done, and no matter how much we want an instant fix, there's nothing we can do. There's no point stressing about it. It won't help the situation.

"You already trying to work on your communication skills for me, husband," I tease, trying to make light of the situation. "Next you'll be compromising."

He starts laughing then, and I join in.

Sometimes, it's either laugh, or cry.

Chapter Eight

"Do you think after one night he's going to lose fifty percent of his assets?" I hear Dee ask Temper as he puts gas in his bike. Temper simply shakes his head in annoyance. "Renny, say good-bye to your second Harley!"

"Dee, you need to shut the fuck up," Renny replies, gritting his teeth. Dee just laughs; the man must have a death wish.

Temper hasn't said much about the whole thing, and I wonder what's going on in that mind of his. I don't know why, but he's not someone I want to disappoint, and I feel like I haven't really shown him and everyone else the best version of myself on this trip.

"Is Temper angry about what happened?" I ask Renny as he pumps gas into his own bike. "He's been even quieter than usual."

Not that I've spent a lot of time with him, but on the ride here and on our night out, he was a little more open and chatty. Just a little. I don't think he's the overly friendly type.

"No one is angry at you," Renny assures me, frowning. "But

that doesn't mean that they're not going to give us shit from now until the end of time."

"Your assets are safe," I promise, smirking. "I'm the last woman you need to worry about that stuff with. I'm too proud to take anything from a man, or anything I haven't earned myself."

Not to mention with only one night of marriage, I hardly doubt that would hold up in court.

"I know," he murmurs. "Don't listen to Dee. He's an asshole, and he loves to stir up shit. I'm not worried about any of that. I'm just a little pissed because I planned on asking you out on a proper date when we got home, but after this bullshit, you're probably going to run home and never look back."

My eyes widen at his honesty. "You were going to ask me out?"

I don't know why I'm surprised, but I am. There is definitely something between us, I'm not too blind to feel and see that, but we live completely different lives and I don't know if I fit in with his. Yeah, we kissed last night, but we were completely intoxicated, and if we weren't we might have been smarter about the whole thing and not given in to temptation.

Sometimes, the best decision is to walk away instead of getting involved with someone, especially when you know that in the end, it's just not going to work out. If my mom had done that, it might have saved her a world of pain.

And I'm not volunteering myself for any heartbreak.

Been there and done that.

He nods slowly. "Why do you sound surprised? You're beautiful, smart and funny, and you never complain or ask for anything. Not to mention I've been checking you out since the day you moved in."

"I hope you added that line in your vows," I joke, feeling my face heat. "Not that either of us would remember."

I hope no one else remembers either.

Renny studies me for a few seconds, not missing my deflection. "Can I take you out on a proper date one night this week?"

Fuck, he knows how to put me on the spot, doesn't he?

"Well, we are married now, so I guess it's the least we can do," I say, once again using humor as a defense mechanism.

"Izzy—"

"I do like you, Renny," I blurt out, glancing out at the road. "But can we talk about this when we make it home?"

With everything that has happened, my emotions are all over the place.

I also can't think straight when I'm around him. It's like he turns me into this other person and I don't know if that's a good thing or not. He brings out the life in me, but that isn't always the safest way to live. He's also way too good-looking, and yes, that's a thing. Everyone knows you can't trust a man who looks that good. I mean, look at Merve. I just told Renny I like him, laying all my cards out, like I usually do. I was never good at bluffing, but I don't want to play games either.

I do like him.

But this is all a bit much right now.

"Yeah, of course," he replies, brows furrowing. "Do you want me to get you anything? More water? Snacks?"

"No, I'm okay. Thank you." I force a smile.

He's been nothing but a gentleman, and it's not only his fault how this entire thing played out, so I can't hold it against him. It takes two to tango, or two to get married in this case, and I saw the video—no one was holding a gun to my head. In fact, my face screamed *I've won the man lotto!*

I cringe just thinking about it.

"Okay, let me know if you want to stop again," he says, and then we're off.

Riding hungover has to be one of the worst experiences of my life, and all I have to do is hold on for dear life. It's Renny who has to concentrate and make sure that we stay safe.

I rest my cheek against the warm leather of his cut and take a few deep breaths.

I can do this.

Without throwing up on him.

We finally make it home, and when my eyes land on my house I'm so relieved, I almost cry. Renny helps me off the bike and I remove my helmet and hand it back to him.

"Thank you so much for everything," I tell him, staring directly into his eyes. "You saved my ass by getting me to my sister, and I really appreciate it."

"What are husbands for?" he says, then grimaces and rubs the back of his neck. "But seriously, it was no problem at all. I was happy to help. I guess I'll see you around?"

I nod. "Yep, I guess so."

Especially considering we have to get an annulment.

"Bye, Renny," I say, giving him a little wave and then turning toward my door. I'm safely inside when I hear the rumble of his engine driving off. After I message Ariel to let her know that I'm home, I take a long shower and drink a lot of water before jumping into my bed and lying there, enjoying being home.

Ever since I got on Renny's bike, my life has been turned upside down, and it's going to take a little time to process everything.

When I fall asleep, though, I dream about him, and if that doesn't mean something, I don't know what does.

"Hey," I say, opening the door and smiling at him. "How are you?"

"Good," Renny replies, dangling my car keys in front of him. "I brought your car back."

I've spent the last few days catching up on work and life in general, and I've barely even left my house. Mostly because I haven't had my car.

"Thank you. How much do I owe you?" I ask, stepping outside to have a look at the car.

"Nothing," he says. "She should run smoothly from now on, but let me know if you have any more issues."

"What do you mean, nothing?" I ask, frowning. I've always paid my own way, and that's not going to stop now. "Will you please let me pay you? I don't want you to be out of pocket for me."

Brown eyes pin me to my spot. "You owe me nothing, Izzy. Don't worry about it, it didn't cost a lot, and I promise you my bank account won't even notice."

I roll my eyes. "That's not the point." I take a breath, pause and then add, "Seriously, thank you, Renny. I mean it."

"It's not a big deal," he replies, waving it off.

But he's wrong. It *is* a big deal. These days it's rare to find people that are willing to help others without asking for anything in return.

"I owe you one," I tell him quietly, glancing over at him. "I mean it."

"Stop it," he replies, placing the keys in my hand and closing my fingers around them. "I almost forgot," he adds, opening the passenger door and pulling out a brown bag and a coffee. "I brought you something."

"Aren't you the gift that keeps on giving?" I grin, shaking my head. "What have you brought me?"

"Just something to keep you going while you work," he murmurs, scanning my outfit. "Is this your work uniform?"

I glance down at my very well-worn and loved Harry Potter pajamas and then back up at him. "This is me looking fancy." His lip twitches as I take the goods from him. "Would you like to come in?"

"I'd love to."

As he steps inside and closer to me, his familiar scent hits my nostrils and makes me want to rub myself against him. I don't, of course, because that would be weird. And probably be considered assault.

"Cool place you have," he says as he wanders into my domain.

"Thanks. It's my little slice of heaven," I admit, leading him into my living room where the TV is still on, and my laptop is sitting upright on the black leather couch. "And this is where I work. Or sometimes I work in bed. I like to mix things up every now and again."

"You don't have an actual office?" he asks, brow furrowing as he sits down on the couch. He takes up so much space in my house, but I don't know if that's because he's such a commanding presence or because my place is too small to accommodate his big frame.

"I do, but I don't really use it," I say, sitting down and opening the bag to see what he brought me.

"A bagel and doughnuts," he says, watching me.

"You remembered." I had told him before we left that bagels and doughnuts were two of my favorite foods. The fact that he remembered means a lot.

He listened and took note.

I didn't know men like that really existed.

"I remember everything you say," he says with a shrug. "I made sure they put extra cream cheese, too."

"I'm impressed, Renny, I'm not going to lie."

He smirks, and then eyes my laptop screen. "What are you working on today?"

"A company wants me to design a new logo for them, in addition to coming up with a whole new promotional package. So I'm working on that, and some brochures and flyers for them," I explain. "What about you? What do you have on the agenda today?"

"The Knights run a few businesses, and one is a bike shop we just opened. We sell custom bikes, that sort of thing, so I'm working in there today."

Interesting. I've wondered how a motorcycle club like them makes money without doing something illegal.

"Custom bikes, that sounds pretty cool," I say, breaking my bagel and offering him the bigger half.

He takes it, our fingers touching in the exchange. "Yeah, it only just opened, so I'm going to be spending a lot of time there, getting the business on its feet." He takes a big bite and moans. "Fuck, this is actually pretty good. It's been years since I've had one of these."

"Told you." I grin.

"Everyone has been asking when you're going to come over and say hello, so this is me officially inviting you over to the clubhouse for drinks and dinner tomorrow night," he says, licking cream cheese off his finger, brown eyes pinned on me.

That takes me by surprise. I never thought I'd ever go to the clubhouse. But I did have a good time with the guys in Vegas, despite getting married. Uh, yes, I keep forgetting that I'm married to Renny. I guess I should get to know his family.

"I guess I can do that," I find myself agreeing. "What time do you want me over?"

"I'll come get you at like seven, if that works for you?" he suggests.

"It's a two-minute walk. I think I can manage getting there without getting lost," I say, rolling my eyes.

He barks out a laugh. "I know you can manage, but I don't want you walking around alone in the dark."

He stands up and flashes me a smile, like it's all sorted then, even though I didn't agree, and heads to my front door, making a quick exit.

It's only after he's gone that I realize we didn't even discuss getting our annulment. After calling two lawyers and playing phone tag with them, I need to find out where he is on the whole situation so I know what I have to do to move the process along.

We obviously can't just stay married, can we?

Chapter Nine

Wrapping my trench coat around myself, I'm glad I wore jeans tonight as the evening chill hits me. I walk through the vacant land toward the clubhouse. I don't like being told what to do, and if I want to walk myself down the damn street, I'm going to do just that.

I can hear the music before I can see the brown brick building, and I don't miss the extra bikes out front. I have no idea what to expect tonight, but after spending some time with Renny, Temper, Saint and Dee, I don't feel too nervous. If I want to leave, I can at any time, and I know without a doubt that Renny will make sure I'm kept safe.

Safe from anyone except him, that is.

Renegade. What the hell am I going to do with him?

"Izzy?" I hear him call from the open metal fence. "I told you I was going to come and get you!"

He looks good. Black leather boots, black ripped jeans and a black V-neck T-shirt, tattoos covering all of his skin barring his neck and face, and a scowl that should intimidate me, but doesn't.

"And I said I'd be fine walking," I say as he approaches. "And see, I made it alive. All on my own."

"Smartass," he mutters, but grins and offers me his hand. "Come on, let me give you the grand tour."

We pass a few men who nod in our direction, and then enter the large building through a wooden door. "This place is bigger than I thought," I admit.

"There's plenty of space," he agrees. "The backyard is huge, and that's where you'll usually find us. Bedrooms are down there." He points down a hallway. "And the kitchen is through there," he says as he points to a door in the other direction.

The place is surprisingly neat, rustic and has a very bachelor feel to it, but I don't not like it. It has ample space, like he said, and a cool vibe to it.

"Do you want something to drink?" he asks, laughing when I instantly shake my head.

"No thank you, I'm only just getting over that hangover, and the last thing I want is more alcohol. I think I'm going to be sober for the next few months, at least."

"We do have nonalcoholic options," he suggests, handing me a can of soda. "I'm with you, actually. I'm not drinking tonight."

I don't think we could make any worse decisions than last time, but I don't want to test that theory. I just want to hang out with Renny, with my wits about me, and I'm a person who can still have fun without drinking.

"Hey, look who it is!" Dee calls out, coming over and giving me a quick hug. "Welcome."

"Thank you for having me," I say, smiling when I see Skylar coming over.

"Hey, Izzy," she says, pulling me into a warm hug. "Nice to officially meet you, and on much better terms this time. How have you been?"

"Good, and yourself?" I ask her, studying the beautiful woman. With her sharp green eyes and stunning red hair, I don't know who is luckier, her or Saint.

"I'm great. I hear that you tied the knot with a Knight, which means you're family now," she snickers, pulling me aside from the men. "I need to hear the entire story from you, because I know men like to leave shit out." She leads me inside to the kitchen and pulls out a chair for me. "Tell me everything."

"Well," I start, unprepared for this interrogation. "We thought having one night out would be a good idea, because I've never had a wild night out in Vegas, and one thing led to another. We all ended up drinking copious amounts of alcohol, and at some point in the night we walked past a chapel and thought tying the knot was a wonderful idea."

"Man, you must have been seriously wasted," she says, eyes wide.

"Enough that I only remember snippets of the night, and if I didn't see the video footage with my own eyes, probably wouldn't even believe that we were that stupid," I admit, cringing. "This is so out of character for me, I don't even know what to think at this point."

I don't really make rash decisions normally, and I don't usually do spontaneous. I don't know what came over me that night, but no one is more surprised than me.

"So what's going to happen now? Everyone has been giving Renny so much shit, but he hasn't really said much. And you're here now, so does that mean—"

"We aren't going to stay married, no."

"But—"

"I don't even know him," I whisper-yell, shaking my head. "I'm waiting to hear back from a few attorneys that I called. I have no idea how I got here," I admit, covering my face with my hands.

"It's not that bad," she assures me, reaching out to touch my arm. "We're here for you, and we know a great lawyer that can help get it sorted out. Have you heard of Bentley & Channing Law Firm? We can give them a call. I'm sure it's something that can be sorted out fairly easily."

I have heard of them before, or at least I've seen their advertisements on TV and social media, but I didn't call them because I know they are largely out of my price range. I called a few local, smaller law firms and I can't even get a call back from those ones.

"I hope so," I say, frowning.

"It will be sorted," she promises. "But are you sure that's what you want to do?"

I move my hand away from my eyes and look at her. "Yes, I'm sure. I know Renny is a very sexy man, but if I ever get married let's just say I want a cuter, more romantic story to tell instead of we got drunk and couldn't remember getting married, but we did it anyway. That screams more that we are irresponsible alcoholics rather than cute and romantic."

Skylar laughs, her shoulders shaking. "You're hilarious. You're gonna fit in here so easily. And I'm happy to have another woman around the place, because the sausage fest is getting old."

I almost choke on my mouthful of soda.

She just grins. "What? It's true."

"Tell me about him," I say, wanting to learn all that I can about my current husband.

"I know that he's been a member ever since he turned eighteen," she starts, running her index finger along her bottom lip. "Saint trusts him with his life. The MC is his family. He's always been a bit of a joker, and somewhat distant if I'm being honest. Still waters run deep. I think that you're going to see a side of him that none of us have," she says like she's contemplating something. "Oh, and he's had a crush on you since you moved in. At least that's what I've heard."

I smile at her last comment. "I've never met anyone like him," I admit, considering her words. The man definitely lives and breathes the MC, something that will have a huge impact on us if we progress into something.

"Renny is a good man though, that I can promise you," she continues, looking me in the eye. "I trust him completely."

I don't admit that I already agree. "Well, I suppose that's good considering he's my—"

I glance out the window, and see something that makes any humor slide away from my face. "Who is that sitting next to my husband?"

Skylar lifts her head to look in my line of sight. "I don't know. Want to go out and find out?"

I do, and I don't.

He's not mine, I mean, I guess he is legally, for now, but he's not really mine. Still...

"Yeah, let's go out there," I decide. Whether he's mine or not, he invited me here tonight, and there's no way in hell I'm hanging around if he's going to be sitting there and flirting with other women in front of me. We both stand up and head back outside, which has now filled up with more people, laughter and chatting almost overpowering the music.

I sit down right across from Renny, who smiles with his eyes as they land on me. He puts his phone away, as if to give me his full attention. I check out his new friend, who is chattering away, and arch my brow at him. Skylar sits down next to me and stares at him, having my back.

Renny looks confused for a second, but then glances next to him, eyes widening with realization. He instantly shakes his head. "Seriously? You think I'm going to flirt with a woman in front of the woman I want and am trying to impress?" he asks me, lip twitching. "I've got balls, Izzy, but I'm not that stupid." He looks to the woman next to him. "This is...uhhh."

"Bec," she inserts, frowning. "I was just introducing myself to all the men."

"I bet you were," Skylar says, rolling her eyes. "Renny is married. See that ring on his finger?"

I'm surprised that he's still wearing the ring, considering that

I took mine off when we got back here. Maybe he hasn't really thought about it, or maybe he's just owning it to his friends.

"I was just saying hello," Bec backtracks, placing her hands up in surrender. She stands and then walks away, sitting down next to Dee instead. Much safer territory.

"Never pictured you as the jealous type," Renny mutters, unable to wipe the grin away from his face. "I kind of like it."

"I wasn't jealous," I assure him. "I just wanted to make sure my hubby wasn't out here making me look stupid by entertaining some other woman."

His expression sobers at that comment, and he leans forward and takes my hand in his. "I only have eyes for you, Izzy. I'm not here to waste anyone's time. I'm too old for that shit, all right? Women are easy to find, but women like you? They're rare. You are rare. And you wouldn't be here right now, around my family, if that didn't mean something to me. I know we don't know each other well yet, so I'm going with my gut here, and just from what I've seen from you so far. I'm trusting that you're being as genuine as I think you are."

Swallowing hard, I nod, feeling a little sheepish, and lift my soda up at him. "To you not being stupid."

Skylar laughs out loud. "I love this girl already."

"Hopefully she sticks around," Renny replies, eyes locked on mine.

I wasn't planning on it, but I keep getting in deeper and deeper with this man. I'm so attracted to him, but it's more than that. He intrigues me, and the more I learn the more I want to know.

"Well, I'm here, aren't I?" I remind him, smiling at Saint when he comes over and pulls Skylar onto his lap.

"What have I missed?" he asks, nuzzling her neck.

"Nothing much, just the cutest interaction with a woman I've ever seen Renny have," she says, sighing heavily. "You two are super sweet."

"Never thought I'd hear the words *Renny* and *cute* in the same sentence," Saint mutters, looking over at his friend and slapping him on the back. "Another one bites the dust, hey, brother."

"And they got married before us," Skylar points out, frowning. "You need to up your game, Saint."

Saint cups her face and kisses her. I don't know if it's to shut her up or what, but it works. "Our time will come. For now let the newlyweds have their moment."

I can only imagine how much grief the MC must have been giving Renny, but he seems to take it well. Or at least he does when I'm around. Who knows what he's thinking and saying when I'm not?

I never thought that I'd be one to have trust issues, but with the dating scene how it is and with Renny being so good-looking, and a biker... I don't know, it's just a little hard to believe that he's all for me. I don't even have low self-esteem or anything like that. It's just my brain working overtime, not wanting to get hurt or to be made a fool of.

I know that love doesn't work like that, and I need to be in it to win it, so to speak. I need to put myself out there and hope I made the right choice in Renny. I didn't even realize until this moment that I actually wanted to try to make a relationship with him work. Over the last few days I did a lot of overthinking and told myself that nothing else was going to happen between us, but the second he comes to my house and invites me over, here I am.

"So where are we going on our honeymoon, hubby? I've always wanted to go to Croatia," I tease, taking a sip of my drink and staring up at him.

Saint barks out a laugh. "When you're married to someone on probation, I think the only places you can travel to are within the country, Izzy."

What?

Well, shit.

Chapter Ten

"I think this is how we got into this mess in the first place," I laugh, letting Renny spin me around and dance against me. Hours later and the party is still in full swing, and I'm having a great night. "I'm having flashbacks."

"I think you might be right," he says into my ear, hands on my waist, my back pressed against his hard chest. "It's not my fault that you're such a good dancer."

"You're not so bad yourself, but you already know that, don't you?" I say coyly, raising my arms above my head and behind me, so that I'm holding on to the back of his neck. "It's nice to see that we're still like this without the aid of liquid courage."

He chuckles. "That wasn't even a concern for me. I was just worried the whole thing scared you off, because I don't think you're usually the reckless type, which makes me the bad influence."

"You are right there," I say, spinning around to face him. "You're definitely the bad influence in this marriage."

He smirks and softly cups my cheek. "Never gets old saying

that, does it? Never thought I'd get married at all, never mind this week."

"Why not?" I ask him, curious. "Not the commitment type?"

"No, I don't think it was that. I can definitely commit, for the right woman, and be loyal and all of that. I guess it's just been a long-ass time since someone piqued my interest, so I was losing hope."

"Yeah, I'm sure you were sobbing, alone," I mutter, rolling my eyes. "Don't play innocent, Renegade, it doesn't suit you."

His smirk grows. "Never claimed I was innocent. However, there is a deeper side to me, if you look through all the bullshit."

"Buried deep in there, is it?" I ask, tone laced with humor.

"Very deep, just how I like it," he whispers into my ear, pulls back and winks at me.

I shake my head. "You're something else, you know that?"

"Hey, you married me," he reminds me, not for the first time. "Not that we were coherent, but you know…"

"Skylar was saying you guys know some top lawyers that can sort our little situation out."

He places my hand over his heart. "Ouch. So desperate to get rid of me? That hurts, Izzy."

"Not as much as it's going to hurt if my sister finds out what happened," I groan, wincing at the thought. "We'll both be dead. She won't care if I'm her baby sister and you're a badass biker, we're both going down."

"One problem at a time," he says. "Look, I know the situation isn't ideal and I'll speak to a lawyer about sorting our shit out this week."

"Thank you."

"But I want to keep seeing you," he continues. "What are you doing tomorrow night? How about we go out for dinner?"

"Okay," I reply without hesitation.

"Okay?" He actually sounds surprised, which is endearing.

I nod. "Yeah, okay. Why, do you want me to put up a fight or something? Trust me, I considered it. But I like you, too, okay, and there's no point fucking around and pretending I don't. Our story isn't starting off in the traditional sense…"

But no true love story ever is.

He flashes his straight, white teeth at me. "You won't regret it."

"Famous last words," I reply, laughing as he dips me back, my hair flowing and almost touching the ground.

Apparently I'm a little more flexible than I thought I was.

We have something to eat, and I chat about nothing and everything with Skylar and the rest of the men.

"I basically grew up in the clubhouse," Skylar tells me, explaining how she ended up here with Saint. "My mom used to be the former president's—" her face crumbles a bit "—old lady. Hammer was the only dad I've ever known, but I moved away when I was in my teens. He passed away last year. And then Temper took over."

I don't miss the flash of pain in her eyes that she quickly tries to mask.

"I'm sorry to hear that," I say, ducking my head. "I know what it's like to lose a parent, and yeah…" Tears prickle my eyes as I think of my mom. "It's the worst thing anyone can go through."

When I lift my eyes Skylar smiles sadly at me. "I'm sorry that we share that."

"Me, too," I whisper. "So how did you connect with Saint?"

"Well, Mom moved me away for a few years and I had no contact with the MC or my dad, until Saint wrote me a letter." She pauses, and then adds, "From prison, actually."

Skylar mentioning prison reminds me about Renny being on parole—something I haven't asked him about yet.

"Why did you lose contact with them?" I ask her, brow furrowing.

"Mom didn't want me to have anything to do with them," she admits, lips tightening. "It's a long and complicated story, but when Hammer broke up with her, she didn't want them to have any contact with me, either. But I came back and fell in love with Saint, who I had the biggest crush on as a teenager, and the rest is history."

"That's quite the story," I tell her, eyes widening and processing everything Skylar has been through.

"Ever think you'd be here?" Temper asks me as he sits down, catching the end of the conversation. I noticed that he's been nursing his one beer all night. Maybe he's not much of a drinker, but I don't miss the fact that he's always scanning the group, as if making sure everything is okay. I know he's the president of the MC, but is this what being president means? Always being on alert, always watching. I wonder if he ever takes a break.

"No," I admit, leaning back and studying him. "I'd hear the music from afar, but never once did I think I'd be inside these walls. It's a whole different world over here."

"Feel free to bring all of your hot friends over," Dee says as he walks over, winking. "You know what they say, the more the merrier."

"I don't know if that counts for STDs," I fire back, making everyone laugh.

Dee's jaw drops open, and then he bursts out laughing, too. "And I thought you were a nice girl."

"I am, but not too nice. I don't think I could survive here if I wasn't."

More laughter, but I'm being dead serious. The men love to tease and joke. But I'm learning that anyone who is overly sensitive wouldn't last here, not to mention that I feel like everyone in here can sense weakness. The men are all strong, and I've only met Skylar, but I can tell she is, too.

"Ain't that the truth," Renny agrees, studying me. "We've all been through a lot here, and our brotherhood comes with a price."

"And what price is that?" I ask unwaveringly, but I already know.

Trouble.

That's the price.

These men aren't saints even though one of them is named such, and I can only imagine the type of things they have to deal with on a daily basis. Yet when I sit here with all of them, I don't feel scared, or worried. I just feel like I'm hanging out with a bunch of friends. I feel safe, at least with Renny next to me, and I know that he will do anything to protect me.

I've never felt that with any man before, my father included.

I've never had a boyfriend I just knew would jump in front of a bullet for me, one I could trust infinitely. Hell, other than my sister, I don't have anyone I would trust on that level. It's a powerful feeling, and it gives me strength.

Although being around the MC would mean that my chances of getting hurt or being put in danger increase drastically, I can't help but like being here.

Maybe that makes me crazy, but it also makes me feel alive.

And for someone like me, who simply breezes through life being as closed off as I can, that is *huge*.

"Where do I start?" Renny asks, touching the stubble on his cheek with his palm. "Any time one of us has a problem, it becomes all of our problems, so let's just say we deal with a lot of shit on a daily basis."

"You trying to scare me off now, Renny?" I ask, arching my brow. "I thought you brought me here tonight to try and make me give you a real chance."

"She's bold," Dee mutters, shaking his head. "Fuckin' bold."

"Just letting you know what you're getting into," Renny says, pushing my hair back behind my ear. "So you can't say that I didn't warn you further down the line."

"Warning noted," I reply, looking around at the group. "How about the rest of you? Have any other warnings for me?"

"Yeah, Renny snores," Temper informs me, eyes filled with amusement. "And he's the main reason we have to get a fuckin' cleaning service coming in, because when he cooks, he trashes the whole kitchen."

"But he does cook, right?" I ask, sounding hopeful to even my own ears.

"I can cook," he assures me, laughing softly. "Is that important to you?"

"Well, I like to eat," I reply with a shrug. "And yeah, it's kind of sexy when a man knows his way around a kitchen."

And a clitoris, but I'll save that one for another time.

"Maybe I should cook for you tomorrow night then," he says so only I can hear. "Blow you away with my skills."

That actually does sound kind of nice, and a little more personal than just going out for dinner. "Okay, sounds good. There was actually something I wanted to ask you."

"What is it?"

"Well, it was mentioned that you were on parole. Care to clear that up for me?" I ask, studying him.

He licks his lips before he speaks. "I *am* on parole, but only for another few months."

"He got into a fight," Dee adds, shrugging like it happens every day. "For assault."

My eyes widen.

"They started it," Renny grumbles, watching me.

"They?"

"Yeah, there were three of them, and somehow I'm the one who was arrested for it," he replies, scowling.

"So three against one and somehow you're the bad guy?" I ask, frowning.

"I'm a Knight," is all he replies. "Goes with the territory."

I know these men aren't all sugar and spice, but that sounds kind of unfair. I guess when you're in this world and your reputation precedes you, it does go with the territory. However, never in my wildest dreams did I imagine I'd be married to someone who has any kind of criminal record.

Renny did try to warn me away, so I'm not going into this blind.

The messed-up part? Despite the revelation, all I can think

about is our date, and whether he is going to cook for me here, with everyone around. That wouldn't exactly be romantic, and I imagine everyone will also want to eat, so it wouldn't exactly be a date. Still, it's his date to plan, so I don't say anything.

Hopefully he thinks things through, especially if his aim truly is to blow me away.

Renny walks me back home around midnight, and even though the party is nowhere near being over, it was time for me to leave and get some sleep.

"I didn't realize how loud our music is until right now," he admits as I search in my handbag for my house keys. "I'm surprised you haven't called the cops in the past."

"It doesn't bother me," I say, opening the door. "Would you like to come in, or do you have to get back to the party?"

"I can come in," he murmurs, stepping inside with me and closing the door behind him.

I know I shouldn't have invited him in, but I guess I'm not ready to say goodbye just yet. "I'm going to make coffee. Do you want one?"

"I'd love one," he says, following me into the kitchen and sitting down on my wooden barstool. "Being the only sober people at a party requires a lot of patience."

"It does, but at least we will remember everything that everyone did and said and can give them shit about it tomorrow," I say, grinning. "It's one of my favorite things to do."

"You're evil," he states, eyes flashing with approval. "I knew I liked you for a reason. Well, other than your good looks, kindness and intelligence…"

"How do you know I'm kind and intelligent?" I ask, arching my brow in challenge.

"Well, let's see, you dropped everything and ran to help your sister, the way you speak about people, the kindness in your eyes… I could go on. And intelligence? Again, the way you speak. The fact that you run your own business means you must be talented. And before you ask, I Googled you so I've seen your website and images of some of the work you have done. Temper even said we should ask you to design a new MC logo for us."

My eyes widen at his reply. Not only is he extremely observant, but he looked me up. While it could be considered a bit stalkerish, who hasn't Googled someone they've dated? "You're a little bit cute, you know that?"

"I do now," he whispers, coming up behind me and wrapping his arms around me. "I don't know what the fuck you've done to me, girl."

"I've done nothing."

Yet. And that word lingers between us.

Turning around I lift up on my tiptoes as he lowers his face, our lips close but not touching. This is that point, the one that I won't be able to come back from.

I make the first move.

Pressing my lips against his, my eyes flutter closed as we kiss. I know we kissed that night in Vegas, but for me, this counts as our first official kiss, because that whole night is a blur. As my heart begins to race, I know it's one I'm never going to regret.

He cups the back of my neck and takes control of the kiss, his soft lips mastering mine, his tongue gently dancing with mine.

My head starts to feel dizzy, lost in his taste, scent and touch, and when he pulls away with those brown eyes looking into my soul... I know that I'm in big fucking trouble.

"You're so beautiful," he murmurs, scanning my face. "I better let you get some sleep. Big day in the office tomorrow?"

"Something like that." I grin, leaning into him and resting my cheek against his chest. "You smell good. I wanted to tell you that all night."

"Why didn't you?" he asks, tone amused. "I guess I wanted to tell you that you looked stunning all night, but I didn't either."

"Really? I was the most clothed person there," I point out, laughing.

"And still the most attractive," he replies, kissing the top of my head. "I don't know. I guess we're both still testing the waters with each other because we don't know where we stand. It's not the easiest of positions to be in. I mean, we're technically married, but not actually together. And I don't really know what the fuck I'm supposed to be doing. I know what I want, but you kind of need to be on board with that, too. We both need to actually communicate with each other and tell each other what we want, up front, no fucking around."

"I know what you mean. I never thought of it like that, but you're right."

Married but not together. Now I understand why people are so into that show *Married at First Sight*. I always thought it was the lamest idea. But now I'm proof that maybe, just maybe, there is something to it.

I laugh internally—I sound like an idiot.

And he's also right about our communication. I think we've both tried to let our actions do the talking, but we both are kind of unsure on where the other is at, because no one has straight out said what they are feeling.

"I want you," he declares. "And this is me telling you, no mixed signals, no nothing. I want to try to see if this can be something."

"I want that, too," I reply, swallowing. "And I have to be honest, I'm not the best at talking out my feelings or giving compliments. I'll think them but sometimes won't say anything, almost like I'm a little shy to. It's something I'm trying to work on," I admit.

My ex-boyfriend Leo always said that I never said nice things about him. I thought he was ridiculous and that he just wanted me to stroke his ego, which I wasn't going to do. But I've realized that I could have been more complimentary. Everyone likes to hear that they are doing well or that they are attractive, and I know that now.

I have to remind myself to do it, though. I'm lost in my own head a lot, and sometimes it's hard for me to be present. I think this is because I don't feel like I need many compliments. I mean, they are nice to hear, but I don't need them. Mom complimented me like any doting parent would, but my dad never did, always pushing us to do better and achieve more. Like nothing was ever good enough. As a result, I taught myself that I never needed to hear praise, which I think made me stronger. But as an indirect result, I in turn never give compliments either.

"You have a shy side?" he jokes, eyes smiling. "No, I know what you mean. Everyone has little issues with communication, but if you know what they are then you're already ahead of most people. I know that when I get angry I tend to just walk away to calm down instead of talking it out, which a lot of women don't like. But I prefer to have a clear head before I have a proper conversation, or who knows what the fuck will come out of my mouth."

"That's probably a blessing in disguise then." I grin, reaching up to touch his leather cut. "I have a lot of pride, and I know it's supposed to be a good thing, but I can tell you now that it's a flaw. Add being stubborn and I'm not always the easiest person to be around."

"Sounds like you're warning me now."

"Well, now you can't tell me that I didn't warn you," I reply, winking at him.

He smiles and kisses me again, and then I'm smiling against his lips in return, and all is right in the world.

After we linger for the next hour or so, I walk him to the door.

"Make sure you lock it," he tells me, stepping through the threshold of the door, but then leans in for another quick kiss, as if he's unable to help himself.

After he goes, I rest my back against the door, grinning like an idiot, touching my lower lip with my thumb.

I feel like a fucking schoolgirl with her first crush.

After a quick shower, I jump in bed, listening to the music from the clubhouse until I fall asleep.

Chapter Eleven

"So I've started packing up the house," Ariel tells me, and I can hear Mila making little noises in the background. "Are you sure you are still okay with us moving in?"

"Yes, of course," I assure her. Ariel and Mila are the only family I have left, and I can't wait until they are here.

"Are *you* sure you don't want me to come back and help you?" I ask, not for the first time.

"Yes, you have your own life there, Izzy, don't worry about me. I'm fine. I'm just taking my time and enjoying this stage with Mila, you know? How is everything over there? What's new with the biker gang?" she asks.

"It's not a gang," I grumble, then roll over onto my stomach on the bed, my shoulder holding the phone to my ear. "Yeah, I might have gone there last night for a party."

I hold my breath waiting for her reply.

"You went to the clubhouse?" she asks, not sounding angry or even surprised, maybe just resigned to my current situation. "How was it? What happened? You're clearly alive to tell the tale."

"Yes, I'm very alive," I reply, rolling my eyes. "It was just a really cool party with all the Knights, and a few women were there. Good music, and good food…"

"And good eye candy?"

I picture Renny. "Yeah, definitely good eye candy."

"I can't believe that after living next to them for so long you're finally friends with them. Or is it more than friends with Renny because you're purposely not mentioning him?"

No one knows how to call me out on my shit like my sister.

"I like him," I tell her. "Nothing has happened besides a kiss, but he's cooking me dinner tonight, so we will see how it goes."

"Stay safe, all right? Don't do anything stupid."

"I'm not going to do anything more stupid than I already have," I promise.

I mean, is there anything more stupid than getting drunk and marrying a near stranger?

Oh actually, yes, there is—not telling your big sister about it.

"Good," she sighs. "You know I worry about you."

"And I worry about you, too. Any more run-ins with Mila's sperm donor, or is he back to being MIA?"

"Haven't heard anything from him. It's been peaceful," she admits. "I only hope it stays that way and I'm gone by the time he decides he needs another photo to show his family on his social media."

"It pisses me off that he's probably playing father of the year to them. Meanwhile, he hasn't done a damn thing for Mila," I growl, wishing the man would just disappear from their lives already.

"I know, but he's her father, and that's never going to change. We're going to have to always be the bigger person, for Mila, and to set an example for her. We can't talk badly about him in front of her. That's half of her, whether we like it or not," she says, ever so wise.

"So mature, Ariel, I'm proud of you," I tell her. "But I'm way

pettier than you, and she's a baby right now and won't understand what we're saying."

She laughs out loud. "You're right, we can speak freely until
she does."

"I miss you," I say, smiling at the sound of her laughter. "I
can't wait until you're finally here. We can grow old together."

"What about Renny?" she asks.

"He can live in the garage."

We both laugh at that.

"It's still early times with Renny. I don't know what's going
to happen," I admit. "I don't want to have too high expectations because then there's a chance that I'm going to get hurt,
but the way he's making me feel right now... I didn't know if
I was ever going to meet someone that was going to make me
feel that way. You know what I'm usually like with guys—I
can take or leave them. It doesn't affect me that much, but the
way it's going with Renny... I think he could really hurt me."

"You're such an Aquarius," she mutters. "And I know, he
seems different for you, which is why it's so scary. And he's not
exactly the man I would have chosen for you. I mean, couldn't
you go for a lawyer or a doctor or something? I don't know."

"Easy paths are boring," I respond, laughing. "I didn't choose
this, though, Ariel. He fell into my lap. He literally came to the
front of my house and into my life. And now that he's here, I
don't want to go back to how it was before him."

"I don't think I've ever heard you speak about a man like
this," she says, sighing. "You usually just brush it off. I just hope
you know what you're doing, Izzy. I'm too old to go around
punching your exes in the face; this isn't high school anymore.
And Renny is no Larry."

I snicker remembering when my sister punched a boy named
Larry in the face after he broke up with me because I wouldn't
sleep with him in tenth grade. "I forgot all about that. You're
such a good sister, you know that? I don't know what I would
have done if I didn't have you looking out for me."

Renny is definitely a whole different ballgame than Larry, but I still don't see Ariel backing down. She's a gentle soul, but when someone she loves gets hurt, she goes into mama bear mode, and nothing or no one can save you from her.

"You looked out for me, too," she says, and I can hear the smile in her voice. "Especially when Mom died."

We go silent for a few moments.

After we say our goodbyes and hang up, I'm about to open my laptop and start my work for the day when there's a knock at the door.

When I open it and see Renny standing there with a bouquet of flowers, I can't wipe the smile off my face.

"Good morning," he says, handing me the beautiful sunflowers. "I'll be here at seven to pick you up, if that works for you?"

"Good morning, and thank you, these are beautiful," I tell him, bringing the flowers to my nose. "And I can just walk over again you know. It's literally down the road."

"We aren't going to the clubhouse," he says with a wolfish grin. "I'm going to take you to my apartment."

"You have an apartment?" I ask, brows furrowing in confusion. "Since when?"

"Since always," he says, putting his hands in his pockets. "I'm hardly there because I'm always at the clubhouse, but when I want a little peace and quiet, that's where I go."

"I was wondering how a romantic evening would work at the clubhouse," I admit. "I was going to tell you that we could come here but you didn't say anything, so neither did I."

"Who said it was going to be romantic?" he asks with a straight face. "I was actually going to make you cook and clean while I played video games."

I roll my eyes. "Try me, I dare you."

He laughs and glances out at his motorcycle, which is sitting pretty on my driveway. "I better get to work, but I just wanted to tell you that I'm looking forward to tonight, and that you look beautiful, and I hope you have a productive day on the couch."

He's standing here in his faded jeans, white T-shirt and boots, and saying everything right. If he doesn't leave soon, I might be having a productive day on the couch, all right.

With him. Under him. All over him.

"Don't look at me like that," he says, brown eyes narrowed to slits. "You're trouble, you know that?"

"Says the outlaw biker," I fire back, distracting myself by smelling the flowers once more. "I can't help it if I find you attractive, and really fucking cute when you do stuff like this. I don't think I've ever gotten 'just because' flowers before, but I've read about them."

Not to mention this is my first time seeing him in something other than black, and it looks good on him.

"You'll be getting them so much now that you'll be sick of them," he promises, leaning forward and giving me a sweet, sensual, yet way too quick kiss. "See you tonight."

"Yes you will," I murmur, staring at his tight ass as he walks away.

I close the door and find a vase for the flowers, suddenly too excited and giddy to concentrate on work.

I need to find something to wear tonight, and it needs to be amazing.

Because tonight is the night I'm going to consummate my marriage.

Chapter Twelve

Crossing the road with my hands full of shopping bags, I enjoy actually being out of the house, wind in my hair and sunshine on my face. After treating myself to a movie and lunch, which is something I know most people don't enjoy doing on their own but something I do for some me time every now and again, I head down the main shopping area in the city, only to be confronted with a hell of a lot of drama.

Pressing myself against the wall of a clothing store, I watch with a crowd as three police officers try to arrest two resisting bikers, a fistfight breaking out in the middle of the street. I eye the bikes and leather cuts and wonder who they are. Even if they were Knights, I wouldn't recognize them, knowing nothing about the patches on their cuts and unable to see their backs to search for the Knights emblem.

A child scurries past me, crying, with no adult around, so I bend down and speak to him. "Are you okay?"

"I can't find my mom," he cries.

"Come here," I tell him, pulling him next to me. "I'll help you find her. Let's just wait until it's safe to walk through."

Maybe I can even tell one of the police officers once the men are both safely arrested.

The little boy stops crying, thankfully, probably feeling a little safer now instead of being lost in a crowd. "What's your name?" I ask.

"Billy," he replies, just as I hear the gunshots.

Grabbing him, I pull him in the direction I just came from, away from the crowd and chaos going on in the middle of the street. Everyone is in a panic, women screaming and trying to usher their children out safely. I've never seen anything like this before and my first instinct is to get the hell out of there.

With my back against the wall of a building and Billy crying beside me, I take a deep breath and try to calm myself. I don't know how much time passes, ten, fifteen minutes maybe, but the whole time my mind is running.

Is this normal for bikers? Do they just not care about any kind of authority? Or public safety? What if these men are Renny's friends?

All these questions are running through my head as a blonde woman comes running over to us and pulls Billy into her arms.

"Thank God you're okay. I told you not to wander away from me, Billy. It's not safe." She glances up at me. "Thank you so much."

"No problem," I tell her, forcing a smile. "I think I'm going to go home now, because that's enough drama for one day."

She stands and nods. "The bikers have been arrested and taken away in the police car now, so it's safe. The Destined Killers MC is nothing but no-good criminals. It's not safe to even walk around here anymore." She takes her son and leaves.

Destined Killers MC?

They sound like a lovely bunch.

This is the same brush all bikers are painted with, including the Knights, but it just reminds me that I have no idea who they are. They could have a whole different side to them that

I don't know about, and it would be naïve of me to think that they didn't.

"What are you doing, Isabella?" I ask myself as I get into my car.

Deep down I know Renny isn't like that, though. I'd like to think I'm a good judge of character and I haven't picked up on any vibes from him or any of his friends.

He's been nothing but kind to me, and has given me no reason not to trust him.

I need to go with my gut on this one.

And just hope that one day it's not going to be the Knights on the road getting arrested.

"Holy shit," are the first words out of his mouth when he sees me. "I'm not taking you on the bike in that."

I glance down at my short, long-sleeved yellow floral dress and block heels, and frown. I forgot about the whole bike thing. "We can just take my car," I suggest, smiling when I look back up at him and see his eyes still on my legs. It's probably the first time he's seen them bare, besides the time he saw me in a bikini, because I'm usually in jeans.

"Yeah, maybe we should do that," he murmurs, giving me another long once-over. "You look…"

Grabbing my handbag and keys, I try and contain my amusement at his reaction and step outside with him. He offers me his hand, and I take it. I unlock the door, but he opens it for me. "Such a gentleman," I note.

"Not many people would agree with that." He smirks. "You don't mind me driving your car?"

"Not at all," I reply.

He waits until I'm inside before closing the door and heading over to the driver's side. It's weird sitting in your own car with someone else driving, and it's not the best car to start with, and I'm sure he's used to driving much better.

"You need a new car," he says, obviously on the same thought process as me. "This just doesn't seem like something you should be driving."

"It's vintage," I tell him, frowning. "I've had it for years; it's become like a member of the family."

"Well, sometimes family members retire," he says, pulling out of my driveway. "And that doesn't mean we love them any less."

I laugh at that. "You have something to say for everything, don't you?"

"As if you don't," he fires back. "You give as good as you get, and I like that."

"Do you only wear black or white?" I ask, taking in his long-sleeve black sweater and dark jeans.

"No, sometimes I mix things up and wear gray, or navy blue," he replies, eying my bright dress. "Do you ever wear black?"

I nod. "Yeah, my wardrobe has a little bit of everything."

"I like your bright clothes," he admits, shrugging. "It's like a dose of happiness. That's why I got you the sunflowers. They're bright and happy…like you, and pretty much the opposite of me."

"Opposites attract," I say, reaching out and resting my hand on his thigh, a pretty bold move for me. Without missing a beat, he holds my hand, acting like it's something that we do every day. "So what's on the menu tonight?"

"I'm going to make us steak with creamy prawns on top, mashed potatoes, corn and salad," he recites. "And garlic bread."

My eyes widen. "That sounds delicious. And like a lot of food."

"Yeah, so I hope you're hungry."

It's only about a ten-minute drive to his apartment, and I can tell from the outside that it's quite a flashy place by the sheer size of it, and how new the building looks. He parks in his allocated bay and opens the door for me, helping me out of the car. I tug on the hem of my dress as I get out, then walk next to him to the elevator.

"So how many nights a week do you spend here?" I ask him, wondering why he even has his place.

"Maybe once a week? I don't know, it just depends, really," he replies, pressing the button for level ten. "The clubhouse can be filled with so many people at different times, it's just nice to have my own space I can retreat to if need be. Many of the members have their own investment properties and houses, and this is just one I decided to keep for me to use."

Just one of his? Just how much money does the MC have? Now don't get me wrong, I'm no gold digger, and everything I have I've worked my ass off for, but the fact that they are so loaded has me wondering exactly how they make so much money for each member. Or is Renny already independently rich with family money or something like that? Either way, it doesn't bother me, but it does have me curious.

When he opens the door to his apartment and gestures for me to enter, I'm taken aback by how big and lavish the place is. It doesn't look like any other apartment I've been to, with spacious rooms, a stunning white-and-marble kitchen and all light-colored furnishings.

"Did you decorate this place yourself?" I ask him, jaw dropping. "It's beautiful. It looks like a display home."

"No. I hired someone and told them the vision I wanted, though," he admits, pulling a seat out for me at the kitchen table. "Have a seat. Can I get you something to drink? Wine?"

"I'd love a glass of red," I tell him, still taking in my surroundings, in awe of this man's second home. He pours me a glass and sets it in front of me, then starts pulling out ingredients from the fridge.

"Do you want me to help with anything?" I ask, looking toward the hallway, wondering what the rest of the apartment looks like.

"Would you like a tour? You can go have a snoop if you like while I start on dinner," he says, laughing softly.

"Do you mind?"

"Go ahead," he says. "My bedroom is on the right."

"What makes you think that's what I wanted to see?" I call out as I head straight there. I hear him laugh as I open his door and take in the huge four-poster bed. While the rest of the house is light, decorated in white, creams and crystal, his bedroom is the epitome of a man cave, in dark mahogany, leather and furs.

"I hope that fur is fake," I mutter to myself, stepping inside and even having a look in his bathroom, which has the nicest, biggest shower I've ever seen, with two heads and plenty of space for more than one person. If there was an orgy shower, this would be it, which suddenly has me feeling a little suspicious. What if this place is like his sex den, the spot he takes women so he has some privacy and quiet away from the MC?

I suddenly want to set the place on fire.

After checking out the guest room and the laundry, I head back to the kitchen and sit back down. "That's a big shower you have there. How many people can you fit in it?" I ask, eyes slightly narrowed.

Back to me, he laughs. "I don't know, that's never been tested, but it is pretty roomy. I'm guessing you think it's a bit much?"

"No, it's beautiful," I tell him, tone not as enthusiastic as it was when we first arrived.

"But?" he prompts, leaving the stove and moving in front of me. He scans my eyes and then tilts his head to the side. "What's going on in that head of yours?"

"It looks like you designed it for orgies," I blurt out, unable to help myself.

He studies me for a few seconds, and then starts laughing out loud. "Fuckin' hell, Izzy, it was not designed for orgies. I just wanted a big shower. I'm a big man and I like to have some space, and yeah, it's a bit over the top, but why the fuck not?"

"Just saying," I reply, backtracking and feeling stupid now. I clearly have a worry that Renny is some kind of ladies' man, and that he's been with a lot of women, which—even if he has been, I know it's not fair to hold against him, long as he knows how to be loyal when in a relationship. I mean, I've only slept with three men, so my experience might pale in comparison to his, but I still know what I'm doing in the bedroom, so I shouldn't feel nervous. Maybe I'm just trying to self-sabotage, looking for a reason to walk away from this before I get hurt.

"I've never brought a woman here before, Izzy," he says, leaning over the counter, his face in front of mine, our bodies not touching but our eyes connected. "So if that's what you're worried about, this isn't some secret place I take women for sex. This is my space, and no one has been here besides Saint, who came here looking for me because there was a fuckin' emergency and they needed me."

"I'm sorry," I say, leaning forward and pressing my forehead against his. "I shouldn't assume."

"I'm not an angel, and I've never claimed to be one," he says, pulling back and watching me. "But I'm also not the devil." He grins, flashing me his teeth. "Now I better finish cooking, or you're going to be a very hungry woman."

"Let me help," I say, getting up and moving next to him. "What do you want me to do?"

"You can make the salad, if you like," he suggests, giving me something to do other than overthink. I get the ingredients out and start to make a Greek salad, popping a square of feta cheese in my mouth along the way. Renny puts some music on his phone and the two of us work in the kitchen together.

"We make a pretty good team," he notes as he serves us the plates.

"We do," I agree. "And the food looks amazing."

I only did the salad, the rest was all him, and it's clear he knows what he's doing in the kitchen. I'm impressed.

He's so much more than just a pretty face.

He refills my glass of wine and we dive in. "This steak is amazing."

"It would have been better if you didn't want it burnt."

"Medium to well-done isn't burnt," I say, rolling my eyes. "I haven't had any meat since Vegas."

"How come?"

"I cut down my meat consumption. So I still eat it, just less regularly. Some nights a week I'll have vegetarian meals, too. I like to mix it up a little," I explain.

"You make everything so complicated," he muses, shaking his head at me. "Next time I'll make you my stuffed mushrooms. You'll love those if you're partial to vegetarian dishes."

He's already talking about next time, which makes me smile.

After we finish up, I try to help Renny clean, but he doesn't let me. "I thought you're the messy one, that's what Temper said," I say.

"You remembered that, did you?" he asks, smirking. "I'm trying to be a little better trained, so I cleaned as I went this time. If I don't, the whole kitchen gets trashed, which is probably what he was talking about."

"Hey, if that's the only shit he could find on you, I'd say you're doing quite well," I tease.

"I forgot about the dessert," he murmurs, pulling out ice cream bars from the freezer. We sit down snuggled next to each other on the couch, eating them while something on Netflix plays in the background.

I start to overthink again, wondering if he wants me to stay the night or not, or is he suddenly going to say *okay, it's time to go home*?

I want to stay, or I want him to come back to mine—either or—but how do I know if he wants the same thing?

I hear him make a sound deep in his throat, and look to my left at him, to find him watching me eat my ice cream.

"Do you eat your ice cream like that in public?" he asks, licking his lips. "You're never having dessert at the clubhouse."

"I'm just eating it normally," I say, frowning.

He imitates me, letting his tongue seductively lap at the milky goodness.

"That is not how I look!" I laugh, gently nudging him with my elbow. We end up kind of wrestling and I land over his lap, in the position someone would be in to get spanked, and I can feel that he's hard.

I can also feel that the bulge is *very* large.

I still, not wanting to squirm on his cock any further, and then casually continue to eat my ice cream, which is still safe in my hand.

What a sight we must make right now.

I glance up at him. "You're trying not to spank me right now, aren't you?"

In this position, how can he not? And not to mention I've always been told I have a pretty decent booty.

He nods. "Not sure what the protocol is on that yet."

While laughing, I accidentally spill ice cream all over his T-shirt. "Oops. Sorry." I pause and then add, "I guess you're going to have to remove that now."

He finishes the last bite of his ice-cream bar and then does just that, removing his top and revealing that amazing toned body I got a glimpse of back in Vegas.

"How much do you work out again?"

"We have a gym in the clubhouse, so every other day or so," he admits, shrugging. "I struggle to sleep if I don't tire myself out."

I blink slowly a few times.

I mean, I wouldn't want him to be unable to sleep tonight, so I guess I could take one for the team and tire him out tonight.

I know, it's a hard job, but somebody has to do it.

Sitting up, I move to straddle him and finish the last bit of my ice-cream bar, then place my hands on each side of his neck.

"So beautiful," he murmurs, before leaning forward and kissing me. He tastes like ice cream and sin, and my hands on his soft skin over his hard body feel like heaven and hell. The kissing soon deepens, and turns heated, and his hands move to the backs of my thighs, sending goose bumps all over my skin as he inches closer and closer to my ass.

Pushing my knees onto the couch, I lift myself up, giving him more access and me more control of the kiss. My breasts pressed against his bare chest, I run my hands through his dark, thick hair, moaning as he sucks on my bottom lip before moving to my neck, trailing his lips down my sensitive skin.

I don't know how it happens, but in a blur of kisses, touching and stroking, I end up naked, pressed back against the couch, Renny on top of me, his hard cock pointing right at me.

"We need to use protection," I tell him, eyes bulging at how big he is. "I'm on the pill, but…"

But I don't know where he has been.

And we might even need some lube, because that is a really fucking huge weapon he has there. He gets off the couch and grabs a condom from somewhere, rips the packet open with his teeth and slides it on like a pro. I think he's going to slide himself inside of me, but he pauses, licking his lips, looking torn.

"I need to taste this pussy first," he says, getting on the carpet—on his knees—and positioning me with my thighs on each side of his head. He starts to lick and suck until I'm wild. I don't think I've ever been this uninhibited before, lifting my hips so he can get more of me, pulling his hair, and all but grinding my pussy against his face. I'm so turned on, so wet and just wanting everything he has to offer and more.

He's made me crazy with lust.

I come louder than I ever have before, whimpering, panting, just blown away by the pleasure this man is giving me. He stands and lifts me in his arms, carrying me back to his bed, to have his wicked way with me. He lays me back and slides inside me, and I'm so dazed and so wet, all I can do is take what he gives me, loving every second of it.

This.

This is what has been missing from my life.

Chapter Thirteen

I wake up feeling deliciously sore, satisfied and hungry. Rolling over, I almost yelp in surprise when I see Renny's face right in front of mine, his eyes still closed.

Shit. It's going to take a little while to get used to sharing a bed with someone, and waking up with them.

Silently stretching, I smile as I think of last night.

We had sex four times.

Four.

I don't think I've ever met a man with such stamina.

That's definitely my new record, but for him, I wouldn't be surprised if he could have kept going. What's more impressive than the four times was the number of orgasms I had.

Five.

That's definitely a record, because it takes me a lot to come, and I usually only come from clitoral stimulation during oral sex, but this guy.

This guy.

He made me come just with his penis.

Either I've been sleeping with guys who are really bad in bed or he's really good, and I'm thinking it might be the latter.

Sitting up, I glance down at him, so boyish in his sleep, his dark lashes crescents on his face. He's such a good-looking guy, but it's more than that. There's just something about him that makes me feel like I'm in the right place, and I'm feeling pretty lucky this morning.

After sliding out of bed quietly, not wanting to wake him up, I use the bathroom, and have a quick shower and brush my teeth with the toothbrush I was smart enough to pack in my bag when I knew I intended on spending the night with him. He's not in bed when I resurface, back in the same dress from the night before. Instead I find him in the kitchen cooking us breakfast. I enjoy the view for a few moments before letting him know that I'm here, admiring his bare, muscled back and his ass in the gray sweatpants he has on. The tattoos covering him are truly beautiful, even the Knight, which is currently looking right at me.

"Good morning," I say, eyes still on his body. "Is that bacon I smell?"

"Bacon, eggs, hash browns and toast," he says, turning around and opening his arms for me.

Resting my cheek against his chest, I reply with, "Cooking bacon with no shirt on—ballsy, but damn, this is a nice view to wake up to."

"I could say the same," he murmurs, kissing me on the forehead. "Do you want some coffee?"

"Coffee would be amazing. I can make it," I offer, moving toward the kettle.

"Nope, you sit down, I've got this," he says, lifting me up into his arms, carrying me to the barstool and placing me down. "Let a man spoil you a little."

"You're going to be in big trouble if I get used to this," I tease, sitting back and watching him work.

This has been the best first date ever. I tell him as much.

"That's what I was aiming for," he replies, beaming. "Next time, though, I'll take you out somewhere."

"That will be nice. I'll have to cook for you one night this week at my house. I have a few recipes up my sleeve I save for special occasions that I'm quite well known for," I brag.

"I'd love that."

That's two dates we've already set up, and I haven't even left his apartment yet. We have breakfast together, amazing coffee, and then we drive back to my house.

I can't remember the last time I had a date where I left just grinning from ear to ear, and feeling so excited to see that person again.

I must have been doing it wrong this entire time.

"You're glowing today," my mail carrier says as he drops off today's package.

"Why thank you, Frank," I say, smiling. "I'm feeling pretty good today."

Renny drove us home and then walked back to the clubhouse. I made a joke about asking if he needed me to walk him, which I think he found amusing, and after I got changed into some fresh clothes, I've been trying to get some work done. But all I can think about is last night. And Renny. And even the mail carrier can tell that there's something different about me, although I hope he can't tell that it's because I got laid last night.

"Have a good day!"

"Thank you," I say, box in my hands. Closing the door with my hip, I head back to my spot on the couch and am opening my package when my phone rings.

I glance at the caller: Dad.

Yeah, not going to pick that one up.

I don't know why he's calling me, because he usually only calls on my birthday and Christmas, but he's not who I want to talk to right now, because he will definitely put a damper on my good mood. If he wants to ask about Mila, he can call Ariel and ask her himself.

Opening the box, I pull out the new clothes I ordered for Mila—in a bigger size, of course—and place them in the wardrobe of my spare room. Before they get here, I'm going to turn this room into the perfect haven for them both.

Ariel and Mila here.

Renny down the road.

I can't see life getting much better than this.

I wish I could take a photograph of Renny's face every time I offer to pay for something. It's a mixture of confusion, disbelief and offense.

"You haven't let me pay for anything since I met you," I tell him later that day, scowling. "I'm paying for dinner, and that's that. You freaking fixed my car and paid for it. A relationship is give and take. You aren't my sugar daddy, and while I think it's sweet you like to take care of things all of the time, I'm a capable, strong, independent working woman. Even though I might not be loaded and dripping in properties like you, I can afford to take us out to eat."

He opens his mouth to argue, but I flash him a look, one that dares him to press me.

"Izzy—"

I give the waitress, who looks like she'd rather be anywhere else right now, my debit card, while Renny sits there, scowling and silently brooding, what I assume is his version of a man tantrum.

A mantrum.

"I don't like having someone else pay for me," he finally says. "Especially my woman. I'm the man, and I should be paying for our meals or activities. You pay for your own life, your own house and bills and all of that, so let me at least cover anything we do when we're together."

"You paid my mechanics bill," I remind him. "It's 2019,

Renny. Modern times. You aren't any less of a man if you let a woman pay for you now and again."

He still looks extremely unhappy, and for a second I wonder if it was worth it, if I should have just let him pay to not spoil what was a beautiful evening up until now, but then I think, no.

Fair is fair.

"Did you think that maybe sometimes I want to spoil you back, too?" I ask, trying a different approach. "I don't want you to put in all the effort—I want to show you how much I like and care about you, too."

"You can do that in other ways," he suggests, a thoughtful expression on his face. "Massages, hugs, cooking…sex."

I roll my eyes. "You're incorrigible, you know that? I paid, you survived it, and that's it. Now stop having a mantrum and ruining the rest of the evening, because we still have to sit through a movie together."

"A what?" he asks, brows pulling together.

"A mantrum. A man tantrum. It's a thing," I say, shrugging.

He starts laughing, softly at first, but then louder. "I seriously never know what's going to come out of your mouth. You know, most people would be too scared to say something like that to me."

"I'm not most people," I reply, arching my brow.

"I know, and I respect that, and you," he says instantly, throwing some money on the table for the tip.

A lot of money.

Which I'm sure is his way of having the last word.

Raising my eyes to his, I state, "I'm paying for the movies."

"No fuckin' chance," is his reply, which he says with a smile. "You paid for dinner, I'll pay for the movies. That's fair, right?"

I eye the money he just dropped on the table for the lucky waitress, which is about the same amount as the entire meal cost in the first place, and shake my head.

"You're a control freak," I decide.

"I'm just old school," he says, shrugging. "That's how my mom raised me, to be a gentleman, open doors…"

"And to pay for shit?" I fill in, smirking. "Well, I'm happy she raised you as a gentleman, and we'll work on the money thing. I guess you're allowed to have one flaw."

"You're the only woman I've met who has considered me wanting to pay for everything a flaw," he grumbles, standing and offering me his hand. "Come on, we better get to this movie."

Taking his hand, I let him lead me out of the restaurant and to his motorcycle. I'm cooking for him tomorrow night, which means three dates in a row.

I've never done anything like that before, but I guess I'm experiencing a lot of firsts since I've met Renny.

Even our first argument over money.

Chapter Fourteen

Knock knock.

Raising my head from my laptop screen, I wonder who could be at the door, unless Renny forgot something when he left this morning.

"Hey," I say when I open the door and see Skylar standing there with food in her hands.

My house hasn't had so much traffic since…well, ever. No one really comes here, but all of a sudden there are people dropping by every day, and surprisingly I don't mind it.

"Hey, are you busy? I picked up some lunch and thought we could hang out," she asks, smiling warmly at me. "Don't be shy to say no and kick me out."

Grinning, I open the door wider. "I'm not busy at all, come on in."

She enters and looks around. "You're really good at decorating," she muses, taking in the bright art on my wall. I've made my space as warm and homey as I can, surrounded by memories and little bits and pieces I've picked up over the years. "Interesting, I wouldn't have pegged you as having a boho style."

"I'm full of surprises."

We sit down at my dining table and she starts to unload the food. "So, I thought we could hang out just us two, because it's hard to get to know someone with all the men around, and it looks like you and Renny are becoming serious. Three date nights in a row? Jeez. Has anything changed now that you guys have actually consummated the marriage?"

"No, nothing has changed," I reply, wincing. "And yeah, I know, apparently we aren't sick of each other just yet."

But that doesn't mean that I want to be married to the man.

"I'm sure it will be fine," she replies, shrugging it off. "Or maybe the two of you will just stay married and live happily ever after and have pretty green-eyed children."

"Yeah, I don't know about all of that." I check the amount of food that she keeps pulling from the bag. "Dude, who else is coming for lunch?"

"I know, but I wasn't sure what you liked, so I thought I'd cover all my bases. Food won't go to waste—I'll just take it back to the clubhouse. Trust me, it will vanish within the second," she says, admiring her spread. "Help yourself. I recommend the burger, personally, but everything is pretty good. It's from the café just down the road from here."

I pick up the burger. "Thank you, this was really nice of you."

"You're welcome, least I can do," she replies, opening the wrapper on her own burger. "Renny says that you're an epic graphic designer. How did you get into that?"

"Just something that I was always good at that I turned into a career," I say, shrugging. "I was always good with editing photos and making little graphics and things like that, and my media teacher actually pushed me toward it when I was in high school. I do enjoy it, and it gives me the freedom to be my own boss. If I didn't have work coming in, though, I'd have to find another real-life job."

Skylar makes a sound of amusement. "A real-life job, hey?

I'm a paramedic. I don't think it gets any more real life than that."

"No, you're probably right," I say, grinning. "You must be pretty badass to dive into such a field—you should be proud of yourself."

"I am," she laughs. "I had no idea what I wanted to do for such a long time, but now that I've found it, it's been worth the wait."

We end up chatting for two hours before she stands to leave. "By the way, I asked Renny if he called the lawyers, and he told me to mind my business," she says at the door, scowling. "I told him that I'd call them for you, and he said he will speak to them when he's ready."

"So he hasn't even called them?" I ask, mouth dropping open. "He said he would handle it."

She smirks as she steps through the doorframe. "Guess he likes you being his wife more than he wants to let on."

I grit my teeth but wave bye to her as she heads back to the clubhouse. I don't have many friends that I see regularly, and it was nice to chat with her. While I still speak to several of my high school friends and we usually do monthly catch ups, I don't have a close friend I get to see all of the time. I think Skylar might just become that.

Renny comes over at about seven and I've already started cooking our dinner, so it's too late to cancel. I'm really pissed off that he hasn't even called the lawyers yet. He promised me he would.

"Something smells like it's burning," is the first thing he says to me.

"Fuck," I curse, rushing to the oven to find my chicken now black on top. I was too busy thinking of all the ways I'd tell him off that I burned the fucking thing. "Goddammit."

Renny takes it out of the oven and inspects it. "It will be fine. We'll just cut all the skin off."

"You mean cut all the flavor off," I grumble, sighing. "Man, this was meant to be the best chicken you've ever tasted."

"Izzy," he murmurs, turning my body to face him, hands on my shoulders. "Look at me." I lift my face. "It's just a chicken. There will be other chickens, and it's fine, we can still salvage it. Come on, I'll help you."

Fuck, he can be sweet, but I'm not going to let him get off easily about this lawyer thing. "Did you sort things out with the lawyer yet?"

"I'm waiting for them to get back to me," he replies. "Why?"

Eyes narrowed, I want to call him out on what I heard today, but I don't want to get Skylar into any shit. "Can you give me their number? I'll call them myself, which might hurry it along," I push, seeing what he's going to say next.

"I told you I would handle it, you don't need to worry."

"You did say that, but it's not handled yet, so I'm a little concerned," I fire back, studying him. "I would have thought that you could make things happen a little faster."

I'm pushing him now, but I know he's not being honest about it and he's clearly taking his time, if he's even called them at all.

"Which lawyers are you going through again?"

"Bentley & Channing. The best in the business," he says without a thought.

"And you've called them?" He pauses, and his hesitation is answer enough. "You haven't, have you?"

"It's on my list of things to do," he admits, wincing. "I'm going to get it sorted, I told you that, and I will, okay? Just give me a little time."

"How about you just be honest?" I say, brow furrowing. "Didn't we have this conversation about no games? And here you are lying about calling them. Don't tell me what you think I want to hear, tell me the truth."

"I'm sorry," he says, sighing softly. "But I will take care of it, Izzy. Look, I'll even send them an email right now, asking them to call me tomorrow."

He types out an email on their website contact page, shows it to me, and hits send. "Done."

I'm still not happy about how he's handling this whole thing, but I let it go.

For now, I decide I'll give him the benefit of the doubt.

I don't like the fact that he didn't tell me the truth, though. It's like he thinks he can do whatever he wants and it will be fine, because he isn't actually hurting me, or however he manages to justify it to himself. But life doesn't work like that. He's clearly used to doing what he wants without having to explain himself, but you can't be like that in a relationship. At least not in the type of relationship I want to have.

We save what we can from the chicken and place it on top of the salad. It actually ends up tasting pretty good, even though it wasn't the original meal I had planned. Renny has a proper look around my house and suggests I let him upgrade the security, so he can put in some cameras and a better lock system. I mention to him that I've even been thinking of getting a guard dog, and he tells me he thinks it's a good idea. With my new ties to the MC, I think I need to start being a little more careful.

"I want a do-over of tonight. Don't judge my cooking skills based on this meal, please."

He laughs, shaking his head at me. "Babe, I wouldn't care if you served me two-minute fuckin' noodles, I'll still be here every night if you'll have me."

Our eyes lock and hold.

He pisses me off, makes me question everything and then he goes and says something like that, something that makes it feel worth it.

Only time will tell if that's true or not.

The next time I invite him over for dinner, I make sure that I've pre-cooked everything beforehand so there is room for error in case anything goes wrong this time around. It doesn't, and my

lasagna turns out perfect. Renny shows up with dessert, flowers and a sexy smile.

"How was your day?" I ask him, rising on my toes to give
him a kiss. I haven't seen him since last night, and although
I'd hate to admit it, I spent a lot of today thinking about him.

"Good. We sold a few more bikes," he says, handing me the
beautiful mixed bouquet of flowers. "And these are for you."

"Thank you," I say, smelling the flowers and then eying the
cheesecake in his hands. "You bring me the best gifts, they're
beautiful. What's the occasion?"

He grins and glances down at the dessert. "Just because.
How about your day? Did you actually get any work done, or
did you procrastinate?"

"I got some work done," I admit, wincing. "But I also cleaned
out my entire linen cupboard and organized it all into labeled
categories."

He laughs softly and follows me into the kitchen. "Nothing
smells like it's burning."

"Very funny," I say, organizing the flowers into a vase and
turning to face him. "Are you hungry now?"

"Always," he replies, glancing down my body.

"Food first." I smirk and settle the lasagna, garlic bread and
salad on the table, hoping he loves my mom's recipe.

"Smells good. Can I help with anything?"

"Nope, just take a seat," I reply, grabbing two plates and cut-
lery and joining him at the table.

"I missed you today," he says, staring at me over the food.
"You should come and work in the shop office, and then I can
sneak in and annoy you and bring you food."

I roll my eyes but secretly think he's pretty damn cute right
now. "That's a little codependent, don't you think?"

"You're the most independent woman I know, I don't think
you could be codependent with anyone," he replies, lip twitching.

"I don't know, I'm getting pretty needy with Mila," I tease, serving him a big slice. "I want to cuddle her at least ten times a day. And, Renny?"

"Yeah?"

"I missed you, too," I admit, looking him in the eye.

I don't know how the hell this happened, but I think I'm falling for this man.

Shit.

"Happy birthday, dear Temper, happy birthday to you," the crowd sings to the birthday boy's displeasure. He didn't want a party or a cake, but he got both anyway, and everyone seems to delight in spoiling the man who would probably rather be alone to celebrate. I can't help but smile, seeing him sit in front of a cake covered in thirty-five candles, and someone even put a fucking party hat on him.

"Hip hip, hooray! Hip hip, hooray!" everyone cheers, clapping as he blows out each and every candle. Skylar passes him a knife and he cuts the first slice before she takes over and cuts the rest of the cake up for everyone to eat.

"Thank you all for coming," Temper calls out, cracking a smile. "I couldn't be surrounded by a better bunch of people."

"This cake is amazing," I tell Renny, licking my lips.

He groans next to me. "You're seriously the most sensual eater I've ever seen. And I don't think I've ever seen anyone enjoy food as much as you do."

I purposely lick some vanilla frosting off my fingers. "Let me eat my cake in piece, Renny."

He makes a choking sound deep in his throat. "I'm going to get a drink. Do you want something?"

"Bottle of water, please," I tell him.

After finishing the cake, I head to the bathroom to wash my sticky fingers. I stop in my tracks when I hear my name. I can hear Renny's and Dee's voices as they stand on the other side of Renny's bedroom door, the door I was about to walk into.

"What the hell are you doing, Renny?" Dee says. "You weren't meant to fall for her."

"You think I don't know that?" Renny replies, sounding extremely unhappy going by his dire tone. "But she's mine, and that's the end of it. Messing with her car that day was the best thing I've ever done."

"Now isn't the time to talk about this."

Messing with my car? Are you kidding me right now? He's the reason it wouldn't start? What if something happened to me? Did he not care if he put me in danger?

Anger, betrayal and hurt hit me, right in the chest, the impact causing me to lean against the wall for support. This relationship with him felt too good to be true, and I guess it was, but I still don't understand what they had to gain from this.

It makes no sense.

What does Dee mean, Renny wasn't meant to fall for me?

Renny exits the room and sees me standing there. "What is he talking about?" I ask him.

Dee comes up behind him, wincing when his eyes land on me. "Fuck, Izzy—"

"Tell me," I demand.

Renny reaches out to touch me, but I step back. He hasn't been honest about something, and I need to know what it is, I need to know if everything between us is real. If he wasn't meant to fall for me, what was he supposed to do with me? Is it not a coincidence that I am here right now?

What use could I be?

Dee quickly makes an exit, leaving me alone with the man I only just thought I was falling in love with. How things can change in an instant. I went from inexplicably trusting him to not being able to look him in the eyes without it hurting.

"You tampered with my car?" I ask, gritting my teeth. I mean, who does that?

"I did," he admits, eyes filled with pain. I'm sure that they mirror my own right now, brown at war with green. "I wanted you to trust me, and I wanted an excuse to talk to you."

"Why?" I ask, tone harsh even to my own ears. "You could have just said hello, like a fucking normal person. Why did you fuck with my car, Renny? You could have put me in danger! Did you even think of that? Or were you too busy just thinking about your damn club?"

He exhales before answering me. "You weren't in danger. I just crimped the fuel line, and you had no gas in there, so the car wasn't going to move. I'm surprised it even made it out of the driveway. We came up with a plan that we would make friends with you, get you to trust us and then... I don't know, okay? We didn't even know what we were going to do, but we know who your dad is, and we know that's going to be useful to us. He's a powerful man. With the shit going on with our MC right now, if we had him at our backs it would benefit us."

My dad. Of course.

I didn't even think of that, because I rarely connect myself to him.

I thought Renny was my Knight in shining armor. Instead he's just a lying biker in leather.

"Well, unfortunately for you, I have nothing to do with my father, and he couldn't care less if anything happened to me, just in case your mind was wandering toward kidnapping me for ransom or some shit like that," I fire at him, stepping closer to him and lifting my head so I'm looking him right in the eye. "I never want to speak to you again. You are dead to me."

And that's how a Knight broke my heart.

Chapter Fifteen

There's a reason I don't tell anyone my dad is the mayor of the city I live in. We have different surnames, because I took my mom's maiden name, so no one normally figures out the tie between us. But the MC obviously got their hands on that information somehow.

Ariel and I cut off ties with him long before the cancer took my mom. We stopped talking to him when he left her for his mistress after years of affairs, treating her less than she deserved. He's not a good man. I do think he loves us, in his own way, but it's not enough. He's known for being a dirty mayor, and yes, for being powerful with his connections, too. I can see how having an in with him would benefit the MC, because he does control a lot of what happens in this city, and having him on their side would be an asset.

I've never felt so used, though, and so betrayed. I thought Renny was…well, the one. My one. I'd never been so hopeful in love than I was less than twenty minutes ago, and now I'm sitting on my couch, crying, alone and destroyed.

I know he followed me home to make sure I got there safely

after I ran out of the clubhouse, but I don't care. I know he's hurt, too, but it's too bad, because he caused this.

"What did I do to deserve this?" I whisper to myself, taking a deep breath. I'm a good, honest person. I don't lie, I don't cheat.

They went as far as to break my car so they could fix it and I would feel indebted to them. That's going above and beyond in the betrayal department. That's manipulative, cunning and well planned. Did they sit at a fucking drawing board, trying to make a plan on how to make me fall in love with Renny so they could use me however they saw fit? Did they even need to go to Vegas, or was that all bullshit, too? Were they going to use me to blackmail my father? I have no idea, and neither did they, I think.

Their plan was simple: Use Isabella.

And Renny was the one they sent to execute it.

And how well he did.

Even though it's late, I pick up the phone and call Ariel. Along with Renny, I just lost everyone I've been spending my time with and giving my energy to, including Skylar. The whole thing hurts, and to be honest right now, I just want to leave.

Maybe I should.

After speaking to Ariel, I do the one thing I never thought I'd do: I book a flight.

That's how badly I need to get out of here. I'm going to face my biggest fear—flying—because the thought of that is less scary and painful than the thought of Renny.

Rather than deal with the fallout of what's happened with the MC, I'm going to run.

Tag, you're it.

"Mila, you're the best thing in my life right now," I tell her, blowing raspberries on her little stomach. "I missed you, beautiful girl."

"You know you're going to have to face him eventually," Ariel says to me, standing in the doorframe, watching me play

with her daughter. "He's your neighbor. This is why they say
don't shit where you live."

"I didn't shit. He did," I reply, sitting up and turning to her.
"I know, Ariel. I just need a little time to get over him so I'm
not weak and can just pretend I don't know him."

"Very mature strategy," she replies, rolling her eyes.

"Maybe I should sell my house and move away. We could
live by the beach or something. Far away from betrayal on a
motorcycle."

"Dad always told us to be careful with who we trusted," she
sighs, coming to sit down on the other side of the bed. "I'm
sorry this happened, Izzy. It's not going to be easy for you, but
you're going to be okay. You're a good person, and you're beautiful inside and out. You deserve someone who wants nothing
from you but your love."

"I know," I agree. "I just have to wonder if it was all fake,
because if it was, then he deserves a fucking Oscar for the per-
formance he gave me."

She's quiet for a few moments before she replies. "I don't
think it was. I do think he cares about you, but he didn't come
into this for that. I think it just happened. I think he obviously
thought you were attractive, but like you overheard, he started
falling for you, which wasn't the plan. But in the end that obviously won out over anything else."

"That doesn't justify it."

"No, it does not," she agrees, nodding thoughtfully. "He had
an ulterior motive, clearly, but did he ever ask you about Dad?
Or for anything?"

"No," I admit, glancing down at Mila, who is sucking on her
fingers. "He never asked anything about Dad, which I don't get.
Shouldn't he have been trying to get information on him from
the get-go? This whole thing just makes me feel so yucky, you
know? I would have done anything for that man."

And I guess that was the point.

If the club got into shit and they needed Dad's help, I probably would have reached out to him and asked for it, because I would have wanted to help and support them in any way I could.

And that's exactly what they wanted.

Renny didn't even have to ask about Dad—it would have been me thinking of that plan, so I would have thought it was my idea, not theirs.

I mean, I can't guarantee what would have happened and if Dad would have helped, or what the fallout would be if he knew I was dating a biker. But for them, for Renny, I would have tried.

And I would have been an idiot, because that's the only reason they wanted me around, to use as a wild card, to try to save them if they ever needed it.

Their secret backup plan.

"We don't know what he's thinking because you never let him explain," Ariel points out, eyes gentle on me. "Don't get me wrong, nothing excuses him for what he's done, but I don't know... Have you checked your phone since you left? I'm sure he's trying to contact you so he can try to explain what happened from the start."

"No, I haven't," I grumble, crossing my arms over my chest. "And I don't want to. I don't care if he's trying to contact me. I don't owe him anything, even an explanation on my whereabouts."

"He did one good thing for you," she adds, grinning.

"What?"

"He made you get on your first flight in fifteen years." She laughs, shaking her head at me. "Let me tell you, I thought that day would never come, but it did and you survived it."

"Barely."

I didn't tell her I had a few alcoholic beverages in the airport before I boarded the flight, but I did, and they did help. Still, I was terrified, and now have marks on my palms from where my nails dug into them. I was scared, but I wanted to be away from home so badly, and I knew I had to stick it out to do that. I could have driven, but that car is tainted for me now, and God

knows what they did to it. Besides, let him see my car there and
wonder where I am. Let him hurt as much as he has hurt me.

All is fair in love and war.

"Are you going to fly home?" she asks, picking up Mila and
gently tapping her on her back. "I guess you could take a bus."

"I haven't thought that far ahead," I admit. I know I'm going
to have to go back and be an adult, and I can't just have my
house sitting there alone and unattended, but right now I'm just
enjoying the distance. Even if it is an avoidance technique, I'm
going to use it for now. "At least this time I brought my laptop so I can work, and I can help you pack up the house so you
don't have to do it alone. Or I can watch Mila while you pack,
because I know how long that takes you."

"You know I'm happy to have you back here," she says, smiling at me. "But you look so sad, and I want to fix it for you, but
I can't. I was hoping he'd look after you, which he did in some
ways but apparently not in others. I don't know. Can I call him
up and yell at him?"

Laughing, I tell her no. "Besides, I'm going to ghost his ass.
That means no contact, and basically I'm going to act like he
never existed."

Ariel grabs my phone from her side table and puts in my
code.

"How do you know my code?"

"You use the same code for everything," she replies, rolling
her eyes. "And you have since high school."

It's true. Dammit.

"He has called you fifteen times, and you also have missed
calls from Skylar," she says, scrolling through. "And ten messages in your inbox."

Sighing, my shoulders drooping, I wonder if I've made the
right move, or if I should just hear what he has to say. If I don't,
this is just going to drag on and on, and if I'm going to get over
him and move forward, I'm going to need some closure on the
whole thing.

"Are you going to put him out of his misery?" she asks, watching me. "Or are you going to continue to make him suffer?"

"I'll hear him out," I decide. "But only so that we can just move on and forget this whole fake relationship ever happened."

I'll sort out the annulment myself, since he seems to be taking his sweet time with it, probably so he can tell Dad he's married to me now. He's probably telling everyone that the mayor is his father-in-law.

"Izzy," Ariel chastises, frowning at the phone. "He's calling, so now's your chance."

She hands me the phone, and with a deep gulp I press accept. "Hello?"

"Izzy, where are you? Your car is here, but you're not home," he says, sounding worried.

"How do you know I'm not home? Did you break in and check?" I ask him, pursing my lips.

When he goes silent, I know that he did exactly that. "You are unbelievable, you know that? You think no rules apply to you and that you can do whatever the fuck you want with no repercussions!"

"I just wanted to see if you were okay, and try to speak to you about what happened—"

"You mean me finding out the truth that you broke my car, lied to me over and over again, and planned on using me to get to my dad and his connections?" I ask, cutting him off. "I never thought you were anything but genuine, Renny. Perhaps you should become an actor?"

"That's not fair," he says, sounding angry now. "Yes, I went into this with different intentions, but when I met you, everything changed. The conversation you heard was nothing new to me—the men have been giving me shit about this the entire time because I told them I had feelings for you. I also told them that no one was to go near you or say anything to you, and that if we wanted to save Temper's brother, then we will have to find another way."

Temper's brother? What does he have to do with any of this? I make a mental note to ask about this after I get to the bottom of my part in it.

"So everyone knows? And I'm some laughingstock to the MC? They all sat with me, laughed with me, got to know me, and they all knew I was only there because everyone wanted to see what you can get out of me?" I ask, yelling now.

He goes silent. "Temper didn't know and Skylar didn't know, but yes, the rest of the men knew."

Temper didn't know? So they all did this without the approval of their president?

"Well, you're all a bunch of assholes," I say, my tone going flat. "You know, if this whole thing had been genuine, and my car really had just broken down, and everything was true, I would have done anything to help you and the MC. I can't believe you would use people like that. It's so unattractive, and not the person I thought you were."

I know he said that he told the men the plan wasn't going to go ahead and that I was his, as I overheard, but it doesn't change how we came about.

It doesn't change anything.

He still tampered with my car, still acted like it was a coincidental meeting, like it was fate playing its hand when really it was a really well thought out, elaborate plan to get me under his thumb... How am I meant to forgive that?

Chapter Sixteen

"I'm sorry," he whispers, taking a deep breath. "I am so fucking sorry that this is how we met, but I'm not sorry I met you. Everyone at the MC knew that I thought you were so fuckin' beautiful, which is why when Dee came up with the idea I wasn't going to let any of the other men come near you—"

"How considerate of you," I snarl, shaking my head. "You didn't know me then, and that you couldn't have known we would end up having such a connection, but the fact that you would do that to someone, anyone...that doesn't sit well with me, Renny. I don't know what you want me to say, or do, or how I'm meant to get over this. How can you expect me to? I've been nothing but honest and myself with you, and to find out that I didn't get that back in return? It's heartbreaking."

"I know," he says, sounding hurt. "Trust me, I know. But I'm fuckin' crazy about you. I know I can't expect you to get over this, but you can't expect me to just let this go either. I've never felt about anyone the way I do about you, and I'll do anything to make this up to you."

"I don't know if there is a way to make this better," I say, swallowing hard. "I'm safe, you don't need to worry about me, and I'll be home when I'm ready."

"Izzy—"

"Goodbye."

I hang up before he can say anything else, then glance up at Ariel, who was listening to the entire conversation.

"Come here," she says, placing Mila down in her crib and opening her arms for me. "It's all right."

She rubs my back while I cry. I've never felt so weak, and I hate that he did this to me.

How dare he?

I was right, he was trouble from the beginning, and I should have trusted my gut instinct and stayed away from him. I should have resisted temptation, but I didn't, and now I have to pay the price.

God help the next man who tries to love me.

"Dad is calling me again," Ariel says, frowning. It's been a week since I spoke to Renny. A very long week. "What do you think he wants?"

"I don't know, he called me last week, too," I admit, shrugging. "Maybe he's having another kid or something."

After my dad married his mistress, Angie, and moved in with her and her children, he went on to have two more kids with her, another two little girls. I've only seen my half sisters a handful of times over the years and am not really close to them, which is sad because they did nothing wrong. My dad's brother once joked that my dad must have done something terrible in a past life to be given four daughters and no sons, which kind of shows what type of men they are.

On top of all the bad blood with our father, Angie hates us and will go out of her way to make us feel like we don't belong anywhere near their family. When Mom was alive Angie was rude and nasty to her, and tried to rub in her face that she stole her husband.

"A good man can't be stolen," my mom replied to her once, and that line has always stuck with me, because it's true. A good man can't.

"How many kids does he need?" Ariel grumbles, then sighs and picks up. "Hello? Hey, Dad. Yeah, I know, I've been really busy." She pauses. "Ummm, no, why? What have you heard about Isabella?"

Oh, fuck.

"Nope, I don't know anything about bikers, Dad, but you know she lives near them, so maybe that's why someone is saying that," she lies, looking at me with wide eyes. "Of course I'm looking after her, someone has to."

And there it is.

None of our conversations can end civilly. The past is always brought up, the bad blood between us seeping through.

"Yes, I will make sure Isabella is making good decisions and not riding on the back of criminal bikers' motorcycles so it doesn't look bad on you. Anything else, Dad?" More pausing. "Okay then, until next time. By the way, your first granddaughter is doing well, thank you for asking."

She hangs up, her jaw tense. "He is such an asshole. How did we come from his sperm?"

"I have no idea," I admit, pursing my lips. "At least he gave us nice green eyes and thick dark hair."

She laughs, relaxing a little. "Someone apparently saw you on the back of Renny's bike and told him, that's why he's been calling. He said for us not to do anything that will make him look bad."

"Yeah, because his cheating looked good for him?" I groan, scowling. "He's a piece of work, isn't he? If only the MC knew the truth. They would probably have better luck on their own making some shady deal than using me to get to him."

Sad, but so true. It's been years since I even felt like I had a father, which is hard when I see him all over the media and on billboards around the city. I kind of learned to bury it and to disassociate myself with him and his life, which is maybe why this whole thing is such a kick to the chest. I can't believe someone saw me and reported back to him, especially when we have nothing to do with him.

"I wonder what they need him for," Ariel muses.

"Renny said something about Temper's brother needing some help, but he also said Temper didn't know about their plan for me. Maybe they were trying to help him, I don't know," I reply, my mind racing. I've never heard of Temper's brother being mentioned before, but they obviously all don't speak freely in front of me. "Dad has a lot of connections."

"Must be important for them if they went through this whole thing just to try to help him," she replies, shrugging. "And knowing Dad's influence, he probably could help them."

My lips tighten. "Are you saying I should help them? You heard Dad just now—he doesn't want me being associated with them. What makes you think he's going to help them for me? He hasn't done anything for me except show me the type of man I never want to marry."

"I'm not saying you should do anything," she replies, studying me. "I'm just thinking out loud here. I know you, if you can help, you're probably going to help."

I puff out a breath. "I like Temper, and he didn't know about what was going on, so he and Skylar are the only Knights who aren't on my shit list right now. But I just don't see how I can help, Ariel. And I don't see *why* I should. For all we know Temper's brother could be a murderer or something."

"Yeah, maybe," she murmurs, glancing down at her phone. "I don't know how you got yourself into this mess, but now we're going to have to get out of it. Renny is going to fight for you, Izzy, like he said, but eventually he will give up, and you need to make sure that you're truly going to be okay with that."

"I'm perfectly fine with that," I tell her, scowling as I think of him. "He played me, and I'm not going to give him a chance to do that a second time. I'd never be able to trust him and I'd always be wondering if he has ulterior motives..."

I'll miss him, that's for sure, but I'm just going to have to deal with it, because that's not a reason to forgive someone if they don't deserve to be forgiven.

I spend the next few days helping pack and clean up the house, or looking after Mila while Ariel does so. My sister agrees to move back with me sooner than she planned, which means once I head back home I will have her with me. That makes me feel much better about life.

I'm singing softly to Mila when there's a knock at the door. "Ariel! Can you get that?"

"Yeah," she calls back and jogs to the door with packing tape in her hand. "What are you doing here?" I hear her say, and my hackles instantly rise.

"Who is it?" I call, frowning.

"Merve," she replies, sounding extremely unimpressed.

I glance down at Mila, her big green eyes staring up at me, and sigh. "You're in for a world of pain, my love, just like Ariel and me."

The cycle we promised would never continue has, and now Mila has a similar unstable, in-and-out-of-her-life father like we have. But where our dad has ambition, Merve just has stupidity, which he proves as he pushes into the house, eyes coming to me and Mila.

"I just want to see my daughter," he says, clearly unhappy that I'm still here. "Not that I have to explain myself to you."

"You can't just show up here whenever you feel like it, Merve," Ariel tells him, coming to stand next to me. "If you want to see her, message and organize it properly."

"I don't have to do that," he says with a shrug. "It's not like you're doing anything anyway. Are you so busy that I have to schedule in a date with my own fucking child?"

"Do you only have a daughter when it suits you?" I ask, narrowing my eyes. "Need more social media likes? What are you really doing here, Merve, because I think we all know you don't really care about Mila. So cut the shit."

He lifts his chin and crosses his arms. "Does it matter? She's *my* daughter, Izzy, and you guys can't keep her from me even if you wanted to."

"No one is keeping you from her," Ariel tells him, moving closer to me and Mila. "I'm just saying that this is my house and you can't show up every few weeks whenever you feel like it. It doesn't work that way."

He comes closer to us, and I can smell the alcohol on him from here.

"Are you drunk? Because there is no way you're coming near my niece if you are." I quickly hand Mila to Ariel and stand in front of them. "I'm going to call the police if you don't leave—now. Come back when you're sober and then you can hold her."

Hopefully we'll have moved away by then, because he doesn't even deserve to breathe the same air as Mila.

I slide my phone out of my pocket and hit the keypad. "What's it going to be? Do you really want to be arrested right now? I'm sure our dad could make sure you're put away for longer if he feels like it."

Great, now I'm using the Dad card.

How the mighty have fallen.

The threat must work, though, because he swears at us but then leaves. We lock the door behind him, but share a look with each other. Something has to give. "You can't keep going on like this," I say.

"I know," she replies. "I need to get sole custody of her, and I need it now."

I nod. She's right.

We're going to have to do what we need to do to keep her safe.

Chapter Seventeen

Three Weeks Later

"I didn't get to finish your room," I tell Ariel, opening the door and showing her the progress that I had made. "I figure that you can put the crib in the corner, and I'd already started stocking the cupboard with clothes for Mila."

"You're so cute, you know that?" She beams, sitting down on the queen-sized bed. "It feels good to be here, a fresh start, you know?"

It may be a fresh start for her, but for me, I'm going to have to face Renny, and everything that I left behind. After that one conversation I never spoke to him again, ignoring all of his messages and calls. I haven't even read any of the messages, and although it did take a lot of willpower, I just didn't want him to sweet talk his way out of what he did, because there are no excuses for it.

"Someone You Loved" by Lewis Capaldi plays as we unpack Ariel's belongings and it doesn't help the situation one bit, my mind unable to escape Renny knowing that he's just down the road again and that we have unfinished business between us. Part of me wants to hide, and the other part of me wants to storm into that clubhouse and give everyone who looked me in the eye and lied a piece of my mind. If I hadn't overhead that conversation with Dee and Renny, I might have never known the truth, and I would have looked like an idiot to the club for the rest of my life. One of my biggest fears in a relationship is someone making a fool out of me, and Renny did just that.

We've only been home for a few hours when he shows up, knocking unapologetically at my door. He must have seen Ariel's car here and knew I was back.

I open the door, and there he stands, dressed in all black, a scowl on those lips I once loved kissing, brown eyes staring daggers at me. "Yes?" I ask him, my tone saccharine sweet.

"Seriously?" he asks, giving me a quick once-over. "That's all you have to say right now? Yes?"

"It's more polite than what I really want to say," I reply, shrugging. "I'm helping my sister unpack, so if you don't mind, I'd like to have this confrontational conversation another time. Maybe next month? I'll have to check my schedule."

Without missing a beat, he pulls me against him, and kisses me. I push at his chest, but my lips move against his, giving him mixed signals. I don't know what to think or feel right now. I'm angry, I'm hurt, and I've missed him, which only pisses me off even further. Things are so complicated, and I don't know if I should follow my heart or my head.

Eventually, sanity reaches me and I push him off. "What do you think you're doing?"

"I missed you," he says, scanning my eyes. "Like really fuckin' missed you. Let me take you for a ride so we can speak."

"I just said I'm busy," I tell him, frowning. "Look, we obviously do need to speak, but not right now. I want to get Ariel and Mila settled in first—they literally just got here."

"Do you need any help? I hope you two aren't carrying heavy shit," he says, brows drawing together. "Tell me what you need."

"I don't need anything, we have it all under control," I assure him, pursing my lips. "Don't worry about me, Renny. We can talk later."

"How am I meant to not worry about you? You left before we could speak, without telling anyone you were leaving or where you were going, so we didn't even know if you were safe or not. Of course I'm worried about you, about us, about fuckin' everything, and I want to make sure that you're okay," he says, shifting on his feet. "Fuck, Izzy, you sure know how to make someone feel bad."

"And you sure know how to lie and use people," I fire back, eyes narrowing. "Don't try to blame any of this on me, Renny. You fucked up, you lied, and you made me think you were a fucking hero when you've been the villain all along."

"I prefer anti-hero," he grumbles.

"Villain," I repeat, smirking. "You're a wolf in sheep's clothing."

He taps his hands on his chest, on his leather. "I'm a biker—how the hell did you ever think I was a sheep? I'm a Knight, Izzy, and I know you've heard about us."

"Fine, that was a bad analogy," I say, waving my hand into the air. "I just thought at the end of the day you were a good man and that I could trust you, and now you've broken that trust. There's no coming back from that."

His lips tighten. "I'll come and pick you up tomorrow at lunchtime."

"I'm busy tomorrow. How about next week?"

"Izzy—"

"What? I owe you nothing, Renny. And don't look at me like I do," I snap, lips pursing.

"You don't owe me anything, and I never said you did. I just want a chance to speak to you, and that's all," he says, taking a deep breath as if to calm himself.

"I need some time before we have this conversation, okay?" I need to wait until it doesn't hurt when I look into his eyes, but I think that's probably going to take longer than he's going to give me.

"Okay," he says, ducking his head. "Next week then."

"Can't wait," I reply sarcastically, watching him walk away and back down the road toward the clubhouse. I don't know what he thinks we have left to discuss, because I don't think that we're going to get past this.

Some things you just can't take back.

He does and doesn't give me a week.

Although he doesn't come and see me directly, every day he sends something to the house.

Day One: sunflowers.

Day Two: red roses.

I appreciated Day Three, a bottle of expensive vodka and a food hamper filled with bagels, doughnuts and other baked goods.

Day Four was special, though. Instead of getting something for me, he sent presents for Ariel and Mila. And not just normal presents—he sent her a voucher for a chef to come in and cook for a month, and a voucher for a cleaner to come in and clean our house for a month, too. I don't think I've seen Ariel so happy. Mila was spoiled with a gift certificate for the biggest toy shop in our city.

Day Five was back to me, and a low blow with a marble-framed photograph of us, a photo taken on our wedding night. Even drunk, we both look good, and like a happy couple.

Day Six I got a brand-new laptop, one that is perfect to do my graphic design work on, and which I've been eying for the last few months but couldn't afford. Damn him.

Day Seven I don't know what to expect, but when he arrives on my doorstep with an envelope in his hands, I wonder what he's up to now.

"You need to stop wasting your money, I don't need your gifts," I say, crossing my arms.

"I think this one you will really want," he says, expression blank as he hands me the envelope.

Hesitating, I take it from him and rip it open, pulling out the document and reading it.

"You finally did it," I say, reading the approved annulment papers. After I sign these, we are officially no longer married. Lowering the piece of paper, I look him in the eye. "Thank you, Renny."

It's a bittersweet moment.

This is something I have wanted and pressed for from the beginning, but I can't deny the little bit of sadness that I feel right now. Either way, it was the right thing to do, regardless of where our relationship goes. If I'm going to get married, I want to do it right, not when I'm drunk and barely remember it.

"You're welcome. And I know it doesn't fix things, and I know you're still mad at me and you have every right to be. I just wanted to show you that you can trust me." He takes my hand and looks me in the eye. I see remorse and a little bit of trepidation. "Please, will you let me explain things to you? Just hear me out."

Shifting on my feet, I sigh. I know it's time for me to hear what he has to say. I've put it off long enough. "Okay, how about tomorrow? I have some work due tonight that I need to finish."

He nods. "Great. Tomorrow."

I watch him walk away, then glance back down at the annulment papers.

Why does everything have to be so complicated?

Nerves hit me when I hear his motorcycle.

"I'll be back soon," I tell Ariel, who is nursing Mila. "Wish me luck."

"Good luck," she calls out. "Hopefully you don't kill him. Is he coming in here? Because I might throw my shoe at him if he does. It would have been more than a shoe, but that was before he sent me presents."

"You are so easily bought. Well, on that note, I'll meet him outside," I say, exiting and closing the door behind me. He's taking his helmet off when I approach, and eyes my boyfriend jeans, black belt and thin red knit sweater. He grins and hands me my helmet.

"Where are we going?" I ask.

"For a little ride," he replies. "I'll take us somewhere quiet to talk."

"Okay." Probably good so that no one can hear me yell. "Let's do this."

Being pressed up against him on the bike brings back fond memories, and I make sure not to lean into him like I used to. I don't want him to think that everything is fine and that I'm over what happened, because I'm not. I'm sure I'll forgive him eventually, but I'll never forget, and it will probably always be something between us.

After about fifteen minutes Renny stops at a big park, with beautiful gardens and a lake. It's the type of place someone might get married at, and I wonder what made him choose it as our place to talk. We're both silent as we get off his bike and walk side by side down the path. He leads the way to a large, beautiful tree, and we sit under it.

"I never meant to hurt you," he starts, studying my profile while I stare out at the ducks on the lake. "I know it was a shitty thing to do to anyone, but once I met you, I knew I would never do anything to hurt you, Izzy. I know I've fucked up and broken your trust, and I'm sorry. But please know I told them straight away that we weren't going through with the plan, because I wasn't going to do that to you. It didn't feel right."

"And what was the plan?" I ask, turning my head so I can look him in the eye. "You never said what the exact plan was, and knowing the MC, there had to have been one. Was marrying me part of it? To get me drunk and then tie the knot to get to my dad, so you'd be married to his daughter and could use that against him?"

"No!" he exclaims, looking surprised. "Us getting married was not part of any plan, and I'm pretty sure it was your idea. How could you think that?"

"How could I not?" I ask. "It works to your advantage, does it not? You could have called him up and told him you were going to make it public that his daughter married an outlaw biker. He probably would have given you anything you wanted to keep that quiet."

He takes a deep breath. "After I met you, everything changed. Nothing else mattered. What we had planned no longer mattered. I wish you could see that. I had the club on my back to try to use your dad's connections to help save Temper's brother, but I couldn't do that to you. I couldn't use you. And I wouldn't. So yeah, I went into this with ill intentions, but I never went through with any of it, and I've given you all of me from the moment you got on my bike. I didn't hurt you, Izzy. I couldn't."

"Where is Temper's brother?" I ask.

"He's in jail," he admits, sighing. "He didn't do what he has been accused of, and now his kids have been put in foster care, and the whole thing is a cluster fuck. But that's not your problem, it's ours, and we'll handle it within the club."

Temper's nieces and/or nephews are in foster care but he doesn't want me to worry about that? I've just become an aunt, and it's one of the most important roles of my life. They've made this my problem and I can't just pretend I don't know about it.

"What is he accused of doing?"

"Someone planted drugs in Trade's house," Renny explains. "And before you ask how I know he's not guilty, Temper's mom died of an overdose in front of both of them. Neither have ever touched any drugs. So trust me when I say Trade is not fucking around with having drugs in his house with his kids."

"Who would want to frame him?" I ask, curious.

"We don't know. Could be another MC, the cops… We aren't sure. Someone was out to get him. It could even be his ex-wife, who lost custody of the kids and wasn't happy about it. Trade used to be heavily involved with the Knights, but when he became a full-time dad he left the lifestyle behind," he says. "He's still a Knight, and always will be one, but he stepped away, and we all respected that."

Shit. "How am I supposed to believe everything you're saying right now?" I ask, lifting my chin.

He cups my cheek and looks me in the eye. "You know me, Izzy, and some part of you still trusts me. Otherwise you wouldn't be here right now, sitting alone in the middle of nowhere with me. If you truly thought I was capable of holding you as a ransom or kidnapping you, would you be next to me right now? You heard what I was saying to Dee, but you also heard him saying that I'm falling for you, and that I've gotten myself into a shitty spot because of my feelings for you. So you know that what's between us is real, and you can't deny that."

He makes some valid points, but I don't know, it feels like before we were a fairy tale and now we're just your average fucked-up couple. Okay, maybe not average, but you know what I mean.

"I'm not denying anything," I say, swallowing hard. "I was falling for you, too, and I think you knew that. But now I don't know what I'm supposed to do. I just need some time to think. I don't know if I can trust you again, and without trust, we have nothing."

"You can have all the time in the world, I'm not going anywhere," he promises, lifting my fingers to his lips and placing a kiss there. "It's been shit without you here. I've missed you so much. Skylar was really upset that you didn't reply to her or call her back."

"I just didn't want to talk to anyone involved with the MC," I admit. "But I know that she wasn't in on this, so I should have replied to her."

"She was really pissed at us," he says, puffing out a breath. "The clubhouse has been filled with tension, especially when

Temper found out the truth. Skylar told him what happened, and he wasn't happy about it."

"At least someone was on my side," I grumble. I know he was trying to save his friend, this Trade guy, but it was at my expense. And yeah, he's changed his tune, but that doesn't change what happened.

"I hope that you can forgive me and know that I will always be honest with you and have your back from here on out. You can trust me, okay? And it might not feel like that right now, but I will prove it to you."

"Okay," I say softly, nodding. "Thank you for explaining everything to me."

"Thank you for listening," he replies, leaning back on his palms and looking up at the tree. "I used to come here as a kid and try to climb this tree."

"I was wondering why you chose this park." It obviously means something to him, if this is where he spent some of his childhood. I've noticed he rarely talks about growing up, or his family, so it's nice that he's opening up a little and speaking about these things.

"I come here to think sometimes," he admits, pointing to the lake. "And the little ducklings are kind of cute. I usually bring some bread to give to them."

"You don't really talk about your family," I decide to point out. To be fair, besides my sister, I've never really spoken about mine. I clearly never spoke about Dad and what happened with our family, and my mom's passing. I guess we both never opened up about our pasts, happier to focus on the now, and the new and exciting relationship we were building together.

"The MC is my family," he says, studying me. "I was an only child and my parents passed away in a car crash. None of my family wanted to take me in, so I was put in the system."

Another reason why he might have wanted to save Trade's kids from that.

Fuck.

"I lost my mom to cancer," I blurt out, staring down at my hands. "Ariel doesn't really like to talk about her, because she gets so upset, so Mom is kind of like the elephant in the room sometimes. We loved her more than anything, and losing her was the hardest thing we've both ever been through. And my dad, well…as I've said, we aren't close, and probably never will be."

"I'm sorry about your mom," he says, gently touching my arm to comfort me, but then backing away. It's like we don't know where we are anymore, and it's kind of awkward. I don't want him touching me, but at the same time I do. I want my space, but I also want him to keep pursuing me.

Basically, I don't know what the hell I want.

Which is why I need a little time to clear my head.

"Want to go down and walk around the lake?" I ask, standing up and offering him my hand for once.

He takes it and laughs as I try to pull him up, but then gives in and helps me by pushing to his feet and leading me toward the water.

"What else has been happening while I've been gone?" I ask, enjoying the fresh air and sunlight on my face.

"I've just been working," he replies, and I'm sure I hear him mutter, "And miserable," under his breath but I pretend that I don't. "So is your sister going to give me a beatdown?"

"She was going to throw her shoe at you if you stepped inside my house," I tell him, grinning. "And she would have, too. Baby in her arms and all."

He laughs softly. "Maybe I'll drop you home and take her for a ride to beg for her forgiveness, too."

"Not a bad idea," I reply in all seriousness. Ariel and Renny have to get along. She's my only family, and she's also my best friend. Her opinion does matter to me.

"I probably deserve the shoe," he admits after a few seconds. "I would have taken fifty shoes instead of you up and running away to Vegas. I thought about finding you, and making you listen to me, but I figured you'd come back when you were ready, and I knew I'd be waiting."

I did wonder while I was away if Renny would just show up at Ariel's door, taking control of the situation and demanding I listen to him.

"You said that I don't think any rules apply to me, that I can do whatever I want, so that's why I didn't follow you, because I didn't want to prove you right. You wanted space from me, so I let you have that, even though I didn't want to."

"Because it's not always about you," I remind him.

"I know that, but I also knew I had hurt you, and of course I wanted to fix it." He sighs, glancing over at me. "You're so far under my skin, and yeah, I guess it's been so long since I've actually cared about a woman that I haven't been handling it too well."

"So I'm like the splinter you never wanted but got anyway?" I ask, making him laugh out loud.

"You're a surprise splinter I never thought I'd be so lucky to find," he jokes back, then sobers. "I don't think you understand—I never connect to women like this. I mean, I'm nice to women, I love women, but I've never actually had an emotional and mental connection with one like this before."

That's kind of flattering, but also kind of sad.

"Guess you just never met the right one," I state, and he nods, agreeing.

"Nope, not until now, and then I went and fucked it all up," he admits, ducking his head. "You make me a better person, Izzy."

I'm glad that I do that, I really am, but does he make *me* a better person?

Or is he pulling me in the other direction?

Chapter Eighteen

"You were gone for a while," Ariel points out as I step in the door. "How did it all go?"

"Pretty well," I admit, giving her a rundown. She laughs when I tell her how he suggested taking her on a ride next so he can make her forgive him also.

"So are you going to forgive him?" she asks, no judgment in her tone.

I've always thought it was weak to forgive a man when he doesn't do right by you, but maybe it requires more strength. Maybe the right man just had to come along for me to want to fight for the relationship, I don't know.

"I said I needed some time to think," I tell her, but truth be told, I have softened toward him already. Not completely, but somewhat. If I decide to completely forgive him, we're going to have a lot of work to do, because my trust in him is shattered, and from now on I'm going to be second-guessing everything.

Is it worth it?

I don't know yet.

How I react now is going to set the standard for the future.

I want those standards set very high, because I'm not going to tolerate any kind of lies or manipulation again.

Ariel hands me Mila. "Well, I'll support you no matter what, you know that. I'm going to have a shower and then finish unpacking the last of my boxes."

I sit down on my couch and cuddle the little sleeping bundle in my arms. I don't need to make any decisions now. I can take my time and listen to my head and my heart, and hopefully they'll both lead me in the right direction.

Hopefully.

When Skylar drops by the next day, it's a little awkward.

"Hey," I say, smiling and opening the door wider. "Come on in."

She steps inside and pulls me in for a big hug. "I'm so sorry about what happened. The men in the MC can be such assholes sometimes. I mean, it's good when you're on their side, because they will do anything to help you, even if it's morally questionable, but to be on the other end... You didn't deserve that, and if it makes you feel any better, I yelled at them all and snitched to Temper."

I laugh softly. "I know, Renny told me. Thank you for having my back and not being a part of the whole scheme. It makes me feel a little better about the whole thing."

She nods. "Will you come to the clubhouse with me? Temper wanted to have a chat with you."

"Sure," I agree, even though I've been feeling hesitant about ever going back there. I'm going to bite the bullet and get it over with. Besides, I have been wanting to speak with Temper, especially since Renny told me the whole story.

I lock my door and we walk to the clubhouse together. "Renny was miserable while you were gone," she says, sighing. "I know it doesn't change anything, but he was, and I think he knew how badly he had fucked up. The night you left, he got super drunk and I could tell he was regretting his life decisions."

I never wanted Renny to be miserable, even though I remember angry me saying something along those lines. But I do want him to know he can't manipulate people like that. The MC, like Skylar said, is obviously used to doing whatever they want as long as it benefits them, and not caring who gets caught up in the fallout, as long as it's not a Knight. While I love that they have their brotherhood and that they look out for each other and are loyal to one another, I'm a person who would never step on another human to get anywhere, no matter if I love them or not.

"Yeah, that was a rough night," I admit, glancing down at the road. "I think the hardest part was that mostly everyone knew and was in on it, so it just makes everything fake, you know? Every friendship, every conversation, every laugh."

"Saint truly does like you," she assures me. "He thinks you are perfect for Renny and he's happy for you both, so don't think that they were all pretending to be your friend. It wasn't just Renny who got attached to you. We all did."

It's quiet when we enter the clubhouse, and we find Temper sitting outside alone, tapping away on his phone. "Hey, Temper," Skylar says, letting him know we're here.

He lifts his head and flashes us a small smile. "Hey. Izzy, nice to see you back here."

"I'll make you both some coffee," Skylar says, making a quiet exit and leaving me and Temper alone.

"I wasn't sure if you would come here," he admits, studying me with wise brown eyes. Temper is an old soul, I think.

"I wasn't sure either," I reply in all honesty. "But I know that you didn't know, so you're one of the only people not on my shit list right now."

"They were trying to help me," he says, running his hand over his bald head. "I know it doesn't excuse anything for you, but it's hard be too angry at men who were trying to help your family."

"I heard your brother was arrested," I say. "I'm sorry to hear about his children."

"He gave up the life for his kids, and they must have seen him as a weak link and went after him. I don't know what they want, but I know that something is coming for us. A war is brewing. I just don't know how to help him."

"Who is 'they'?" I ask.

"We've made some enemies over the years," he admits, placing his phone down on the table. "I don't know if Renny or Skylar have told you, but last year we lost her father, Hammer. He was the president of the club before me."

"She did mention that, yes."

"He was a good man. The best man, actually, and losing him was hard," he says, throat working as he swallows. "But there could be backlash from what happened there, which is what I'm thinking it might be. The men must have thought the same and also wanted to help Trade out, especially since he hasn't had anything to do with the club in a few years now. It's a shitty feeling knowing something you did is affecting someone you love, someone innocent."

"So this is the con to the lifestyle, hey," I whisper, feeling for him. "And it's a big one."

He nods. "It is. But there's a reason the men didn't tell me about their plan for you, and it's because I never harm anyone who hasn't harmed me or the club. And you're a nice girl, and you're our neighbor, and I like how happy you make Renny."

I ignore the fact he admitted that he'd happily harm anyone who was an enemy of the Knights, which might even be how they've gotten themselves into this situation right now.

"I'm trying to get his kids back so they can stay with me," he continues. "But they're going to take one look at me and say no, which I'm preparing for, but at least I tried." The sadness in his tone kills me. "I just wanted to say I'm sorry for what they did to your car, and for lying, and trust me, I've had words with them all. I hope you can forgive Renny, because he's a good man at the end of the day and he will do anything for those he loves, which I'm sure you've found out."

Yeah, because I've been on the other end of it.

"My dad and I aren't close," I admit, feeling the need to explain myself. "He's not a great person, and I know that firsthand. I mean, he's not all bad, but if I ask for something like this, I know there are going to be huge ramifications. So I guess the question is, how badly do you want it?"

Am I really considering asking him? One conversation with Temper, and I'm ready to dive in and try and save a man I've never met so his kids, who I've also never met, can be reunited with him. The fucked-up thing is, I probably *can* save Trade. It's just that I know what my dad is going to ask of me in return, and I don't know if I'm willing to do that.

"You don't need to explain yourself. You owe us nothing. And I don't expect anything from you. They fucked up, all right? Don't put this on you," he says, frowning, then shaking his head. "You haven't done anything wrong."

"I know," I respond, and I do. "But I'm the type of person that will help if I can."

"This is a different level of help," he warns. "This isn't helping an old lady pay for her groceries or babysitting for a neighbor. Like you said, there will be ramifications, and if those fall on me, then that's fine. Hell, I've been dodging that shit for my whole life, but I'm not going to let anything fall on you. Especially for something that isn't your problem. You said the mayor isn't a good man? Then it's probably for the best, because we don't need any more problems right now."

Skylar returns with coffee, obviously having taken her time to give us some privacy and a moment to chat. I think about Temper's words, and I know that he's right. This isn't my problem, and bringing my dad into it will probably only bring out further problems down the line. However, it will also most likely get Temper's brother out of jail. I know the type of contacts Dad has. He could make it happen with just a phone call. Whether he will or not though, I can't tell, because he's extremely unpredictable.

"Thank you," I say to her, holding the mug in my hand. "So, what else have I missed in the last few weeks?"

"Nothing much. I think you going MIA and leaving was the big drama," Skylar admits, smirking. "Renny wasn't much fun to be around, and we were all yelling at each other—"

"I'm pretty sure it was only you doing the yelling, Sky," Temper deadpans, reaching over and squeezing her cheek. "And everyone else trying to calm you down."

"Well, can you blame me? You guys chased away the only other woman around here who isn't a—"

"No slut shaming, Sky." Temper cuts her off, amusement dancing in his eyes.

"The only other woman I'd consider a friend," she concludes, pulling her hair out of its ponytail and letting it fall down her back. "Not to mention I was left out of the loop, too. What other sneaky shit are you guys up to that I don't know about?"

"My worries exactly," I add, sharing a look with her. "I mean, I'm not involved in the club, but anything that affects Renny also affects me."

"It's true," Skylar agrees, nodding. "It's not an easy thing. I mean, I grew up with the MC, but I was always left in the dark about anything they would deem club business. And I know that it was to keep me safe and uninvolved, but it wasn't a nice feeling to be the only one who didn't know what was going on."

"We all wanted to protect you," Temper says to her in a gentle tone. "And you're family, but you're not a member. No women are. And now you're Saint's old lady, so it's up to you how much he wants to tell you. Most of the time, you're in the know."

"Because I proved myself," she states, looking Temper in the eye. "And because I was dragged into some shit. Member or not, I was there beside you all fighting my way out of it." She looks at me and adds, "Which was the day I ended up on your doorstep."

I've always wondered what happened that day. Skylar showed up, frantic and asking to use my phone, looking like she had fallen in a ditch or something. Of course I let her in and did what I could do for her in that moment, which wasn't much other than to let her make the call, and soon the rumble of motorcycles came for her. I don't know why she didn't go to the clubhouse, and I never asked her, but after seeing the gates out front, I'm thinking that maybe it was in lockdown and she couldn't get inside.

"Lucky for you I work from home and was there to let you in," I joke, lightening the mood. "I always thought about that day and hoped you were okay."

She reaches out and touches my hand.

And although we might never be members, maybe our own sisterhood is enough.

Chapter Nineteen

When Renny walks out and sees me, his eyes widen.

"Izzy," he murmurs, smiling. He's wearing a gray T-shirt today, and it looks good on him, clinging to his every muscle, yet not too tight, letting me imagine just how ripped he is underneath. I mean, I know the answer to that is very, but I wouldn't if I hadn't already seen him naked. "You hanging out here without me now?"

"Yep," I reply, popping the *P*. "Skylar dropped by and told me to come over, so here I am." I don't want him to think that I just invited myself over or something, because that would be awkward.

He kisses the top of my head and sits down next to me. "It's nice to see you here."

"Nice to be here." They must have been worried I would never return, too angry with everyone over what had happened. And if you had asked me before, I probably would have said the same thing. At the end of the day these guys were my friends, and they will always be my neighbors, unless I up and sell my house, so it feels good to speak with them all and make peace, no matter what happens with myself and Renny.

"Are you going to stay for dinner?" he asks, pulling my chair closer to his. "You can bring your sister and niece over, too."

"What are we doing for dinner?" Temper asks, sounding confused.

"I think Renny's going to organize something because Izzy's here," Skylar whispers to Temper, making me laugh.

"Don't organize a dinner on my account," I tell Renny, grinning. Although it is sweet, and even nicer that he invited my family, it's very unnecessary.

"We can order pizza or something," he says on a shrug. "Or Chinese."

I know my sister won't want to come, especially not with a newborn, but I could send her a message inviting her so she feels included. They are her neighbors now also, but if she doesn't want to have anything to do with the MC, that is also okay, and very much up to her.

"Yeah, let's order Chinese," Skylar says, rubbing her hands together. "It's been ages since I've had any dumplings. I love the ones that have the soup in them."

"It's Izzy's choice," Renny pointedly tells her, scowling at Skylar.

Don't try and steal my thunder, I mouth to her, making her laugh out loud.

"Chinese is good," I tell him, smiling.

Eventually Saint and Dee show up, along with another two men I've never seen before. "Who are they?" I ask Renny, eying the two young, attractive men.

"New recruits," he replies, scowling. "Why?"

"I've never seen them before," I explain, rolling my eyes at him for obviously assuming I was checking them out. "What are their names?"

His lips tighten. "I think you better stop looking in their direction or they're about to get kicked out of the fucking club."

I look to Skylar with wide eyes, only to find her looking back at me with a similar expression.

What the fuck? I mouth to her.

"He's jealous," she replies, lip twitching.

I pause, and then ask, "Seriously, though, what are the new guys' names?"

Ignoring the growling noise that comes from Renny, Temper introduces me to the prospects: Crow, who is tall, lean and blond and blue-eyed, with neck tattoos peeping out of his Hawaiian shirt, and Chains, whose dark hair and eyes are almost menacing.

"Nice to meet you both," I tell them, smiling politely.

"You, too," Crow says, winking at me. "I can tell that I'm going to like it around here."

Renny steps in front of me, staring Crow down. "She's mine. Don't even breathe in her direction, because I will end you."

Crow throws his hands up. "Noted. Just being polite."

Even after everything that has happened, there's no way I'd have eyes for anyone other than Renny, especially in his clubhouse. Tugging on his hand, quietly telling him to cut it out, I pull him away from poor Crow and lead him into the kitchen.

"I wasn't checking them out, I was being polite and curious," I quietly tell him, frowning. "I'm supposed to be the one who has trust issues with you, not the other way around."

"I didn't like the way he was looking at you," he grumbles, opening the fridge and getting us two bottles of water. "And he needs to know now that he has no fuckin' chance, either."

"He was just being nice," I reply. "He's new here, he's going to be nice to everyone."

"Chains hasn't been nice to anyone," he fires back, smirking. "Crow should be more like him."

Stepping closer to him, I look up at him. "I know we're in a weird place right now, but that doesn't mean that my eyes have started wandering, all right? Especially around your friends and family. I'd never do that to you."

"I know," he admits, tucking my hair back behind my ear. "The thought of you with someone else just kills me, all right? And yeah, I don't even know if we're together or not, I don't think you even know either, so I'm a little on edge right now."

"I'm here, aren't I?" I say, resting my hand on his chest. "I don't know what's going to happen, but that has to mean something."

Dee enters into the kitchen, stopping in his tracks when he sees us. "Can I speak to her?" he asks Renny, avoiding my gaze.

Renny glances down at me, silently asking if that's okay.

"Sure." I nod.

He hands me the water and then leaves, eying Dee on the way out.

"I just wanted to say that I'm sorry," Dee starts, pulling a chair out and sitting on it. "I'm the one who found out that you were the mayor's daughter, who came up with the plan, and I'm the one who put pressure on Renny when he called it all off."

"Yes, I know, but you aren't the one I was falling in love with, so you telling me these things doesn't hurt me as much as Renny ever being a part of the whole thing," I admit, sitting down next to him. "I appreciate the apology, I really do."

"You're a gracious woman, Izzy."

"Did you guys even need to go to Vegas, or was that just an excuse to get close to me?" I ask, something I just realized I've never asked Renny.

"We were planning on doing a trip to visit the Vegas Chapter of the Knights," he admits, wincing. "But did we need to leave right then and there? No, we didn't."

"I thought as much," I say, taking a deep breath.

"Yeah, it's fucked up, I know. But for the record, Renny made the right call."

He stands up and kisses my forehead, then leaves the kitchen. Taking a deep breath, I lean my head back and try to pull myself together. The men are so forward and confrontational, and

I know it's a good thing to put everything out in the open so we can move on, but it's also quite draining and a lot to take in.

The food arrives, and we all sit at the outside table and eat together, chatting and laughing like nothing has changed.

Except it has, and I don't know what's going to happen next.

When the name *Dad* flashes on my phone a few days after, curiosity has me picking it up this time. "Hello?" I say.

"Isabella?" he replies in greeting. "How have you been, daughter? I've called you a few times now, but you haven't answered."

"I know," I tell him. "I've been busy with work, and helping Ariel with Mila."

He goes silent at the mention of his first grandchild, the one he's yet to meet. "I'm sure Ariel told you about what we discussed the last time I contacted her."

"Yes. Someone saw me on the back of a motorcycle, and somehow thought it was their business to tell you," I say, rolling my eyes. "And you think it will be a bad look for you, so you rang to tell me to only take transport with four wheels?"

"Cute," he grumbles. "It has nothing to do with what looks bad for me, Isabella. I'm worried about you. Who is this man that you've been seen with? Is he your boyfriend? I heard he was wearing a cut, that means he's part of an MC."

"That's a lot of assumptions you're making there," I say. "Why, what does it matter if he's a biker or not? I can't even remember the last time I saw you—was it last Christmas? Or maybe the one before? I don't know. I don't see how what I'm doing with my life affects you at all, Dad. Nobody even knows we're related."

"That's what you think," he replies, sighing heavily. "I'm still your father, and of course I care about what's going on in your life."

I go silent, my mind running. "I have a question for you, Dad."

"What is it?" he asks, sounding suspicious.

"If I had a friend who was in jail, is there any way you would be able to get him released as a favor to you? He didn't do what they've accused him of."

I know how bad that sounds. Everyone says they didn't do what they've been accused of, and I'm just going by the word of others—others who have lied to me before. But my gut is saying that Temper was being honest, that this Trade guy has been put in a shit place to get back at the MC.

"What did this *friend* do?" he asks. "And who are these people you are keeping company with these days?"

"They found drugs in his house," I reply, ignoring his other question.

"I mean, I could see what I could do, yes," he replies, but then says no more.

"Yes or no, Dad. Just how powerful are you?" I challenge.

One thing about my dad, he has a huge ego, and he doesn't like it one bit when you question him.

"Yes, of course I can," he replies, scorn filling his tone. "Why should I, though?"

"You're still my father, aren't you?" I ask, using his words against him.

He's silent for a few moments as he thinks. "I can get your friend out of jail, but if I do, I want you to lose the biker."

I knew this was going to happen.

I just knew it.

These are the ramifications, and they are going to solely fall on me.

To save Trade, I'm going to have to give up Renny.

I know how important family is, and if Ariel was in trouble, or Mila, and someone could help them, I'd want them to do that. Sibling love and loyalty mean everything to me, and if I can help Trade, I want to do that.

I asked Temper just how badly he wanted it, and he said he'd do anything as long as the consequences fell on him, but they're not going to. They're going to fall on me, and on Renny.

And I need to decide what I'm going to do.

Chapter Twenty

"He said *what*?" Ariel asks, pacing. "He wants you to cut all contact with Renny? Does he know that you live down the road from him? It's going to be kind of hard to do that even if you wanted to, which is why you faced your fears and jumped on a damn plane."

"I know. And Dad's never been to my house, but he has to know where I live, right?" I ask, wrinkling my nose. "My dad has never been to my house, how sad is that?"

"Pretty sad," she muses, sitting down next to me and sighing. "How are these your life problems right now?"

"I have no idea," I groan, covering my face with my hands. "And how is he going to ensure I stick to my word? I could just not ride with Renny, but it's not like he'd know who is going to be in my bed, or who I'm spending my free time with."

"Maybe he doesn't care as long as you're not out in the open where people can see and tie it back to him?" she guesses, resting her cheek on her palm. "I don't know. Maybe he has some secret ulterior motive we have no idea about, and he's going to drop it on us like a bombshell."

"Like when he left Mom for another woman?" I add, pursing my lips.

"Yeah, like that."

"You just never know with him," I agree. "I'm just going to think on it for now. Maybe I should run it by Renny and see what he thinks? I don't know. Bringing Dad into the mix is dangerous, he's such a wild card, but after hearing about Trade…"

I feel bad for a man I don't even know, and he means something to the MC, to Temper. I'd like to help them and his children.

"What do you think I should do?" I ask my big sister.

"I think you should speak to Renny," she replies, nodding. "Yeah, I think that's the best bet. Don't try to be some martyr and just do this and not tell him. He will be pissed. And I think you should just be honest and work with him, not against him."

Work with him.

I could do that.

"You're right," I whisper. "I need to speak to him."

I could have just agreed, not told Renny, and then he would have been left confused and hurt when I withdrew from him, which isn't fair to him. He's invested in me, and I don't want to hurt him, but maybe I can save Trade and make it work with Renny, too?

Can I have my cake and eat it, too, or is my dad going to expect something like this and be one step ahead of me?

I stand up. "I'm going to go over there now. Do you want to come?"

"No, I'm going to stay here and watch movies," she says, smiling at me. "I'll leave the excitement up to you."

"Okay, I'll be back soon," I promise. "How do you feel about us getting a guard dog? I feel like with everything going on, we're going to have to up the security here. Renny said he can sort it out for us."

Although there hasn't been a direct threat to us, and there might never be, I'd rather be safe than sorry.

"I think that's a great idea," she says, brow furrowing. "Between Dad, Merve and the MC, we never know what the hell is going to happen around here."

"I've wanted a dog for so long," I admit, smiling widely. "You have no idea. How do you feel about a Boerboel? They are huge, so cute and pretty much bred for protection."

"I knew you were going to want one of those," she says, smiling. "I'm happy with whatever you want."

"How did you know?"

She rolls her eyes. "You've mentioned them a few times. And I remember everything you say."

"Oh. Well, you know what they say, an elephant never forgets."

I leave her laughter behind in the house and jog down to the clubhouse. I send Renny a message to let him know I'm coming over to chat on the way, then enter through the open gate and knock on the door.

Temper opens it, inviting me in when he sees me. "Is Renny here?" I ask.

"He's in the gym," he says, pointing me in the right direction.

"Thanks."

He's lifting weights when I step into their makeshift gym, which is actually a really cool spot and has everything they could need. Renny is alone in the room, shirtless, and in nothing but a pair of black basketball shorts, his arms moving up and down with each lift.

I wait until he's finished before speaking, not wanting to scare him and have him drop the bar on his head.

"Need a spotter?" I ask him, my heart skipping a beat at his smile as he sees me.

"Isn't this a nice surprise?" he murmurs, taking me in.

My eyes can't help but roam his body, especially his abs. None of the men I've been with before have had a six pack, and all I want to do is run my tongue down it once more.

He strolls over to me, grabbing his towel along the way. "Probably not a good idea to look at me like that."

I kind of think it's a great idea actually, especially since it's been weeks since we last slept together, and with him looking like that... I want him.

"Why is that?" I ask him, placing my hand on his sweaty chest and taking a step closer to him.

He makes a soft growling sound and leads me to his room, locking the door behind us and then taking us into the bathroom. He turns the shower on, drops his shorts and briefs and stands there in all of his glory.

"You going to join me?" he asks, heat in his gaze.

I pull down my leggings and lift off my white top, throwing them on the ground and leaving me standing there in black cotton. I didn't exactly plan for us to have sex, so I didn't put anything racy on, but the way he's looking at me makes me feel like the sexiest woman alive.

When the bra and panties join the pile on the floor, I step into the warm water with him, and before you know it I'm back in his arms, his lips on mine, our bodies pressed together, droplets of water falling all over us. He lifts me up and pushes my back against the glass screen, hands on my ass, squeezing and kneading each globe.

When he pulls back and looks me in the eye, the emotion there is nearly my undoing. He needs this as much as I do.

Cupping his face, I kiss him again slowly at first, but then harder, deeper, and when he presses his cock against my sex, I'm more than ready for him. Making a sound of encouragement in his throat, he slides the tip in, slowly, gently. He has all the control in this position, and I'm so hot and horny right now that I just want him to fuck me, but he plays it out, kissing my neck and taking his time, teasing me.

"Renny," I plead, which must work on him, because he thrusts inside me, both of us moaning at the same time, then continues to slowly work himself in and out, all the while kissing me, touching me and stroking me. It's not long before he makes me come, scoring my nails down his back and whispering his name as I do so. Lifting me up higher, he moves against me faster, deeper, until he finishes inside me.

"Fuck," he grits out, body jerking.

Once he's done, he kisses me again, pushing my wet hair off my face and gently rubbing his hands down my arms and back up to my cheeks. "I missed you."

"I could tell," I reply, smiling against his lips. "I missed you, too."

He places me back down on the floor, my legs feeling like jelly, and then squirts some soap into his hands and gently rubs it all over my body. I let my eyes fall closed and just enjoy it. It's been a long few weeks without being touched like this.

"I'm glad you dropped by," he says into my ear, making me grin.

"Me, too. I did come here for a reason, though, you know, other than to come."

He chuckles softly. "I thought as much."

We finish up in the shower, dry ourselves and jump in bed before I tell him what I came here to tell him.

"So your dad will help Trade so long as you stop seeing me?" he repeats, jaw going tight. "Over my fuckin' dead body."

"And I don't even know if he will keep his word, which is the same thing he could say for me, so it's a pretty iffy deal. But it's all we have right now if you want to get Trade out of jail as soon as possible," I tell him, shrugging. "I don't know. You guys need to let me know what you want to do."

"I'm not giving you up for anybody," he states, pulling me against him. "If your dad doesn't like that you're with a biker, too bad for him, because it's too late."

"Too late for what?"

"Too late for either of us to walk away from each other," he says, rolling on top of me. "I know you're still angry at me, but come on, Izzy. I think we both know we're in too deep now.

I've fallen in love with you. I can't just walk away and I'm not going to let you do the same, especially when it's not you who wants to do so."

"You're in love with me?" I ask, searching his gaze.

"Yes, I am," he replies, brown eyes gentling. "Very much."

Am I in love with Renny?

I think I am, but I'm not one hundred percent sure, or maybe I am but my pride won't allow me to say it yet. We're supposed to be on some break while I figure out if we can be together, but we've already broken that by sleeping together anyway. I don't regret being with him, not one bit, but it doesn't change anything.

I open my mouth to speak but he shakes his head, stroking my hair. "You don't have to say anything. Are you going to sleep here tonight?"

I nod. "Yeah, I better message Ariel."

It wouldn't feel nice to sleep with him then not stay the night. I've missed his cuddles more than anything, and spending the night wrapped up in him sounds perfect.

I send her a quick message, then lie back down with Renny.

"We'll talk to Temper about this whole thing tomorrow," he says, sighing. "We'll find a solution, okay? One that doesn't involve you walking away from me. I'm glad that you came to me and didn't consider doing it."

I go silent, because I did consider it, but I'm glad that I didn't go through with it because it would have been silly. I'm not going to lose the man I love because my dad doesn't think it will look good for his image.

Love.

Shit. I *am* in love with him.

I decide to keep it to myself until the right time makes itself known, until we are in a good place again.

For now, it can be my secret.

Chapter Twenty-One

"Well, at least we know the mayor's view on bikers," Saint muses, turning to look at Temper. "Thoughts, prez?"

"His request is stupid," Temper replies, pacing up and down the kitchen with a scowl on his face. "I think I need to speak to him, man to man. Do you think you could arrange that for us, Izzy?"

"Sure."

"That's where your involvement in this will end, though," he says, pausing in his steps to look at me. "I don't want you to give anything or lose anything, all right? You've done enough to help the MC, and because of how this whole thing came about, I don't want you feeling used in any way, shape or form."

I open my mouth, but he cuts me off before I even say anything. "And I hope you didn't even consider taking any deal he offered you, because this isn't your problem, it's mine." I decide to nod, agreeing, and to let him continue. "I'm going to speak to him and see what I can do to get him in our court."

"I'm going to spend the day working on the clubhouse security, and Izzy's security at her house," Renny inserts, looking at all of the men. "I think we need to hope for the best, but be prepared for the worst."

I know there's something they're not telling me, and I think it has to do with Hammer's death. Is someone coming after them? Temper said they have enemies, but who, and why?

"All right," Temper mutters, then turns to say something to Skylar that makes no sense to me. "Do we have eyes on your mom?"

"She's on the farm," Skylar tells him.

The little meeting ends, and Renny escorts me back home, joining me on my walk of shame, wearing last night's clothes. "I'm going to get a guard dog."

"That's a good idea," he agrees. "Temper suggested getting a few rottweilers or something for the clubhouse, but I know that if the cops step inside and the dogs are barking at them, they'll probably just shoot them, and then we'll all be devastated."

"So you didn't get dogs so the cops can't kill them? That's really sad." I hope no cops ever come to my house, although I don't know why they'd have reason to, considering I've never done anything illegal in my life. Still, I guess I'll now be guilty by association from here on out.

"I can see why your dad wouldn't want you to be with me," he says quietly, eyes down. "But know that the club and I will protect you with all we have, and that we will do everything in our power to make sure that nothing touches you or your family."

"I know," I assure him. "I'm not dwelling on what he said, trust me. I don't need his approval to be with who I want to be with. If he were a different person and we had a close relationship, maybe, but he isn't and we don't, so you don't have to worry that his opinion will ever make me change my mind about you. I knew exactly who you were before we started dating, and I'm never going to ask you to change anything about you. I mean, besides the whole lying thing."

"I know I deserve it, but man, you know how to hold a grudge," he grumbles, taking my hand as I walk along the curb. "But I'm glad that his comments don't have you running away. Not that you'd get very far, considering you're just down the road."

"Dad jokes, hey?" I tease, smirking. "Nope, I haven't run since high school, so I don't think you have to worry about that."

We stop at my front door, and I give him a hungry kiss before we enter.

"I'm home!" I call out, placing my bag and keys on the table near the door and heading to the kitchen.

"Hey," Ariel replies from the couch. "I'm guessing your vagina trumped your grudge-holding skills, eh?"

I cover my face with my hands. "I probably should have told you that Renny is here with me, coming to up our security game in the house."

I chance a look at his expression, but he's just amused, eyes dancing.

"My comment is still valid," she replies, coming into the kitchen with Mila in her arms, her eyes narrowed. "Renegade."

"Ariel," he says, smiling at her full-naming him. "How are you?" He glances down and adds, "Just making sure you're not wearing any shoes that you can throw at me."

Ariel's lip twitches. "Not too bad, and yourself?" she replies, as I hold out my arms for Mila.

"I'm okay," he says. "Going to upgrade all the locks and install a security camera in here."

"Isn't she the cutest?" I ask Renny, introducing him to Mila.

He glances down at her and grins. "She is the cutest baby I've ever seen, I think." He then proceeds to baby talk to her. "Hello, Mila. Aren't you just gorgeous? You look like a mini version of your mom and aunty."

Ariel and I share a look while he continues to fuss, eventually taking her from my arms and holding her. He looks really good with a baby. A little too good—my ovaries are about to burst.

"Well, I've forgiven him," Ariel whispers, watching him with her daughter. "And also can he babysit, so me and you can go out to the movies or something? Because that would be great."

"I love kids," he says, gently rocking Mila. There's something about seeing a big, built, sexy, tattooed man holding a little vulnerable baby, and him being so gentle and sweet to her, that is really, really sexy.

He hands Mila back to Ariel with a smile, then turns back to me. "I'm going to check the house, then go and get what I need."

"Sounds good. I'll make us all some lunch."

Renny does the recon while I make some nachos and guacamole. Flashbacks of us last night keep hitting me, and the fact that we had sex twice more after in the shower doesn't make me want him any less right now.

Will that ever go away?

I hope not.

I can't believe that I've unconsciously decided to give him a second chance, my actions speaking louder than my words.

I just can't let go of him, not yet.

Maybe not ever.

"Now when someone comes to the door, we don't even have to get up, how good is it? We can see who is there on our phones and decide whether we want to answer it or not," I say to Ariel, my feet up on the coffee table as we watch a movie together. Renny installed the cameras, upgraded all of the locks and blocked off one side of the house so no one can enter from that area. Something about a controlled setting. The cameras come with two screens, one for Ariel and one for me, which are portable, so we can put them wherever we want and have a constant stream of everything happening on our property.

"I know. No more dealing with salesmen," she agrees, tossing some popcorn in her mouth. "And less walking around for no reason."

"When we get the puppy, we're going to have to do daily walks, though," I tell her. "It will be cute, little family outings.

We can put Mila in her stroller and walk down to the local dog park."

"I suppose I could lose some of my baby weight," she says, wrinkling her nose.

I eye her. "You don't have any baby weight. You look exactly the same." And she does. Yeah, she has the slightest stomach, but it just looks like she ate a whole pizza or something. Even my stomach does that. "I'd totally be rocking the mom bod if I were you. This is the time to let yourself go."

She laughs and throws a pillow at me. "Maybe you'll be pregnant soon, especially with the way Renny was looking at you today, like he wanted to eat you whole. I felt like I was watching the beginning of a porno. He was the handyman fixing shit, and you were the housewife, cooking lunch and watching him."

I blink slowly a few times. "Do me a favor and never say anything like that ever again. Ew."

She just laughs, and it's nice to watch and hear her do so. She has been so stressed lately about Merve, and the lawyer appointments she made, which he never showed up to or responded to. We have no idea where he is or what he's going to do, but at least he doesn't know where Ariel lives now. I guess he will contact her when he wants to, as she still has the same number.

"Maybe it's just because the last time I had sex was when I got pregnant with Mila," she muses, continuing with the oversharing. "And it wasn't even good sex. Merve isn't exactly what I would call a generous lover."

"Why does that not surprise me one bit?" I reply in a dry tone. "You were always way too good for him. I mean, I'm not going to say I wish he was never born, because then we wouldn't have Mila, but what the hell were you thinking?"

She sighs heavily and presses pause on the movie, giving me her full attention. "He's good-looking, we all know that, it's the one thing he does have. But I don't know, he was kind of charming back then, and had the whole bad boy thing going on. I mean, come on, you know the allure. Look at who you're dating."

"Hey, Renny is nothing like Merve. He's funny, kind, smart and *really* generous in bed. And if he had a kid, I'm sure he'd be a great dad." Also unlike Merve. "And he's smoking hot. You should see him naked," I add, giggling.

"I'd rather not," Ariel deadpans, lip kicking up at the corners. "Does he have any hot friends?"

I arch my brow. "Yeah, he does. Bikers in all shapes, ages and sizes. Come to the clubhouse and let me show you."

She unpauses the movie and continues to stare at the screen. "No way, at least not now. I just had a baby—I don't have time for a man right now. Mila is my priority."

"You might not have time for a man but surely in a few months or so you'll have time for a little penis," I reply, snickering to myself.

"I don't want to have time for a little penis," she replies, smirking. "Only big ones, please."

There's nothing better than having a sister. You can say whatever the hell you want, no matter how uncensored or immature, and she won't bat an eyelash. She'll just feed off you and keep the conversation going.

No judgment, no sensitivity, just pure, unconditional love.

The best kind.

Chapter Twenty-Two

I'm pretending to work the next day, but really am just scrolling through my social media when I see a post pop up about a dog someone is giving away because apparently they don't have time for him anymore. If nobody wants him they are going to hand him into the shelter.

"People are such assholes," I mutter to myself, looking at the picture of the sad-looking staffy-Rhodesian ridgeback mix.

"Why are people assholes?" Ariel asks, stepping into the living room with the mop in her hands.

I show her the post. "They are giving away this two-year-old dog, and look at his little face."

She looks at it and then back at me. "Want to go have a look at him?"

I grin, stand up and get changed.

Twenty minutes later we're at this family's house, and we see Shadow chained up in the backyard, looking miserable.

"Why is he chained?" I ask the man, unable to hide my disapproval.

He glances at me from the corner of his eye. "He barks at

the slightest noise or when anyone walks past, and he also tries to jump the fence."

"Do you exercise him?" I dare to ask. Maybe if he went for a walk or something, he wouldn't be trying to escape to take himself for a walk.

"He pulls on the lead," is all the man replies, so I'm going to take that as a no.

"How is he with kids?" Ariel asks, Mila in her arms.

"Great. He loves our kids," the man says, sounding genuine about that fact. "He's a good guard dog but loyal to his family. I trust him with my three for sure."

"You wait here," I say to Ariel, just in case Shadow jumps up on her or something while she has Mila. "I'll suss him out."

Ariel agrees and waits by the car, while I enter this man's garden through the side gate. I pretend I don't see the marijuana plants and head straight for Shadow, who barks when he sees me, but stops when the man says, "It's okay, Shadow."

Then he starts to wag his tail as he runs over, all but jumping in my arms and licking my face. "Aren't you a good boy?" I say, patting the ridge of hair on his back. He looks more staffy, but has the coloring and markings that I've seen on purebred Rhodesian ridgebacks, just with a little white on his chest. He is beautiful, and one look into those brown eyes and I'm in love.

"Do you want to come home with me?" I ask him.

He licks my cheek.

"I'm going to take that as a yes," I say, laughing as he licks me more.

Looking at his owner, I say, "I'd love to take him, and I'll make sure he has a permanent, loving home."

Leading Shadow to the car, he jumps right in the front with me, which is good so he can't lick Mila in the back.

Ariel looks over me and smiles. "He's so cute! Welcome to the family, Shadow."

That evening, when Renny comes over, Shadow runs to the door, barking and growling his head off.

"It's okay, Shadow," I say, using the same command his previous owner used.

He calms instantly and sits, looking at the door. I open it to see a confused Renny, who glances down at Shadow and then back up at me. "You got a dog?"

I nod. "This is Shadow. Isn't he great?"

Renny steps in and Shadow just eyes him. "Is he going to bite me?"

Wrinkling my nose, I glance down at my new best friend. "I don't actually know—we only got him a few hours ago, so I can't make any promises. Also I'm pretty sure he was used as a guard dog to protect the drugs the man had growing in his garden."

"Do you trust him around Mila?" Renny asks, closing the door behind him, not taking his eyes off Shadow. "Did you think this through or did you just rush in to save some dog from a drug dealer?"

"He's great with kids," I tell him, frowning. "We introduced him to Mila, and he just sniffed her and loved her. It was fine. He grew up around children."

Renny takes a step closer to me and Shadow growls a little, so I lean down and say, "It's fine, Shadow. Come on in, just ignore him. I'm sure he will warm up to you." Taking Renny's hand, I pull him into the living room. "We love the security cameras, by the way. Thank you so much for installing them for us. And with Shadow, we already feel so much safer."

"You're welcome," he replies, sitting down. "Did you speak to your dad?"

"Yeah, I called him just before, and he said he'd have a meeting, but Temper has to go to him. I gave him Temper's number so tell him to keep his phone handy," I say, shrugging. "I don't know how this is going to play out, but I could tell he was intrigued by meeting the president of the Knights of Fury MC."

And also highly unimpressed that I knew Temper well enough to be facilitating this meeting, but that's another story.

"Okay, well, that's a good sign," Renny murmurs, eying Shadow, who is sitting right in front of him, staring. "I'm your dad, why are you looking at me like that?" he says to him.

"You're not his dad. We aren't married anymore, remember?" I tease, smirking.

"Just because we aren't legally married right now doesn't mean we won't be again one day," he fires back, shrugging.

"I'd like a proper proposal this time around, and all the trimmings," I tell him. "Not a wedding that I can't even remember."

I glance up to see Ariel standing in front of us wide-eyed. "What?"

Oh, fuck.

Cringing, I open my mouth, close it, then open it again. "Renny and I got drunk and married in Vegas and I didn't tell you because I knew you'd kill me. But don't worry, now it's all annulled so no one needs to ever speak about it again. We can all just pretend it didn't happen."

"Isabella Marie Johnson," she growls, shaking her head. "You are a walking cliché and I can't believe you didn't tell me this! And you," she grits out, pointing at Renny. "How did you let that happen?"

"Are you angrier that I did it, or that I didn't tell you?" I ask, wincing.

Green eyes narrow. "Both! I'm actually going to kill you, Izzy. Mom is probably rolling in her grave right now."

Okay, ouch, that was a low blow.

She storms off all dramatically, stomping like a baby elephant, while I sit there groaning. "That went better than I thought it was going to. Imagine if it wasn't annulled, she actually would have killed me."

"Really?" Renny asks, confusion all over his expression. "You thought it would be worse than that?"

"Yeah." I nod. "I think I got off lightly. We got married, Renny. It's kind of a big deal, you know?"

"Oh, I know," he whispers, standing up. "I'm going to go and talk to her."

"Are you sure you want to do that? I usually let her cool down before I try and speak to her."

Which, I think, is the smart thing to do. Otherwise people say all kinds of things in anger, and words are something that, once spoken, cannot be taken back.

"Yeah, I'm sure," he says, following Ariel.

"Your dad has big balls," I whisper to Shadow, who gives me a head tilt in response. I pat him and try to listen for any yelling, but the house remains quiet, so it must not be going too badly. When Renny resurfaces it's with Ariel by his side, who studies me for a few seconds, a scowl still settled firmly on her pretty face, but she says, "I can't believe you didn't tell me."

"I didn't want to see the disappointment on your face that I see right now," I admit, biting my lip. "And it's all sorted now, Ariel. We handled it."

"And I've never done something stupid? You've seen my baby daddy," she says, rolling her eyes. "We all make mistakes, and yes, I will yell at you and tell you that you're stupid, because that's what big sisters do, but after that I'm going to be there for you to help you get out of said stupid situation."

"I was going to just hide it under the rug," I admit, exhaling deeply. "I didn't know Renny and I would start dating, I didn't know any of this would happen, and I was just going to pre-tend it didn't happen. And if I told you that was going to make it very, very real."

She sits down next to me and gives me a big hug. "Don't censor me from anything, okay? You know I'll always get over it."

"Okay, the next time I get married, I'll make sure that you're there," I promise her, grinning.

Renny mutters something, but I don't hear him. "What did you say?"

"Nothing," he replies, flashing me his teeth. "Aren't you happy everything is out in the open now?"

"Yeah, I am. I actually forgot that I didn't tell her, to be honest, which is obviously why I brought it up without even thinking about it," I admit, shaking my head. "All the other stuff that has been going on has kind of overpowered the marriage debacle. Who would have thought?"

"Not me," Ariel replies, standing up when she hears Mila cry. "Never would have thought that you'd be married before me."

She leaves the room and Renny sits back down next to me.

"What did you say to her, Mr. Smooth-talker?" I ask, kissing him softly on his cheek, his stubble pricking me.

"The truth," he replies, kissing my lips. "I'll go tell Temper about the meeting. What are your plans for the rest of the day?"

"I'm going to buy Shadow some new things, like a bed, bowl, lead and collar, and then take him for a walk. Apparently he doesn't do too well on the lead, but I think he'll be fine."

"Do you want me to come with you?" he asks, giving Shadow a dubious look.

"Yeah, that would be nice. We don't know if he's good with other dogs. I might get a muzzle until we know what we're working with here."

"Probably a good idea," Renny agrees, reaching out to pat him.

Shadow doesn't react negatively at all, he just lifts his head up for more love.

"See, he's a big softy, he just looks tough," I say, watching the two of them interact. "He's a great guard dog, too. He will bark if someone he doesn't know even comes near the property."

I can see Renny already warming up to him, especially when he pats the couch and lets Shadow sit next to him on it.

"Is he allowed on the couch?" he asks me afterward, looking a little sheepish.

"Yeah, why not? He's a member of the family now, and I'm pretty sure he's spent most of his life on a chain." But all that is over for him now, and I'm going to make sure he's the most happy, spoiled pooch around.

We go to update Temper, then head to the shops to pick up Shadow's new belongings. When we return home with his new lead and collar, he starts jumping, so excited.

"We should probably avoid the dog park until we know what he's like," I tell Renny, stepping out the front door. Shadow begins to pull straight away, almost yanking my arm off, so Renny takes the lead and lets him pull until he gets tired of it. Only when he relaxes does he start the walk, and although he does pull a little and walk on each side of us, getting himself tangled, he's not as bad as he was made out to be. He ignores the other humans and dogs as we pass them, and I think he's just happy to be included and getting some fresh air.

"He's a good boy," Renny finally admits on our way home. "The pulling thing we can fix; he just needs a little training and patience."

"I'm so glad I went on a whim and got him," I say, holding Renny's hand and smiling up at him. "He fits into our family so well—come on, admit it."

And I helped save him, which is much better than forking out thousands for a puppy.

Adopt, don't shop.

"He does. We'll have to bring him to the clubhouse so everyone can meet him."

"Sounds good."

We head home and I catch up on some work while Renny cooks us all dinner.

We might not be your normal family, but we definitely are becoming one.

Chapter Twenty-Three

"There's no way I can concentrate knowing Temper is sitting somewhere in a meeting with Dad right now," I say to Ariel, tapping my foot nervously. "What if it's a setup? Could you imagine? What if he plants some bullshit on Temper and now he's in jail with his brother?"

"Temper is the president of an MC—I doubt he'd have to plant anything," Ariel reminds me, arching her brow. "These aren't choir boys you've decided to align yourself with."

"I don't need your logic right now," I groan, covering my face with my hands. "It's Dad. Dad always has a plan."

And they say you end up with someone just like your father. Great.

Renny always has a plan, too.

"I'm sure Temper didn't get to where he is without a plan, too. Have some faith," she says, bringing me some lunch. "Here, eat. Food is always the answer."

I take a few bites of the sandwich she made, but I keep checking my phone for updates from Renny about how the meeting went. Is Dad going to demand that Renny leaves me alone?

What if that's the only thing he wants from the MC? I don't want to lose Renny, and I know he won't give me up, but we still need a plan to get Trade out of this pickle he's found himself in.

A knock at the door makes Shadow lose his shit, and my eyes move straight to the screen to see who it is. A cute, petite, middle-aged lady stands there, holding a piece of paper.

"There's a lady at the door," I tell Ariel. "Shadow!"

He comes back to me, which is a good thing, and I hold on to his collar while Ariel answers the door. I hear a muted conversation, and then she returns with a flyer. "Just some lady looking for her dog."

"Aw no," I say, frowning. "I haven't seen any dogs roaming around here."

"Me either, but we can keep an eye out." She hands me the picture, and it's of a golden Labrador.

"What a gorgeous dog." I look down at Shadow. I'd be devastated if he got away and I had no idea where he was or what had happened to him. "Maybe we could help her look for him," I suggest.

Before she can answer, my phone rings with Renny's name popping up on my screen. "Hello?"

"Hey, I'm coming over now," he says.

"Okay." He says goodbye and hangs up, and I share a look with Ariel. "I guess we're about to find out how much of an asshole our dad is."

"I hope you're not expecting much from him," she replies, kissing the top of Mila's dark head. "Because you know he lets us down, every damn time."

I know, but still.

How did we turn out so different from him?

Surely there's some good in him?

When Renny steps through the door with Temper, I'm a little surprised to see the president in my space. Still, I make sure he feels welcome, introducing him to my sister and niece and telling them to come in and sit down. My mom once told me that only people with class introduce others to each other, and that line has always stuck with me.

"So he said he'd help me get Trade out and get his kids back," Temper starts with, cracking his knuckles.

"And what did he ask for in return?" I ask him, brows drawing together.

"At first he said all he wanted was the MC to stay away from you," he admits, glancing over at Renny. "But I pointed out that that is impossible to govern, and impossible in general. So he came back with a counteroffer."

"And what is it?" I ask, looking at Ariel. What does our darling father want from the Knights?

"We owe him a marker, no questions asked. One he can call in at any time," he explains, crossing his arms over his chest. "He mentioned that he's been getting some threats and a little bit of blackmail, and apparently we have a mutual enemy, so I think he'll want our help with something to do with that. But he just doesn't know what that is yet."

"Does that make you allies?" I ask, surprised at this turn of events. "Your enemy's enemy is your friend, right?"

"I wouldn't go that far," Temper replies, frowning. "But yeah, for the time being, I think we're on the same level with everything. He's working on getting Trade out right now."

Feeling a little suspicious, I ask, "So, you're saying things are looking up, and everything might work out?"

"We can only hope," Renny mutters, shaking his head. "Let's wait and see if he gets Trade out, and go from there. If he wants us to owe him, something shady must be going on, and there's definitely shit he's not telling us."

"If the Destined Killers MC is involved, you know shit is going to get messy," Temper adds, standing up. "I'm going to get back to the clubhouse. Saint has Tory there, and I'm going to go and hang out with her."

"Who is Tory?" I ask.

"Saint's daughter," Renny explains, laughing at my surprised reaction.

"I had no idea that Saint has a kid… Skylar?"

"Skylar's not her biological mother," he says, explaining that Saint had Tory before he and Skylar got together.

"That makes more sense." I can't imagine Skylar having a daughter and not even mentioning it to me. Moms love to talk about their kids.

My phone rings and I stare at it when I see my dad's name. I know instantly that this isn't going to be a pleasant phone call, but curiosity has me answering anyway. "Hello?"

"Please tell me what your long-term plan is with this biker?" he asks, and I can just imagine him sitting in his office on his big chair.

"Dad," I start, taking a deep breath. "My life doesn't affect yours. No one will connect us. I'm sure the person who saw me on the bike was one of your spies, am I right? It wasn't just someone random. No one even knows who I am. The media only knows your new family."

"I don't have a new and an old family, Isabella, I just have a family," he states with such conviction that, if I hadn't experienced being left behind by him myself, I probably would have believed him. "You are all my children and I love you all the same. I'd love it even more if you and Ariel spent more time with your baby sisters."

"Don't pretend we are welcome there, Dad. Your wife has been nothing but rude to us and made sure we knew our place from the very beginning. Either you didn't care or you allowed it anyway, which is the real reason this family isn't close. Never mind how you treated my mother, who was a good woman."

"How many times are we going to have this same argument?" he asks. "And it has nothing to do with the fact that you are now dating a criminal. What happened to my smart little girl? I don't even know who you are anymore."

This comment hurts and angers me at the same time. He

hasn't known me in years, and that's because of his decisions and his actions.

"We're probably going to have this same argument forever," I tell him, gritting my teeth. "Maybe I chose a biker because I have daddy issues that you caused. Don't worry about what I'm doing, it's not going to affect your latest campaign, I can assure you of that."

"Isabella—"

"I really appreciate you helping Trade," I continue, my nails digging into my palm. "So thank you for that, Dad. But if you've just called me to lecture me and tell me everything I'm doing wrong with my life, I'd rather not hear it." I pause and then add, "And by the way, if you love us all the same, how come you haven't even seen or asked about your granddaughter? Surely that should mean something to you?"

"She was born out of wedlock—"

"You cheated on your wife," I remind him. His hands are far from clean from his own judgment. "You can't just choose how you sin and decide that it's okay, but judge everyone else for their life choices. It doesn't work that way."

He takes a loud breath, like he's trying to calm himself. "At the end of the day, I'm still your father, whether you like it or not, and I'm never going to accept you being with this biker. You think I'm going to walk you down the aisle? Be there when you start a family? Leave you anything in my will? Because I won't if I don't agree with the way you're living your life."

"As if you're leaving us anything anyway, that wife of yours will make sure of that," I tell him, rolling my eyes. There's no way she's going to let him give us anything in his will; it will all go to her and her children. "I don't want any money from you, Dad. The one thing I wanted you've already destroyed, which is my childhood."

I hang up, feeling worse after my rant instead of better.

There are some people who just bring out the worst in you, and those are the people you need to avoid.

Even if they are your own flesh and blood.

Chapter Twenty-Four

About a week later I find Ariel staring at the security screen, Shadow barking like mad at the front door. "Izzy, there's a really hot guy at the front door. Who the hell is he?" she whisper-yells, pointing.

I close my laptop to give this my full attention. "I don't know, I've never seen him before."

The man at our front door is tall and tattooed, with dark features and a man bun tied on top, but underneath he has it all shaved off.

"What do we do?" she asks, throwing her hands up in the air. "Who knew living with you would be so social? You used to be a hermit."

"Come on, let's go and see who it is." Surely someone that meant us harm wouldn't just knock on the door? Although I've seen burglars on television use this technique to gain entry and then push right in with force.

"Yes?" I call out to the man.

"Hey, Izzy? I'm a friend of Renny's," he says.

I pick up my phone and call Renny.

"Hello, beautiful, I was just thinking about you."

"Do you know some brunette young guy with a man bun?" I ask him. "Because he's here and name dropping so we'll open the door."

"What? Oh, that's Trade. He wanted to say thank you, although I told the bastard to wait until I got home. I'm on my way now."

Trade? I hang up on Renny and open the door. "Hey," I tell him. "Sorry, just had to check who you are. You know, stranger danger, and all of that."

He smiles widely, flashing white teeth. I tell Shadow to stop his barking, and he does, instantly.

I don't know why but I pictured Trade as being...well...an old man. He has kids and got out of the life, so I was assuming he was older than Temper, maybe in his forties or something, but the man in front of us looks young, maybe late twenties, and doesn't look like a dad at all.

Ariel has gone oddly quiet next to me, and I know that Trade is just her type.

"No problem. Renny told me to wait for him, but I was bored and I wanted to say thank you to you both." He looks over at Ariel, and just stares for a few seconds.

I glance between them both, watching as they both visibly check each other out.

"Come on in. Renny said he's on his way. Ignore Shadow, he'll stare you down but won't bite you." Unless I tell him to.

Trade steps inside and glances around. I lead him to the kitchen, and offer him a drink. "I'd love a coffee," he replies, so I get to making us all one.

"You don't need to thank us, we didn't really do anything," I tell him. "The MC did all the hard work. I just made a phone call."

"Still, I appreciate it," he says, looking us both in the eye. "Without your dad using his contacts, who knows when I would have gotten out, and who knows if they would have given me my kids back, so thank you."

"How many kids do you have?" Ariel asks him, suddenly having found her voice.

"Three," he replies, smiling at the thought of them. "Two girls and a boy."

"Nice. They must keep you busy," she says, leaning forward on the counter. I bet she's wishing she was wearing something other than her unicorn silk pajamas, with her hair in a messy bun on top of her head. She still looks beautiful, though.

"They do. I'm a full-time dad and I work full time, so my life is pretty hectic," he replies, the two of them now having a private conversation between them as if I'm not even there anymore.

"What do you do for work?" she asks, conducting a full interview.

"I work in construction," he says, brown eyes pinned on her. "I own my own company, actually. So I can be flexible when I need to, but it also requires a lot of my time and energy. So it's basically like having four kids."

They both laugh, while I'm standing here wide-eyed, adding sugar into their mugs.

Shadow runs to the front door, letting me know that Renny is indeed here. He storms in, scowl etched onto his handsome face, dressed in all black. "I told you to wait for me."

"I was bored," Trade muses, standing back and scrubbing his hand down his freshly shaven face. "I've been at the clubhouse all day, sitting around, waiting for the call that I can go and pick up my kids. I needed a distraction."

"My woman's house isn't a place you or any other man gets to go to for a distraction," Renny seethes, staring him down. I don't think I've ever seen him this angry before.

He comes to my side and kisses my temple. "I'm sorry you both had a random fresh-out-of-jail biker showing up at your doorstep, especially when we've just told you to be more careful."

"It's okay," I assure him, wrapping my arms around him and resting my cheek against his chest. "And before you lecture me on leaving the door unlocked, you said you were right around the corner."

He purses his lips, but chooses his battles and lets it go, too busy directing his anger at Trade, who is currently making love heart emoji eyes at my sister.

"Would you like a coffee, babe?" I ask Renny, distracting him.

I can see why he's annoyed at Trade, especially since we're all kind of waiting for the shoe to drop at any moment, but the man did just get out of prison, and like he said, is waiting for his kids to return to him. It's nice that he wanted to thank us, not that I needed to hear it because I didn't actually do much, but I appreciate the sentiment.

We all sit on the couch. I put out some snacks, and Renny and I watch Trade and Ariel hitting it off. Mila starts to cry, so I get up before Ariel can, and bring her back to the group.

Trade looks at her with wide brown eyes. "Renny?"

"Not mine," Renny replies, smirking.

Trade then eyes me, but I also shake my head and nod at Ariel.

"Mila is my daughter," she says, smiling as I hand her to her.

Realization hits him. He doesn't look disappointed or turned off, just really surprised. "You don't look like you have a newborn child."

"Told you," I tell her.

"Well, thank you," she replies, ducking her head and giving her attention to her child. "She is an unexpected surprise, but now that she's here I can't imagine my life without her."

"I thought you were going to be an old man," I admit to Trade after a little while.

He barks out a laugh. "Why is that?"

"Temper said that you walked away from club life for your kids," I explain with a shrug. "So I thought you'd spent years with the club or something. I don't know, I just thought you were in your forties or something, older than Temper."

"I started having kids young," he says, amusement in his gaze. "I was seventeen when I had my first, so yeah, I guess I can see why you thought that. But nope, I'm the younger and better-looking brother in the family."

Ariel and I share a look, because we make similar jokes about each other all the time. I guess no matter where you live and how you grow up, one thing doesn't change, and that is that siblings are always going to give each other shit.

"And the modest one, clearly," Ariel adds, arching her brow. "How did you fit into this house with a head that big?"

I snuggle into Renny and let them have their banter. "You smell nice," I tell him, staring up at him beneath my lashes. "Were you at the bike shop?"

"Yeah, been there all morning. I'm going to hire someone else, someone who knows their shit, because the place is taking off," he says, eyes alight with excitement. "You looking for a new job, Trade? All legitimate, nothing shady."

"You assuming that I know my shit?" Trade fires back, grinning wolfishly. "I've been doing nothing but building houses for a long time now. I haven't even gone for a ride in months."

"You forget who you're talking to? I know you, brother, and I know how fuckin' good your bike looks," Renny replies, lip twitching. "Whether you've had the time to ride it or not. She's in mint condition."

Shadow runs to the door, barking, and my eyes dart to the screen. "Who else is joining us today?" People dropping over unexpectedly used to give me anxiety, but now I feel like I'm just rolling with the punches. I like to be a good host, though, and making sure everyone is fed and watered has always been a priority of mine.

Temper stands at the door. "I'll let him in," Renny says, standing up.

"Is our house the new clubhouse?" Ariel asks, laughing to herself.

She shouldn't be complaining, though, because if Trade hadn't invited himself over here, she never would have met him, because she's never stepped through those clubhouse doors.

"What the fuck are you doing here?" Temper asks his baby brother as he enters the room. "I've been looking for you."

Trade sighs, leans back and lifts his feet up on the coffee table. "I came to visit with our lovely neighbors here. What did you want me for?" He starts to pat Shadow, who just sits there, loving the attention.

"We can go pick up the kids now," Temper says, sighing in relief. "I just got the call. Come on, let's go."

"Really?" Trade asks, jumping to his feet. "We can get them, just like that?"

Temper nods. "Yes, just like that. A deal is a deal, and the mayor came through with his end. Next month we need to come through with ours."

The two of them leave, and I feel so happy for Trade.

"So," I start, grinning at my sister. "What the hell was that?"

"What the hell was what?" she asks, kissing Mila on the forehead.

"You and Trade were eye fucking each other from the second he stepped inside," I blurt out, smile so wide my cheeks start to hurt. "Mrs. I Don't Want A Man totally wanted that man."

"He was nice to look at that's all," she replies, scowling. "I'm allowed to admire a man—that doesn't mean I want him." She turns to Renny. "And don't you dare go and say one word to him."

"My lips are sealed," Renny promises, amusement radiating from him. He rests his arm behind me and turns to me. "Do you want to come back to the clubhouse with me? I'm going to work out, and then we can go out for dinner?"

"You two eye fuck each other all the time," Ariel adds, glancing between us. "Like right now... But when I do it once..."

Renny stands and lifts me up in his arms. "Yeah, and look where we are now."

"I'm not going to marry him, that's for sure," she grumbles, standing up and heading to her room.

Hand in hand, we walk outside to his car.

He sits me on the hood of his car and kisses me, leaning me backward with a hand on my nape.

God, I love this man.

Chapter Twenty-Five

"I don't know how we're supposed to just sit here," I tell Skylar, pacing up and down the clubhouse kitchen. "What if something goes wrong?"

"I know exactly what you mean, but in this case there's nothing much we can do. If we were there we'd just be a distraction to them, and they need to concentrate on doing their job," she replies, tapping long red fingernails on the table. "Trust me, I hate it as much as you do."

The men left an hour ago when my dad called in the favor the MC owes him, which ended up being them doing security for some political event. Considering he will also have his own personal security there, it doesn't sound like it will be too much of a risk, which makes it a bit fishy. There's more going on that I don't know about. It's also highly likely that Renny left some information out when briefing me on what was going down, even though Temper admitted that there might be some added issues with a rival MC of theirs.

"When did life get so complicated?" I ask myself, sighing. I never thought I'd have to be worrying about anyone's enemies, never mind a motorcycle club's, and I never thought I'd have to worry about whether or not my man will come home.

Most of all, I never thought my dad would be involved in the same situation as all of this.

"When you accepted a ride on Renny's bike when your car fake broke down?" Skylar reminds me.

"Ahh yes. That's right." How can I forget?

Skylar studies me, a thoughtful look on her expression. "Come on, we can't just sit here and do nothing."

"Where are we going?" I ask her, following her out to her car.

"To the event."

"What about that speech you just gave me?" I ask, frowning. I don't want to be a distraction or make things harder for them in any way. I'm so out of my element right now. At the same time I'm glad that she has a plan, because sitting there and waiting is killing me.

"We won't just rock up there, we can hide and just see what the hell is going on..." She trails off when we see Crow and Chains sitting on her car.

Crow grins, crossing his arms over his chest, an amused glint in his blue eyes. "Saint told us you might try this, Skylar."

"What did he tell you? That we'd get hungry and head out to grab some food?" she lies, acting casual and relaxed. "We will be back soon."

"We've been told not to let either of you go anywhere unless we accompany you," Chains adds, seemingly unimpressed with his babysitting gig. "So if you want to get food, then we'll all go."

Shit. Saint really knows his woman, and I know how angry Skylar must be right now—he essentially left these men here to make sure she does as he had instructed.

Crow brings those blue eyes to me. "Saint said you'd corrupt Izzy."

Yeah, Saint really does know his old lady.

I throw my hands in the air. "We're going to get some food. Now if you're all coming, then come. I'm hungry."

We all get into the car, Skylar and I grabbing the front seats before they can, so the two of them are stuck in the back and unhappy about it, but too bad.

No one has a plan here, but as we drive away from the clubhouse, I'm wondering if all we're going to be able to get is some food.

"So what are we eating?" Crow asks, sticking his head in between our seats. "I heard about this new fried chicken place that just opened."

Skylar and I look at each other, having a silent conversation.

She asks me if I have a plan.

I tell her no, I don't, and that we're fucked.

She winces.

I tell her we need to get as close to the event as we can without it being obvious we're going in that direction.

"I don't know, I kind of feel like dumplings," she says, shrugging. "What do you think, Izzy?"

"Dumplings and a cocktail sound amazing right now," I agree. "Do you like Asian food, Crow?"

"Sure, why not?" he replies, sounding a little suspicious. "It might be better if we stay a little closer to home, though, don't you think?"

"Don't try to bullshit us," Chains states from the backseat. He has this growl in his tone that's kind of scary, but kind of sexy at the same time. "Tell me what you're up to."

"What if the men are in trouble?" Skylar asks them, giving up on the pretense. "I'm not going to lose any of those men, and if I can help in some way, I want to be able to. And yes, I know I'm not some badass biker, but I'm not useless. I'm smart, I'm scrappy, and I'm capable, and so is Izzy. I'm a damn EMT! Not to mention it's Izzy's dad running this whole thing, so if something goes wrong, she might be the only person who can fix it."

I never thought of it that way, but she's right, especially if my dad has plans to screw them over. He might not be father of the year, but he wouldn't want me to get hurt or to see him being shady, because he still maintains his façade of being a decent human being.

"Nothing is going to go wrong," Chains assures us. "They are staying in the back, just making sure the Killers MC doesn't decide to come to the event and start some shit."

"Which is dragging the Knights back into a war we only just got out of," Skylar replies, swallowing hard. "A war that lost me my father. So excuse me if I'm a little paranoid that something can go wrong again this time. If something happens to Saint…"

"Nothing is going to happen," Crow tells her, sighing. I can tell he's not sure what to do and has been put in a hard place between Skylar's emotional plea and what his president and patched club members have ordered him to do. "We need to be back at the clubhouse, which is where Temper wanted us to be, not driving around trying to convince you two to follow orders. The clubhouse is empty now—what if someone goes there right now?"

Skylar and I share another look, because he's right, we did leave the clubhouse empty.

"What does the clubhouse matter if one of the men die?" Skylar fires back, scowling. "The people make the clubhouse. There's nothing in there that can't be replaced."

My phone rings, and it's Renny.

Fuck.

I need to answer this.

"Hello?" I say quickly.

"Where are you?" he asks me, anger in his tone. "I got a message saying that you've left the clubhouse."

Damn, one of them snitched, and my bet is on Chains.

"We're fine," I assure him. "We're just worried about all of you. What's going on there? Is everything okay?"

"Get back home now," Renny growls. "Just listen to me, Izzy. You and Skylar get home and stay there."

"No, tell Izzy to get here. We need her, maybe she can fix this," I hear Saint call out in the background.

"What does he mean? What can I fix?" I ask Renny.

"Nothing," Renny snarls. "Just listen to me and get home. There is nothing you can do."

"Okay," I whisper, staring down at the phone as he hangs up. "We have to go back… I think."

Something has gone wrong, I can feel it in my bones, and I just hope that none of the men are hurt—or worse.

"What do you mean, you think?" Skylar asks, taking deep breaths, and I can tell she's trying to stop herself from freaking out and panicking. "What did he say?"

"Renny told me to get back to the clubhouse, but I heard Saint in the background, and he said that maybe I can fix…whatever is going on there," I explain, closing my eyes and resting my head back. "I don't know, what do we do?"

I love Renny, and I know he wants to protect me, but if I can do something to help, I'm going to.

"Saint wants you to go?" she asks, frowning.

"Yeah, and I think we should go," I declare, turning to face the men in the backseat. "Something has happened, and we need to go. I don't give a shit what either of you have to say."

"Fuck," Chains grits out, looking at his friend. "We're screwed if we do, and screwed if we don't. If we let them go and get hurt, they'll have our fuckin' heads, and if we kidnap them and drag them back to the clubhouse, they're going to make our lives hell."

"Fuck it, let's just go, they might need us," Crow agrees, nodding. "Let's do it."

He pulls out a gun from his jeans, which has my eyes boggling. "Fucking hell."

What am I getting myself into right now?

My mind flashes back to the shootout I witnessed a few weeks back, and little Billy crying next to me.

"It will be fine," Skylar assures me, reaching over and touching my shoulder. "We're all in this together."

And I guess that is the one part that makes you want to fight for this, because these people will always have my back, and I want to give them the same loyalty in return.

Skylar steps on the gas, and I hold on to the seat belt, wondering what the hell we're about to walk into.

And if we're all going to make it out.

Chapter Twenty-Six

There's a lot more people at the event than I thought there was going to be. It seems like the whole city has come to hear the mayor speak and to meet the guests he has invited. Skylar parks the car, and we all get out and slip into the busy crowd.

"What now?" I ask her, glancing around to find Renny. "I can't see any of them."

My dad is standing in front of a microphone, speaking about all of the ideas he has to make the city a better place. He has his security behind him, but none of them are the Knights.

"You stay here," I tell Skylar, Chains and Crow, pushing through the crowd, ignoring Skylar calling my name, trying to stop me. I'm the only one safe here, because Dad won't hurt me.

I stand right in front, where he can see me if he looks down, and search for any of the Knights, but come up short. I know when he lays eyes on me, because he stumbles in his proposal, then clears his throat and continues.

I look him in the eye, my expression blank. If anything has happened to Renny, I will never forgive him, because I know he had a hand in whatever has transpired today.

After the speech is over and someone takes over the microphone, my dad takes a seat, and I decide to send Renny a text message. I'm here. Tell me what has happened.

I know how angry he's going to be, but I can deal with that later. Right now I just need to get everyone out of here alive, well and hopefully without a target on their backs. I don't see any other bikers around, unless the Killers are here incognito.

Renny doesn't reply, the first sign that the plan has gone south.

It's then that I see them, to the right of the building, standing in front of a police car. Temper is in handcuffs and is being held on the hood, facedown with two officers pinning him.

I rush over to my dad as he walks offstage. "What is going on? Why is Temper being arrested? Did you plan this?"

"No, I did not," he assures me, fixing his suit jacket and glancing around to make sure no one can hear our conversation. He pulls me to the side, farther away from anyone else. "He had a gun on him, the cops showed up. There's nothing much I can do, Isabella."

"You asked them to be here to help you," I tell him, anger making me wild. "You set this up! Didn't you? What do you get out of this?"

My father looks strained, and much older than I last saw him, the lines in his forehead more prominent, the gray hair around his face more visible. "It's not me calling the shots with this, okay?"

"That doesn't make it okay," I reply, clenching my teeth. "Dad, Temper is a good man and he doesn't deserve this. They came here to help you and to stick to their side of the deal. It's up to you to make sure they don't get arrested and go to prison over them keeping their word! Please, for me."

He studies me, scanning my eyes, just like his. "Fuck."

He walks over to where the cops are now placing Temper in the back of the police car, and says something to the officer, who looks surprised but nods.

They then let Temper free, uncuffing him.

Just like that.

It's a pretty terrifying concept, really, the fact that if you don't know someone, you're fucked, but if you do you're able to get out of any situation you manage to get yourself into. What a messed-up world we live in.

I rush over to Temper, grabbing onto his arm. "Where is Renny and the rest of the guys?"

"They went after the Killers MC," he admits, stretching his neck from side to side and cursing. "What the hell are you doing here?"

"I'm here with Skylar and we dragged your prospects into it," I say quickly, leading him in the direction of her car. "You can yell at us later. We just need to get you out of here, and we need to make sure everyone else is safe."

When he says they went after the Killers, I don't picture the best outcome. I might have been able to help in this situation because of my dad, but I don't think there's much I can do to stop two motorcycle clubs trying to kill each other.

Skylar is waiting at the car, looking worried as hell, and confusion takes over when she sees me with Temper and Temper alone.

"Rest of them went after the Killers," I explain, hoping it makes any sense. "Temper was about to get arrested."

"Go back to the clubhouse," he demands. "I'll meet you there on my bike."

We nod, and this time, do as we've been told.

I just hope that Renny is okay.

"No one is answering their phones, Temper included," Skylar says to us, pacing. "It's been over half an hour, he shouldn't have been this far behind us. He's gone after them! He made us go home, and then he went to help them."

"Makes sense." Crow nods from where he's sitting on the

kitchen counter. "I'd have done something similar. He won't just sit around while his men are at war."

"We're back in the exact same spot we were in." I groan, covering my face with my hands. "This is a lot of stress and anxiety."

We hear the rumble of motorcycles and all rush to the front to open the gate as they all pull in. Renny, Temper, Saint, Dee, Trade…they're all there, along with a few faces I don't know.

Once the bikes are all parked I run to Renny and jump into his arms, kissing his face as soon as his helmet comes off.

"Thank fuck you're okay," I say as he squeezes me tightly, carrying me in his arms and walking back into the clubhouse, my legs wrapped around him and my face buried in his neck.

We all sit down at their big table, in a room I've never been invited into before.

"What happened today was a clusterfuck," Temper starts, sitting at the head of the table and eying us each in turn.

"What happened?" Skylar dares to ask.

"We did the security, everything was going fine. No drama. And then the Killers showed up, with their new president. At first it was obvious they had their eyes on Izzy's dad. But then they saw Temper and all hell broke loose," Saint explains.

"They tried to shoot him, but then the police were called in and Temper was arrested. They took off on their bikes so we went after them, along with the cops, who ended up arresting a few of the Killers members. With the cops there we just bailed, letting them handle the Killers. Eventually the whole event was shut down, and everyone had to leave."

"I think they were supposed to take out your dad," Temper admits. "Which is why he wanted us there, because he would have got wind of that. But then they saw me, and they didn't want to miss that chance."

So my dad didn't plan for Temper to get arrested, he just wasn't going to do anything to stop it. I don't know why they'd want him dead, other than his personal agenda doesn't work

with theirs. I really don't know much about how these motorcycle clubs work, so who knows? My dad and I might not be
close, but that doesn't mean that I want to see him hurt or killed.

"Are the cops going to come here now?" I ask, considering
everything that happened today.

"Maybe," Temper replies. "Hopefully they're too busy with
the Killers, who openly branded weapons and fired shots. I had
my gun on me, but it's registered, and I didn't use it, openly
or not. It was concealed at all times until they searched me."

My head suddenly hurts. They continue their meeting, breaking down everything that happened and what they think should
happen next, and then finally I'm brought up.

"Skylar and Izzy, we told you to stay behind for your own
safety," Temper says, scowling. "However, if you hadn't come,
Izzy, I would have been behind bars right now, because they
arrest first and ask questions later. It would have been a fuckin'
messy ordeal, so thank you. I know you both just wanted to
help, but I'd appreciate it if we could count on you both to follow orders in the future.

"Crow and Chains," he continues, glancing at the two prospects. "I know these two are headstrong, but you let the women
lead you. It all worked out this time, so I'm not going to be so
harsh, but what would have happened if one of the women got
killed? Could you imagine the fallout of that? If the men leave
their women under your watch, they do so knowing you will
do anything and everything in your power to keep them safe."

Crow nods. "It was hard, especially when we knew Saint
wanted Izzy to go and Renny told her to stay. They made their
decision and I wanted to be there to protect them during it."

"I couldn't let them all go alone," Chains throws in, clearly
pissed off at the turn of events. "Like you said, our job was to
make sure that they were safe, and we did that to our best abil-
ity."

"I know you did what you thought was right. But next time

you have to do everything you can to just follow orders." Temper is not giving in on this.

Crow and Chains have enough smarts to just take the lashing and say nothing in response. Temper turns to Skylar, but addresses the group. "Georgia was there, too."

At the mention of this person named Georgia, all the men go on high alert as Temper continues. "I don't think that that is a coincidence. She's working with the Killers again, and while I don't quite know what she's up to, I know she wants to take us down."

"She was there?" Skylar asks, brow furrowing. "I thought she had let it all go and was moving on with her life."

"That woman can never let anything go—she's always up to something. I don't know what she wants this time, but we're going to find out," Temper bites out.

"Who is Georgia?" I whisper to Renny.

"Skylar's mom, who was behind getting her father killed," he says.

Her mom?

Shit. I don't know why I'm so surprised that an MC would have so much dysfunctional drama. Maybe because they preach loyalty?

I guess not everyone gets that memo, though.

I head back home to have a bath and a well-deserved glass of wine. Ariel is sitting on the couch breastfeeding Mila as I walk inside, and one look at my face and her expression turns from content to concern.

"What happened?" she asks, sitting up straighter. "You look drained."

"Well, the Knights were shot at and then gave chase to the bikers who shot at them. Then Temper got arrested and I had to ask Dad to tell them he was part of his security team to let him go," I start, sitting down next to her and lifting my feet up.

"And apparently Dad is on the Killers MC's shit list because of something or another and they want him to disappear."

She opens her mouth, then closes it, brow furrowing in thought. "I've literally been sitting here with Mila, cleaning the house and cooking us dinner, and this is what has been going on in the meantime? Jesus Christ."

"Where's Shadow?" I ask, realizing that he hasn't come to greet me.

"He's outside," she says, lifting Mila up to burp her. "And I can't believe Dad actually helped Temper."

"To be honest I think he realized he needs the Knights. They're the only ones who can stand up to the Killers, or at least the only ones who have done so in the past," I admit, thinking over everything that I have learned from today. "I don't know, Ariel. There has to be a way out of all this bullshit without someone getting hurt. Skylar's dad, Hammer, died the last time they faced off with the Killers. Now they both have new presidents but don't want to let go of what happened."

"If someone killed someone that you loved, could you let it go, or would you forever want revenge, just waiting for the right moment?" she asks, kissing the top of Mila's head.

If anyone hurt her or Mila, I wish that I could say I would be strong enough to forgive and move on, but I don't know if I could. I don't think you ever know until you are in that situation.

"These men are a brotherhood, Izzy, and now it looks like you're involved in all of this. Are you sure you can handle it? Nothing bad has happened yet, but it almost did today. And it most likely will."

She's right. And I knew it from the start. I didn't go into this blind.

But now? I'm in way too deep to get out.

I'm in love with a Knight, and this is what comes with it.

For better or for worse.

Chapter Twenty-Seven

"Hello," I say to the lady at the door. She's holding flyers in her hand, just like the one she gave Ariel. "You still haven't found your dog?"

"No," she says, sighing with sadness, her green eyes teary. She's petite and wearing a headscarf over her hair. "I've looked everywhere. I was hoping someone might have seen him, but I'm afraid I'm having no luck."

"I'm sorry to hear that. I've been keeping an eye out," I promise. "Do you live around here?"

"A few blocks over," she admits, pointing to the right, away from the clubhouse and toward the city. "Who knows how far he could have gone by now? My name is Gia, by the way."

"I'm Izzy," I say, offering her my hand. "It's nice to meet you. I kept the flyer with your number on it, so if I see or hear anything I will give you a ring."

"That would be perfect, thank you," she says, smiling sadly. "I've met some really nice people around this neighborhood, it's just a shame that this is why. I haven't gone to the MC clubhouse, though... I wonder if they have seen my dog."

"Oh, I can ask for you," I suggest. "I don't have many other friends to ask around here, but I can ask them, at least."

"That would be great," she says, perking up. "You know them well, then?"

"Not well," I backtrack, shrugging. "But I do know them, yes. They are nice people."

She opens her mouth to ask another question, but I cut her off before she can. "I'll call you if I find anything out, all right? Good luck."

She nods, smiles and walks away. I can't help but feel terrible for her—she must really love her dog. But talking about the MC with a total stranger isn't something I'm going to engage in any further. I wish I could do more to help, but my hands are a little full right now with everything going on with the MC and my dad.

Closing the door, I puff out a breath and walk back into the kitchen, where Renny is carrying Mila while Ariel is lecturing him on what's going to happen if I get hurt in the crossfire.

"Just remember, I know where you live," she concludes, pointing her finger at him. "And stop being so cute with my daughter while I'm trying to yell at you."

"I can't help it," he says in his baby voice. "Mila is just too cute, aren't you, Mila? How do you feel about your mommy yelling at me? You don't like it either, do you?"

I shake my head at him in amusement. "The lady came back looking for her dog."

"Aw, no. I was hoping she'd have found him by now," Ariel says, stirring the pot of pasta she's making. "I haven't seen any dog around, and I've been looking."

"I know, I said the same. Don't be getting clucky over there, mister," I say to Renny, who is looking at Mila with a little too much love in his eyes. "I know she's cute, but the best thing about her is that you get to return her."

"Can men get clucky?" he asks, grinning. "She's just really cute, all right? Give me a break. Don't worry, I'm not going to ask you for a baby." He pauses, and then adds, "For at least the next three years."

My mouth gapes.

I can't believe he just said that.

"What? We were already married, isn't that the natural progression of things?" he asks, chuckling at my unamused expression.

"No, getting remarried would be next." Ariel smirks, glancing between the two of us. "In due time, of course."

"I have a plan, don't worry," he replies, winking at me. I don't know what plan he's talking about, but if things are going how they are going and we do remain a couple long-term, I'd like a proper proposal and wedding, because that one definitely didn't count.

"Are you going to share this plan with me?" I ask, arching my brow.

I've always said that I'd only get married once, but for the same man, I'll make an exception.

He just laughs and continues to fuss over Mila. Ariel throws me an amused look, and I know she's thinking the same thing as me.

Renny wants to remarry and have kids with me one day.

I'd say that I don't know how to feel about that, but the smile on my lips speaks for itself.

When Dad calls and asks if he can come over for a chat, I hesitantly agree. One, he's never been to my house before. I've always gone to his mansion instead. But we definitely do have things to discuss, and it would be nice for him to finally meet Mila. Not to mention that if I'm going to see him, I'd rather do it without his wife present, because no one needs that in their lives.

I hate that we tidy the house and cook a meal knowing he's coming, and I hate that we get dressed and look decent, presenting this picture of us having our lives all sorted and put together.

I guess no matter how far you come, some things will never change, and secretly wanting parental approval is one of them. Or maybe we just want to show him how much we have succeeded in life without him. Without his time, without his money and without his support, we have banded together as our own mini family, and we are thriving.

And we want to show him we don't need him.

He shows up straight from work, in a navy blue suit jacket with a white shirt, his dark hair unkempt and messy, like he's been running his hands through it in frustration.

"Hey," I say to him, opening the door and letting him inside. I can hear Shadow barking from outside, but ignore him and offer my dad a seat. "Do you want a coffee or tea or something?"

So formal. Any other parent would probably just walk in and make themselves at home, I imagine, but with him it's almost like having a stranger enter your premises.

"Coffee would be nice," he replies, sitting down and looking around.

Ariel walks out with Mila in her arms. "Hey, Dad."

"Hey, Ariel. So this is Mila," he murmurs, standing up and walking over to them. He holds out his arms, and although Ariel hesitates, she ends up letting him hold her. "She looks just like you did as a baby."

"I know. I did a comparison photo and we look pretty much exactly the same. Same green eyes, dark hair and lips. I think she only got her nose from her dad."

Dad sits down and just watches Mila. "I'm sorry I'm only meeting her now."

He doesn't say anything else, no explanations, no *I'll come around more*, just a sorry. Ariel doesn't say anything in return, and I don't know how she's expected to answer.

"What did you want to discuss?" I ask, placing his mug on the coffee table and sitting down.

"We can start with what happened the other day," he says,

eying me. "You were reckless. You knew something could have gone wrong that day, but you showed up anyway."

"And if I didn't you would have let Temper get arrested, and they would have found some bullshit reason to keep him locked up," I say.

Or legit reason, but that doesn't sound too good for my argument.

"At the end of the day, the Knights were there to protect you, and you need them to handle the Killers, who you've apparently pissed off," I continue, using what I know will work on him.

"We kicked them out of their clubhouse and knocked it down," Dad admits, handing Mila back to Ariel and wincing. "And yeah, I made the final decision on that. I was hoping they'd leave town, because they're all a bunch of criminals and make the city look bad."

My jaw drops. "Yeah, that would do it."

Imagine how angry everyone would be if the council did that to the Knights?

"How did you kick them out? Isn't it their property?" I ask, wondering how the hell that could have been legal.

"We have our ways," he replies, sniffing.

"So you bribed someone," I guess out loud, shaking my head. "You guys are basically like an MC without the bikes—you still do shady things, you still think the law doesn't apply to you, and you have no problems running over other people to get what you want."

"And you have no problem dating one of them," Dad reminds me, scowling. "So don't throw stones at glass houses, Isabella. You can't judge my character, because look at who you have surrounded yourself with."

"Renny is a good man," I defend, lifting my chin. "And if that's why you're here, you're wasting your time because I'm not walking away from him."

"I'm here because I'm worried about you both. You have a baby to worry about now, so it's not exactly the time to be getting mixed in all of this. And if the Killers are targeting me, you don't think they're going to try and go after my family? Especially considering one of them has ties to their other enemies."

The man has a point.

"Well, your other family is safe behind those massive gates back at the mansion," Ariel adds, shrugging. "Don't worry about us. Most people don't know about your connection to us, and we have the MC for protection."

"You're both alone here, with a newborn," he states, tone full of disbelief. "Yeah, I'm sure the MC will protect you, but they aren't exactly here twenty-four seven, are they?"

"We will manage," Ariel says, no emotion on her face. "Don't worry about us, Dad, worry about yourself, because you might have been shot dead the other day."

"I know, and the cops are on them. The Knights being there has drawn most of them out. A few of them have been arrested, which is why things might be quiet for a while, but they couldn't place all of them at the event," he admits, rubbing the back of his neck. "And I let them know the Knights were there to help me, so the cops will be leaving you all alone."

"Thank you," I say, meaning it.

"You're welcome," he replies, taking a sip of his coffee, then glancing into the mug. "It tastes just like how your mom used to make it."

We all go silent.

Mom taught me how to make coffee, so of course it tastes just like hers, but as usual when he mentions her we all freeze up.

"I do miss her," he continues, either not picking up on the sudden frost in the air or just not caring. "Regardless of what you two think, I did love your mom, and I always will. She was a great woman."

"We know," I finally say. "She never said a bad thing about you, even after all that you did to her. She was graceful right up until the end. I don't know if I could have had that strength."

In fact, I know I couldn't, because I'm holding on to her grudge for her.

"You do have her strength," he finally says, standing up and looking between the two of us. "If you need a safe place to stay, call me. I can put you in one of my houses, or you are always welcome to come and stay at mine."

"Okay, thanks," I say.

"You stay safe, too," Ariel says before he leaves the room.

"Don't worry, before I'm through all of the Killers MC will be behind bars," he calls out. I hear the door close behind him.

I can't help but think the real reason he wanted the Knights there was to draw them out, as he said, so he could get rid of them once and for all. I wouldn't put it past him—he's always one step ahead, using whoever he needs to get what he wants.

"Well, Mila, that was your grandfather," Ariel says to her daughter.

"We should have taken a photo or something," I muse. "For when Mila is older. But I guess she can always just search him online."

"I'm surprised he didn't lecture me on Merve. He always did hate him."

"I guess I'm the bigger disappointment to him right now so I'm taking all the heat for you," I grumble, reaching out to let Mila hold my thumb in her hand.

"I appreciate that," Ariel says, laughing softly. "How did we turn out so normal?"

"Did we turn out normal?"

She thinks about it. "At least we aren't assholes."

"Fair."

"And at least we have each other," she says, reaching out to squeeze my face. "We're a two-woman army."

I smile.

And she's right, we are.

Chapter Twenty-Eight

I can tell that something isn't right the second I step onto my property. Shadow, who is on the lead with me, starts barking, but it isn't his usual bark. There's an aggression and a panic in there that I haven't heard before, and it sets me right on edge.

Rushing to the front door, which is unlocked, I step inside the house and let Shadow off his lead. He runs around the house, sniffing and barking.

"Ariel?" I yell, rushing to her room, but she's not there. And neither is Mila.

I call her phone, but she doesn't pick up, so I contact Renny straight away. "Hey, babe," he says, and I can hear the smile in his tone.

"Can you come here now?" I ask, rushing the words out. "Ariel and Mila aren't here, and the door was unlocked..."

"I'm on my way," he says, then hangs up.

I try to call her a few more times, but she doesn't pick up. There's nothing missing, no sign of struggle in the house, and her car is still here, so I know she hasn't gone anywhere. I asked her if she wanted to come for a walk with me and Shadow, but she declined because Mila was asleep, so it makes no sense for her to go for a walk either.

Renny rushes into the house and I give him a quick rundown. He goes to the security monitor and checks the footage. I don't know why I didn't think of that, probably because I was freaking out and not thinking straight.

"Here," he says, pointing to the footage. A man comes to the front door, and Ariel opens it. He then pushes inside and pulls out a knife, demanding that she and Mila leave with him or he's going to kill the baby.

My heart in my throat, tears drip down my cheeks. I've never been this scared in my life. If something happens to either of them… "What if he's hurt them already?"

"Don't think like that. We're going to save them, all right?" he assures me, cupping my face with his hands. "I need you to tell me all the information you know about the man, okay?"

"It's Merve, Mila's father," I say.

"Write his full name, address, anything you know about him down for me, while I ring Temper," he commands, taking control of the situation.

I pull out the pad of paper and pen from my bag and write down any information I know about Merve that might help them locate him. I hear Renny calling in Temper, telling him we need them all, and for them to all come to my house because it's an emergency.

I can't believe Merve did this. We always knew he was a lowlife, but I didn't think he'd actually harm his own child, or threaten to. I don't know how he found us, but he must be angry that we moved away without telling him. He never tried to contact Ariel, though. Like she said, her phone number was the same, and he never bothered reaching out or asking when he could see Mila next.

This whole time I've been worried about what the Killers

might do next, I didn't even peg Merve as a threat, and now he's blindsided us by pulling this bullshit.

The rumble of motorcycles comforts me. It's not long before all the men jump off their bikes and pile into my house.

"What happened?" asks Trade, brown eyes filled with worry. "Tell me everything."

Renny gives everyone a quick recap, shows them the footage and then hands them the paper with Merve's information on it. "From the camera footage I managed to get the license plate number off the car he was driving, so I'm going to run with that," he says.

"We'll find them," Temper assures me, touching my hair. "And we will deal with that piece of shit once and for all."

I nod and watch as they all scatter, trying to find this man before anything happens to my loved ones. "Do you need someone to run that plate?" I ask Renny. "I can call my dad."

"That might be the quickest way," he admits, kissing the top of my head. "You call him and tell him what has happened. If we can use his contacts, we'll find them a lot faster."

Dad answers on the third ring. "Hello? Isabella?"

"Merve kidnapped Ariel and Mila," I say, voice breaking. "We have the license plate number of the car he was driving. Any chance you could run it and help us find them?"

"Fucking prick," he mutters, but agrees. "Yes, of course. Text me the number. I'll get the cops on it right away."

He hangs up and I look up at Renny. "I'm going to kill him with my bare hands."

"Not if we get to him first."

Dad said the MC would bring us down, would get us hurt, but they're the ones that are helping us right now.

And I know they won't stop until Ariel and Mila are home, safe, where they belong.

And as for Merve?

He'll get what's coming to him.

* * *

"He's using a stolen car," Dad says when he calls me back. "It belongs to a woman who reported it missing a few hours ago."

At least we can add that to his "reasons he should be in prison" list, which is quickly accumulating bullet points.

"So now what?" I ask, frowning. Merve's not from here so where the hell would he go and who would he stay with?

"The cops are on it, we're going to be tracing him," Dad says. "Don't worry, they will be found."

He hangs up and I turn to Renny, who is on the phone to Trade, discussing their plan of action. Everyone has been out searching for the car, knowing he can't be too far away, and Temper has been checking all the local motels and hotels.

I'm not sure what I can do to help. I feel so useless. I know that someone has to stay here at the home base just in case, but it's really hard having to sit here and play the waiting game, hoping someone finds them.

What is Merve's plan for them? I see cases like this all the time on the news, and they never end well. Maybe he wants to scare Ariel, or maybe he wants to keep Mila and get rid of Ariel. I don't know how I'm going to cope if anything has happened to them.

I wish I had been home when this happened, although he was probably waiting for the moment when I wasn't there, along with Shadow.

In the video he says he just wanted to see Mila because he missed her. Ariel let him in because she was trying to do the right thing and never wanted to keep Merve away from his daughter, and look where it got her. She should have never answered the door. Instead she should have called me, or Renny, or anyone, and told us that her baby daddy was there.

Renny hangs up with Trade and comes over to me. I know he's itching to get out there and look for them, but he doesn't want to leave me here alone.

"You can go and join them if you want," I tell him, brow furrowing. "The more people out looking, the better." I also need to stay here in case Dad or the cops drop by asking for more information.

He's about to reply to me when his phone rings. I see Temper's name pop up.

"Hello?" Renny says. "Yeah? Oh, fuck. Okay. What do you want to do with him? Okay. Message me the address. Bye.

"They found them, let's go," he says after he hangs up, grabbing my arm and leading me to my car. "Temper saw the car out the front of an old dingy motel about fifteen minutes from here."

I message Dad and tell them we have located them. "Do we want the cops there to arrest him?" I ask Renny.

I know they'd probably prefer to hand out their own form of punishment, but if he's arrested and put in prison, that's the best outcome we can get.

"Yeah, that's probably the safest bet," he replies, pressing on the gas, trying to get us to there in record time.

"Are they safe?" I ask, wringing my hands in worry. "Is Temper waiting outside or did he break into their room?"

"He was speaking with the front desk and asking them which room," he explains. "So I imagine he's breaking into the room right now."

"He found them pretty fast," I say, relief filling me. I wasn't sure if we were going to find them, because potentially Merve could have just kept driving over to the next state, and then our chances of finding them would have been low.

"I wish we could say that this is our first kidnapping rodeo, but it's not," Renny admits, reaching over and touching my hand. "We all know what we're doing and we work as a team."

"I can see that," I say. "You found them before the police even did."

And I've never been more grateful.

When we pull up to the motel I see Temper's bike there, and point to it. Renny parks next to him and we get out. A quick check of Renny's phone gives us the room number, and we run there, finding the room door wide open.

Stepping inside, I want to cry in relief when I see Ariel, sitting on the bed, mostly unharmed, Mila in her arms. Rushing to them, I wrap my arms around my sister, taking deep breaths, stroking her hair and thanking God that she is okay.

If anything had happened to her...

Ariel has a red mark on her face, like she's been backhanded, but she's alive and well, and that's all that matters right now. "Is Mila okay?" I ask her.

She nods, tears falling. "She's fine."

"Good," I whisper, glancing down at my niece. I have so much love for these two, and words can't express how broken I'd have been if we hadn't been able to locate them before Merve did something stupid like hurt them.

I turn to find him sitting with his back against the wall, Temper in front of him with a knife in his hand. It must have been the knife Merve used to get Ariel and Mila into the car.

"You're such a piece of shit," I say to him, hands curling into fists. "I hope you rot in prison for the rest of your life."

"And if you don't, we'll be right here waiting for you," Renny adds, smirking. "You fucked with the wrong sisters."

"She should go to prison for taking my daughter away from me!" he snarls, staring daggers at Ariel. "She moved away without even telling me! Who does that? It's her who should be punished. You will all get what's coming for you, don't you worry about that."

He's completely lost it. He starts laughing, and the sound sets me on edge.

"You didn't show up to any of the lawyer meetings," I remind him, shaking my head. "You didn't answer your phone, and you've only seen your daughter twice for like twenty minutes each, so stop pretending that you're father of the year, because you're not. This just proves Mila is so much better off without you."

It never ceases to amaze me how people try to justify their actions, or never take any responsibility. It's always someone else's fault, never their own, even though he kidnapped them and had who knows what planned.

I don't know if he's on drugs, or maybe just needs some mental health assistance, but something is not right with him, and I know he hasn't always been this way. The Merve I met was charming, witty and intelligent, so I'm unsure how he became the person he is right now, but I hope he gets some help.

The cops arrive, and with my dad, luckily, because I'm sure otherwise they would have also arrested Temper for standing there with a weapon in his hands.

Dad hugs Ariel and kisses her temple, and it's the most affection I've seen him give her in years. Afterward, he comes over to me and does the same. "I thought I'd lost them both," he admits. "When I hadn't even got to spend any time with them." He turns to Renny. "Nice to see you again, Renny."

"You, too, sir," Renny replies, taking my hand in his. "Thank you for helping us."

"You don't need to thank me. I'd do anything for my family," Dad replies, smiling sadly, before leaving. He doesn't even stick around. Obviously just knowing that Ariel and Mila are okay is enough for him, or maybe he doesn't feel like he's wanted here.

I feel kind of bad for him, but at the same time I don't, because it's his choices that have led us all to this position right now, where we're family but we're not close, because he felt it was all too hard.

"Let's go home," I tell Ariel after the police finish their questioning, wrapping my arm around her. "Don't you ever scare me like that again, you hear me?"

"I'll try not to," she replies, cradling Mila against her chest and walking with me to the car. She stops and turns, as if she suddenly remembers something, and gives me Mila. She then walks back up to Temper and gives him a big hug.

"Thank you," she says. "To you and all of the Knights."

She then runs back to me.

Thank you, I mouth to him before getting into the car.

I almost lost my heart today, and if that doesn't make you appreciate life more, I don't know what does.

Chapter Twenty-Nine

"How is she doing?" Renny asks, coming up from behind and wrapping his arms around me.

"She had a shower and is now in bed," I say, turning around to face him. "I think she just wants to sleep it off and pretend that it never happened."

If only it were that easy.

"I don't think I've ever been so scared in my life than I was today," I admit, burying my face against him, his familiar scent a comfort.

"I know, but it's over now and they're safe. Merve will be locked away, and we won't have to worry about him," he assures me, rubbing my back. "And when they let him out...we can worry about that then."

"She needs to get the sole custody paperwork sorted now," I say.

"I know, Trade is going to speak to our lawyer about it today, don't worry. We will take care of it all."

Pressing my palms against his chest, I glance up at him. "How did I get so lucky?"

"Well, it all started when you wore that red bathing suit to wash your car…" he teases, lifting me up on the counter and kissing me. "You know I'd do anything for you, right?"

I nod. "I think you proved that today."

Renny and the MC had my back when I needed it most, and I've never had anyone other than my mom and Ariel be like that for me. To me, blood has always been thicker than water, but the MC treats each other just like blood. Now I know that family is what you make of it, and you can choose who you want to be in your family.

"We look after our own," he murmurs, kissing me again. "I love you, Izzy, and I want you to be mine, now and forever."

Cupping his stubbled cheeks with my palms, I look into his brown eyes. "I love you, too, Renny. And I'm grateful to have you in my life."

Pressing my forehead against his, I close my eyes and just savor the moment. Right now under my roof I have all the people who are important to me, and they are all safe and healthy. That makes me extremely lucky.

"Thank you for believing in me and giving me a second chance. You won't regret it," he says, kissing me again, pulling back and looking into my eyes, and then kissing me once more.

I don't miss the heat in his gaze, but we're both going to have to wait for that.

Trade stops by with flowers, which is really fucking cute, and when I tell him that Ariel is asleep but he's welcome to wait for her, he places the bouquet on the kitchen table and leaves.

"His kids are at the clubhouse right now," Renny explains after he disappears. "I think he's going to stay for a few days before returning back to his old life."

"So he's not going to be around after that?" I ask, frowning. I know the timing is far from right, but there's definitely something there between him and Ariel, and I didn't miss how frantic and worried he was when she went missing. There's a connection there, and it would be sad if he just went off the grid and we never saw him again.

"I'm not sure," Renny says, running his palm down his stubble. "You never know with Trade. He's always been a bit of a nomad."

"It was nice of him to bring Ariel flowers."

"Yeah, it was," Renny admits, suspicion in his tone. "I didn't think he was the flowers type."

"Were you the flowers type?" I tease, moving across the couch to sit on his lap, my arms around his neck.

"Nope. The right woman makes you the flowers type," he says, eyes widening in realization.

"Really, you're only getting this now?" I ask, smirking. "They've been eying each other since the moment that they met."

"I'm usually only paying attention to you, not who the other Knights are checking out," he mutters, then adds, "Unless they're checking you out. I definitely notice that. Like with Crow."

"He wasn't checking me out," I groan, rolling my eyes. "And you have nothing to worry about. You're the only one I want."

"I better be," he murmurs, trailing his finger across my breast, just a light touch, but it sends a shiver down my spine and makes me tighten my thighs together. "Because I'm crazy about you."

Ariel wakes up and wanders into the room, stopping when she sees us. "Don't let me interrupt you."

"You have flowers," I tell her, pointing to the table.

"From who?" she asks, bringing them to her nose and smelling them. "They're beautiful. I can't remember the last time someone sent me flowers."

"Trade. He dropped by to see you, but you were asleep," I say, watching her reaction. She smiles like an idiot, but then puts the flowers down and heads into the kitchen to have a glass of water.

"Who knew that 'sorry you've been kidnapped' flowers are a thing?" she says without emotion. "I can't believe today even happened. I'm so glad I don't have to worry about Merve anymore."

"We all are," I say on a sigh. "We all are."

I try to bring some normalcy to my life the next day and stick to my usual routine. I do some brochures for a new company that wants to change their brand, and design a website for another. I keep an eye on Ariel to make sure that she's okay, and although a bit shaken up, she seems to be doing fine, even cracking jokes about it.

"I need to get out of the house," she declares, stepping into the living room dressed up in jeans and a tank top, Mila in a car seat. "Where can I go with a six-week-old baby? She's too young to do anything."

"You're wearing jeans? I've seen you in nothing but leggings since you gave birth," I point out.

"I know, I thought I'd change it up a little," she says, shrugging.

"I don't know where you can take a baby that young that she'd actually enjoy, but I'm sure you can go out for coffee or something. You know I can always watch her for you if you want some me time," I say, placing my laptop to the side. "You know I don't mind."

"I know, but I thought it would be nice to get her out of the house, too," she explains. "And look, I dressed her up in one of the outfits you got her. How cute is she?"

"Adorable," I say, smiling at the little matching headband, dress and leggings. "Red is definitely her color. Do you want me to come with you?" I don't want her to feel like I'm trying to baby her, but the ordeal did only happen yesterday, and I want her to look after herself and take it easy.

"No, I'm fine, Izzy," she assures me, picking up Mila and heading to the front door. "I'll be back soon!"

I close my laptop and glance down at Shadow. "I'm being ridiculous, aren't I? Merve is gone, what else can possibly happen?"

Shadow sighs.

"I feel the exact same way, buddy."

I decide to walk over with Shadow to the clubhouse, where I find Renny and Saint boxing each other out in the backyard. I sit down next to Skylar, who is watching them with a cocktail in her hand. "Enjoying the show?" I ask her, amused.

"You know it. You missed Crow and Chains beat the crap out of each other, it was a good fight," she says, taking a sip of her cocktail. "Would you like a drink?"

"No, I'm good, thanks. I'm meant to be working but I thought I'd drop in and see what my man is up to," I reply, wincing when Saint's fist goes just a little too close to the face I love.

"Your man. I heard you two are officially back together now," she says, smiling at me. "I'm so happy for you both. I was worried there for a little while."

"So was I," I admit, looking away as Renny hits Saint hard in the stomach. "I don't know how you can watch this."

"I grew up around this kind of stuff," she says with a shrug. "It's normal life for me. It used to be a lot worse, trust me. I also have brothers, and you know boys, they fight a lot."

We couldn't have had more different upbringings. "I have no brothers," I tell her. "So this is kind of rough for me."

"Is it just you and Ariel?"

"I have two other younger half sisters, but I rarely see them," I tell her, closing my eyes as Saint gets in a shot on Renny's pretty face. "So yeah, pretty much it is just me and Ariel. Can you leave his face alone, Saint?" I call out.

Skylar laughs softly, just as Crow comes out to sit with us, sporting a black eye and a grin. "Look at you, Skylar, still sitting here with your drink, enjoying the blood and violence."

"Hey, I was sitting out here first, enjoying the sun. You guys are the ones who came out here and tried to kill each other," she says, sticking her tongue out. "You sure you don't want a drink, Izzy? I feel like an alcoholic over here."

"I'll have one," Crow says, removing his black sneakers and putting his feet up. "I think we all deserve one, it's been a long month."

Understatement of the year.

"Sorry if we got you in trouble," I say, patting him on the shoulder. "I'd like to say that we'll behave and actually listen to you next time…"

"But that would be a flat-out lie," Skylar finishes, grabbing a glass and pouring from the jug she has made. She fixes Crow a drink, even with a lemon garnish on the side, and slides it over to him. "I'm here all week."

Renny comes out and kisses me, pressing his sweaty body against mine. "I thought you were working all day."

"I am," I reply, pushing him away and laughing as he tries to kiss me more. "I just wanted to see what you were up to."

"Everything okay?" he asks, pouring himself a drink. "Do you want one?"

"No, I'm good, and yes, everything is okay. Ariel went out with Mila, and I was alone in the house, so I thought I'd bring Shadow over."

"Where is he then?" he asks, glancing around the yard.

"He went straight into your room and jumped on the bed for a nap," I admit, laughing. "And it's your fault for letting him up on there last time."

"Ariel probably needed to take control back over her life, make her feel like she's in control and independent," Renny says, pushing an errant lock of hair out of my eyes. "She's strong, and she will be fine. Don't stress. There are some things you can't save her from, she needs to figure them out for herself."

I know he's right, but that doesn't help the fact that she went through something yesterday. She could have died, and we all know that.

My sister, my best friend, my family.

And I almost lost her and her daughter.

It's a hard pill to swallow, and it's even harder to know that from now on, I'll always have to watch my back.

Chapter Thirty

Renny steps into the kitchen, freshly showered, dressed in his black leather. "Ready to go for a ride?" he asks me, leaning over to kiss the top of my head.

After all the drama and commotion, Renny wants to take me for a ride and out to eat, and just have some relaxing alone time with me, which sounds really nice. Over the last week I've really struggled with leaving the house without Ariel. My anxiety kicking in and making me want to be near them at all times, just because I never want to come home to them missing again. I know the chances of that happening again are extremely low, but I never want to be in that position again.

Renny has been slowly encouraging me to relax, because I can't live that way, he's right. I can't live in fear, because it will drain me, and I won't be able to enjoy life like I want to. Life is short enough, and I need to live in the moment.

"Yeah, I'm ready," I reply, finishing the last of my morning fuel.

We stop back at the park that will forever be known as his

park, to me anyway, and Renny pulls out a little picnic I didn't even know he had packed in his leather saddlebag.

"I love this park," I say, sliding my sunglasses on to shield my eyes from the bright light. "I just imagine you playing here as a child, getting into trouble."

"The view is definitely amazing," he replies, looking at me.

After we eat, we lie down on the tartan picnic blanket, wrapped in each other's arms, whispering sweet nothings and laughing. When you're with someone and you don't need to be doing anything, you can just enjoy being next to them, touching them, I think that's when you know you've found the right person.

The person who makes you happy by just being around them.

You don't need anything else, just them.

They become your home, your comfort zone, your happy place.

Renny is all of that for me, and more, and I'm thankful for the day he rode into my life and never left.

We stop at his apartment on the way home, and the second the door is closed behind us, my back is against the wall and his lips on mine. The tension has been building between us all day, and I've been waiting for the moment I can get him alone like this, my body craving his.

"I've been looking at those red lips of yours all day, waiting for this," he says against my mouth, removing my cardigan and letting it fall to the floor. My shoes and jeans are next, leaving me in my black lace panties and a black strapless top.

He reaches for me but I step aside, arching my brow at him, then running to his bedroom, or at least trying to. He grabs me before I make it there and spins me around and kisses me more—hungry, deep kisses. He holds the back of my nape, controlling my body, then picks me up and carries me the rest of the way to his black-satin-covered bed, and all but throws me on there. He hastily removes his clothes, and I watch through heavy-lidded eyes as he returns to the bed in all his naked glory, pulling down my top and panties so we're both on an even playing field.

He flashes me a smile as he spreads my thighs and lowers his head, his pink tongue peeking out for a taste, moaning, before going down on me properly. I want to look but my head falls back and eyes close of their own accord, pleasure overtaking my system. I've never been with someone who enjoys and actually gets turned on from this act; I wasn't even sure if men like this existed. He makes more moaning noises which have me so wet, I can feel it all over my inner thighs. I can feel myself close to coming, so I try to squirm away a little, because I'm not ready for this to be over yet.

Not even close.

"Not yet," I tell him as he continues to deliciously torture my clit.

He lifts his head, wipes his mouth with the back of his hand and leans over me, pressing his hard cock against me and slowly pushing inside. I hold on to his thighs, lifting my hips up and pushing back against him. He plays with my nipples with his tongue, gently nibbling at them, shooting pleasure straight to my lower stomach.

"So beautiful," he murmurs, staring down at my body and then my face, looking me in the eye. "I'm such a lucky man."

Yes, he is, but my mouth won't seem to work right now, too lost in my head and in my body's reactions to his lovemaking.

He pulls out again and lowers his mouth back to my pussy, and this time I can't stop the orgasm from hitting with full force, my back arching off the bed as each wave hits me. He drags it out for as long as he can, his tongue never stopping its movement until I'm limp on the bed, sated and sensitive, and only then does he slide back inside of me and continue.

Flicking my hair off my face, he presses his body against mine and kisses me. I can taste myself, but I don't care, I kiss him back, holding on to his neck and pulling him closer to me. Pushing at his chest until he rolls over, I take control, placing my hands on him and riding him. I love watching his facial expressions—the pleasure that crosses over them is my undoing every time.

Sitting back, I play with my breasts as he watches, grinding my hips on him so slowly, I know it must be driving him crazy. Proving me right, he soon moves me off him and lays me on my stomach, sliding into me from behind. He reaches underneath us and plays with my clit until I come a second time, and only then does he join me.

"Fuck," he grits out as he finishes, making growling sounds that have me wanting to jump him again.

We lie next to each other afterward, our fingers touching as we both stare up at the ceiling.

"I love you," he says.

"I know," I reply, lip twitching.

And I do.

A love like this is something that's hard to find, and although it's not perfect, it will always be enough for me.

I roll over and rest my head on his chest. Even though I'm hot and sweaty, I still want to be close to him. "It's been a while since we've been back to your sex den."

Renny chuckles. "Our sex den. I can't believe you thought this is where I brought all of my women."

"Come on, it's a valid conclusion to make," I reply, frowning. "Your own private space, where you can be as loud as you want and no one can hear you."

"You think we're shy about being loud in the clubhouse?" he asks, chuckling deeper. "We're not. No one cares. We're all men and we all have needs, and we're all adults."

"Yeah, I think you should stop talking," I tell him, rolling my eyes.

He pulls me back down next to him. "Any women I've been with in the past don't matter. The only thing that matters now is you, and trust me, I'd be an idiot to fuck this up. I'm not going to do anything to lose you, all right? It's me and you against the world."

"I know," I say. "I trust you. I wouldn't be here right now if I didn't."

We take a long, hot shower together and then head back home.

And yeah, Ariel and Mila are still there when we arrive.

Chapter Thirty-One

Chapter Thirty-One

I wake up to voices. Throwing my robe on, I head into the kitchen, where I see Trade holding Mila while Ariel makes some breakfast.

"Good morning," I say to both, eying them in turn. Trade hasn't been here since he dropped the flowers off, and I wonder how he invited himself over this time.

"Trade dropped by on his way to work to see how I was doing," Ariel explains after I just stand there, staring at them. "Do you want some breakfast? I'm making us bacon pancakes."

"I'd love some," I say, smiling as Trade coos at Mila, similar to the way Renny acts with her. "Where are your little ones today?"

"At school," he says, glancing up at me. "My youngest just started kindergarten. It's kind of weird not having any of them at home during the day, but easier with work because I don't have to put them into daycare."

He's obviously a hardworking man, and a good father. He might be a little rough around the edges, but not more so than

Temper. From what I've heard they didn't have the best child-hood and found the biker lifestyle appealing at a young age.

"You should be proud of yourself," I say. "Working and kids sounds like two full-time jobs put together."

He just smiles. "Someone has to do it, hey?"

I nod, because I know what he means. It's amazing what you can do when you have no choice.

Disappearing into my bedroom, I give them some time alone and have a shower and get ready to start my day. I never thought I'd see Ariel with a biker, especially after the shit she gave me at the start for being with Renny, but as long as she's happy and safe, I will always support any decisions she makes.

By the time I make it back out there, my food is on the table but Trade has already left for work. "What was that?" I ask, eyes wide.

"What was what?" she asks, playing dumb.

"That felt like a date I was intruding on," I admit, grabbing a fork and sitting down at the table. "I felt like a third wheel and you guys haven't even spent any time alone together yet."

She purses her lips. "He's just a nice guy, checking up on me because I was kidnapped."

"Most of the men at the clubhouse are nice and care about us, but I don't see any of them dropping in with flowers to see how you are."

"Well, he's obviously the nicest," she says, shrugging. "I don't know, and don't give me any shit, because I already have no idea what I'm doing."

I nod, staying quiet for a few moments. Unable to help my-self, I say, "If you two get together, you'd have gone from hav-ing no kids to having four within a few months."

If looks could kill, I'd be dead before any bacon even hit my mouth.

"You're getting a little ahead of yourself there," she replies, sitting down with Mila in her arms. "I'm not going to rush into anything, okay? If he wants to be a friend, that would be nice, but that's about all I can take on right now."

"Friends are good," I agree.

It's also a great foundation to start a relationship on, if ever they are ready.

"Is Dad still coming over today?" she asks, changing the subject.

"Yeah, he's meant to be dropping in with Eliza and Lucy," I reply, referring to our younger half sisters. "He said he wants them to meet Mila."

She tilts her head to the side, considering. "Do you think he genuinely wants to be a part of our lives now? You know he's probably getting a lot of shit from his wife for coming here, especially with the girls."

"I know," I agree, chewing and swallowing thoughtfully. "She must hate it, and is probably making his life a living hell. She's not coming today, is she? Because I might not call Shadow off if she is."

"Nah, he wouldn't," she says, smirking. "Or more to the point, she wouldn't."

"I don't know why she hates us so much. It would be like you hating Trade's kids and not wanting him to have anything to do with them—it's stupid." I groan, rolling my eyes just thinking of her. "How can you want to have kids with someone who wasn't a good dad to the kids he already had?"

"I don't know," she says, glancing down at Mila. "I could never be with someone who didn't love my daughter. She will always come first to me."

"That's how it's meant to be," I say, finishing off my meal. "Thank you for breakfast, it was delicious." Even though she was really making it for Trade, and I just happened to stumble across it at the right time.

"You're welcome."

We both tidy up, and then I do some work until Dad arrives. I put Shadow outside so he doesn't scare the girls. I wish I didn't feel awkward around them, but I don't know them, so it doesn't feel like my sisters are coming to visit. More like distant cousins or something.

"Hello," I say to them both, smiling. "You've both gotten so big."

They both look like their mom, with light hair and eyes, both lean and very feminine looking. "I'm fourteen now," Eliza says proudly. "Only a few more years and Daddy says he will buy me a car."

"An expensive car," Lucy adds with an eye roll.

I share a look with Ariel, one that says *and this is why we don't see them often*. Their mom has raised them completely differently from how we were raised, and they are very spoiled and entitled. Still, they are family, and I'm older than them, so I try to make an effort.

"Can I get any of you something to eat or drink?" I ask, while Dad sits down and holds Mila in his arms. He even brought a gift with him this time, something Ariel thanks him for but doesn't open just yet.

"I'll have coffee," Dad says to me, looking to the girls. "Do you want something? Eliza? Lucy?"

"No thanks. Can we get something on the way home instead? I want a smoothie," Eliza says, sitting down and staring at Mila. "So this is my niece?"

"Yes," Dad says, watching me from the corner of his eye. "You are both Mila's aunties. Isn't she cute?"

The girls don't reply. And then Eliza says, "Mom said that Ariel was stupid to have a baby when she wasn't married and that the dad tried to kill her."

My jaw drops. I knew the girls could be a little rude, but I had no idea that they had become this bad. At one point, they were kind of sweet, but I can see that teenage years have brought out a different side in Eliza. She's never reminded me more of her own mother than at this point.

These two might be kids, and they might be my half sisters,

but no one is going to talk shit about Ariel in front of me, and I'm not allowing anyone to be disrespectful in my own house.

"Eliza, I'm not going to allow any rudeness toward me and Ariel in my house, so if you don't have anything nice to say, you can go wait in the car," I tell her, then look to my dad, daring him to argue with me. "Or next time, feel free to just stay with your mom."

I've had it.

I don't even care.

"Dad?" she asks, pouting. "You said we'd have fun coming here." She's a little brat, and I don't know how he can deal with this on a daily basis. I feel bad—she's only a kid, after all—but wow.

"Why don't you come and hold Mila? You love babies, remember?" he says, ignoring her complaints.

"No thanks," she grumbles, sighing. "Mom said she's not really related to me anyway, so it doesn't matter."

Ariel, who I think is suddenly feeling a little protective, picks up Mila and cradles her. I think I'm actually speechless, because I have nothing to say right now. They are only kids at the end of the day, but I can't believe how rude Eliza is, and how Dad tolerates it. My mom never would have. We never would have dared to be so rude to anyone, never mind an adult.

"Well, this has been great," Ariel announces, wincing at the lie. "I can see why we only see each other once a year or so."

Probably going to be even less than that after this.

"Why don't you come alone next time, Dad?" I suggest, but then Lucy comes and sits next to me.

"I think Mila is a pretty name," she says. "There's a girl in my class named Mila, and all the boys like her."

My lip twitches at that. Lucy must be about twelve now, but she has a younger vibe about her. "Well, let's hope that's not the case for this Mila, because then Ariel and I will have to put her in an all-girls school."

"Probably a good idea. Boys are trouble," she says, nodding. "Dad said you got a dog. Where is he?"

I let Shadow in, and he steals the hearts of not just Lucy, but Eliza, too. We spend the next hour together, and when they leave, I feel a little better about it than when they first walked in.

And when Ariel opens her present from Dad and inside is a photo album of all her baby photos, an engraved gold chain for Mila and a check for five thousand dollars to start off Mila's savings account, I know that there is a good side to him.

Somewhere in there is the dad who used to come home and kiss us and tuck us in. The dad who made good choices.

And that's something I'm going to hold on to.

Chapter Thirty-Two

Shadow with me, I head to the clubhouse and find the men sitting outside, chatting. I'm about to leave, not wanting to interrupt, when Renny sees me.

"Hey, where are you going?" he calls out, coming over to me.

"You guys look busy," I explain, letting him lead me out there with them. "Hello, everyone." I glance down on the table and see photos of different people lying there, photos from surveillance footage. "What's all this?"

"We've been keeping an eye on all the members of the Killers MC who aren't in prison," Renny explains, sitting down and pulling me onto his lap.

"We wanted to make sure no one was coming for us," Temper adds, leaning back and studying the photos. "We've got eyes everywhere."

One of the pictures captures my attention, so I reach out and pick it up. "Who is this?"

"Why?" Temper asks, glancing between Renny and me. "Have you seen her before?"

I nod. "She has come to my house twice now, saying she lost

her dog. She didn't come inside or anything. Ariel spoke to her once and then I spoke to her at the door. Both times she came by for a few short minutes and then left."

"Fuck," Renny mutters under his breath. "This is Skylar's mom, Georgia, the lady we were talking about before. She might look all *Little House on the Prairie*, but she's dangerous and not to be underestimated."

Fear fills me. I got no weird vibes from this woman—she appeared friendly and genuinely concerned about her dog. I'm a person who generally is good at judging someone's character. She had me completely fooled, and I would have been comfortable inviting her in for coffee or something without thinking about it.

My mind is blown right now, and I'm completely speechless. Why did she come to my house? I have to wonder how I factor into her plans here.

"What is she playing at?" Renny asks Temper, holding on to me tighter.

"I think she was trying to get Izzy to trust her," Saint adds, jaw tight. "She looks so sweet that no one would think she's a threat. Maybe she wants more information about something, because she's probably already got some plan up her sleeve."

"I thought she was out of this lifestyle," Dee comments, crossing his arms over his chest. "Yet she's showing up every fucking place we are, first at the mayor's speech and now here. Do I have to go back there? Because that place is a hole. I'm not cut out for the country life."

"She's probably still here," Temper says, turning to Saint. "Keep an eye on Skylar at all times."

"Already on it," Saint says, typing on his phone.

"I can't believe she came to your house," Renny says, looking into my eyes. "Next time tell me if anyone you don't know comes around, okay? I know you wouldn't have thought twice about this, especially a little older lady looking for her dog, but from now on even if it seems like nothing, just let me know."

"I will," I promise.

"Just when we think we can relax a little, we're back on alert thanks to the she-devil," Temper groans, scrubbing his hands down his face.

He looks tired and frustrated, and like he is in desperate need of a long holiday.

"I think I'm going to need to hear this story," I tell Renny, cuddling up to him. "Why is this woman so dangerous?"

Renny tells me the quick version about the story behind Georgia and Skylar. My jaw drops with several plot twists, and by the end of it, I have even more respect for Skylar, if that's possible.

"Holy shit." This woman sounds like the devil incarnate. She's clearly very intelligent, manipulative and a sociopath, and I can see now why it would be a stupid decision to not be wary of her.

"Now that Hammer is gone, though, you'd think her need for revenge would be satisfied," I say to the group.

"We thought so," Saint agrees, nodding. "But at the end of the day, who knows what goes through her mind? She hates the fact that her daughter sits here, not there with her, and that Skylar is loved and protected by the club. She's twisted. And I know she's Skylar's mother and all, but I'd feel a hell of a lot better if she was six feet under."

I can't imagine how Skylar must feel. At the end of the day, that's her mom, and you only get one of those.

The men make a plan to track Georgia and make sure they know where she is at all times. Security is to remain on a high level, and everyone is not to put their guard down.

I think in some ways, though, it's always going to need to be like this.

Because when the guard is down, bad shit happens.

Epilogue

Six Months Later

"Hey," I say as Trade steps into the clubhouse with Ariel and Mila at his side. The two of them have been taking things extremely slow, but I think it's safe to say that they are dating. He's at our place almost as much as Renny, especially when his kids are at school, like today, and I like having him around. He's so sweet to my sister and my niece, so what more could I ask for? "How was the zoo?"

"Good," Ariel replies, smiling down at her daughter. "I think we enjoyed it more than Mila, who slept through most of it, but it was a beautiful day out."

"You going to watch this movie with us?" Renny asks them, glancing down at his phone.

"Yeah, we got the message," Ariel replies, wrinkling her nose. "Who knew a whole MC would get together to watch a superhero movie."

"Secret nerds," I say, patting the spot next to me. "I brought snacks, though, so I know it's going to be a good time."

"Dee is bringing beer," Renny adds, grinning at Trade. "And Temper is ordering pizza as we speak."

"No wonder you guys have these giant couches," Ariel muses, while Trade picks up Mila, who starts to fuss as she wakes.

Sky steps into the room, smiling at us all. "Oh good, I'm not the only one who's early." Her eyes widen as she spots Mila. "Trade, let me hold her. You hog her."

Trade holds Mila closer to his chest. "I do not."

"Someone needs to have another baby so we're not all fighting over mine," Ariel adds, glancing between me and Sky. "Come on, one of you take one for the team."

"Shotgun not," Sky calls out at the same time I shake my head.

The rest of the men arrive, and we all pile into the lounge room together.

I love moments like these, moments when we're nothing but a normal family.

When Renny whispers into my ear that he has a surprise for me, and leads me away from everyone, I have to wonder what the hell he's up to.

"Where are you taking me?" I ask Renny, so tempted to remove the blindfold covering my eyes.

"We're almost there," he promises, carrying me in his arms when my blind walking is taking too long.

Apparently we're both extremely impatient today. I don't know what surprise he has for me up his sleeve, but I'm excited for it. Life has been nothing short of amazing being with Renny, letting him in and truly trusting him. I never thought I'd feel for someone the way I do for him, the love, respect and loyalty he gives me on a daily basis is more than I ever thought I'd have.

When the blindfold comes off, we're at his park, standing in the middle of a circle filled with red roses.

"When did you do this?" I ask, eyes widening as I do a full spin. "It's beautiful, Renny."

My jaw drops open as I see him drop to his knee.

"Izzy, I love you more than anything or anyone in this world, and I want to give you everything. You deserve a proper proposal, engagement and wedding, and I really wanted sober me to pick the ring this time…"

I laugh at that.

"Will you marry me?" he asks, opening the black box to show me the most beautiful pear-shaped halo ring I have ever seen. "For the second time?"

"Yes," I say to him, tears of happiness dripping down my cheeks. "Yes, of course I will."

He slides the ring on my finger, and it fits perfectly, just like the last one did.

Then he stands and kisses me, a long, sweet kiss filled with love and promises.

Staring down at my new ring, I can't believe what the world has handed me in the last year.

One thing I know for sure though, I'm in love with a Knight.

And drunk me knew back then what sober me knows now.

Renegade was meant to be my husband.

* * * * *

Acknowledgments

A big thank-you to Carina Press for working with me on the Knights of Fury MC series!

Thank you to Kimberly Brower, my amazing agent, for having my back in all things.

Natalie Ram—I miss you, bestie! It's hard doing life without you, but I know you are just a call away. I love you. Thank you for always reading my work and supporting me, even though I know how busy you are.

Amo Jones—Thank you for always being there when I need someone to talk to, for the badass writing sprints and for encouraging me to be the best writer I can be. You just get me, and finding someone that does that is so rare. I love you, wifey.

Brenda Travers—Thank you so much for all that you do to help promote me. I am so grateful. You go above and beyond and I appreciate you so much.

Ari—You are one of the best souls I have ever met. You are kind, generous, and I'm so lucky to have you in my life. Thank you for always caring about me. I love you!

Tenielle—Baby sister, I don't know where I'd be without you.

Thanks for all you do for me and the boys, we all adore you and appreciate you. I might be older, but you inspire me every day. When I grow up, I want to be like you.

Christian—Thank you for always being there for me, and for accepting me just the way I am. I always tell you how lucky you are, but the truth is I'm pretty damn lucky myself. I appreciate all you do for me and the boys. I love you.

To my three sons, my biggest supporters, thank you for being so understanding, loving and helpful. I'm so proud of the men you are all slowly becoming, and I love you all so very much. I hope that watching me work hard every day and following my dreams inspires you all to do the same. Nothing makes me happier than being your mama.

And to my readers, thank you for loving my words. I hope this book is no exception.

About the Author

New York Times, Amazon and *USA Today* bestselling author Chantal Fernando is thirty-two years old and lives in Western Australia.

Lover of all things romance, Chantal is the author of the best-selling books *Dragon's Lair*, *Maybe This Time* and many more.

When not reading, writing or daydreaming she can be found enjoying life with her three sons and family.

NEW RELEASE

BESTSELLING AUTHOR

DELORES FOSSEN

Even a real-life hero needs a little healing sometimes…

After being injured during a routine test, Air Force pilot
Blue Donnelly must come to terms with what his future
holds if he can no longer fly, and whether that future
includes a beautiful horse whisperer who turns his life
upside down.

In stores and online June 2024.

Subscribe and fall in love with a Mills & Boon series today!

You'll be among the first to read stories delivered to your door monthly and enjoy great savings.

MILLS & BOON SUBSCRIPTIONS

HOW TO JOIN

1

Visit our website
millsandboon.
com.au/pages/
print-subscriptions

2

Select your favourite series
Choose how many books. We offer monthly as well as pre-paid payment options.

3

Sit back and relax
Your books will be delivered directly to your door.

WE SIMPLY LOVE ROMANCE

MILLS & BOON